David Hallwood was born and bred in Northumberland and despite living in Kent for the past 56 years remains proud of his 'Geordie' roots. A busy and successful career in the world of Licensed Property Brokerage and Brewery Companies continually prevented him from following his first love – writing.

An after-dinner speaker for many years, David's work will always have a strong line of humour running through it. He is married to Vanessa, and has a married son and two stepdaughters. His loves are family, friends, Canterbury R.F.C., cricket, crosswords, and Newcastle United.

The Brewer's Wife

David Hallwood

THE BREWER'S WIFE

Olympia Publishers
London

www.olympiapublishers.com

OLYMPIA PAPERBACK EDITION

A CIP catalogue record for this title is
available from the British Library.

ISBN: 978-1-84897-419-7

(Olympia Publishers is part of Ashwell Publishing Ltd)

This is a work of fiction.
Names, characters, places and incidents originate from the writer's imagination.
Any resemblance to actual persons, living or dead, is purely coincidental.

First Published in 2014

Olympia Publishers
60 Cannon Street
London
EC4N 6NP

Printed in Great Britain

This book is dedicated to my darling wife Vanessa and my family for loving me so much!

Acknowledgements

To: Alison and Chris for reading the book from start to finish and being so enthusiastic and supportive. Ladies, I am so grateful.

CHAPTER ONE

1978 – AN UNEXPECTED INVITATION

Stella opened the hastily scribbled note that Dale had slipped to her during the few moments they had been alone together following their earlier meeting in the Brewery Marquee during Canterbury Cricket Week. Circumstances decreed that the content could not have been more clear or more to the point: *"My dear Stella, I realise that this is completely crazy but if I don't do something today then I might never get the chance again. I can't believe that events have turned out as they have but I have no intention of allowing this almost unbelievable situation to pass without making some effort to rekindle what we had together thirty years ago and what I believe we can enjoy even more in adulthood. I believe that deep down you are still the girl I knew and worshipped in my boyhood days and whom I must admit, I've never forgotten. If I'm right then hopefully you will indeed be able to come to Croft House next Thursday at say one o'clock and wallow in an afternoon of sheer nostalgia. I'm not embarrassed to talk about such things because I really believe you and I still want the joys that rubber and bondage can bring. Nobody has ever come anywhere near to creating the excitement you did, I've never forgotten you in your shiny Wellington boots with your wonderful gang games and the fun you and I had together. I still remember vividly how, having tied me up, you kissed me full on the lips. Yes, of course we were children then but so what? That was a huge 'first' for me. Do you recall that moment? We can't just let our meeting today go by as though nothing has happened. I suppose I've been waiting all my adult life for this moment without ever thinking it would come about. All I ask is that you come, **please**, and bring with you a pair of glossy high black rubber boots, a pair of black rubber gauntlets and a bikini…I'll have everything else. I'm sorry this* *note is so rough and ready but I can't let you go today without making you aware of the feelings I have always had for you. Forget all about being the wife of a Brewery Chairman, ignore thoughts that you are a JP and a School Governor or whatever, just please be there – you will never forget the afternoon I'm going to give you and that's a promise! If you don't appear then I shall know that I've embarrassed you and made a fool of myself. Whatever your decision I swear that no one will ever know about you and me Stella – it will always be our secret but do try and come to Croft House **please***! *All my love. Dale"*

"The nerve of the man," thought Stella as she re-read the note. What, possibly was annoying her more than anything was that despite her high position in local society, her safe and secure married status and the satisfaction of her life-style she was actually excited by Dale's words. She was well aware that the wearing of Wellington boots at all times by her Gang had been her idea and possibly this was motivating Dale in some way. Rubber boots had not been readily available to children during the war but the smart shiny black and brown Wellingtons that had then come back on sale had appealed to her for reasons about which she was still unsure. Her memory banks began to work overtime as she recalled, not for the first time she had to admit, all the bondage games that the Gang had enjoyed and the very 'special' relationship she had had with Dale. The very idea of being in a 'tied up' situation had simmered below the surface of her inner consciousness for the first few years of married life but had gradually filtered away as Richard had organised their sex life in a conservative and rather unimaginative manner.

That Richard loved her was not in doubt but so many other things seemed gradually to have come into his busy life and she had become accustomed to his occasional 'roll-on / roll-off' sexual ferries. She smiled to herself at the very thought of jumping into bed with her rubber riding boots on as Richard peered over his spectacles with eyes full of astonishment, horror and real fear! He would not have the faintest idea of what was going on and would honestly have felt that his dear wife was suffering some sort of mental breakdown.

"Of course the whole idea is ridiculous," she thought as she pulled on her tight-fitting boots. 'The man must have an ego as big as the Albert Hall,' she muttered as she slid into the sexiest bikini she owned. 'How dare he invade my life like this with his clumsy innuendoes. Who does he think he is? I…I…' She caught sight of herself in the dressing mirror. 'Do you know, I don't look too bad at all in this kinky gear. Oh damn the man.'

The next two days saw Stella in total confusion. The arrival back into her world of Dale Ingram had thrown this very confident and organised lady out of her stride. On JP duties she found herself giving judgement and wagging the finger at some poor miscreant whilst imagining how he would have taken her words had she been dressed in her bikini and boots instead of a light grey suit. Chairing the School Governors' meeting her mind wandered as she mused on whether the rather 'dishy' Head Teacher would approve of her in Dale's fantasy clothing.

In Keymarkets she purchased a pair of shiny long black rubber household gloves. 'Strictly for kitchen use,' she prompted herself. 'I can keep them for the heavier tasks and for weeding etc… oh God, I wonder if he really wants to tie me up?'

Stella wore her new gloves in the kitchen the following morning. As she washed up the early morning coffee cups Richard wandered in and started complaining that the English middle order batting had collapsed yet again and he may not bother to go up to the Oval this year. She wafted her gloves at him whilst commiserating with him in his despair… absolutely no reaction.

'I couldn't get any normal coloured kitchen gloves in Keymarkets yesterday,' she found herself piping. 'So I had to buy these **black** ones. What do you think?' The look Richard gave her was somewhere between '*What a funny little world my funny little wife lives in*' and '*I think I am married to a half-wit!*'

'I'm sure they will be fine darling, no toast for me this morning,' was what actually emerged.

On Thursday morning Stella had booked an appointment at the hairdressing salon and entered shaking with guilt, misgivings and a sense of total excitement. The mundane chit-chat no longer interested her as the sheer terror of what lay ahead continually forced its way to the forefront of all her mental aberrations. As she drove towards Croft House in her metallic grey BMW she glanced down at the black carry-on flight bag on the passenger seat and wondered what any paramedic team would make of the contents of same in the event of her having a road traffic accident.

'I must be bloody mad. I must be absolutely bonkers. What if this is a "wind-up" and he's not serious about me dressing up and becomes terribly embarrassed because of my actions? I won't go. I'll remain aloof and pretend I thought he was joking about us meeting up. I'll make him spell it out if he is looking for something from me. I will not be treated in this way by Dale Ingram!!!!'

Croft House was an ideal venue. Some thirty miles from Canterbury and set in deeply wooded countryside this small private Guest House was run by an elderly and most discreet couple. As the BMW rolled into the driveway Dale emerged from the house looking smart and so pleased to see Stella.

'I've been hoping and praying that you would turn up Stella, he remarked enthusiastically. 'I haven't been able to think of anything else but today since I first saw you. Stella, we are going to turn the clock back and have a lot more fun than we ever did in Northumberland all those years ago. You look fabulous by the way.'

Stella smiled and replied, 'I trust all this stuff about yesteryear is really on the level Dale. Nobody but Dale Ingram could possibly have got me to carry out the instructions you penned in your note to me. I've brought all that you requested and hope I'm not going to regret this afternoon for the rest of my days! You have got me so bewildered I can't think straight!'

'Stella, I promise you that you will not regret anything. Those times we spent together as kids were magical, quite unforgettable.

Stella you have always been *so special* to me! I can't wait to see what you've brought in this bag. Feels very sexy.'

Stella took a deep breath to try and calm herself down and followed him into the small hotel.

CHAPTER TWO

1978 – FIRST MEETING

It was indeed a most pleasant start to Dale's day to receive an official invitation to attend Ladies' Day at the Canterbury Cricket Week Festival as a guest of one of the Firm's best clients, the local Brewers, Messrs Wetton Ackeson of Sandwich. They were having a marquee this year and it was sure to be a splendidly organised affair for the Company had an excellent name when it came to such things. Kent were having a great season and as well as being in contention for the County Championship they were also looking favourites to lift the Benson & Hedges Cup for the third time in six years being a particularly efficient 'one-day' side under the captaincy of A G E Ealham. The match was against Leicestershire, never an easy side to beat under the canny control of Ray Illingworth.

The St Lawrence Ground is surely one of the prettiest and most gracious cricket grounds in the world with its huge lime tree set well inside the playing area where it had stood long before the cricket ground had been established, its half circle of gaily striped marquees stretching for almost half the perimeter of the boundary showing their various flags and the old and new stands taking up the remainder of the viewing space. It always brought back memories of his childhood when, as a young Geordie schoolboy, he would be dropped off by his uncle who was on his way into work at nine o'clock in the morning and reminded to be outside the ground again at five forty-five for the pick-up and return to his holiday home.

He had got older but the magic of the place had not receded one iota. The white or cream flannelled ghosts of Les Ames, Arthur Fagg, Les Todd, Doug Wright, Fred Ridgeway and the incomparable Godfrey Evans, all his boyhood heroes, still haunted the atmosphere and he had always found himself in total awe if any of that band of men who were still living appeared at the ground. The constant television viewing of all the big matches had lessened the charisma of the present international players but these stars of the Paramount Newsreels etc, shown briefly at the local cinemas in black and white, had retained their own sense of mystique and this was never to leave them as their playing careers had drawn to a close.

Entering the ground on foot, when the day arrived, knowing a day of heavy drinking would most certainly exclude any thoughts of driving home, Dale saw the colourful Brewery Standard billowing in the breeze above a large marquee and strolled in to be met by the Company Secretary George Banyard and Ron 'Tubby' Norton who was one of the older and more senior Area Managers on the Tied Trade side of things. They greeted him warmly and he was directed to the bar counter where a young lady gave him a cup of coffee. The talk was of cricket and of the success the County side were enjoying. George had been an excellent club cricketer in his earlier days and when he talked one listened for his knowledge was sound and his comments always interesting. Tubby, on the other hand, was strictly 'here for the beer' and was obviously dying for George to leave them so that he could tell Dale the latest obscene but very funny story he had heard before some of the other Area Managers arrived and got in before him.

Tommy Thornhill and Bernard Brazier, two partners from Dale's biggest rivals in the region, Messrs A W Spatwell & Creed of Tunbridge Wells, sauntered in and joined them. Dale had grown up in business with Brazier whilst Thornhill had been a 'thorn in his side' albeit a very pleasant one, for over fifteen years. Bernard Brazier was a tall slim individual with a long nose and steel-rimmed spectacles whilst his colleague Tommy Thornhill was small, dapper and was seldom seen without a floral button-hole. Neither were cricketers in so far as he knew but neither were naïve enough to allow such an invitation to pass them by and they would be around until the final ball had been bowled and every last piece of goodwill extracted. He wondered where David Queen, their other partner had got to. David was a fine cricketer and they had played against each other on many occasions.

'Where's the third 'Stoogie' or are you just coming as Morecambe & Wise today?' asked Dale 'I can't believe old Queenie is missing out on a day with Wetton Ackeson.'

'Unavoidable dear boy,' trilled Thornhill. 'He's on holiday in Cyprus and his wife wouldn't come home three days early.'

'Selfish cow,' laughed Tubby Norton.

The Brokers were all good friends and although bitter rivals in business they were incapable of any unprofessional or underhand treatment of each other's firms and all genuinely liked each other. The guests flowed into the tent in a fairly continuous stream with several of the Brewery Company's hierarchy joining the fray accompanied by their wives and in one or two cases, their children also. Dale had been told by George Banyard that the Chairman and his wife were coming for lunch and hinted that this was quite an occurrence as Mrs Rigden-Ackeson did not normally have too much to do with Brewery activities.

With the weather not being particularly kind and rain a distinct possibility Kent's pretty feeble first innings total of the previous day began to look very respectable as old 'Deadly' Derek Underwood carried on where he had left off, the previous evening taking wickets at regular intervals much to the undisguised joy of his faithful followers.

Just before lunch Richard Rigden-Ackeson walked in with his wife who was a dark-haired lady in a quite stunning very pale brown silk dress and cream high-heeled shoes. Sensibly, she had a milk chocolate coloured cardigan slung over her cream leather handbag. Dale happened to be in Tommy Thornhill's company at that moment.

'Wow!' Tommy exclaimed. 'My opinion of our Lord and Chairman has gone up one hundred fold in the last thirty seconds… what a woman!'

'You know your place Mr Thornhill,' laughed Tubby Norton. 'She's in a different league to you.'

'More like a different planet to you Tommy,' added Dale, with a smile.

'Ah my dear boys,' sighed Thornhill. 'I know my place. Mind you I'm not a proud man and would fuck her leather handbag if given the opportunity!!!'

'Having seen you in the showers may I respectfully suggest that you limit your desires to that of her purse?' replied Dale. Such outbursts between these characters was absolutely par for the course and they all enjoyed the 'ragging' that went on and would continue to go on whilst they had breath in their bodies.

'Yes our Stella is quite a "looker" isn't she?' Tubby continued. 'She's a JP you know, but she doesn't deal with licensing applications for obvious reasons.'

At the mention of 'Stella', Dale's pulse quickened. That name would always make bells ring in his head for it was not a common Christian name and brought to mind immediate vivid memories. He studied her again, this time taking in her finely chiselled features, her lips and her hair. Her hair was so similar, dark and so thick and curly.

"Could it be her? Could it possibly be Stella? My Stella?" he thought.

Certainly her age would be right for she looked a few years younger than the Chairman and her hair was exactly the same colour that he remembered. By this time he was more excited than he could ever recall and knew, deep down inside himself that he would have his hopes dashed or raised to dizzy heights before the day was out. It mattered not one jot that she was Richard Rigden-Ackeson's wife and that he could well be prejudicing future dealings between his firm and the Brewery Company. What did matter that if this was his Stella Ward then he had to talk to her.

He tried to make conversation with the chaps on his table as a delicious banquet of prawn and crab cocktails followed by cold meats and umpteen salad dishes were served together with bowls of hot new potatoes. The wines flowed, the chatter rose to a crescendo as guests and their hosts tried to be heard over the clatter of crockery and cutlery and the music from a military brass band who were playing on the playing area beside the marquees. The Chairman began to circulate as the cheese and biscuits was served together with a decanter of port on each table. Mrs Rigden-Ackeson did not move but chatted to one or two of the Directors and their wives. She glanced round the tented space and failed to recognise any of the assembled guests but Dale caught her eyes for a second and smiled straight at her.

Stella hadn't really wanted to come to the cricket but Richard had insisted that it was a social occasion that she should not miss. Rather than cause a row or be accused yet again of failing to support her husband she had agreed and would make the most of it. As she sat down to what she had to admit was a fine luncheon she found herself talking to Sophie Fanshawe and Maggie Gunnerstone who were both wives of Directors. Sophie was a sweet lady who deserved so much better than her idiot husband Toby. Toby was simply rich... he was rolling in it and as such one could only suppose that Sophie had been overwhelmed by all that he could give her. He could not talk about anything on an intellectual level and at work was led totally by his management team. At any meetings with the Chairman he would have his number one man, Tom Spanswick, by his side and it would be Tom who would answer the queries and put forward the policies for consideration. The Chairman knew this of course and

Toby realised he knew, but nothing was ever said. All Toby wanted was respectability and all Richard wanted was to keep his Aunt Maude, Toby's mother, out of his hair. Sophie had a flat in Knightsbridge and spent quite a bit of time up there. She had never actually admitted anything to Stella directly but had given the distinct impression that there was more to her life than poor old Toby.

She gazed round the tables and caught a bronzed handsome gentleman staring straight at her with a smile hovering on his lips. She quickly looked away, thinking to herself, "Do I know him?" and then admitting to herself "No, of course I don't. One doesn't forget faces as nice as that one." She waited for about five minutes then glanced again his direction. "Oh God! He's still looking at me," she thought to herself. Maggie Gunnerstone was a real regular at such 'do's' as this and Stella turned to her and said:

'Don't look now Maggie... but who is that rather good-looking character sitting next to Mr Norton on the table by the door? I think I've met him and it would be embarrassing if we meet later and I don't know to whom I'm talking.'

After a minute or two Maggie looked and squealed, 'Oooh! That's Dale Ingram. He's with that Brokers' firm in Canterbury, Tremletts I think they call themselves. All the girls at the Brewery fancy him rotten. He's such a nice fellow and has never been married so they tell me... what a waste!!!'

'Dale Ingram!' Stella didn't really catch much of what Maggie was enthusing about as she caught her breath and let this absolute bombshell of news take effect. Thirty years had passed since he had explored her helpless body. Thirty years had passed since she had trussed him up tightly then explored his helpless body with nervous but firm hands and kissed him as warmly as she had ever kissed any man including her husband confessing her undying love. She had never forgotten him, but had filed him away in her memory bank under the heading 'Excitement'.

She now knew who he was but did he know who she was? He really was a most handsome guy, and as the coffee cups were taken away she found herself glued to the seat and unable to look one way or the other.

'Are you coming for a stroll around the other tents darling?' Richard's voice shattered her thoughts.

'No darling,' she replied. 'I think I'll do a wee spot of PR round our own tent.'

'Waste of time my dear. They all need us a great deal more than we need them,' he snorted.

"At times Richard can be an arrogant sod," she thought. "He is always at his worst when meeting people who depend on him. It's so much easier to be pleasant and courteous."

She then thought to herself, "Am I already defending my Dale? Oh dear, did I really think *my* Dale?" she asked herself.

Richard accepted her words and wandered off with one or two of those sycophants who always seemed to be at his beck and call. She had never discussed this particular band with Richard but knew that her husband was no fool and could only presume that he enjoyed being told how wonderful he was so many times each week. As he disappeared out of the marquee she found herself looking across the tables once more and once again Dale Ingram's eyes were focused on her. She could not contain herself any longer and got up as if to start wandering around the tables. Most of the guests had already gone outside again and were settling down to watch the afternoon session. Dale moved quickly and was beside her before she had moved more than a few yards.

'May I introduce myself Mrs Rigden-Ackeson. We haven't met before but my name is Dale…'

'I know who you are Dale and I have a strong suspicion that you know who I am,' she interrupted. 'I just don't believe that we are meeting here after all these years.'

'So it is Stella Ward. My darling, darling Stella Ward,' he said quietly. 'I can't believe this is happening. After all these years my dreams have come true and I'm with you again... do you realise how much I have missed you and how much your departure from Monkseaton has had on my life?'

'I promise you, I did mean to write Dale but what with a new school down in Kent and new friends it seemed so pointless and in no time at all I was at Cambridge University, and the North East began to fade from memory.'

'Did I fade from your memory Stella?' he asked.

'If I'm honest with myself I have to say "no". You never really left me Dale. You were the first man to genuinely excite me but you know all this.'

Dale persisted with his questioning. Underwood was still creating havoc with the Leicestershire tail and the spectators were enthralled by his magic.

'Do you still like wearing shiny rubber boots?' he asked. 'You were never out of them as I remember and insisted we all wore them all the time we were on gang business. Does the idea of being tied up still appeal to you?'

The questions were so straightforward that she was thrown out of her stride. Up until now she had been totally in control of herself and the situation but this reference to her former uniform footwear and possible preferences made it clear that Dale had remembered everything about their past adventures and, like her, had given a great deal of thought as to why she had insisted on the wearing of Wellington boots at all times and had needed to be tied up on so many occasions. Being interrogated by Dale thirty years later and having nowhere to hide made it very difficult to give him a satisfactory reply.

'What questions,' she remarked, desperately fighting for time and space. 'I really can't give you any positive answers I'm afraid. I seem to remember that the boots were a whim at the time and we were stuck with it. I never minded being tied up by you or any of my gang, it was fun and it was harmless. Why do you ask?'

'I ask because I want to see you again Stella. We have got to talk. Not here, not now, but soon and at a place where we can reminisce, laugh, play and catch up with what has happened to us over the past thirty years. May I say you are a stunningly attractive woman? Do you know a small hotel the other side of Maidstone called The Croft Hotel? It's just outside West Malling and…'

'Are you OK Mrs Rigden-Ackeson?' interrupted George Banyard who had seen the flustered look on the face of his Chairman's wife and thought it was time he rescued her from the clutches of young Ingram. 'I have a gentleman who is longing to meet you and wondered if you could spare him a few minutes of your time before the Chairman returns.'

'Yes I'm fine,' she hastily reassured the Company Secretary and getting up from her seat she gave Dale a dazzling smile and said, 'It's been so nice talking to you Mr Ingram and I think I agree entirely with what you say. Sounds an interesting project.'

As she stumbled across the room to be introduced to some diminutive fellow in a pin-striped suit with a large yellow floral button-hole she found herself thinking, "He called me *stunning,* he called me *attractive,*" and felt a confidence flow through her that had certainly not been there for a very long time. As Tommy Thornhill twittered on about something or nothing she turned and took in Dale again as he stood at the bar in conversation with two or three gentlemen who were obviously not terribly interested in the cricket. Dale Ingram was over six foot tall and still had a mane of dark brown hair which seemed naturally to fall into place without looking over-groomed. He was sun-tanned and extremely good-looking and she recalled what a nice-looking boy he had been at the time of their parting. He looked over in her direction and smiled.

"Oh dear," she thought. "Dear Dale, after all this time, dear Dale."

CHAPTER THREE

NORTHUMBERLAND 1946

In 1946 the sun never seemed to set over Monkseaton. The ending of the war had brought joyful homecomings of sons, fathers and husbands and a wonderful summer for the folk of this small Northumbrian town, set about a mile inland from the busy bustling holiday resort of Whitley Bay which proudly boasted of a huge stretch of golden sands, a wide promenade, well-kept links, a stream of amusement arcades, the famous Spanish City Fairground, a theatre, four cinemas and the imposing lighthouse set at the end of the bay on a tidal causeway island.

For Dale Ingram his tenth birthday was to prove of special significance. Stella Ward and her gang were a band of pirates, cowboys, gangsters, soldiers or whatever the mood took them. However to become a member Dale was well aware that he had to be ten years old. Their departure from the streets around Dale's house always filled the lad with sadness for he knew they were off on another exciting day of adventures and that he would not be allowed to join them until his wretched birthday arrived in July.

Stella was his hero, or heroine I suppose one should say, and he had worshipped her from afar for two years. Aged nearly thirteen she could out-run, out-fight and out-think any boy of her age in the area. She was tall, intelligent and being educated at a Convent School in Newcastle. Every weekday afternoon she would walk past Dale's house from the station on her way home. Her chocolate brown school uniform and cream Panama hat looked totally wrong on this fiery goddess but Dale knew that within an hour or so the gang would be out and about with their leader back in a shirt, shorts and her shiny brown Wellington boots. The uniform of the Stella Ward Gang was well-known to every child in the area and whether the snow lay crisp and even, the rains descended or a heat-wave threatened to melt the tarmacadam-covered farm tracks the gang wore shirts, shorts and wellingtons with coats or jumpers as necessary.

The Shilton twins, Diane and Claire, had tried to bring about a change by wearing print summer frocks one day but both had been sent packing and never promoted their cause again. Even parents seemed to know that the gang had their uniform and accepted it all with a smile for Stella was a popular lass and liked by all.

The other two gangs in the immediate vicinity were 'Stempy's Gang' led by Johnny Stemp, a boy from the local Orphanage and the 'Goofy Grafton Gang' or 'Three G's' as they were known and master-minded by Graham Grafton. Johnny Stemp had a huge gang but they were more of a threat at school where they would roar around the playground at the Bygate Infant School or rush through the streets surrounding the school as soon as lessons had finished for the day roaring their defiance at the world. The 'Three G's' were a different kettle of fish and although much smaller, numerically speaking, compared to Stempy's Gang they were far more dangerous if you strayed into their territory. Only Stella herself seemed totally unconcerned by Graham Grafton and his bunch of cronies. She seemed utterly fearless and oblivious of any danger. Dale had such a clear recollection of the time, as a nine-year-old, he had been walking home in the snow after he had swopped a fine birds' egg collection with Bobby Dodsworth for several sets of cigarette cards. To his delight Stella had joined him en route only for them to be waylaid by about ten of the '3 G's' Gang. After a furious struggle about eight of the gang managed to tie Stella to the 5-bar gate leading to James' Farm field whilst the remaining two had little difficulty in securing

28

young Dale in a similar fashion. With much hooting and crowing, snow was packed tightly into their wellingtons and down the backs of their necks. Dale remembered Stella's look of sheer fury as she hissed, seeing his bottom lip begin to quiver, 'Don't you cry! Don't you dare cry!!!'

On his tenth birthday Dale awoke feeling six feet tall knowing that by six o'clock that evening he would be a fully-fledged member of the gang. Stella had promised him as much and she would never have a more faithful ally than he. He was unaware of the initiation rites but felt that anything was worth enduring for the ultimate joy of full membership to such a secret society.

By eleven o'clock most of the gang had gathered and had made their way across James' Farm field to the single track railway line that linked Monkseaton to the coastal town of Blyth. Suddenly the party veered off the track and plunged through thick undergrowth before arriving after about ten minutes at a wooded glade with a thick mossy carpet and signs of past camp-fire ashes.

His initiation was frightening, thrilling, humiliating and yet strangely wonderful. Staked out in Red Indian fashion he was closely examined, to the accompaniment of much laughter, by all present who wallowed in his obvious embarrassment and discomfort. He had promised Stella to follow her leadership and to never disclose any secrets of the gang. Dale would have promised Stella anything, anywhere and at whatever the cost may have been.

The next two years were the best of his young life. The gang needed no one else for they were a happy self-contained unit of fun and friendship. Their 'wide' games were many and varied and always played in the woods, by the railway, on the sands or links of Whitley Bay or along at St Mary's Island reached daily by tidal causeway and dominated by the lighthouse standing tall and watchful as it tendered to the needs of the River Tyne and North Sea traffic.

Stella Ward was the keystone to everything. She was never lost for ideas. She knew where the biggest newts could be found and was able to uncover birds' nests and rock pool crabs with uncanny skill. She knew of so many secret haunts that appeared to have been fashioned for the games of her gang. They all adored her but none more than Dale who saw in her a kind of perfection he had not thought possible. So different from his silly elder sister Daisy and her girlie friends. Stella could do no wrong and the bond between them grew over these years. On one occasion, whilst re-enacting a particular Saturday morning cinema serial featuring hero, heroine, villains galore, kidnap and rescue, Stella had been trussed up and left in the care of Dale and Claire Shilton whilst hero Roy Banks searched for her and tried to avoid capture himself. Claire wandered off to 'spend a penny' as was her usual ilk and Dale took the opportunity to tease and torment his adored but helpless leader. Stella writhed most convincingly but submitted to a full kiss on her cheek and then another and another. Claire returned and the episode was not mentioned but something had happened that afternoon that neither the teenage tomboy nor her young fan could understand or explain.

The months came and went and the friendship of Dale and Stella strengthened as they became closer and closer. Dale, growing physically and mentally almost by the day, had achieved a position of some seniority in the gang. Only Roy Banks, aged thirteen, was stronger than he and there was a serious doubt as to whether Roy could run faster than his young colleague.

The week before the school summer holidays of 1947 came to an end a wonderful game, incorporating the Foreign Legion, marauding Arab tribesmen, a captured princess and a dangerous but heroic rescue attempt, had been thought up by Stella. Dale had been assigned the position of the leader of the tribesmen and it was he who was to capture the princess and then ensure that the gallant legionnaires did not find her. To his delight Stella was to be the princess and with all members of the gang other than 1947 newcomers Timmy Court and Donald Witts sworn not to commence their search for half an hour, Dale determined that the feelings he had experienced for Stella would be put to the test once more.

Using their old 'forced march' tactics of running 100 yards then walking 50 paces Dale, Stella, Timmy and Donald were soon well into the woods and midway between Monkseaton and the village of Earsden. Tim and Donald were delegated to 'lookout' positions some distance from their camp and instructed that if seen they were to draw off the searching rescue party. The camp was secluded and difficult to trace.

Dale tied up his princess with two football laces and got out his handkerchief. Despite Stella's assurances that she would not call out or make any sound whatsoever and her obvious reluctance to be gagged with a far from clean cloth that had already that day held marbles and had wiped blood off Diane Shilton's cut knee during horseplay in the street, Dale nevertheless duly silenced her protests and then stood up and surveyed his prisoner. Once more there was an embarrassment between them, a feeling of unease that did not exist amongst the other gang members. To Dale, his only thoughts were that he had his wonderful leader, the peerless Stella Ward, completely at his mercy. Nearly twelve years old and hardly aware of sexual matters other than investigative probings at initiation ceremonies of new members he could not understand the joy he experienced as he bent down close to Stella and looked into her eyes, fiery and still sparkling notwithstanding her helplessness. Despite initial protests through the gag and the flailing of bound boots in his direction, Stella eventually lay back and allowed her young captor to give her another clumsy and faltering kiss on the cheek. It was all so strange to Dale but a low whistle from Tim Court soon brought his mind back to more important matters. The rescuers were closing in and without further ado he rolled Stella on to her tummy, tied her hands to her feet, checked out her gag and was off on a long run to take the pursuers way off track. Stella could wait.

Upon his return some fifteen minutes later Dale was astonished to find no trace of Stella nor of Timmy or Donald. Excited by what had gone before he felt saddened that his teasing of Stella was apparently at an end. He could not understand his actions but knew deep down that what he had done had been quite natural and extremely pleasurable. It had appeared that Stella had enjoyed the episode too despite her stifled moans and theatrical writhing around. Her eyes had been round, warm and twinkling with delight as her young admirer took advantage of her plight. Dale had remembered too that it had been Stella's idea that she be the princess on this occasion and that he be her chief captor.

Dale's day-dreaming as he wandered back towards the railway track was suddenly brought to an end as he was attacked from behind by an assailant who was soon to show herself as his gang leader in all her ominous power. Their struggle was furious, fast and, for a few moments, fairly even. However Stella's fighting technique was far superior to Dale's and within four minutes and with growing horror and mounting excitement of what may be in store, Dale had his hands fastened securely behind his back and Stella was binding his wellingtons together using the very same football laces that he had used on her.

Stella sat back on her haunches and laughed at Dale's embarrassment. She explained that her bonds had not been too difficult to escape from and she had decided to veer from the story line of their 'wide' game by finishing off the game that Dale had started with her.

The next half hour was to live with Dale for the rest of his life. Stella teased and tormented Dale for almost twenty minutes before making him lick both her boots and confess his undying love for her as urges he could only guess at surged and re-surged through his body and his brain. She made no attempt to untie him and ended by kissing him fully on the lips whilst professing her love for him too.

'You are too young for me Dale,' she had whispered. 'You are too young but I truly love you.'

In 1948 Stella moved away with her family. They went to live in London somewhere and their departure was sudden and heartbreaking for Dale and the rest of the Gang. To be honest Stella had not seemed quite so available since the Christmas holidays with school-work and school activities filling up her days. She was wearing pretty floral dresses, heeled shoes and going back into Newcastle on Saturdays to see her school chums. Without her leadership, her ideas and her constant laughter the gang were lost. Games were not the same and Roy Banks left altogether because of increased homework and the fact that he was playing regularly for his school's 'under 14' soccer team.

Stella had promised she would write but no letters ever came from the south and gradually the memory of her faded to them all except for Dale who ached constantly for the sight and smell of her and found life intolerable without her. He had no idea why Stella Ward was so different from all his other pals and certainly no other girl had even touched him as he prepared for a new school and all that such things would produce for him.

CHAPTER FOUR

STELLA

Stella Ward left the North East of England with a heavy heart. Her childhood had been such a happy period in her life and she had made so many friends both in Monkseaton and amongst her fellow pupils in Newcastle. She would always remember her gang and especially the latter two years of leading it. Dale Ingram had given her that very first awkward kiss and they had both confessed their love for one another. He had explored her young body and produced new sensations that had made her tingle from head to toe. At school she had started attending dances and boys from the Royal Grammar School and Dame Allens prestigious City schools had attracted her notice. Older than her by a couple of years they had that inner confidence she had not come across before in her Monkseaton boys and she was beginning to find their talk and body language most interesting and exciting. One or two exploratory embraces outside the School's Main Assembly Hall, where the dances were held, before the boys were whisked away in their respective coaches, had shown Stella that she was an object of some desire and the fact that many of the girls from higher classes did not enjoy her popularity pleased her enormously. But throughout this period Dale Ingram still figured largely in her thoughts.

The gang had gathered outside Stella's house on the morning of her departure. It seemed that they really did care for her so much and their downcast expressions told the whole story. She chatted to them and promised that she would write and the Shilton twins hugged her warmly admitting that it would never be the same without her... they spoke for everyone. Dale tried hard to say something but nothing of any substance came out and as he knew he was very near to tears he stayed at the back only rushing forward at the last moment before she climbed into the family saloon and giving her a 'smacker-rooney' of a kiss on her surprised lips and muttering, 'Please don't forget me Stella, I'll never forget you Stella... NEVER!'

Stella's father, who was in the world of insurance, had been moved to South East London and had bought a house in Bromley giving him quick and easy access to the City each day. Stella was delighted with her new school which had an excellent reputation for academic studies and sporting prowess. She was a first class athlete excelling in sprinting and long jumping and her skill on the hockey field had soon established her in both the school senior eleven and then the County School Squad. The school-work was advanced to that of her old school and the first few terms were difficult for her as she struggled to catch up, with only her lovely nature and growing sporting reputation saving her from scoldings on several occasions as work was handed in that was far from satisfactory.

However, improve she did and gradually the prospect of a good University degree began to look more and more hopeful. Less and less she thought of her days in the cold North East but, just occasionally something would happen that would jerk her back to Northumberland. On a Field Day the sixth form had visited a wild nature reserve park and sitting on a tree stump she noted that nearly all the girls were wearing Wellington boots as they ate their packed lunches. She looked down at her own feet and remembered how many times those brown rubber boots had been tied together in past days. It was a mere passing memory that did not linger but it was a memory nevertheless of her gang and of Dale Ingram and she was glad that it was there.

'Dutch' Holland came into her life in her final year at school. Graham was a young Estate Agent in Bromley and they had met through their mutual love of athletics. Dutch was a fine sprinter and also played rugby for the local club's First XV although his running took precedence on all occasions. He was good-looking, confident and, to be honest, a wee bit arrogant. He knew he was good and saw little point in denying it. Stella thought he was wonderful and trained two evenings a week at the local track with a happy heart knowing that she would end up with Dutch who always would walk her home and kiss her goodnight. She had not got any taller since moving South but her body had changed shape and was now slimmer in adulthood. She moved with the grace of a big cat and was aware that she looked good and was attractive to the opposite sex. She was also proving attractive to her own sex as one or two of the younger girls in her House appeared highly smitten with their Captain. Their 'crushes' were harmless and Stella enjoyed this little bit of hero worship as she performed great deeds for the School and her House on the sports field.

Two episodes, hardly a week apart, ended her innocent relationship with Graham Holland. One afternoon she was waiting for her bus when three girls of about her own age surrounded her. Two of the grabbed her arms and held her tight whilst the other, a peroxide blonde with a leather jacket covering her ample upper body, got a hold of Stella's lips and crushed them together.

'How do you feel now Miss Goody Two Shoes? Not so bloomin' clever now are yer? This is just a warning. Stay away from Dutch Holland if you know what's good for yer. If we see you wiv 'im agin we'll make today seem like a bleedin' picnic.'

'Blondie' walked away and the other two girls released her arms and threw her forward as they sauntered off in the wake of their companion. Stella wasn't frightened, she was furious that she had not been able to say anything or do anything, so swift had been the attack, and frustrated that if she carried on the dialogue then quite obviously she was going to get more of the same from them. She was dressed in her school uniform with short heeled court shoes whereas her assailants were all in jeans and heavy boots. She sighed and wondered if she should tell Dutch about it all or wait to see if they re-entered her life. She decided on the latter plan of action for the time being.

The following weekend she and Dutch had finished training and were sitting on a park bench as the sun faded and dusk began to eke into the atmosphere. Dutch was edgy and finally spoke.

'Stella, you find me attractive don't you?'

'Was this a statement of fact or a question?' she pondered.

'Well I think it's about time we got it together don't you. We love each other and therefore it is the natural thing to do. I've been wanting to make love to you for ages but you haven't shown the slightest interest in such things and so I suppose it's up to me to make the first move. Look I've got a French letter so there's no worry on that score. Come on Stella, let's go over in those bushes and just do it.'

Stella realised that he was serious and couldn't believe what was happening and what had been said. It was his words that had shocked her so much. Obviously it had not occurred to him that in his wildest imagination she would not want to have sex with him and, just as obviously, old 'Blondie' had been and still was, very happy to oblige.

As silence had greeted his request he slid his arm around her and gently pulled her up from the bench.

'That's my girl,' he said. 'Now let's get it on… it'll be brilliant.'

Stella finally spoke and continued speaking until he was well out of earshot. She told him what she thought of him and his morals, she told him what she thought of his little blonde playmate and she told him that he would never make an international athlete as long as he had a hole in his bottom. She was still shouting as he disappeared over the horizon but he heard the epithets 'arrogant', 'conceited', 'loathsome', 'immoral', 'dirty', 'slow' and 'deceitful' quite clearly.

'Slow?' he mused. 'That's a bit hard… I'm never slow… I'm a 'ten point one' man for heaven's sake!'

Stella had excellent examination results and on the strength of the same was accepted by Newnham College, Cambridge where she had decided to read for a Degree in History. In the fifties colleges were all either all-male or all-female institutions but this suited Stella down to the ground as she had always attended all-girl schools to date and would have found being educated along with young men difficult enough without having to live in college with them as well. The course would last three years and that would be the end of her academic life for Stella could not wait to get out into the world of business, high finance or whatever. In those days females holding degrees were still something of a rarity and Stella's degree and her time at Cambridge would not be wasted and would be the icing on the top of a fairly impressive cake. Her final school report had been extremely effusive in its praise of the considerable impact she had made at the school on a very broad canvas covering most of the learning and sporting facilities that the school offered. Stella Ward was indeed a pupil of whom the redoubtable Miss Jean Brodie would have been most proud!

May Balls and all the joyous merry-making that was a constant companion to these quite unique social events were something to which all under-graduates looked forward. Despite their title they were held in mid-June to celebrate the end of the summer term and the end of 'final' examinations for some and mid-course papers, theses or whatever for the majority of the other under-graduates. The Magdalene College May Balls were to play their part in Stella's career for after two weeks' partying, drinking, climbing over walls to gain re-entry into her locked quarters and generally behaving outrageously she attended the Ball as the partner of one, Robbie Patterson, and having danced, laughed and talked for nine hours finally lost her virginity in what she could only describe later to herself as a ten minute frantic exhibition of lust, giggling and utter unfulfillment on her part, capped, almost inevitably by an enormous alcohol and banquet-induced fart from her exhausted and spent 'hero'. Robbie was great fun but completely mad, and with a career all ready and waiting for him, 'my Dad's quite big in steel' he was using his days at Cambridge to ensure that by the time he had to settle down under the watchful eye of his family there was nothing left to regret. He was clever and despite his antics he was to get a fairly decent degree and return to Sheffield from where Stella heard no more of him. This was of no consequence as although he was fun to be with she had never had any serious thoughts about him from a romantic point of view but knew that in his company there would always be loads of parties and a great deal of silliness which was a perfect antidote to the oppressive work regime she had set herself. Stella knew that she was intelligent but she was not a true academic and progressed by way of hard slog consisting of hours and hours of revision.

In her final year, during the May Ball party season, she met Richard Rigden-Ackeson. Richard was the elder brother of Toby who was a fellow History student and one of the gang with whom she seemed to spend much of her leisure time. Richard was strikingly handsome and quiet in comparison to Toby who tended to bound about the place like some demented Labrador puppy. In conversation Richard mentioned that he worked in the family Brewery Company down in East Kent and that he too had attended Cambridge and gained a degree in Law some six years previously. Stella liked him immediately and was flattered by the obvious attention he paid to her. Toby organised for his big brother to attend the Magdalene May Ball and to her delight invited her to come as his own partner knowing full well that he would see little of her but happy that such things pleased Richard immensely. Toby admired his elder brother enormously and Stella began to fall in love with the whole idea of a relationship with what must be a lovely family to have produced such smashing boys.

Richard arrived late on the evening of the Ball owing to work commitments but found Toby and Stella immediately and fell deeply in love for the first time in his life with the lovely vision that stood before him. Stella had taken time and trouble to look her best and with her dark hair and a quite stunning emerald green ball-gown she took his breath away, quite literally. They spent the entire evening together and talked and laughed and danced until dawn. Stella had eyes for nobody else and their love affair was off and running.

She obtained an excellent degree and was glad in a way that Richard had come into her life at this late stage in her academic career for she doubted whether she would have committed herself so diligently to her college work had the distraction of this young Brewer been around a year previously. She soon found herself a position with the City firm of Braithwaite & Whitehead who were Property Developers on a grand scale and wanted Stella to head their newly-formed public relations department. Stella was not sure at the time as to whether Richard had had anything to do with her getting the post but he assured her it was all down to her and subsequent conversation at a much later date proved this to be the case. She loved the work and the day-to-day contact with interesting and high-flying businessmen. Richard pursued her in his quiet but wholly determined fashion and exactly twelve months to the day from their May Ball date he proposed to her and she said 'Yes' as composedly as she was able with a thumping heart and tears in her striking green eyes.

Her family were delighted at the news for they had become very fond of Stella's handsome young beau and the wedding was arranged for the first Thursday in November of that year. It was 1956 and Stella was twenty-two years old. Richard's family were also pleased that their elder son had found such a lovely young lady to become his wife. The Rigden-Ackesons were a family whose traditional home had always been in Kent and they had been brewing beer for almost two hundred years in the historic Cinque Ports Town of Sandwich. Richard's father was not in the best of health and had gradually been taking less and less of a managerial role in the running of the Company. He had been a quite splendid Chairman but a mild stroke some three years ago had made the position clear to all and Richard's mother was determined that he should retire from active involvement at the earliest opportunity. Richard had grown in stature over the past seven years and already his new ideas and enthusiasm coupled with his tendency to be a workaholic where Brewery matters were concerned had made him the driving force of the Board of Directors. Having a beautiful and intelligent wife by his side was a real bonus for him at this stage in his career and their future looked both bright and exciting.

The Rigden-Ackesons took over the wedding arrangements from Stella's family but there was no rancour or unhappiness as their staging of the grand event could not have been bettered. Stella was as beautiful as everyone knew she would be and the social set in the County talked of nothing else for weeks after. A whole page in the *Tatler* devoted itself to the wedding with a large photograph of the happy couple. They honeymooned in the West Indies and returned home three weeks later to their new home, *Clover Leys*, a rambling manor-house situated in deep countryside between the villages of Wingham and Ash. The grounds were spacious and there were stables, greenhouses and a tennis court. A beautifully landscaped walled garden to the right of the house boasted a kidney-shaped swimming pool and tiled patio area with built-in barbecue. Stella had chosen the house having fallen in love with it on sight.

She resigned from Messrs Braithwaite & Whitehead and commenced her new life as the wife of the youngest Chairman of a Brewery Company in the land for Richard's father had retired almost as soon as they returned from honeymoon having established that

Richard would take over as Chairman, a move that was heartily supported by the remaining members of the Board. They had no doubts whatsoever that his keen financial brain and almost uncanny knack of doing the right thing at the right time would serve them admirably and it had to be said that two or even three of the present Board could not have organised a booze-up in a Brewery never mind be responsible for the continued success of their Company. The sixties had seen the end of most of the Kent Brewers with Mackeson, Cobb & Co, Tomson & Wootton, Gardeners of Ash and Fremlins being swallowed up by the Whitbread giant brewing conglomerate. Only Wetton Ackeson and their only real rival local Brewery, the even older Company of Messrs Shepherd Neame Ltd of Faversham, had managed to retain their independence during this pretty traumatic period.

Stella joined committees for this and Charitable Institutions for that and became a Justice of the Peace within a few years. She learned to ride, but not to hounds, and in later years was a familiar sight around the local area on her lovely chestnut mare Chance, accompanied on most occasions by their yellow Labrador Simon. As Richard became more and more entrenched in the modernisation of his Brewery so Stella found herself leading a life away from her husband but she was happy and although rarely getting involved with Messrs Wetton Ackeson she provided a warm and loving home environment and was the perfect hostess for all Richard's entertaining needs.

Neither of her parents were to live to an old age with her father suffering a massive heart attack at the age of fifty three and her mother losing a battle against cancer in her sixtieth year. Being an only child of two 'only children', Stella had no relatives and it was a great sadness to her that she and Richard did not produce any children themselves. All the tests were made after three or four years and it was diagnosed that there were no anatomical or physiological reasons why Stella had remained barren. Their sex life was not very active or exciting and had not played a great part in their relationship it was true but Richard had certainly done all in his power to try and produce a son and heir or a daughter as lovely as Stella.

'Don't you worry my dear,' he would say. 'If you stop trying so hard and relax I'm sure we'll be successful.'

"Thank you for those words of wisdom," thought Stella.

CHAPTER FIVE

DALE

Upon reaching the age of sixteen Dale had made quite a name for himself in the district. He was a natural sportsman and was playing cricket for the town and captaining the First X1 at school despite only being in the Junior Sixth Form. On the rugby field he had represented the County at 'under 18' level and was being groomed by the local club enjoying games with their third team, made up from past stars and budding youngsters. It was the era of Newcastle United's famous FA Cup exploits when the 'Magpies' actually won the cup three times in five years and Dale and his pals were regular Saturday afternoon visitors to St James' Park to watch the wondrous deeds of 'Wor' Jackie Milburn and the rest.

Dale had gained a state scholarship to a minor public school in Tynemouth at the age of eleven and wallowed in happiness in this new environment where discipline was strict but fair and an appreciation of sporting prowess more than held its own against the academic side of things. Dale was a good lad and before long had left his 'Gang' days behind him gaining new friends from within his classmates. David Welch, John Jeffcoat, Ian Lee Francis and he were soon inseparable buddies and remained so throughout their days at Tynemouth. All were talented sportsmen and all represented the school at the various age levels as they progressed.

Girls were something of an anathema to them in that they 'hated' them because that was the thing to do but also leered at the nudes in the 'Health & Efficiency' magazines that David used to pilfer from his elder brother's bedroom. Dale hinted that he knew more than the others and told vague stories of a past girlfriend but even to him members of the female sex were classed as 'rather silly things who dance backwards'.

It was at about this time that Una Smith came into David's life and Peggy Graham bounded into the world of Dale. Una was still at school but Peggy had left her school and was working at the town library. Peggy was pretty and full of fun and Dale fell madly in love. She was far more experienced than he and during the course of their romance she taught him so much about the techniques of pleasing a woman sexually. Dale found to his bewilderment that his penis was a strict and unerring pointer to sexual arousement and constantly was embarrassed by surges in his loins as Peggy played tennis or danced or did any of the things that the Whitley Bay gang did in those carefree days.

One day they had cycled to Seaton Sluice, some five miles away, to spend some time by themselves lazing in the sand dunes, swimming, kissing and cuddling. After a brief but exhilarating dip amongst the North Sea rollers they ran up the beach and flopped onto their towels. As Peggy went to unclip the chin-strap of her white rubber swim cap Dale stopped her.

'Don't take it off yet Peggy... I... I... I think you look incredible in it,' he found himself saying without really understanding why.

Peggy kept the cap on and queried the motive behind his odd request.

'Don't you like my hair?' she laughed. 'Or have you got a **thing** about rubber?' Seeing his cheeks colour Peggy cottoned on immediately and squealed, 'Oh Dale! You have got a **thing** about rubber haven't you, I'd have worn my wellies if I'd known!'

Peggy, being Peggy, found the whole thing hilarious and a definite subject to explore from this time forth. Dale couldn't cope and sulked for the rest of the day but realised that all Peggy had said was absolutely true. He had found the look and the scent of Peggy quite unbelievably erotic as she donned her rubber hat and her mention of wellingtons drove his memory banks back to Stella and all the joy she had provided.

'Why oh why does this have to happen to me!' he moaned to himself.

The very next day was as wet as the previous day had been sunny and a ring at the door bell was followed by his Mum's voice exclaiming:

'Oh hello Peggy love. My! You are dressed for the weather and no mistake!'

"Oh my God," thought Dale with a mixture of terror and anticipation flooding his mind. "What is she wearing?"

Peggy was wearing a bright pale blue short rubberised mackintosh with a sou'wester to match and on her feet were a pair of brand new shiny black Wellington boots. She looked wonderful and, of course, she knew that to her boyfriend she looked wonderful and very sexy.

'How do you like the outfit Dale? Do I look stunning?' she laughingly goaded him as she stood there with her legs apart and her hands on her hips.

Life was never again going to be the same for Peggy Graham and Dale Ingram. For the next eighteen months Dale and Peggy were seldom apart out of school and work hours. She followed his sporting career with enormous enthusiasm and caused quite a stir at the School versus The Staff annual cricket match when she turned up and sat with the Headmaster as Dale led his team to a rather easy victory in one of his final matches before departing.

Peggy spoiled him rotten over his love of seeing her in rubber and wore her boots whenever possible and would even don her bathing cap when saying goodnight to him on her front porch. Had there not been National Service to interrupt his life then Dale felt certain he would have married Peggy for there had never been anyone else in either of their lives from the moment they first met. They were well matched and both families approved of their child's choice of partner. Sexually they grew in experience with Peggy proving to be a quite superb lover. She could produce almost any emotion out of Dale and was a very skilful mistress in the arts of holding him back from that huge bursting climax that is wasted on so many teenagers. He was a willing pupil and loved to have his teacher gasping for breath and unable to think of anything more erotic to scream than 'Oh Yes!! Oh Yes!! Fuck me! Fuck me! Fuck me!'

However, Dale, having obtained reasonable A level marks decided that he would carry out his National Service before going on to University and duly joined HM Forces in the September of 1955. Twelve weeks' square-bashing and then a posting to BAOR as a clerk in the Royal Army Service Corps at HQ Field Records stationed at Bad Oeynhausen saw Dale quickly establishing himself in the local rugby team. The work was plentiful but not mind-blowing in its content and Dale's duties were to keep a watchful eye on all those serving men who did not return from leave on time. Sick on Leave or SOL was perfectly acceptable provided Doctors' certificates substantiated the information but AWOL or Absent without Leave was a totally different matter and Dale's duties included having the miscreants arrested by the civil or military police and the latter bringing them back to Germany to serve their sentence.

In mid-service HQ Field Records moved to Viersen, a pretty village setting some three miles from Munchen Gladbach, where a brand new camp accommodated them. Here Dale found the chance to ride first class horses and play rugby with the HQ BAOR XV as well as turn out for Field Records at soccer and hockey. Having obtained the rank of Corporal he met an attractive young German female groom who introduced him to her family and was very eager to make their friendship into a deeper association. Several times, after a wonderful ride in the flat countryside surrounding the stables Dale could not control his feelings at the sight of this blonde and bronzed young woman in her tight breeches and boots and their subsequent love-making in the stable hay was both noisy and not without tension, as one of her brothers had no time for the British Army in Occupation and even less time for Corporal Ingram whom he thought might just be 'knocking off' his little sister and as a result tended to spring out of the shadows at the slightest pretext. Marlene Shroeder was not Peggy Graham but Dale's lack of corresponding to his girlfriend and clumsy handling of their separation meant that within a year of leaving the North East Peggy had given him up as a bad job and was soon engaged to a Master Butcher from Newcastle. Dale was still deeply concerned by the fact that he was, according to Peggy, a real dyed-in-the-wool rubber fetishist and wondered if he would ever be able to find another girl who enjoyed his 'kink' so much. He never discussed the problem with Marlene but noted that she never wore one article of rubber clothing during the entire period of their affair. He was not really sorry to say goodbye when the time came for his departure from Germany as it was clear that she and he were going nowhere.

As demob' drew near, Dale thought about his future life and decided that he wanted to live in Kent where he had spent many happy holidays staying with relatives in and around the Canterbury area. The idea of going back to college did not appeal to him at all and he was grateful when one of his uncles let him know that there was a pupil valuer's position up for grabs in the City and was he interested? With David and John both at University and Ian already fixed up with employment in London his school chums were not going to be around and the idea of working in such a lovely part of the country became more and more appealing to him. He let the firm in question know of his interest and that he would be free to attend for an interview within six weeks. To his delight a letter came by return giving him dates and times for his meeting with the Senior Partner.

After a week of celebration following his departure from the Army, and including sister Daisy's marriage to Frank Cowell, Dale duly attended his interview in Canterbury. The Senior Partner, a Mr Tremlett, was in his sixties and was dressed in a black jacket, striped trousers and spats covering his highly polished shoes. Dale took to him immediately and he sensed Mr Tremlett liked him in return. They talked of cricket, rugby and golf and discussed Dale's starting salary and, in general terms, the business life that beckoned. He agreed to the terms that were offered and left the old but very distinguished office feeling really good about the meeting he had just had.

Two days later a letter arrived in Monkseaton informing that the position was his and they expected him to commence work in four weeks' time. Dale was overjoyed. Leaving the North East was not the wrench it might have been without the upheaval of National Service and he knew that his home and his parents would be there at holiday times. He found Peggy and on neutral ground apologised for his boorish behaviour. She was still a most attractive young lady but made it very clear that he had hurt her badly and there was a wound inside her that would never heal.

'I really loved you Dale,' she admitted. 'I loved all your funny ways and couldn't ever believe that you would dump me like you did. Do you still prefer your ladies in rubber by the way? How did the frauleins take to that I wonder?'

Dale had no answers and having kissed each other they left and never saw each other again, although Dale continued to check up on her whereabouts for the rest of his life for Peggy Graham, like Stella Ward, was special, very special.

Dale threw himself into his new job and was working with the Senior Partner for most of the time, learning the art of valuation of licensed property whether it be a four-star hotel or a bent tea spoon. Property and chattels had to be assessed alike and he found the whole thing so interesting. Most of the public houses belonged to the various Kent Brewers and were let to tenants and it became clear as the weeks went by that C G Tremlett & Son were a kind of specialist Estate Agent who carried out all the needs of the tenant licensee.

Dale's rugby prowess soon had him playing regularly for the Canterbury club much to Mr Tremlett's delight who, unknown to Dale at the time, wallowed in the most complimentary match reports of his pupil in the local paper each week. He made many friends and because of his startlingly good looks attracted much interest from the young ladies of Canterbury and was especially popular with the nurses from the nearby Kent & Canterbury Hospital who smuggled him into their quarters on many occasions for an exciting and most rewarding end to a night out.

For three or four years he dated a Carol Cooper whom he had met at the Saturday Dance at the Abbots Barton Hotel, the Mecca for all young folk in the late fifties. Carol was lovely to look at but not too bright and worked in the office of a Coal Merchant dealing with orders etc. Dale enjoyed her chatter and the fact that she never really wanted any commitment from him for he was determined that no girlfriend of his would ever be badly treated by him again.

After about a year he bought her a swim cap and asked her to put it on for him. He explained that he loved the look of such things and that the smell of rubber was a real 'turn-on' for him. Her response was not in the Peggy mould at all for the lass could not get her head round what he was saying. Dale tried to explain about fetishism and the broad canvas it covered over all sexual preferences. Eventually Carol pulled the cap over her blonde locks and buttoned up the chin-strap feeling desperately embarrassed and completely bewildered by Dale's behaviour. She could not have expected the powerful and immediate response from her Dale as she found herself being stripped and carried to Dale's bed where he made love to her in a manner she had never experienced before, either with Dale or any other man with whom she had been. He simply overwhelmed her with his lips, hands and feet all combining to stroke, kiss and caress every part of her body. Her climax was utterly fulfilling and as she dressed herself some sixty minutes later she made a mental note that wherever she went from now on the bathing cap went with her.

'Talk about Superman and his Kryptonite,' she murmured. 'God knows what will happen to me if I can get hold of a wet-suit!'

Their lovemaking was wonderful for them both after that and Dale was grateful for all the things that Carol did to titillate his whimsical wants. Like Peggy had done in those pre-National Service years, new black wellingtons were purchased and often donned for sessions in Dale's small flat. Carol seemed to know instinctively that she was pumping up her lover's libido to bursting point and this gave her enormous confidence in herself. Eventually she allowed Dale to experiment with bondage games and although she found these to be a bit frightening at first she soon realised that sadism is not in the tool-kit of your run-of-the-mill rubber fetishist, and to be sexually aroused and brought to a climax when utterly helpless and at the mercy of your lover is one of life's real 'turn-ons'. Wearing rubber she felt herself attaining the stature of some kind of Superwoman and although never telling anyone of her antics she longed the world to know how sexually content Dale Ingram had made her. She was falling very heavily in love with him and yet, to be fair to the man, he had never allowed her to believe that this was anything other than a 'bit of fun' with nothing asked of either partner other than total discretion. It was a real dilemma for Carol and she was at a loss as to how to solve the growing problem.

Dale loved his sessions with Carol but treated them purely as just that... sessions. She was fun to be with and loved all the extra things he would call upon to make their lovemaking that much more interesting and exciting. He had never thought of Carol as anything but a good mate and was upset and unsettled when she eventually told him of her love for him and her desire to settle down to married life with him. His abject refusal to entertain such an action had to be very carefully worded for he would not have hurt this pleasant lass for all the tea in China. Carol was hurt but could not hate her Dale no matter how hard she tried.

"There has to be more than just sex and sex games," she told herself, "and if Dale doesn't want a home and a family life then I'll find somebody who does before it's too late."

They continued to see each other for a few months but then decided that it wasn't helping anybody to allow the relationship to dwindle on in this way and a tearful Carol departed from his life.

Dale's business life was progressing in leaps and bounds. He had become, under Mr Tremlett's wise counsel, a most competent and popular valuer with Tenants and Brewers alike and enjoyed the cut and thrust of valuation work, agreeing settlement figures with other valuers and physically attending the various public houses all over the South East of England on the days that tenants were moving in and moving out to carry out the business transaction of the 'Changeover'. He made friends in the trade very easily and with the social side that this brought to him and his rugby and cricket sporting days each week his life was full. There were two or three 'Carol' characters who drifted into and out of his life but none were anything but playthings to him, although one did threaten to tell the world about their kinky goings-on when they approached the end of that particular road, but was eventually talked out of such things by Dale who pointed out that she would come out of it looking a wee bit silly herself particularly as she had purchased quite a number of rubber garments during their affair and had paid for same herself.

As the years rolled by Dale's life quietened as most of his friends married and began to produce families. He noticed that being a single man with no girlfriend meant fewer hostesses tended to invite him to their dinner parties and for the first time in his life he began to think about the idea of finding himself a wife. But what sort of a wife? She would have to be lovely-looking, full of fun, intelligent, in love with him and in love with all his sexual deviations, a great home-maker, tolerant of his sporting life, and, and... all rolled into one gorgeous female! One or two public house landladies had been out with him unbeknown to their husbands and one or two had been extremely good to be with but such an affair would have brought disgrace on the firm and possibly caused the death of the ageing but nevertheless still able Senior Partner. Certainly had he continued to see one little Welsh 'bombshell' from the 'Golden Griffin' in Dover it would have caused the premature death of one, Dale Ingram, for on their first illicit outing she had demanded sex up against his Ford Cortina in a lay-by outside the village of Eastry and then wanted full 'no-holds-barred' sexual intercourse on his back seat in the car park of a country inn near Hythe. His mention, as he lay with one foot over the driver's head-rest and the other stuck in the safety-strap, that he was 'interested in rubber' merely brought out the comment from her as she heaved and sweated under him:

'I couldn't care less what interests you Dale my lovely boyo… the only interest in rubber that I have at this moment in time consists of the piece folded around your old John Thomas. Now let's really get this show on the road… Do you want to try me "doggy fashion" or what about the "wheel-barrow?"…I love the "wheel-barrow"!!!'

Dale felt there had to be more to life than these constant peccadilloes and as he approached forty years there was a real anxiety creeping into his innermost thoughts. The magnificent Rubenesque Dr Maeve Kavanagh, Sexual Therapist Extraordinaire, was to allay those fears however.

CHAPTER SIX

CROFT HOUSE

Stella thought, "Oh my God he's going to tie me up! He's going to see me in riding boots and a bikini! He's going to take the bikini off!"

Stella said, 'I repeat, I nearly didn't come. I have had a hell of a busy morning and couldn't decide whether you were serious or not. But I did pack what you ordered just in case the situation demanded it.' She felt her words sounded ridiculous.

Dale had done all the booking-in and they glided through the homely Reception area without being noticed and were soon in Room Eight. Stella looked round and was pleasantly surprised by what she saw. Much love and affection had gone into the furnishings and the en suite and very modern bathroom was in direct contrast to the warm antique-laden bedroom. She took in the oil paintings, the brass coal helmet and the pair of ornate iron fire dogs in the grate. Stella noted the bed which was five foot wide, made of pine and had four turned corner posts.

Stella thought, "Oh my God he's going to spread-eagle me!"

Stella remarked casually, 'My! What a lovely room… I **love** the paintings.'

Dale did not beat about the bush. It was all too important to him. For thirty years he had carried the memory of this fantastic girl, a girl whom he had totally given up any lingering hope of ever meeting. True they had never been lovers in the full sexual sense but they did have a bond and this feeling of unfulfillment had remained with him for always. It was this lady who had made him the man he was, he was sure of it.

He moved towards Stella and held her.

'Stella, my dear Stella, this is our time. I'm absolutely certain that this is what fate has decreed. Please undress and put your gear on. I can't wait to see you in your boots. You do realise that I've had a *thing* about rubber boots ever since you made us all wear them in the gang.'

'Oh, so it's all my fault that you're as kinky as hell is it Dale? I chose our outfits because we could all wear the same clothes in winter or summer. I had no idea that one day my perfectly sensible and practical planning would come back to haunt me.'

'But you did like to be tied up Stella. You've got to admit that nobody got tied up more than you even though you were quite capable of preventing most of the gang from trussing you up. Do you still get tied up by your Richard? Do you still love it?'

The questions were innocent enough and deserved answers.

'Good heavens, no! Richard does not tie me up. Never has and never will. He's perfectly normal.'

'But do you still love it?' persisted Dale.

Stella smiled, giving herself time to deliver a perfectly sensible reply to a question that she knew, deep down, had one very simple and basic answer.

'I can't say I've ever really given the matter a great deal of thought,' she lied. 'I suppose it's fun in a way if you like that sort of thing and I'm pretty open-minded about all matters sexual. Whatever turns you on, as they say.'

What she desperately wanted to say was "Yes! Yes! Yes! Tie me up! Tie me down! Take me! Take me! Take me!" but her game of cat and mouse continued and Dale once again had to take the initiative. Taking his hands from around her waist he went over to her flight bag and un-zipping it extracted Stella's black rubber riding boots which had been treated to a coating of high gloss rubber and vinyl polish which she had borrowed from Richard's car kit together with her black bikini and gloves.

'Jesus Christ, what brilliant boots! Get 'em on Stella,' he said simply. 'This I have got to see.'

Stella made no comment and disappeared into the bathroom. Once inside she quickly took off her grey suit and high heels, underwear and tights. "This is madness," she thought. "I am not the girl he remembers and this is certainly not the body he remembers." Taking a deep breath and with her confidence fading by the second she slipped into her bikini, pulled on her boots and gloves. She looked at herself in the mirror and under the bright lights of this ultra-modern room she had to admit to herself that she didn't look at all bad. She knew the boots and gloves were sexually going to turn Dale on and if she were honest the smell and look of her rubber gear excited her too. It was all so completely unreal and she still couldn't quite accept that Mrs Stella Rigden-Ackeson JP, a pillar of East Kent Society was about to let a man she had last known as an eleven-year-old boy see her dressed like this.

Taking another deep breath she opened the bathroom door after spraying herself with Oscar de la Renta and primping her already immaculately groomed hair.

'Anyone for riding?' she laughed, whilst standing in the doorway with hands on hips and legs apart.

Dale was waiting for her entrance. He had quickly pulled on his own rubber riding boots and a pair of navy blue boxer shorts. He moved to her and laughingly cried, 'Stella, your gang awaits you! Now let's sort you out once and for all… come and lie on the bed you gorgeous female!'

Dale was in no way inhibited by his own dress and Stella admitted to herself that he looked in terrific shape. She lay down on the bed half-expecting to be showered with kisses but instead Dale motioned for her to give him her right wrist which he bound gently but very firmly to the bed post above her head with golden silken curtain cord. The left wrist followed and then her legs were moved wide apart as her booted ankles were secured to either post at the foot of the bed. Stella was absolutely helpless, she knew it and Dale knew it.

Dale went over to his case and tossed a white floppy object onto Stella's bare midriff. Stella looked down and saw with mounting horror that it was a very new but very old-fashioned bathing cap with a chin-strap.

'**I am not going to wear that bloody thing!**' she shouted at him but it was to no avail and with an expertise that was lost on her for the present the rubber cap was pulled gently over her tumbling tresses until all hair had disappeared and then the chin-strap was clipped firmly in place.

'I can't believe this Dale. I think you had better untie me right now!' she said.

'I'll untie you my sweet if you are in pain or feel ill. Normally, all you would have to say is the word MONKSEATON and you'll be free but I won't free you because you just want me to. You look gorgeous and now you are my Rubber Princess.'

'I must look like a boiled egg in this bloody cap. The last time I wore one of these was at the open air sea-bathing pool at …' she drifted off for a moment, 'at… the open air baths at Tynemouth… and you were there and four of you grabbed me and threw me in the deep end.'

'You put up a hell of a struggle then Stella and I can still see your face screwed up with effort as you tried to escape. You were helpless then Stella and you are even more helpless now.'

Stella watched with growing apprehension as he went back to his case and took out a blue dimpled hard rubber ball almost the size of a golf ball which appeared to have a round leather dog collar threaded through the centre.

'You will be perfectly able to breathe but speaking will not be possible,' Dale said in a throwaway fashion. 'You will not therefore be able to say MONKSEATON but I shall know you are unwell if you blink furiously for a few moments.'

'If you think you are going to put that thing in my...**GROOF...BLOOFER...GROTHLER,**' shouted Stella as the ball was neatly placed on her tongue and rapidly buckled into place. She subsided for a moment or two and then really let her captor have it with both barrels.

'**GROOF...AAAGHLOF...KAUGHKOW...OWKKA...OR GAS,**' she screamed as the gag, without causing any real discomfort, performed exactly as Dale had predicted.

Stella lay there wondering what on earth was going to happen next. Dale went over to the wardrobe and produced two spare pillows which he pumped up and then slid under the base of Stella's back causing immediate much increased comfort despite the new arched position in which she found herself.

'You all right my Rubber Princess?' enquired Dale

'**GAAGHAF...GROOKAN...AAAHHEG...CACCCHHO NAAGHEN!!!!**' Stella replied which, roughly translated, questioned her captor's right to be alive, his parenthood and something about giving him a vasectomy without any local anaesthetic and blunt kitchen scissors!

Dale gently un-clipped her bikini top and then un-laced her bottom leaving her capped, gloved and booted solely in rubber. He produced a pink vibrator from his case and holding it in front of Stella's ever-widening eyes explained that this particular model not only was a dab hand at thrusting in and out but also explored the whole of her gorgeous fanny in a wide sweeping and scouring motion.

'**GORRRR!!!**' gasped Stella

He touched her nipples and almost immediately they hardened. Stella's breasts were in great condition and although not big were nevertheless firm and nicely rounded. They too firmed up at Dale's touch and gradually, slowly he moved down to her stomach which gently rose and lowered under her steady breathing. The pillows having arched her back meant that Stella's vagina was presenting itself almost pushily for attention and having wafted the vibrator under her nostrils he switched it on and Stella gasped through the gag as she saw at first hand the versatility of the wretched thing.

'GORRRR!!!... GLOODDY GELL!!!'

The entry of the vibrator produced one incredible jerk from Stella's arms and legs as they fought for freedom. The creak of bedposts, rubber and bonds was heard as she strained every sinew to free herself from this mechanical love-toy.

'I'm not going to come, I'm not going to come, **I'm not going to come!!!**' she screamed inwardly as the vibrator busied itself hitting the G spot about every 3 seconds. Dale stood over her stroking and caressing her inner thighs, her breasts and stalk-like nipples. He leant over and kissed her lips forced apart by the ball gag.

'I'm not going to come…I'm not going to come…**I'm not going to come!!! OH GOD!! I'M GOING TO COME!!!!!'**

Dale seemed to pick up the final frantic thread of her outburst which came out something like… **'AAH COG!!! AAAHCAWKAN GAA GONG!!!'** and gently removed the super-penis murmuring to Stella as he did so, 'No! No! No! Not yet time, my lovely. Plenty of time for comings and goings.'

Four times the vibrator was replaced inside Stella and four times it inevitably brought her to that point just before the bursting, all-consuming, wonderful moment of blissful climax only for Dale to smilingly remove the battery-operated gadget and allow the moment to pass before the pinnacle of sexual joy had been achieved.

'You're beginning to make me jealous Stella darling. I do believe you are falling in love with my vibrator and that would never do.'

If it was possible to sulk with a blue rubber ball stuck inexorably in your mouth then Stella gave a fair imitation. She raised her head as far as she could and noticed that her spread-eagled body was glistening with sweat, her booted ankles were as secure as ever and there was no give in the cord around each gauntleted wrist. Dale sensed her assessment of her situation and brought a mirror from the dressing table so that Stella could see her face in it. The shock of seeing herself close-up was immense. Her sweat-coated reddened face stood out against the whiteness of the bathing cap and the wretched blue ball gag could be seen behind her gleaming half-opened teeth She wondered what the hell Mrs Stella Rigden-Ackeson JP was doing here and why the hell she was still so excited about all that had happened since Dale Ingram had come back into her life.

'Oh fuck him!!!' she cried out

'**Aaaah gaark urrgk!!!**' Dale heard her cry with venom in her eyes.

At this point the gag was finally removed and Stella was able to converse coherently with Dale. She was well aware that despite being bound and gagged she had nevertheless experienced the most satisfying sexual episode of her life. She had to admit to herself that she was not in any physical discomfort and although the close-fitting bathing cap was hot to wear it was obviously a real 'turn-on' for Dale and this pleased her. It gave her a platform to explore.

'Will you take this bloody cap off me?' she enquired politely.

'I'm afraid not my darling Stella,' he replied.

'Bastard!' was all Stella could think to say as she tugged once again at her bonds only to find that her ankles came away from their posts. Dale had loosened them and before she could lash out at him as she had always done when captured in their childhood days he was on top of her and in between her legs. He kissed her lips, caressing her body and finally her crotch. Stella was wet and over-brimming with her juices... sliding down, his mouth found her demanding and ripe vagina. His tongue flicked and licked inside as though preparing her for some grand finale. Stella sighed and heaved with sheer love of lust. Now free, her legs came into play and Dale found his head clamped inside her crotch by her crossed booted ankles behind his neck. Her longing was something she could neither hide nor make any pretence of indifference about. She desperately wanted Dale to fuck her upstairs, downstairs and in my lady's chamber!!!

Their lovemaking lasted for nearly two hours and although Stella had been untied for over half that time she nevertheless kept wearing her cap, gloves and boots as they explored every crevice of each other's bodies. They climaxed together four times at intervals and Dale was amazed by the almost continual erection he was able to sustain during that time. Later he put it down to the surge of passion that had flowed through him as their boots had interlocked on occasion and squelched together in delightful harmony. He supposed that if this was the height of rubber fetishism then, by God, it took some beating! They both knew it would have to end and slowly their bodies disengaged and they lay, wet and wonderfully exhausted, their passion spent, their needs fulfilled.

Stella sat up and peeled off her black gloves. She then unfastened her chin-strap and removed her cap tossing her head as she did so allowing her cramped lovely dark tresses to tumble down around her shoulders... the riding boots would have to wait. She lay back and reflected on the past three hours. She could not remember having been so happy, so content with herself and so utterly in love with one man. She looked across at Dale as he lay beside her, eyes closed and breathing deeply. This man had come back into her life and turned her whole world upside down. Richard was a caring, loving husband but a man incapable of even understanding the happenings of that afternoon never mind putting them into practice. He could probably buy and sell Dale thirty times over but then business and money were his prime motivations. He simply did not understand that his wife yearned to be **loved** to the furthest outpost of her emotions and not just made to feel safe or put on show every now and then as a prized possession. What was she to do? One thing for certain was that she was not going to lose Dale again.

'I knew it would be wonderful, darling Stella,' Dale remarked quietly. 'I knew you would be the same proud and defiant lady and quite able to cope with anything I threw at you.' There was a hint of genuine admiration in the manner in which he spoke. 'I'm sorry about the gag and the cap but they were so necessary for me and, I suspect, for you. As leader of the Stella Ward Gang you simply thrived on bondage situations and I just knew that deep down those girlhood feelings would still be there. I was right wasn't I?'

Stella smiled.

'What can I say… I had no idea that such feelings were still in me but you have produced the key that has opened up emotions that must always have been inside me. Yes! Yes! Yes! I loved every second of time spent here in Croft House. I hate the gag, the cap and the gloves but I adored wearing them in my tied-up state and seeing how Stella Ward could excite a man like you so much.'

An hour later they were showered, dressed and ready to face their new world. The lines that the inner rubber welding of the tight-fitting cap had ingrained on her forehead had finally disappeared. Stella had suggested a meeting at the County Hotel on the following Tuesday where they could meet for coffee as though by accident and this plan dove-tailed with Dale's commitments.

'I'm not going to give you up Stella,' Dale said.

'You need not worry on that score but I simply have to give some thought as to how I'm going to cope with all this Dale. You have completely shattered my lifestyle and the foundations of my marriage. You have compelled me to take stock of myself and Richard. I'm just grateful for the first time in my life that we have not been blessed with any children to date… it does make things slightly less complicated, if that were possible.'

Dale watched as the BMW rolled out of the hotel driveway and then clambered into his old Rover and began his drive back to Canterbury. It had been quite a day.

CHAPTER SEVEN

Stella spent that evening in some kind of blissful trance. She was racked by inner guilt but utterly overwhelmed by the happenings of that afternoon. How could all this have happened to her? Richard had come home a little earlier than normal muttering something about the gardener and the state of the swimming pool and vanished into his study for an hour before re-emerging downstairs in his oldest clothes.

'I'm going to try and sort out the pool this evening,' he remarked. 'That bloody fool of a gardener hasn't got a clue.'

Stella found herself saying, 'I couldn't agree more! The water is over-chlorinated and it needs a really good cleaning,' whilst picturing herself on the diving board in her new bathing cap posing in front of the admiring Dale Ingram. "Oh damn the man!" she thought. Richard spent the rest of the evening at the poolside eventually coming in as dusk became black night.

'It's fit for a princess,' he proclaimed.

'Am I still your princess?' Stella asked

'Of course you are, you funny old thing. Now are you going to make the cocoa or shall I?'

Stella went into the kitchen and mused about her life with this man whom she loved and knew that he, in turn, loved her. She had betrayed him in the most outrageous fashion and had the tables been turned she had no doubt that she would have left him immediately if his secret had become known to her. And yet she had no feeling of regret, no wish inside her that her meeting with Dale had not happened. She had, after all, known Dale Ingram since childhood days and knew that she had talked of him to college girlfriends whilst up at Cambridge when discussing early sexual encounters. This was the man or rather the boy, who had given her that first real kiss, he was the first to see and squeeze her young formative breasts and he the first to explore, albeit very clumsily, her pubic mound. "Am I trying to justify all this?" she mused.

'Dearest, are you **ever** going to bring cocoa into my life?' Richard queried loudly, bringing her back into the land of reality.

By the time Stella had undressed and put on her nightie Richard was in bed and deeply ensconced in a book about the history of the fight for the Ashes. She did not even switch on her bedside light as she slipped between the covers.

'Goodnight darling,' she said. 'It's been a long and funny old day and I'm whacked.'

'Goodnight my dearest. I'll be off early tomorrow morning so don't be alarmed if I'm not about when you wake up.' He kissed the top of her head as she began to drift off into what dreams she knew not.

Dale had some valuation work to do down in Rye and left the office before ten in order to be down in East Sussex before the public house got busy with lunchtime trade. The landlady was young and pretty and Dale recalled meeting her some four years ago when she and her husband had called for a general interview prior to being accepted for this tenancy. They had been very successful and as a result had been offered a much better house near Ashford with the same Brewery Company, Messrs Wetton Ackeson of Sandwich.

Dale gazed at the young lass and with almost indecent haste quickly transformed her into *a Pirate Captain with silken blouse, tight breeches and shining thigh boots standing on the poop deck with her legs astride and her gauntlet clad hands on her ample hips.*

'Cup of coffee Mr Ingram?' she asked

'AAAAaaaaarrrrrrr.' The 'Robert Newton' impersonation dried on his lips. 'Er, that would be very nice my dear,' he replied.

Throughout his life Dale's vivid imagination had constantly got him into the weirdest of situations and the meeting of yesterday with his beloved Stella had set his sexual taste buds on fire. Dousing himself with the cold water of reality he commenced work on his inventory and valuation of the saloon bar chattels and by the time the coffee arrived he had managed to put a floral dress and white high-heeled shoes back onto his attractive client.

The house was not large and by two-thirty the valuation was complete and Dale supped a half-pint of Wetton IPA as he talked to Vin and Annie Scott of their impending move. Vin was a likeable cove and very ambitious. As he talked excitedly of his plans for the Games Room being made into a small dining room Dale found himself *having a Douglas Fairbanks Sen (or Jun) sword fight with Cap'n Annie Scott, the Queen of the Barbary Coast. Grinning broadly the tip of his sword sliced open her tight silk shirt allowing her swelling breasts to tumble forth…*

'So what do you think Mr Ingram?'

'Wonderful! Wonderful!' Dale cried, trying desperately under the table to clobber his erect member with the tip of his three foot rule but catching instead the pub cat which was napping on the chair beside him and forcing it to leap from its lofty perch with a howl of indignation. Life was never straightforward for Dale Ingram, never had been and never would be.

Annie came out to the car park with Dale to say goodbye.

'Do you really think we'll make a go of it Mr Ingram?' she asked.

'I'm certain of it Annie, and do call me Dale please… all my friends do and I'd like to class you as one of my friends after all this time.' The words were innocuous enough and yet Annie found herself wondering if there had been something more behind them.

'I noticed some riding boots in the bedroom Annie. Do you still ride?'

'Only occasionally Dale, but whenever there's an opportunity I love a morning's hacking over the marshes. I don't have a horse but one of our farming fraternity has always made one available for me. Are you keen yourself?'

Annie, dressed in Doris Day's "Calamity Jane" outfit, was bound to an old tree with the taut ropes sprayed either side of her heaving bosoms. Dale, all in white, galloped up to rescue her as Sinatra warbled 'I Did it My Way' with massive orchestral backing.

'Are you keen on riding yourself?' she repeated.

'Who me? Yes I love riding and there's nothing nicer than to see a lovely young lady astride a powerful hunter. We must have a morning out together when you are settled in Charing. I too know a farmer who is only too pleased to have his horses exercised whilst his children are at college. I'll organise it if you like.'

'Oh I'd just love it Dale. Vin hates anything to do with horses apart from those that race around a track and he ends up hating them as well if the truth be known,' she laughed.

Annie walked back to the house with a spring in her step. Dale was a charming and handsome man who would give her an excellent day's riding and a lovely day out to boot... she was sure of it. Dale drove through Appledore *with Frank Sinatra still singing, Calamity Annie still writhing and he still thinking of untying his damsel in distress... eventually.*

Stella Rigden-Ackeson walked across the Brewery Car Park. She had agreed to be one of the judges in the Company's 'Best Kept Garden' competition and she and her fellow judges were visiting six of the entrants that day. Richard was in London at a Society Meeting and would not be back until quite late that evening. The Brewery Secretary, a tall, pipe-smoking cadaverous individual in his early sixties who listed amongst his hobbies: phillumeny or the collection of matchbox labels, the growing of orchids and the game of cricket, met her at Reception. George Banyard had been at the Brewery all his career and had served Richard's father and uncle as well as the only remaining member of the Wetton side of the Company, Rupert, who had died in rather suspicious circumstances whilst holidaying in Malaga at the age of 74. There had been talk of a young Spanish waitress with an insatiable appetite for multiple orgasms and a liking for unusual positions, but nothing came out in the papers at the time and 'a severe and fatal heart attack whilst in the throes of attempting to slow down the speed of the circulating ceiling fan' was the official and possibly correct verdict.

The other two judges were Mrs Philomena Billshot, the wife of the Tied Trade Director and Toby Fanshawe who was a cousin of Richard's and had been given the title of Marketing and Sales Director despite having the intelligence of an amoeba and the social graces of a starving Jack Russell. Philomena, Philo to her many friends, was a lady with a liking for fun and the high life who was attractive in a rather 'horsy' way, but really didn't have a nasty bone in her buxom body.

The six gardens were all in excellent condition with the various tenants having worked long and hard to produce neat and colourful harbours in which their customers could relax and pass away an hour or two. They were situated in West Kent and East Sussex with the final call being at the Black Swan in Rye. Their surprise visit did not appear to faze the Scotts, who had organised a tray of coffee and a plate of crustless cucumber sandwiches by the time the judges had carried out their inspection.

George Banyard explained to the party that Mr and Mrs Scott were moving to the 'Green Man' at Charing shortly as a promotion for the fine job they had done at the 'Black Swan'. Philo gushed out her praises about the garden, the house and the sandwiches and Vincent Scott's grin of sheer happiness broadened visibly as she spoke.

'Do you think you will like living in Charing, Mrs Scott?' queried Stella.

Her mind still full of Dale Ingram's visit and his kind and thought-provoking offer concerning a day out with him on horseback found Annie replying:

'Oh I'm sure I will Mrs Rigden-Ackeson. The house is quite beautiful with plenty of scope for Vin and I to plant our own personalities into the plan of things and the village itself is just lovely. My own hobby, when I have the time, is riding and our Broker, Dale Ingram, has already offered to give me a day's hacking around the local countryside… everything is just perfect!'

Stella thought, "The bastard! I bet he offered her a day out. The sight or thought of Mrs Scott in tight breeches and shiny boots would set his heart beating far too quickly. What about me? What about his 'rubber princess'?"

Stella replied, 'Well that sounds wonderful' and silently wondered if the Scotts would be disappointed when they heard they had not won the 'Best Kept Garden' competition.

'May Hell freeze over first!' she muttered through gritted teeth.

On the drive back to Sandwich Stella continually found herself at odds with her fellow judges as they extolled the virtues of their tenants in Rye whilst she attempted to point out that their lawns were covered in moss and many of the rose bushes were in drastic need of 'dead-heading' etc., etc… It was all quite pathetic and deep down she knew it. 'Oh damn the man! Oh damn Dale Ingram!'

Dale had explained to her at their unexpected first reunion at the St Lawrence County Cricket Ground that he was directly involved with the Brewery business and had been dealing with Wetton Ackeson since coming down from the North East of England, but he had not gone into much detail. By subtle means she managed to get George talking about Public House Brokers and was astonished to learn how much involvement there was between Brewer and Broker. These people were in the main responsible for distributing sale 'particulars' of all the various Brewery Company tenancies that were 'on the market' at any given time in the same way as any normal

Estate Agent. Some of the larger firms, and he mentioned Dale's firm in this category, had mailing lists of over 500 potential clients and rarely were they not able to supply the Brewer with one or two good couples for interview for every house tenancy that came on the market. The old traditional Brokers also boasted strong stocktaking and accountancy departments so that, in theory, all the professional needs of the self-employed tenant were safely taken care of by their Broker. As each tenant moved in or out they sold their inventories of loose trade goods and effects at valuation and their wet stock at cost price on the day of the changeover. The Brokers were responsible for all this work too and also carried out all the legal work involved with the granting of a Licence to the new tenants including two visits to the Magistrates' Courts. George was generous in his praise of this rather specialised service pointing out that the system of changing public house tenancies had gone on with very little change in procedures for as long as anyone he had been dealing with could remember.

'They seem quite indispensable,' Stella remarked. 'I can't think why I've never heard of them before. Richard has never mentioned such folk to me but, then again, he probably wouldn't think that I'd be interested.'

'To be quite honest I think our Chairman regards them as a necessary evil. You are aware of how fiercely independent he is over all matters concerning our Brewery and I'm sure he would much rather have an 'in-house' Brokerage Department dealing with all our properties. This cannot happen of course, for obvious 'wicked Landlord/poor Tenant' scenarios over the valuation of inventories etc. but I can see changes being made by our Company in the coming years. I love the way business is done at present and have no complaints at all… happily I shall almost certainly be retired by that time.'

'I met Mr Ingram at cricket last week and found out we lived quite close to one another in early childhood,' Stella told her travelling companions. 'It was quite extraordinary and he brought back many memories from those far off days.'

'Oh, I know Dale Ingram,' cooed Philomena. 'He comes to some of the re-openings when we've modernised our houses. He's absolutely charming and scrumptious looking to boot. He's sports mad and is heavily into rugby, cricket and riding I'm told. Tommy got quite jealous over the amount of time I spent with him at the 'Crown' re-opening last month… I loved it!'

Stella thought, "I bet you did, you soppy cow!" Stella replied, 'Well I didn't get into his private life but he was a most charming chap I thought and, to be honest, most folk from Northumberland are charming to a fault!'

By the time they returned to their Quayside Brewery it was agreed that the 'Black Swan' at Rye and the tenants, Mr & Mrs Vincent Scott, would go through to the final representing Area G despite their moss-ridden lawns and untrimmed rose bushes. Stella knew that this was the right and proper decision but she would be talking of Mrs Annie 'bloody' Scott at another time in another place, the County Hotel next Tuesday for instance… a day's hacking indeed!

Now that she knew a little more about Dale's profession she found it difficult to understand how she had not come across him before now. Of course he could not possibly have known that his Stella Ward had become the wife of the Richard Anthony Rigden-Ackeson but he was still Dale Ingram and his name had never come up in conversation with her husband or any of the Brewery gang. She chided herself that she really should take more interest in Brewery matters and attend more of the social functions. It was irksome to know that Philo Billshot had chatted to Dale on several occasions. She privately thanked God that his predilections for rubber and bondage had not reached the ears of Philomena and the vision of a wet-suited Mrs Billshot welcoming him to her poolside for afternoon cucumber sandwiches sent shivers down her back.

"Oh God! I'm becoming totally neurotic!" she sighed inwardly.

CHAPTER EIGHT

Tuesday morning was wet and miserable. Dale had a court application in Margate and then he was free to meet up with Stella. He had really been totally pre-occupied by the events at Croft House the previous week and could not believe that all had gone so brilliantly. Stella had always remained this strange unobtainable female from his past and so many of his wildest sexual fantasies were wound intrinsically around her. Suddenly she had re-emerged into his rather lop-sided world, and although not knowing quite how he was going to manage it, he was nevertheless determined that Stella would be playing a major role in his life from now on. He really loved her, he was absolutely sure of it. He really did love her.

'She will turn up won't she?' he mused as he waited for his application to be heard. 'I wonder what she will be wearing?'

He gazed at the Licensing Justices, two ladies and their male Chairman and having idly dressed the blonde on the left in *a fireman's helmet* he lost interest after a moment or two and concentrated on addressing the application. His client was not exactly out of the top drawer and being very nervous appeared unable to put more than two words together without coming to an abrupt stop. Dale had rehearsed him as to what to say and how to say it and had given him a clear understanding as to what the Justices required of any person applying for a Licence in their Division. The law stated that the applicant had to be a 'fit and proper person' but such a statement covered a very wide canvas and the truth was that if the Justices did not like the 'cut of one's rig' then the application was in trouble. Dale was heartened by the rapidity with which the cases were being dealt with that day and guessed that either there were loads of civil prosecutions to be heard immediately after the Licensing Meeting or the Justices were keen to be in other places. At any rate his client, a Mr Tony Lucan by name, staggered through their basic questioning and when *the lady fire-fighter* made some pathetically weak quip about him not being related to Lord Lucan, Dale threw himself about the court in helpless laughter thereby securing plus points for his client, a dazzling smile from the JP and, in due course, a Licence to sell intoxicating liquor from their Worships. Mr Lucan was duly grateful and thanked Dale profusely as they left the Court Buildings.

'I couldn't 'ave done it wivvart yer Mr Ingram and that's the bleedin' truth. You was bleedin' brilliant in there and if there's ever anyfink I can do for yer or if yer need suits or electrical goods then give me a bell… I can always get anyfink at give-away prices for a bleedin' toff like you.'

Dale wondered as to the true pedigree of Tony Lucan and felt it would not be long before the local Licensing Inspector would be making his presence felt. Oh dear! Oh dear!

The rain continued to fall and Dale cursed the weather that would most surely deny Kent another almost certain victory if it persisted. The office was not busy and his Secretary had sorted out the only real problem of the morning for him. Julie Swift was a splendid lady and had worked for Dale since coming to Canterbury from Newport three years previously. She adored Dale and it always appeared to Dale that her husband Morgan was 'well down the batting order' in her priorities although she loved him quite unashamedly. No, for Julie, Dale was a God-like figure and she held on to every word he spoke. Her 'Welshness' was lovely and Dale was very fond of her, admitting to himself on occasions that this slim long-haired young maiden could well figure in one of his more erotic fantasies.

'I'm popping down the town Julie,' he said. 'If there are any problems I'll be back to sort them out this afternoon. Is that OK?'

'Yes Dale, of course it's OK. The Guv'nor told Colleen that he wouldn't be back until 4.30 but that still gives him or you time to bring yourselves up to date,' she replied happily. Dale relaxed in the knowledge that his Senior Partner was coming back to the office that afternoon. Although in his eighties Mr Godfrey Gervase Tremlett was still a formidably business-like character, admired by friends and business foes alike. 'Gee Gee' took no prisoners and believed that the service his Firm gave was without doubt, the finest possible. Staff who failed to live up to his expectations did not last long and minor complaints from members about such trivialities as being paid overtime for doing work outside office hours were quickly labelled 'Trotskyites' or 'trouble-makers' and told that their services were no longer required. He had taken to Dale and despite calling all his various partners by their surnames at all times he had nevertheless always called his young pupil by his Christian name and had brought him into the partnership in '66 at a quite unheard of early age. Mind you, when he felt it necessary to bring his young pupil down a peg or two he was a master in the art. Sensing that Dale was impatient to value by himself he sent him down one morning to value the chattels inventory at the Maple Tavern in Upper Deal. The tenant was a massive man who had been a miner up to the age of fifty and now ran his pub with a rod of iron. John Stark was aptly named. Dale drove down to the house in the Guv'nor's Humber Hawk and swung into the car park feeling on top of the world. Marching up to the door he knocked confidently and waited. The door was opened by the biggest man Dale had ever seen… He could not have been 'born'… 'Must have been hewn out of solid rock,' mused Dale.

'And who are you?' boomed Goliath.

'I'm Dale Ingram from Tremlett & Son and I've come to carry out your inventory valuation Mr Stark,' Dale stammered.

'Oh have you now, Mr Ingram,' he said very slowly. 'Well let me tell you Mr Ingram that when I engage Tremlett & Son to work for me I expect Mr Tremlett to attend… NOT HIS BLOODY SHIRT BUTTON!!!'

So saying he shut the door quite slowly in Dale's face. Dale thought about knocking on the door again but then thought better of it feeling that if he did so Mr Stark may well assassinate him there and then in a most horrific and very painful manner. Tearing back to the office he almost ran into the Senior Partner's office and related what had happened. Mr Tremlett listened and then picked up the telephone and rang Mr Stark.

'That you Starkie,' he said. 'Tremlett here. What are you doing frightening the life out of my young man? You should be ashamed of yourself. Now I'm going to send him back and you let him carry out the inventory work today… I'll value it tomorrow!'

He beamed at Dale and laughingly remarked, 'His bark's far worse than his bite I promise.'

Dale realised that he had been 'set up' by his Master but the point had been made and he never pushed for advancement again. Mr Tremlett knew the time was not ripe for Dale but ensured that no loss of face had actually been suffered in public. Clients loved him or hated him but they all wanted him to act for them on the premise that if 'Gee Gee' Tremlett was working **for** you then he couldn't possibly be working **against** you… and that thought had made strong men go weak at the knees!

Dale grabbed his umbrella and set off for the County Hotel.

Stella looked out of the window and saw the rain cascading off the stable's roof. It was Tuesday and the day of her meeting with Dale at the County in Canterbury. The forecast had been gloomy and a day of pretty constant wetness appeared inevitable. She chose a pale brown skirt and cream silk blouse with smart high-heeled court shoes. She saw in the back of her wardrobe a pair of cuban-heeled Russell & Bromley fashionable wellingtons in soft white rubber that she had bought in the sixties and was tempted to pull them on for her visit into Canterbury. With a smile to herself she made a mental note for possible future titillation and took out a dark brown belted mackintosh with a matching Armani headscarf to counter the appalling conditions.

Dale was already in the delightful coffee lounge area when Stella strolled in. Despite the awful weather she looked wonderfully composed and carried the air about her of a woman who would always be in control of whatever situation she found herself.

'A real class act,' Dale murmured to himself.

They went through the boring play acting of a surprise meeting and Dale made a show of inviting her to share his table, tucked away in the furthest corner of the room. Two fresh coffees were ordered and as one or two seemingly interested fellow customers lost interest in what was obviously the chance meeting of two friends, they were able to talk.

'Did you get home OK last week Stella?' Dale said feeling their afternoon at Croft House should be brought straight to the surface. 'I can't remember much about the drive home myself… just kept on pinching myself that it had taken place and that you had been so bloody fantastic from start to finish.'

Stella realised that it was pretty pointless trying to maintain a slightly unconcerned air when she recalled the events of that incredible afternoon.

'Yes, you, you lovely, kinky man, I got home OK and began to think straight about four hours later. It was a good job that Richard was pre-occupied that evening as I could not have held an adult conversation with him. Dale, have you **any** idea of what you have done? Do you realise that my life has been overturned and instead of enjoying my lovely social and business world of luncheon parties, charitable work, magistrature and School Governor duties I am now constantly wondering when you are next going to appear and what the hell you are going to do to me when you get me alone!'

Dale chuckled quietly, 'I do know, of course, my darling rubber princess. What happened between us was something that was meant to happen and had I known that you were here and living in East Kent then it would have happened years ago!'

They talked at some length of their childhood days and Stella persisted on the subject of their mutual love of bondage and Dale's fixation for rubber. She wanted to know whether their gang games and childhood sexual foreplay had been partly responsible for the way he was and the fact that she had been so excited as her bonds were tied.

'I realise that all that stuff is very common, particularly amongst men, but not everyone can have had the sort of childhood that we enjoyed,' she said. 'Have you always wanted sex in that way or am I just some ghost from your past that brought all this back to you?'

'I can't answer that Stella. All I know is that ladies in rubber excite me and have done so since as long as I can remember. It's a very common fetish and I did seek reassurance on the subject from a therapist some years ago. She really approved of the way I was leading my life and didn't feel that any serious change in my lifestyle was necessary. But what you must also know is that no one has **ever** excited me in the way you did last week or the way in which you did near the Blyth railway track all those years ago... **that makes you special!'**

What Dale did not add was that the sexual techniques he had used on Stella had been honed over a great many years with a great many ladies in a great many situations including, of course, his therapist, dear Maeve Kavanagh. In his own mind though he had worked out that all that had gone before was a kind of preparation class for the final examination that his Stella was inevitably going to set him.

'More special than the landlady of the "Black Swan" at Rye?' asked Stella.

'Why on earth do you say that?' said Dale feeling only slightly uneasy as he spoke. 'I mean to say I haven't done anything ... yet!' he mused.

'Oh I was talking to her recently and she gave me the impression she knew you quite well and that you would be spending the day out riding with her when she has moved to her next tenancy,' explained Stella. 'You haven't asked me to go riding with you have you?' she added almost pouting as she said so.

Dale relaxed for he knew a case of jealousy when he saw it. Delighted that he had got himself safely ensconced in Stella's own fantasy world he now realised that his own very strong feelings for her were reciprocated and Stella clearly had no intention of allowing anyone to get inside their private world.

'Relax darling... Annie Scott is a nice lass and was genuinely not sure whether she really wanted to move from Rye to the outskirts of Ashford even though Charing is a pretty and convenient village in which to dwell and the pub itself does a far bigger trade than the old "Swan" ever could manage. I sensed that she needed a lift and made it clear that the riding she enjoyed around the marshes that surrounded Rye could easily be duplicated in the countryside near Charing. My offer was nothing more than that and it did the trick 'cos she agreed to the move immediately. Business is business as they say.'

Well, most of what he had spoken was the truth, more or less and it wouldn't have done anybody any good to know that as he clarified the true position concerning Annie Scott the vision of *Calamity Annie's terrified gaze at her hero as he struggled to free her from the railway tracks as the steam engine thundered towards them* surfaced for a moment or two.

His words seemed to allay Stella's fears and she talked of her conversation with George Banyard and all he had told her of the world of Public House Brokers.

'You really are a specialist body of men aren't you. You appear to provide virtually every service that a tenant or a Brewer would want. I got the impression that George approved but that Richard did not. Am I right?'

'I really don't know what your old man thinks Stella. For goodness sake we move in different circles and although he knows me through my sporting connections I can't say he has ever led me to believe that we are an essential and indispensable body. All I know is that Messrs Wetton Ackeson of Sandwich are very important to us. They, along with our other two Kent Brewers are remarkably loyal to the Kent firms and we seldom have to do business in our neck of the woods with London boys. George is a good old stick and although set in his ways and decidedly eccentric at times he nevertheless keeps us in front of all the various Area Managers and their Director James Billshot.'

'Oh yes, that's another thing Dale. Philomena Billshot appears to know you too and spoke about you in glowing terms.'

'She's an awfully nice lady,' Dale replied. 'She has made one or two pub re-opening very bearable and has more humour in her little finger than poor old Billshot has in the whole of his body… how on earth do these people ever get together?'

Stella detected the hint of real affection for Philo in the tone of his voice and voiced her inner thoughts immediately.

'Oh my God, you haven't had her up at Croft House have you?' she laughed.

'Stella, my darling Stella, I haven't "had" anybody up at Croft House but you. How could you contemplate such a thing… and talking of Croft House, what about another afternoon together? Are you free on Friday?'

Stella knew that Friday was not a good day for her. She had an expected long morning in Court and then a working lunch with some of the RSPCC committee at a lovely pub in Chestfield to discuss their approaching 'Bring and Buy' Sale. Friday was impossible.

'Yes. That will be fine for me,' she lied. 'I'll have to change one or two things around but I can make it. I presume you will be wanting to stage a similar production or have you got other things and other costumes in mind?'

'Oh no, my rubber princess is quite exquisite… she could not be improved on I assure you.'

Stella flushed at his words and felt the surge of sheer lust and excitement flow through her from top to toe. The man was incorrigible, outrageous, very, very kinky and utterly wonderful. "I am so happy," she thought despite feelings of inner terror as to what the eventual outcome of all this madness would be.

As they got up to go Dale guided her towards the private telephone booths in the darkest corner of the Reception area of the hotel.

'Let's just pop in here for a moment Stella,' he said. 'I've got something to show you.'

They disappeared into the booth and Dale placed himself between the folding door and Reception. He produced from his pocket the bathing cap and quite calmly gave it to Stella.

'Put it on for me darling, I can't wait another three days to see you in it.'

Stella couldn't believe what was happening. Here she was in the centre of Canterbury, in the Reception area of a major hotel, some fifteen yards from the High Street… and… and this idiot was asking her to put on a bathing hat. She pulled it on and pushed her hair inside the cap and clipped the chin-strap in place.

'This is madness,' she growled and added, as he calmly slipped the strap into her mouth, 'I can't beleesh we are doin' thisshh.'

Dale's mouth found her parted lips and hungrily kissed and explored her half-opened mouth. Stella returned his kiss forcing her tongue over the restricting strap and into close contact with Dale's.

'Thisshhh ishh utter madnishh,' she whispered, trying desperately to conceal her whole person behind Dale's wide frame and again her thoughts were of a brand of terror mingled with the utter joy of knowing that this man, this crazy zany man, loved her and wanted her so much. The hardness of Dale forced itself into her crotch as she gulped through the rubber strap and her emotions once again fought the restraint their perilous position dictated.

'Will you pleash shtop thish nonshense Dale. The way I feel at thish moment I jush might do someshing I will regret forevermore.'

'I'm just cross with myself that I forgot a bit of cord so I could have secured your hands behind you as well my darling,' he murmured. 'I could have tied your headscarf tightly round your rubber-clad head and put your mac' over your shoulders and then walked you back to your car... great adventure!' he enthused.

"Oh my God he means it," thought Stella as she pulled her cap off, shook her hair and tried to take on the identity of Mrs Rigden-Ackeson once more. "Damn it all," she thought. "I **am** Mrs Rigden-Ackeson!!"

They left the booth and Stella went to the Powder Room to compose herself. "Well," she contemplated as she fixed her hair, her lips and her inner confusion. "Nobody saw anything and no harm was done to me or my reputation ...and... and... I loved it! There, I've been totally honest with myself. It was stupid, it was rash and it was indefensible but what on earth is wrong with just 'going with the flow' occasionally so long as it hurts nobody. He's mad and so I suppose I must be mad also but, oh God, it was marvellous!"

'Don't you **ever** try any stunt like that again Dale,' she ranted. 'Don't you **ever** put my reputation at risk in that manner. Have you

any idea of the humiliation I could have brought upon myself and Richard if we had been caught?'

'I would never allow you to be embarrassed in any way my sweet,' he replied. 'I love you Stella and I've always loved you. I'm sorry if my wooing is odd and my behaviour totally over the top but such things fade into insignificance when you think about what we had in that booth together and the sheer electric chemistry that passed between us. **You** matter to me in a way that no one else could possibly do. I want to have you with me all the time and if for part of that time you are in rubber or hanging from a rafter, or whatever, then that's the way it must be. You do understand don't you darling?'

'Hanging from a rafter?? What do you mean, hanging from a bloody rafter?? You never said anything about hanging from a bloody rafter!!' Stella cried just a little too loudly, as this new frightening vision flashed before her eyes.

They walked slowly up the High Street chatting about nothing in particular and in full view of the shopping battalions shook hands warmly and went their separate ways. Dale was exhilarated by his meeting with Stella and made a mental note that he must make it clear to the proprietors of Croft House that he was a stranger to their shores! He had, after all, never dreamt that this fantastic lady would ever come back into his life and therefore, to be fair, his romantic dalliances in Room Eight over a number of years now could be forgiven.

CHAPTER NINE

1971 – SEXUAL THERAPY

Mention of the celebrated Dr Maeve Kavanagh took Dale's mind back some eight years and to his early sessions with her. They had been memorable days as he tried to find out more about himself and times spent with this wild Irish colleen were etched in his memory banks for all time

Dr Maeve Kavanagh loved her work. As a forty-five-year-old Sexual Therapist she was well aware of the tremendous assistance she had given to many poor, tortured souls, lost in a maze of sexual abnormality, unfulfillment, inadequacy, self-doubt or whatever. For almost twenty years she had enjoyed a very profitable income from a constantly growing private practice that she ran from her beautiful detached house near the cliffs at Kingsgate on the Isle of Thanet. Married for almost twenty-one years to Wilfred Skinner, a Chartered Accountant in the nearby town of Broadstairs, her life was comfortable but dull. Wilf was a man of 46 years, looked and lived the life of a man of 66 and sexually performed with the skills and regularity of a man of 86! Maeve had been born and bred in the busy little town of Ardee in County Louth, some 60 minutes' drive from Dublin, and had met her future husband whilst working as a young Houseman at the Margate General Hospital. Wilfred Skinner was a good, kind and decent man and deep down Maeve knew there was a sexual climax in her, waiting to burst forth all over him.

She looked across at her patient and thought, not for the first time, what a lovely-looking man he was. Clearing her throat she continued:

'Mr Ingram, I feel it appropriate at this stage in the therapeutic relationship to reiterate some of the insights gained during these last eight sessions. I feel that you had two related but nevertheless, differing agendas.

'You initially expressed concern that, at 35, you had never had a deep and lasting relationship with a woman. You felt that your relationships floundered when your partners expressed a desire for something more permanent than just an interest in your sexual fetish. It became apparent during therapy, that it was you, who in fact ended or effectively sabotaged any potentially long-term relationships.

'Your rubber and bondage fetish was your other area of concern. Once you appreciated that it was not the cause of your failed relationships you were in no doubt as to its central role in your sexual expression. The origins of this fetish appear to be intricately bound to a very early sexual experience with the then love of your life. As we have previously discussed, she still represents your ideal partner. She was not only powerful but was sexually domineering. You have never allowed any sexual partner since those childhood days to adopt a dominant role, effectively precluding them from being a long-term partner.

'I am now convinced Mr Ingram that these insights should enable you to move forward and take this opportunity to conclude the therapeutic relationship.'

Dale Ingram had been listening intently as the good doctor clarified, reassured and praised the frankness he had shown throughout their eight appointments to date. Rising from his chair he moved across the room and slipped a pinkish vibrator into the wet and gasping vagina of the distinguished and erudite Doctor Maeve Kavanagh.

'There, there, my dear. Let's see how you cope with your first introduction to this little toy. It's not too big but, by Christ, it's damned persistent and it certainly won't go away.'

'Oh for God's sake Mr Ingram! Will you please get on with it and screw me sideways you kinky bastard!'

'All in good time Doctor Kavanagh, all in good time. Now are you comfortable or is there something you need?' Dale asked with infuriating seriousness as he switched on the battery-operated aid.

'Oooooh! Arrrrrrh! Oooooh! For goodness sake take me! Have me! Fuck me all the way to Kilkenny and back you mad bastard!' screeched Maeve.

Dale surveyed the scene. Her therapist's white linen three-quarter length coat was still buttoned up with the fasteners straining as her truly magnificent breasts fought to escape their confinement. On her head, almost inevitably, hiding a wild mass of deep auburn hair was a tight-fitting white rubber bathing cap with the chin-strap clipped in place. Her surgical gloved hands were bound to an antique gas mantle bracket over her head. Her feet, shod in shiny black rubber boots, were secured to the inflow and outflow pipes of a wall radiator, spreading her legs wide open. All other clothing had long since disappeared.

Dale moved over to the side mahogany table and selected a bright shiny green medium sized apple from the glass bowl.

'Open wide, there's a good girl,' he advised, quickly slipping the apple into her mouth and lodging it in and behind her gleaming teeth thus effectively ending all conversation from the by now highly aroused medico. White rubber hat, red face, green apple and silence… well, almost silence.

'Glonka! Arrrh! Glonka! Glonka!' Maeve screeched, which Dale, who was pretty conversant with *Golden Delicious Speak*, translated as being roughly along the lines that she had been demanding for the past few minutes.

He slowly undid her coat and stroked her wondrously proud and very firm breasts. Allowing his tongue to trace a slow passage over her heaving navel and stomach territory Dale arrived at her moist cherry and extricating the busy little vibrator he plunged his tongue into Maeve with a passion and a fury that had the poor lady almost apoplectic as she fought the apple gag and the cords that kept her prisoner. Dale stood up and slowly removed his shirt and then his blue cords and pants leaving him only in the black rubber riding boots he had worn underneath. Maeve saw his penis for the first time and remembering Wilfred's 'Cadbury Chocolate Finger' she beheld the 'Giant Size Tolerate' with growing anticipation.

'Corrrrr! Glonka. Glonka. Glonka,' she squawked weakly, whilst still thrashing about as best she could.

Their love-making was very noisy as once the apple gag and ropes had been removed Maeve was totally without care or caution as she experienced all the passion that had been for so long contained and smouldering inside the very being of this flame-haired Irish girl. Rolling all over the linoleum and Belgian cotton carpet, under the consultation couch and finally against the side of the desk, *Mary Mother of Jesus, Jesus Christ himself, St Patrick, Val Doonican, Georgie Best, the Dubliners, Molly Malone and most of the Disciples at the Last Supper* were summoned noisily and shrill-voiced by Maeve as climax followed climax. She had fallen for the thirty-five year old Mr Ingram at their first consultation as he asked poignant questions without any embarrassment about his love of seeing girls in rubber and then titillating them to distraction after tying them up. Dale wanted to know if such a fetish would seriously harm any future long-term relationship he might desire as he certainly had not met 'Miss Right' yet. Most of his friends were now married with young families and he sensed a slight distancing from them.

'Am I odd or just unlucky?' had been an early question as Dale had introduced himself and his sexual needs to the voluptuous and interested Doctor.

By the third meeting Maeve had moved him to the last appointment of the day on days when Wilfred would not be home early and had left her Wellington boots on show in the surgery with some cords and a strap or two 'lying about'. By the fifth meeting she was masturbating daily. At their sixth meeting she had met him wearing her boots making some pathetic excuse about a 'leaking hose-pipe' in the garden and had chosen not to remove them. As their question and answer games became more and more personal she had admitted to a craving since her teenage days to be 'taken' by a man, albeit in the most civilised of ways.

'I am a powerful female Mr Ingram and I confess that to be helpless and at the mercy of a man is something I've often thought about myself. I would *hate* any pain you understand but to be unable to prevent a man doing exactly what he wanted to you seems so damned exciting to me.'

That specific day then had almost been inevitable, as the 'dare' of the seventh meeting became reality. Dale had trussed her up and then added the swim cap as she settled into the first bondage session. It had proved to be the most stimulating and sexually exciting hour of her life and she had simply wallowed in the joy and fulfilment her 'captor' had provided.

As they drank coffee in the Reception area Maeve tried to reason with herself. She was an educated and very sensible person who loved her husband and certainly did not love Mr Dale Ingram. There was absolutely nothing wrong with this wretched lovely man, as he was well aware of what he was and what he wanted from any relationship. Any female who shrank from rubber or bondage would, quite simply, not fill his bill.

"I'd better finish this before it goes too far and gets out of hand," she mused, thoroughly confused and annoyed with herself for this temporary and quite out of character lapse in her normal exemplary professional conduct. "Mr Ingram certainly doesn't need any more guidance from me and I doubt whether he really needed any advice in the first place. I'll do it now. I'll knock this nonsense on the head before Mr Ingram and I take this relationship along paths neither of us would really wish to travel."

'Well Doctor Kavanagh, that was just fantastic, you certainly seemed to love the old bondage and you look magnificent in rubber,' said Dale. 'Will it be the same time Tuesday week?'

'Yes, I've marked it in diary and I'll see you at 3.30 p.m,' she responded immediately, sighing to herself as she muttered the words, 'Oh God! Why am I so bloody weak?'

Their sessions together had remained a carefree and at times hilarious part of Dale's life and the two of them had formed a friendship over the years without ever meeting each other socially. Maeve loved to be 'taken' and if it meant dressing up as 'Miss Dunlop 1971' or the 'Rubber Hand Maiden from Hell' for Dale Ingram's titillation every now and then, well, what the hell?

CHAPTER TEN

The firm of C G Tremlett & Son had been in business in the City of Canterbury for over one hundred years but only the Ledger Clerk, a Mr Jacob Growser by name, could recall the present Senior Partner's father coming into the office. He would recount stories of the days in the late twenties when, as the office boy, Mr Cornelius Gervase Tremlett would give him a penny if he thought the lad had taken trouble with his appearance but also give him a clip across the back of his head if he failed to carry out instructions 'to the letter'. Growser was well over the retirement age but it seemed inconceivable that anybody could ask him to leave. The firm was his life and despite his very advanced age he made few errors, possibly fearing that 'a clip round the ears' from young Mr Ingram may well follow if he did so. 'Young' Mr Tremlett was a 'chip off the old block' according to Growser but despite the similarity in their ages the Guv'nor treated his Ledger Clerk as some young lad who had to be watched very carefully at all times.

'Knows far too much about our business,' he would announce at partnership meetings. Can't have him going off to pastures new and telling all to any Tom Dick or Harry. We must think about giving him a pay rise... but not this year I feel!'

Dale had gone in to see the Guv'nor and was discussing a pressing and difficult valuation problem when the door burst open and the Senior Stocktaker, Felix Chapman, stood before them in a most agitated state, chest heaving with emotion and tears not far away.

'Yes Chapstone. What can I do for you?' Mr Tremlett asked.

'You may well ask sir!!! You will recall that you heard that old Mr Briggs had passed away at the 'Fern Tavern' in Deal and that I should go down there straightaway and carry out the required stocktaking valuation for probate purposes before any other cowboy got his foot in the door? You assured me that you would lay it all on.'

'Do get on with it Chapfield,' grunted Mr Tremlett who was never very good on names and, after all was said and done, the fellow had only been there a few years... 20 at the most!

'You assured me that you would lay it all on' repeated Felix Chapman as his face became redder and redder 'and what do I find when I get there? WHAT DO I FIND???'

'Well, what do you find man? Spit it out Chapstone, there's a good fellow, before I die of old age and Mr Ingram falls into a coma from which he may never wake!!' cried the Senior Partner.

Felix Chapman's agitated condition appeared to have made him oblivious to Mr Tremlett's comments or Dale's involuntary convulsions of suppressed laughter.

'I'll tell you what I found. I found that Mr Briggs was being buried this very morning and they knew absolutely nothing about me or my visit. I have never been so humiliated in my life. Sir, I just wanted the ground to swallow me up. The door was opened by the poor wretched Funeral Director in his morning suit and silk top hat! The bearers were directly behind him with the coffin covered in floral wreaths. All the family were ready to go off to the Crematorium and Mrs Briggs, bless her heart, **apologised to me** amidst her tears, for my wasted journey. Sir, I have never been treated so shabbily. I am utterly outraged by the position in which I found myself today. I am sickened by the whole wretched business and am here to ask what action you intend to take?'

'Oh... go tomorrow Chapstick there's a good chap,' beamed the Senior Partner and swung round to re-address Dale's problem. Such encounters were quite common and Dale loved the old man's totally outrageous but very effective methods of dealing with matters that he judged to be utterly superfluous to the effective running of the firm. Dale knew that had he had to deal with this normally quiet and most holy of men then Felix Chapman would have pinned him down for at least half an hour. As it was Felix rushed from the room with a heaving chest and pounding heart.

'Dear old Chipstock… he's a remarkable fellow isn't he?' So saying, as far as the Guv'nor was concerned, the matter was at an end.

The twenty years he had spent working under this remarkable gentleman had taught him so much and he would be forever in his debt. Mr Tremlett had ceased to do the actual 'physical' inventory work where only chattels were involved some years previously after an incident with Dale at the George Hotel in Herne Bay. Coming to the end of a long inventory, after working separately for many hours, the two valuers met up with only the contents of the Hotel Entrance Lobby and Entrance Hall to list and value to complete the task in hand. Mr Tremlett looked tired which, quite frankly, he had a perfect right to look, as he approached eighty years of age.

'You call and I'll write for you Guv'nor,' Dale said.

Mr Tremlett began listing all the various contents as he had done for over sixty years including the period of Dale's pupilship as his young valuer hastily scribbled everything down in readiness for typing. Suddenly the old boy stopped… Dale looked up and saw he was staring at a tea trolley which had on the bottom shelf a very modern chromium plated electric twin toaster with the cable and plug disappearing under the trolley. Finally Mr Tremlett commenced his description:

'A three foot six, oak, two-tiered…' He paused yet again as he took in the chrome box and cable… 'A three foot six, oak, two-tiered… **motor-assisted tea trolley**!!!' he declared. Dale felt he had to point out the error and with a sigh the Guv'nor accepted the position and moaned.

'Well I suppose that's it then Dale my boy. I don't think I'll be making any more inventories from now on. I'm just too old for all these modern machines.' True to his word he never made another inventory of chattels and a pupil for Dale was organised within weeks.

His problem solved he called for his Secretary and settled down for a spell of dictation. Julie came bouncing in and sat down in readiness for his outpourings. Dale's lunchtime rendezvous with Stella had teased his poor over-sexed imagination and he went straight into fantasy mode. His charming Secretary had become *the feisty Ann Baxter in the film 'A Ticket to Tomahawk ' and was dressed in buckskins and high boots.* 'Dear Sir, I refer to your letter, blah, blah blah and then do the same three paragraphs we did for that letter to the tenant of the Red Lion at Wingham,' he dictated, trying desperately to find the right music to go with his fantasy and finally settling for Nancy Sinatra's rendering of *These Boots are made for Walking,* although to be honest with himself **walking** was the last occupation he had in mind for them! As he ploughed through seven or eight letters he idly undressed and dressed Julie and by the time he had completed dictation she seemed to be wearing *Miss Baxter's boots* but very little else. As Julie left the room he gave her *a Welsh National Costume hat to wear, one of those tall black ones, and stuck a leek in for good measure!* God, it was all go in the office today.

Poor Stella drove back to 'Clover Leys' with her head spinning still. Her heart pounded as she reconstructed the events of that afternoon and putting the worst but quite possible scenario to what might have happened if she had been caught 'necking' in a telephone booth in a public Reception area with a bloody bathing cap on and the chin-strap between her teeth. How could she have explained it to anybody? She vowed to herself that she would never allow Dale to take such a risk with her again. To her horror though she couldn't help smiling as she passed through the village of Wingham and then giggling like some besotted schoolgirl at the antics of this lovely man who would not allow anything to get in the way of the passion he held for her.

As she drove into the driveway of her home she noted the dark green Jaguar parked and wondered what Jamie Donald, a local farmer, wanted. Jamie farmed about 500 acres and his land more or less surrounded 'Clover Leys' on three sides. His marriage to Kate was floundering due entirely it must be said to his extra-marital affairs and she and Richard had had to comfort both Kate and Jamie in recent months. Jamie had made a move on Stella one morning some two years previously which fortunately had come to nothing due partly to the unexpected homecoming of Richard but both he and Stella were aware of the moment and nothing had been said since that time. Stella, being at least 5 or 6 years older than Jamie had been flattered by his attention and miffed inwardly that he had not made any further advances. She did not feel anything for him but it was nice to know that one was still attractive to the male population. He was a popular chap and liked by the majority of the locals. Kate was a hard-working osteopath and took little or no interest in the farm. Her practice was in Broadstairs on the Isle of Thanet and her hours were long. They had two young boys who were often visitors to Stella's pool and both were capable riders although not in the same class as their mother who had approached international selection levels in Three Day Eventing as a younger woman. Kate still rode and kept her Hunter in one of Stella and Richard's stables for much of the year.

'Hallo Jamie Donald!' Stella cried as she entered their spacious Reception hall and found their neighbour slouched on a settee, dressed in a check shirt with sleeves rolled up, baggy corduroy trousers and muddied brogues. 'What can I do for you?'

Jamie put down the 'Horse & Hound' he had been reading and rose slowly to greet Stella.

'My goodness! You do look good this afternoon Stella. I don't have to ask if everything is chipper in your world at the moment… you are blooming!!!'

Stella smiled, thinking to herself that it is surprising how 'abject terror of the unknown' can put roses in your cheeks.

Jamie continued, 'I'm sorry to have to bother you with all this but Kate's thrown another "wobbly" and has said she won't be expecting me home tonight. Her exact words were "Don't you dare come back here this evening. Go and spend your nights with that trollop in Ash and let the boys and I have some breathing space. Let her put up with you and your unacceptable behaviour and see how long it is before you're not the flavour of the month with her too!" give or take a few expletives. She really was beside herself and I think I had better stay away for tonight at least.'

'You do realise that we can't have you here Jamie, don't you? Kate is a good friend and I know I speak for Richard as well when I state that we cannot be seen to take sides in this matter. Your safest bet is to book into the "Red Lion" at Wingham for one night and let Kate know what you have done. Don't go anywhere near Ash for God's sake. Who is this "trollop" by the way? Anybody we know?'

'It's Amanda Broughton,' he muttered.

'Isn't she the local vet?' asked Stella.

'Yes. She was over at the farm two or three weeks ago dealing with a difficult calving and what with the joy of a new-born healthy calf and Amanda all sweaty in her protective gear.'

'Oh not another bloody man who is into rubber and all that nonsense,' she interrupted without realising what she was saying. Hastily she re-addressed the situation and continued, 'So many of our cases in the Court seem to stem from men who are plagued by some bloody fetish or other which drives them to make fools of themselves. I thank God for my Richard every day!'

Jamie appeared totally satisfied with the content of her outburst and continued.

'It was just a spur of the moment thing. One minute we were hugging each other for joy at Amanda's skill and such a happy outcome and the next minute I was tugging her gum-boots off. We've not had another session and to be honest she's really not the type to behave like that – I'm sure it was just the moment but Kate got to hear of it yesterday from God knows who and she's not at all pleased.'

Stella chided him for his crass stupidity and promised she would try and speak to Kate later in the day letting her know that Jamie would be in the bar of the 'Red Lion' from about seven o'clock onwards. Jamie Donald thanked her profusely and apologised again for his antics and for the trouble he constantly seemed to cause his neighbours. He kissed her cheek and left.

The telephone rang, it was Dale.

'Just rang to say how wonderful it was to see you today. I dream about you, I day-dream about you and I fantasise about you constantly. Have you any idea of how bloody marvellous you look in nothing but your riding boots?' he enthused. 'I'm lying here on my bed and have been in a state of high arousal for almost twenty minutes... what a waste of an erection... don't suppose I could smuggle it over to you could I?' he laughingly cried.

'No you bloody well couldn't,' Stella retorted. 'I'm delighted that you find me both exciting and arousing Dale but I'm afraid you will have to just fantasise all by yourself this evening. By the way I still can't believe what you did today... outrageous! Absolutely outrageous!'

'You enjoy it?' he asked, quietly.

'Yes, you kinky swine, I loved it!'

'Goodnight my darling Rubber Princess,' he murmured softly 'I'll see you on Friday.'

'I can't wait, my darling Dale,' she replied. 'Until Friday... God bless.'

CHAPTER ELEVEN

Their meeting at Croft House on the following Friday was just as intense and just as wonderful as had been their first encounter. Stella had been that much more confident about things and had added to their mutual enjoyment by inventing some games of her own. The clock was turned back thirty odd years as she insisted on trying to avoid the humiliation of being bound by Dale by being allowed to put up a struggle. However Dale was no longer the slightly built youngster she remembered so well and despite her commendable efforts she was soon spread-eagled once again and forced to put up with her ball gag and her cap.

Stella lay there on the bed and allowed every sinew in her body to relax as she simply breathed in the sheer sense of a fulfilment of every possible joyous emotion and sensation one could experience. Dale could do and was doing anything he wanted to her and his attention to detail was awesome. She shuddered as overwhelming sexual urges rushed through her gleaming body and prayed that it would never stop.

When they had completed their lovemaking Stella showered and then sat on the end of the bed watching her lover as he lay there. Dale had not removed his boots and was totally spent from the exertions of the past three hours. Stella wondered if she dressed up again whether he could summon up the strength to continue but felt that it was unfair to put him to the test.

'What are we going to do about us Dale?' she said.

'Well my darling Stella. What we are not going to do is anything silly. I know you are racked with guilt but what we are and what we have is something so special that it defies all the rules of fair play and I am not about to lose you after waiting over half my lifetime for you to re-appear. We will have to get over the problems one by one and if we can do it without hurting anyone then that's fine but if you think that Richard is somehow going to be able to get rid of me then you've another think coming!'

'Do you really believe that you have been "marking time" Dale... waiting for me?' Stella said. 'Have you never experienced these feelings before with any other female? I can tell you straight out that as sure as hell I haven't.'

Dale did not have to lie or even be economic with the truth for his love-making with Stella had been unique in both its passion and in dredging every ounce of lust and love from his body and from his inner soul... it had left him exhausted and devoid of feeling for hours.

'Stella, listen to me and take this in. I have never experienced anything remotely like the feelings I have had here at Croft House with you. You are so special and the fact that I have shied away from marriage all my life may mean that all along I have been waiting for you to return to me. I don't know that for sure of course, but it makes as much sense as anything else in this extraordinary trail of events.'

Yes, Dale had had several ladies in Room Number Eight and many had been treated to a similar form of lovemaking, as to that which Stella had so enjoyed. Dale knew they had enjoyed their afternoons with him but the sight of Stella stretched out before him was a totally new experience for him also and as she prepared to leave he watched her collect her things and thought how striking she looked.

'Shall I take the bathing cap Dale?' she asked. 'I feel so nervous now after your exploits inside the County Hotel and am terrified you are going to demand too much of me in some public place. If I have it then you haven't and I'll feel a whole lot safer.'

'No darling, you leave the cap with me,' he replied and was unable to see the smile that flicked across Stella's face as she walked to the door, dropping the bathing cap on the side table as she went.

'I'll be in touch Dale, within a day or two I promise.' She turned and blew a kiss to him before gliding into the corridor and out of his life once more.

Dale lived in a fairly spacious top floor flat with a balcony overlooking the river Stour as it passed through the City of Canterbury. He was not overlooked himself and thick walls meant a quiet and very private existence although there were several other flats below him. He had a garage and the building had an inner courtyard for one's own and one's guests' parking. He had seen the plans for the building long before publication and knew it was right for him and that any subsequent change in plans would not find him having a problem over the sale of same. The Agent had told him that there would be a waiting list for the flats and that his top floor apartment would be most sought after. He had been living there for four years and was perfectly happy.

A day in the office meant that he could leave the car in the garage and walk to the office if the weather was fine as was the case one day in early September. Waving to car horns that greeted him as their drivers recognised Dale and chatting to fellow walkers on their way to work, Dale was in buoyant mood by the time he reached the office.

'Morning ladies!' he cried as he passed through the Reception area.

'Morning Mr Ingram,' came back their united chorus.

'Come in with my mail when you've sorted it Julie,' he shouted as he disappeared into his office.

Within five minutes Dale found himself talking to a frantic Mr Lucan who, not to Dale's surprise, had had a visit from the Licensing Inspector, 'Andy' Devine, who was not at all pleased with the way in which the house was being run.

"Ee told me that I was breaking abart ten licensing laws Mr Ingram and that if it 'appens agin then 'ee's goin' to throw the book at me. "Ee said that the Royal Mail 'as always been a problem 'ouse and 'ee wasn't going to 'ave any truck from me. What shall I do? My Jenny's goin' balmy here.'

Dale promised he would call later in the day silently cursing that he had left the car at home and thought of one or two other houses he should call on in the Margate area whilst there. Julie came in and plonked his mail down on the desk in front of him and sat down ready for dictation. She was as smart as usual and by force of habit he undressed her quickly as she sat there and saw her as *Ursula Andress coming out of the sea in the 'Doctor No' film with a dagger in her hand, wearing a thong and waders...* **waders?** *No that couldn't be right could it and he hastily discarded those and settled for a semi-unzipped wet suit... the music, unaccountably, was that of the band of the Grenadier Guards playing their regimental march.*

'Dear Mr Thompson,' he began.

Arriving at the 'Royal Mail' Dale found Tony and Jennifer Lucan in a fine old state. Apparently they had been accused of, amongst other things, serving after hours, serving alcohol to under-aged persons, serving alcohol to persons already far too inebriated and to allowing known prostitutes to ply their trade on the premises. The Licensing Inspector had given them one final warning and had made it clear that they were on his 'hit' list from this moment. He told them that it was only their lack of experience that had stopped him from closing the premises down there and then.

Dale went through the licensing laws with them very carefully and was gratified to see that Mrs Lucan was not only paying attention but was actually making notes. Tony twitched and ticked and tutted but really didn't seem to show the same sort of attentiveness as his wife. He had some theory that the local Constabulary "ad got it in for me' which was not the case at all. Tony was a small-time villain, immensely likeable but nevertheless a villain and it had not taken long for the local bobby, Inspector Devine or Dale for that matter to work him out. Dale noticed a bottle of spirit on the decanter counter that was foreign to the brands supplied by his Brewery Company under their Tied Trade Agreement. He asked Tony where it had come from and was told that it was a 'raffle prize' he had won. Knowing this to be patently untrue and very aware of the Brewers' concern about the huge amounts of illicit 'bootleg hooch' that were flooding the East Kent market as a result of individuals purchasing vast amounts of stocks of spirits and beers in the supermarkets and wholesalers of northern France and bringing them back across the Channel for sale to any retailing outlets that wanted them, Dale felt it only right to warn him that the discovery of any 'foreign' stock in his cellars by the Area Manager could mean instant dismissal. Tony smiled and Dale got the distinct impression that he might as well talk to a brick wall... if there were any 'fiddles' going then Tony Lucan was going to be right in the middle of it all.

The tied trade system had been operative since tenancies of Brewery-owned public houses had come into being. It was not a perfect system but changes were being considered and the 'tie' on wines and spirits looked to be under real threat for the major National Brewery Companies. Under the 'tie' the tenant had to purchase all his alcoholic stocks from his Brewery Company unlike the 'free' houses who could buy from whatever outlet they wished provided the correct duty had been paid. Being a comparatively small Company, Messrs Wetton Ackeson ran a complete 'tie' on all the alcoholic products but did appear to have a fairly wide range from which to choose, and their draught and keg beers and lagers were very popular in the South East.

After a couple of calls in Ramsgate, Dale drove along the Sandwich Road and cut off to the pretty village of Ash where he popped into the Chequer Inn to discuss a bit of possible business with the landlord, Bill Warlord. Sitting on a barstool sipping a quite magnificent pint of bitter he caught sight of Jamie Donald, an ex-

Canterbury Rugby Club man and former team-mate of Dale's some ten years ago. Jamie had his back to Dale and was holding hands across the bar table with an attractive lady of some thirty-odd summers. Whoever she was the lady was certainly not Kate Donald whom Dale knew well as she had sorted out problems with his back and ankle over a longish period.

'Who's that with Jamie?' he asked Bill.

Bill was never one to beat about the bush and laughingly replied:

'Oh that's our local lady vet, Amanda, whom I suspect is sorting out a great deal more than his herd of cows and Labradors.'

Dale was already in fantasy land as Bill finished and was imagining *Amanda in rubber gauntlets up to her armpits and very little else other than a long waterproof apron and boots. Roger Miller was singing 'King of the road'.* He strolled over to Jamie and greeted him like a long lost stranger. He had always liked the man and they had enjoyed one or two major drinking and lustful evenings together after Saturday matches. As he was introduced to Amanda Broughton he found himself *taking off the apron and liking what he saw underneath.* She was a good-looker and her smile was most encouraging Dale thought as he shook her hand. She was wearing a tight shirt and jeans and a pair of hard-wearing sensible shoes. They conversed briefly and Jamie made it pretty clear that he did not really want to spend a very valuable lunchtime break talking to Dale. Amanda, however, was more than eager to chat and Dale promised himself that here was a lady worth a wee spot of trouble, provided she was not too married and that Stella did not find out. Nothing must ever spoil what he now had with Stella but... if Amanda was single and if Amanda was available then who knows? Certainly Amanda was making it very clear that she wanted to talk to him. Dale made some comment about a friend who needed advice from a vet and took the card that Amanda proffered, almost too hastily, he thought.

'Tell your friend to ring me any time Dale,' she said. 'That's my mobile number so I'm always on the end of it.'

Dale had a call to make in Kingsgate that afternoon so left work early. Dr Maeve Kavanagh, Sexual Therapist Extraordinaire, had asked him to call and he had spent an interesting hour watching her bound body writhe around the polished parquet tile flooring begging for sexual favours before he had put her out of her misery.

'Oooooh! I really think you are almost cured Dale Ingram. I reckon that in another ten years you will be off the "danger list".'

'I'm pleased to hear it Dr Kavanagh. I must say that over the past few years you have made me feel absolutely normal.'

'Only too pleased to help. I'd like to see you fairly soon as I've got a new shower fitted with extra strong rails and hooks. I feel it will be a good test of your new confident approach to your old doubts if you hang me out to dry in there and then 'do' me with the power shower fully operating. What do you think?'

'You're the Doc so just let me know when this new form of therapy is to commence.'

Dale had never really lost contact with the wonderful Maeve who was insatiable in her quest for new and even kinkier action. He wouldn't hear from her for months and then, almost like a bottle of champagne that had been shaken once too often her cork would pop and there she would be demanding to be hung up, spread out, tied up, tied down, bent over, jack-knifed, hog-tied or whatever.

CHAPTER TWELVE

Dale and Stella continued to meet either at Croft House or, occasionally, at Dale's flat. Stella rather enjoyed the total safety and seclusion of the latter rendezvous where access was only available by speaking through the outside telephonic system and then by lift to Dale's top floor apartment. If Dale did not want visitors then that was that. Dale did not put any pressure on her feeling that these were wonderfully exciting and formative days. Stella wallowed in the sheer joy of all the sexual emotions her relationship was providing. She had no inhibitions left but still retained a fierce pride and her refusal to be bound and gagged without a real struggle made the subsequent and inevitable delicious torment that much more arousing for both of them.

They were never to forget the re-opening of the 'Turk's Head' Hotel, after extensive modernisation of the bars and dining area, in the November of that year. The hotel lay on the outskirts of Folkestone and although old, had nevertheless enjoyed an excellent bar and hotel trade for many years. The Company had placed the house under their 'Managed House' umbrella some years previously at the time of the retirement of their tenant of twenty-five years' standing. This was a practice all too common with all Brewery Companies and left a sour taste in the mouths of all the ambitious tenants who watched as the cream of the Tied Trade Estate were extracted from their market leaving only tenancies that were considered not worthy or not profitable enough for management. Dale remained certain that a good tenant would almost always improve greatly on the trade that a Manager could create because of the obvious personal benefits and that a good tenant would never mind paying a fair rent for the privilege of enjoying the advantages of such a position.

Dale could hardly contain himself as Stella swept into the Hotel with husband Richard. The weather was typical for November, very wet and very windy, and Stella had seized the opportunity to dress for the occasion in a style that was not only both smart and sensible but would also, she was certain, drive Dale to distraction. A white mackintosh, which when opened, revealed a white knee-length fluid jersey dress with a draped cowl neckline and on her feet were the Russell & Bromley white rubber Cuban-heeled fashionable wellingtons. She looked absolutely stunning.

Knowing his place, Dale stayed in the background and chatted to two of the Brewery boys, Area Managers Dick East and Gordon Day who were doing their usual PR work in their normally efficient manner. Stella had smiled at him from across the bar area being well aware that he was dying to get his hands on her. The Chairman, in his quietly effective style, duly 'opened' the modernised portion of the house and laughingly invited the local Mayor to pull the first pint from one of the porcelain-handled beer engines. The local press and the Company's own photographer duly clicked away and took notes as he spoke briefly of the hopes they all had for the future of the Turk's Head Hotel and the plans they had for many of their houses in the coming year. Richard Rigden-Ackeson excelled in such things and Dale admired the man greatly for the immense difference he had brought about since taking on the Chairman's office.

A buffet had been provided for invited guests with the Chairman and his immediate party being seated at the far end of the spacious dining area. The local Member of Parliament and the Mayor chatted animatedly to Richard whilst Stella looked after the needs of the Mayoress and one or two of the other 'special' guests. Dale ate a few sandwiches and quaffed a pint of bitter that was most welcome after the two glasses of warmish white sparkling wine he had been offered to date. He watched Stella from time to time and smiled to himself in the knowledge that the chemistry between the two of them was bubbling away albeit at a distance of some forty yards. She had dressed in the way she had purely to excite him. He knew it and she knew it and Dale determined to ensure that the day was not forgotten... little did he know at that moment how unforgettable and momentous this day would prove.

Dale checked the outside and found that Stella had driven to the house in her own car that was parked in the rear car park. The Chairman's Rolls was in front of the Hotel with the chauffeur sitting in the front passenger seat reading a newspaper. Dale moved his own car and effectively blocked in Stella's BMW by a piece of idiotic parking... there was method in his seeming madness. He sauntered back into the hotel and met Tommy Thornhill and David Queen in the Entrance Hall.

'Bloody good party Dale. I'm a bit pissed but David isn't so we should make Tunbridge Wells by four I should think,' laughed Tommy.

'I can't understand why these Breweries keep on inviting you Tommy,' replied Dale. 'You drink them out of house and home, fart far too loudly in all the wrong places at all the wrong times and then make an improper suggestion to some poor bloody female who is only guilty of looking remotely attractive.'

'I know dear boy, I know. But you've got to admit the Chairman's lady wife looks bloody fabulous. I'm not a proud man Dale... I'd fuck her rubber boots... I really would.' Tommy's old rhetoric never changed but his expression would have altered considerably if he had known what Dale had in store for the Chairman's lady wife, boots and all!

David Queen steered his fellow partner out of the front door and Dale was watching them depart when Stella walked up behind him.

'Good afternoon Mr Ingram. I had heard you were on the guest list today so I made a special effort with my attire. Do you like the dress?' she teased.

'Bugger the dress Stella. Where did you get those boots from? I'm up in Room Number Two and I'll be there for an hour… please join me if you can.'

George Banyard came into view and they drifted apart from what they hoped had looked like a chance meeting. Dale disappeared upstairs and Stella walked towards the Ladies' Powder Room. George puffed on his pipe for a moment or two and then went back into the bar.

Stella had told Richard that she had had enough and would be going shopping in Folkestone before coming home. He had been delighted that she had come down and hoped that this would mean his dear wife showing a bit more interest in his beloved Brewery. Certainly in recent weeks she had asked more questions about all matter of things than he could ever remember and hoped this trend would continue. He left the hotel some minutes after Stella had left the bar, and set off for a Planning Appeal Meeting in Maidstone.

Room Two had a 'DO NOT DISTURB' notice hanging from the door handle but Stella turned the handle and strolled in. Dale sprang off the bed and kissed her with a passion that Stella had learned to know and love. She knew that Dale would make her pay for what she had put him through over the past two hours. She did not have long to wait as within five minutes she was standing in front of him in her white lace bra and pants with her hands tied behind her back, an extra cord round her elbows forcing her breasts to almost topple out of their cup-holders and her Wellington-booted ankles bound tightly together. Despite her usual pleas about her elegant coiffure, her bathing cap had been pulled on and the strap inserted in her mouth. Dale produced a slim-line plastic sausage-shaped object from his pocket and Stella saw with growing anticipation that it was a standard battery-operated vibrator.

At this moment the room telephone rang and Dale went over to answer it.

'I'm so sorry,' he said. 'I'll come straight down and move it.' Turning back to Stella he explained, 'I put my car in a bloody silly position to ensure you didn't leave without seeing me and now I've blocked some prat in who wants to leave. I won't be long but here's something to think about while I'm away' So saying he quickly slid the vibrator inside her and then, after checking it was being kept nicely in place by her pants, he switched it on despite the frantic pleas from Stella.

'Don't swisssh ish onn!!! Pleeesssh don't swisssh ish onn!!!!'

Dale had left the room only seconds when the door re-opened and to Stella's horror and utter dismay the Secretary of the Brewery Company, George Banyard, walked in.

'Oh goodness me... What have we here?' he cried in false alarm staring straight at Stella and taking in every tiny piece of her that was on display. 'Here am I having a look around the hotel and what do I find? What do I find indeed?'

'Georghsss, thish ish not what it sheems,' she lisped through the confines of the strap. 'I am nosh in the habish of ....ooooooooh gloddy gell......oooh no........ ooooohhhhh....ooooohhhh......aaaaaaarrrggghhhh!!!!!' George failed to understand why the Chairman's wife was now jumping up and down on the floor with her eyes wide open and face getting redder and redder. He guided her, hopping, towards the bed where she subsided and allowed her bound body to go through a series of bending and stretching movements which ended with a strangled gasp.

'Georghsss,' she continued. 'Thish ish not whasssh ish sheems.'

'There now, my dear, don't fuss yourself. I'm sure you know what you're doing and there is a logical explanation. We'll talk about it at a later date shall we my dear. Let's say next Wednesday at your house when the Chairman's at his monthly Society Meeting in

London. I'll be there about noon eh? Until then… mum's the word eh?!' He began to leave the room as quietly as he had entered.

'Yesssshh,' she gasped as the bloody vibrator continued to hum away inside her and a fresh and frightening surge began to course through her body. 'Yessssshh! **Yessssshh! Oh guck it. YESSSSSHH!!!!'**

'I heard you the first time my dear,' said George, 'and there really is no need to shout!'

Dale came back about three or four minutes later and apologised for the delay which had been caused by meeting up with a client who wanted him to call at the earliest date possible for a meeting at their house.

'Still, you seem to have enjoyed yourself darling. You look positively soaking!' He tried to ignore the glaring eyes as he switched off the vibrator and decided she looked so angry that a loosening of cords at this particular time would not be wise.

It is very hard to say with great clarity 'I have never been so embarrassed or so humiliated in my whole life!' when one has a rubber strap in one's mouth but Dale got the message loud and clear. Removing her cap and her elbow cord he heard with growing alarm of Banyard's surprise entry into the bedroom and of Stella's attempts to rectify the situation as she reached a magnificent sexual climax and prepared for the second 'coming'. Stella lay in his arms, still tightly bound but secure in the knowledge that she had forestalled any tale-telling for the time being and confident that she could persuade George Banyard not to say anything about what he had seen in Room Number Two.

Dale explained that he had found the 'Disturb' notice on the floor outside their room and supposed it could have come off the door as he shot downstairs to move his car. He felt it strange that he had not met George in the corridor but there again, he could have been inspecting Room Number One next door.

'You don't think he was on to us?' Stella asked, 'and has been biding his time before making his move?'

'Who can tell,' Dale replied. 'But if that is the case then George Banyard is a bloody sight more devious than I gave him credit for! Oh! Sod Banyard, my lovely, lovely darling Stella… Let Wednesday take care of itself. Let's get these ropes off you!' and so saying he pulled her towards him and for the next hour they loved and laughed and kissed and cuddled. The matter was potentially serious of course but neither of them could see how George Banyard could possibly gain anything at all by running to his Chairman and telling all.

They had a lot to learn about the quiet pipe-smoking Company Secretary.

George Banyard had had his suspicions about young Ingram and Stella Rigden-Ackeson for some time. He had seen them chatting quite animatedly at the cricket and knowing that Dale Ingram had a reputation as being a bit of a ladies' man he had decided to keep a watch on his movements whenever in the vicinity of the Chairman's wife. He had heard one or two stories of Stella being seen in Ingram's company over past months and was concerned that a scandal was in the offing. George Banyard's loyalty was to the Brewery Company and this factor was paramount in his thoughts when he watched the two of them chatting in the foyer of the Turk's Head Hotel and then, upon seeing him, part hurriedly with Ingram vanishing upstairs and Mrs Rigden-Ackeson going into the 'Ladies'. Checking at Reception he found that a Mr Ingram had booked Room Two for the afternoon but had promised to leave by seven o'clock thus allowing the room to be booked for an overnight stay if required. Sitting by Reception planning his next move and aware that Stella Rigden-Ackeson had disappeared his next move was made for him when a frustrated guest of the 'opening' came in to complain that a fawn coloured Rover 2000 was blocking him in and could the owner remove same. He gave the registration number and George was able to pipe up:

'I'm sorry to butt in but I couldn't help hearing your conversation. I know that car... it belongs to a Mr Ingram whom I think is staying at the hotel as we speak.'

'You're quite right Mr Banyard sir,' squeaked the receptionist. 'He's in Room Two. I'll ring him and get him to move his car right away.'

George moved silently upstairs as the call was made and positioned himself on the other side of Room Two and waited, just out of sight. After two minutes the door opened and Dale Ingram sauntered down the corridor and out of sight. Moving to the door George quietly removed the 'DO NOT DISTURB' sign from the door handle and laid it on the floor some feet away from the threshold to the room. He turned the door handle and went in.

The sight of Stella Rigden-Ackerson JP standing in front of him wearing only her bra and pants, a white bathing cap and white rubber boots would have been more than enough to have quickened his pulse but to find that she was trussed up with a gag in her mouth and therefore completely at his mercy and no possible threat to him whatsoever gave him a confidence he never realised he possessed. Women had always been something of an anathema to him and he had never really experienced a loving relationship with any female other than his mother and a devoted younger sister. The fact that she was at first begging his indulgence and then suffering from some sort of epileptic fit consisting of jumping up and down on the spot despite her bound ankles and shouting through her gagging bathing cap chin-strap combined with a loud buzzing noise coming from deep down inside her startled him, but once she had hopped over to the bed and kicked the fit out of her system she calmed down and allowed him to make arrangements for the following Wednesday. The Chairman always went to London on the third Wednesday of every month to attend his Brewers' Society Meeting and so, for George, the coast would be clear. A plan was hatching in George Banyard's mind and he felt he might just be clever enough and firm enough to pull it off. As he got off the edge of the bed to leave Stella started to move violently again, almost in time to the buzzing noise she was making which, he concluded, was rather like the deep purring of a contented cat and must be 'something that women just do' when aroused. At any rate she had appeared to concur with the arrangement he had suggested even if her response had been a little on the noisy and excitable side. He felt he must spend quite a bit of time over the weekend working out every detail so that he would be totally immune from any blame and at no time could he be seen in anything but a sympathetic light. To have the lovely and seemingly 'untouchable' Stella in his power was a tasty dream indeed.

Richard felt it had been a 'good' day. The re-opening had gone off awfully well and the modernisation of the 'Turk's Head' was pretty certain to bring in a lot more bar trade as well as making the house one of the better eating houses in the area. Stella had bothered to come down to Folkestone and support him and this was a major plus too. His Appeal to the Planning Authority had been successful and without being too boastful he felt that his presence there had been one of the reasons for the decision going the Brewery's way. On the way back from Maidstone he had called in at the 'Green Man' at Charing and found great satisfaction from seeing how happy and settled Mr & Mrs Scott were, despite having only been in the house a matter of two months. Their trade was up on all fronts and the good folk of the village were giving them excellent support in appreciation of all the new ideas they were introducing to the house.

'Don't try and do too much, too soon,' he warned them. 'We know what a jolly good couple you are and we don't want to see you wearing yourselves out in the first few months of what we hope will be a long and very successful tenancy for you.'

'Oh you don't want to worry about us sir,' replied Annie. 'We are getting involved with the village activities and are having leisure time that can't help to benefit the house in the long run. Vin has got into the village football club and helps with their training and has agreed to be their Secretary next season. We'll sponsor their kit and hopefully they'll use us as a sort of clubhouse in the future. They are a nice bunch of lads and they don't half drink!!'

'And what about you my dear?' asked Richard. 'What do you do in your spare time?'

'Well, I love riding but haven't got out yet but funnily enough Mr Ingram from Tremlett & Son has arranged for us to go out next Wednesday for a hack around the local countryside and I'm really looking forward to it. He's our Broker and such a nice gentleman,' she added thoughtfully.

"I bet he is," thought Richard who knew a wee spot about Dale Ingram and could visualise what he had in store for young Mrs Scott. Half his female staff appeared to go weak-kneed at the mention of his name. He really didn't know the chap but certainly, in his favour, he had built up a splendid reputation as a club cricketer and rugby footballer in the County. The fact that he worked for that old rascal Tremlett meant that there would be no flies on him either.

'You sure about letting your wife go riding with Ingram,' he laughingly posed the question to Mr Scott. 'He's got quite a reputation with the ladies you know.'

'What sir? Mr Ingram? He's been a good friend to us and he was the one who really persuaded us that we were good enough to be successful here. I'd trust him with my life. Without Mr Ingram we wouldn't be here sir.'

'Nor would Mr Tremlett have a nice fat fee from the transaction,' mused Richard but left saying, 'Oh well, that seems fine then. You enjoy yourself on Wednesday my dear and don't do anything too brave will you.'

Upon reaching home Richard went straight into the drawing room and poured himself a strong scotch, which he was savouring when Stella walked in.

'It's been a good day darling,' he said. 'I do hope you enjoyed yourself down at the Turk's Head.'

111

'I wouldn't have missed it Richard... although I did get a bit 'tied-up' with guests towards the end. No, it was a thoroughly pleasant day and the house looked so nice. I really must come to more of these things provided they don't clash with my other engagements.'

Richard was so pleased and they chatted over a light supper that Stella had organised before going up to bed at about ten o'clock. Richard was in an affectionate mood and no sooner were they in bed than he had moved over to embrace Stella and within minutes she was being pumped up and down with great vigour as her 'stallion' satisfied himself in his usual style. She groaned once or twice and sighed long and hard as he rolled off her and lay on his back feeling totally exhausted but happy in the knowledge that he had just transported his dear little wife 'to heaven and back'.

'Mrs Defferary missed those cobwebs in the corner by the dressing table,' she mused, then switching off the bedside light turned over and went to sleep, dreaming of Dale and all the lovely and exciting nonsense that was now part and parcel of her life.

CHAPTER THIRTEEN

Wednesday morning found Dale and Annie Scott out very early on two pleasant-natured horses, a hunter and a young cob, loaned to them by local farmer Tony Cracknell. Tony farmed near Pluckley and with his two daughters away at a Teachers' Training College in Chichester and at Leicester University respectively he was really pleased to have experienced riders willing and able to exercise their horses. Tony and Dale had played rugby together for East Kent representative sides and clashed often playing for the Ashford and Canterbury clubs. The pleasant-natured farmer was delighted to meet Annie, and Dale could see that his client would have no difficulty in getting a ride whenever she had the time so to do. She looked a picture in her tight black breeches, black high boots and tweed hacking jacket. They rode for about an hour and a half and Dale called a halt by a stream and produced a bar of chocolate and a hip flask from his jacket pocket.

'Let's have a sit-down and give the horses a break too,' he suggested.

'Good idea, Dale. Oh! I really am enjoying myself. It's such a long time since I rode out and I didn't realise how much I had missed it all. It is so kind of you to take me out like this.'

She flopped down on the grass beside him and watched the waters of the stream as they gurgled past. Dale watched as her essentially very English habit changed *to the sexy cowgirl outfit worn by Jane Fonda in the comedy western 'Cat Ballou'. She stretched out on the ground, the song was 'I was born under a wand'rin' star' and the singer was Lee Marvin.*

It was all too much for Dale who felt a stirring in his loins and made his 'play'.

'You look absolutely stunning Annie. I don't know what it is about a girl in riding boots but it always makes me feel very, very wicked.'

Annie had been thinking very much along the same lines for quite a time. 'He's so gorgeous,' she said to herself. 'He could have me any time he wanted.' She always felt very erotic when she rode and wondered if it had anything to do with the motion of the horse on her stretched crotch. She tried to think of old Vin back at the pub, she tried to think of all the hard work he and she had put in over these past weeks, she tried to think of their plans for the future and then she tried to think what Dale had in mind for her.

'Just how wicked do you feel?' she enquired. 'I know that this girl in riding boots could be pretty wicked herself if the opportunity arose.'

Dale rose and taking her hand pulled her up and led her some twenty yards from where the horses were grazing into a small glade on the edge of the wooded countryside that surrounded them. Their bed was to be of soft moss and Dale quickly pulled off her boots followed by her breeches as Annie removed her upper garments. To Annie's surprise her boots were then tossed back to her as Dale asked her to put them back on again.

'This is all very kinky Dale,' she said with a hint of nervousness in her voice.

'Annie my love,' Dale remarked as she stood there in front of him. 'If you could see yourself through my eyes at this moment in time you would realise just what an exciting woman you are. I have to admit that since I first saw you I have wanted to make mad passionate love to you.'

With a shriek of sheer lustful delight Annie threw herself on Dale and after a playful struggle he was on top of her and pinning her arms over her head he began to move into automatic mode using all the techniques he had learned over a lifetime starting with the lessons Peggy Graham had taught him as a schoolboy. It was she who had made him aware of what pleasured her most and how to attain that maximum enjoyment… he had been an attentive student and now held a First Class Honours Degree in the Arts of Seduction and Satisfaction. Annie was a very supple creature and found ways of ensuring that Dale enjoyed their session as much as did she.

They lay down by the stream again after they had dressed once more but Annie let her bare feet dangle in the swift flowing waters. She felt so good and couldn't believe that a gentleman like Dale was neither married nor seriously courting some rich privileged bitch. She wondered what the future held for them both. She didn't wonder for long.

'We must do this again Annie. You are a superb lover. Have you ever made love whilst in a 'tied-up' situation? If you haven't, don't knock it 'cos once you have, nothing is quite as good afterwards.'

Dale Ingram was so calm and so cool as he uttered these amazing statements. Poor Annie had just about got her head round being stripped and then wearing her rubber riding boots for sex but now her imagination played havoc as she imagined herself in a bondage game with this dreadful man.

'I ca… can't take all this in Dale,' she stuttered. 'I've never met anyone like you. You are so different to the gentleman I knew as Mr Dale Ingram. But in answer to your question… no I have not been tied up for sex by Vin or any other man. It's something I've thought about… tell me a woman who hasn't and I'll show you a liar. What I do know is that I've 'had a ball' today and do hope you will take me riding again. If you have things in mind then I think you'll find me a willing partner.'

Dale relaxed and smiled to himself contentedly. *As Cat Ballou pulled her boots back on and strolled over to her horse Dionne Warwick crooned 'Our Day Will Come'* and Dale looked at his watch. It was ten past one.

He wondered how Stella's meeting with the Company Secretary was progressing.

George Banyard arrived on the stroke of noon and Stella ushered him into the conservatory overlooking the pool area. He was carrying a rather large and heavy-looking bag that rather mystified his hostess. After getting him a small shandy and pouring herself a stiff gin and tonic she opened up the conversation.

'Firstly George, may I say thank you for the very diplomatic way in which you dealt with my embarrassment last week. I can't begin to think what you thought was going on and yet you showed such kindness by retreating tactfully and leaving me to cope with the position in which I had got myself. I am still shaking with embarrassment and am so pleased that you made the decision to talk about things today rather than get involved with the man who left me in the state you found me.'

'Oh you mean Dale Ingram,' he replied rather too jauntily for Stella's peace of mind. 'Oh I didn't want to spoil any fun that you two were having but, then again, as they say, "There's always a price to pay in the long run," and really I'm here today to let you know what your 'price' is going to be.'

'What on earth do you mean… price to pay?' asked Stella as the hairs on the back of her neck began to bristle. 'I'll have you know…'

'Please let me finish Stella,' he interrupted. 'I have two suggestions to make and leave the choice to you. But let me make it very clear… **there are only two choices**.'

Stella began to feel sick as she watched this up until now quiet, loyal, thoroughly decent and totally reliable rock of respectability begin to weave his web of cunning and degradation.

'Choice number One. I go to the Chairman and tell him exactly what I found when I casually walked into Bedroom Number Two at the Turk's Head Hotel last week. I was checking out the standards of the rooms and came across his lady wife standing in the centre of the room wearing nothing but her bra and pants, her boots and a bathing cap. She was bound and gagged…'

'All right Mr Banyard, no need to elaborate, I get the picture. Now what is the other alternative?'

George Banyard was clearly enjoying watching the very apparent discomfort of the Chairman's wife and had no intention of allowing these precious moments to pass too quickly. 'I assisted her to the bed by holding her left arm as she hopped across the room and then stayed only to check that she was OK physically and mentally, Sir, before retiring discreetly. I did arrange to speak to her about the matter on the following Wednesday at which time I hoped to be given a very plausible explanation that would satisfy me, sir, and would mean that I would not have to trouble you unnecessarily. I regret to say, Chairman, that no such explanation has been given and therefore I stand before you…'

'Yes Mr Banyard. You make the position extremely clear' Stella stopped him once again in mid-sentence. She thought to herself "For Christ's sake he sounds like bloody Mr Chamberlain in 1939 with his 'I regret to say that no such fucking explanation has been received'," but kept her calm and carried on. 'So let's hear what your alternative is,' leaving unsaid, 'before I come across there and decapitate you with Great Grandfather's military sabre that's hanging on the wall over there, in an attempt to wipe that bloody silly self-righteous smirk off your stupid bloody face!!!!'

George went across to his case and returned to his seat holding it on his knees.

'The other choice is simplicity itself,' he said. 'I call to see you on the third Wednesday of every month at noon when my Chairman is in London and you greet me wearing the contents of this case. You wear them for the hour I spend with you and you carry out a small 'kindness' for me before I leave… a 'kindness' of a sexual nature but one that will only involve your right hand if you get my drift. If you decide to take this course of action then the Chairman will never know anything of your extra-marital and rather odd sexual behaviour. I hasten to add that for the remainder of the time I spend with you we will talk and you can serve biscuits and coffee if you wish. One further point I must insist on… our arrangement is strictly private and **nobody** must know about it. At the first sign of you breaking this silence I will go to the Chairman and will, of course, deny any knowledge of our agreement. You will have the 'wardrobe' … not me.'

Stella could hardly believe her ears. She was being asked to dress up in some weirdo costume and then, after polite conversation, give him a 'hand job' and then wave him on his way. All this for George Banyard and all this, once a month.

'I've got to actually jerk you off on a monthly basis dressed in some kinky uniform?' she asked, hardly able to even contemplate the idea of debasing herself in such a way.

'You can always don some rubber gauntlets for the final pleasuring,' he chuckled, adding, almost in an undertone, 'You do seem to have a considerable affection for the texture my dear from what I saw that exciting afternoon in Folkestone.'

'Let's see the outfit,' she said curtly, making a mental note however that her hands would indeed be inside her gloves if she did indeed have to go through with this humiliating charade.

George opened the case and took out a pair of Clarke's highly polished children's leather sandals (size six), a pair of white ankle socks, elasticised brown knickers circa 1942 which came halfway down the thigh, a fairly modern bra, a chocolate coloured gymslip with a white and brown waist band, a starched white blouse, a thin chocolate and gold striped tie and a Panama hat with an elastic chin-strap.

'This will be your summer outfit but from November to April you will wear…' George stopped and took out a schoolgirl's brown belted gabardine raincoat, a brown Panama-styled hat with elastic chin-strap and a pair of size six shiny brown Wellington boots. 'I'm sure these last items will please you my dear… they are all 1939-42 models but in very good condition and the boots are 100% rubber.'

'Will you be my little schoolgirl?' George asked. 'I will call you "Stella" and you will call me "sir" at all times, there must be no sulking or bad humour and you must confirm that you are looking forward to seeing me next month when saying goodbye. I must have your answer now and I won't change a word of what I've said. It's up to you.'

'Damn him! Damn him!' she sobbed inwardly. 'Damn bloody George Banyard and damn bloody Dale Ingram who seems to be getting out of all this without a bloody scratch. Oh! Damn all men.'

'It would appear that you give me little alternative Mr Banyard. Either I become your "little schoolgirl" or you will wreck my marriage to Richard, a man for whom I have the highest regard. What possible pleasure you can possibly get from seeing me in these ridiculous outfits I can't imagine but…'

'Almost as ridiculous as a bathing hat and white rubber boots would you say,' sniggered George who was not going to be talked down to by this young lady. Those days were over.

"Touché you bastard," thought Stella. 'I take your point Mr Banyard and I agree to your terms which make me very unhappy nevertheless. Yes I'll be your schoolgirl, yes I'll jerk you off and yes I'll see you on the third Wednesday of next month… now please get out and leave me alone.'

George felt that he had won so many battles in such a short time that to stay and reinforce the power he held over her was just not necessary.

'Goodbye then my dear, and remember, not one solitary word to anyone. Not even to your dear Mr Ingram. I look forward to seeing you in your winter uniform on the third Wednesday of next month.' So saying, he picked up his now empty case and strolled slowly out of the room. Stella heard his car start up and soon she was alone.

'What a complete mess,' she sobbed. 'That bastard has gone and spoilt it all!' She realised that to tell Dale would be to cause absolute ructions. He would never agree to her parading in front of George Banyard and might even give him a good hiding into the bargain which although giving her and Dale great satisfaction would undoubtedly see the end of her marriage and, quite possibly, the end of Dale's career. She was not ready to think about the possibility of a break-up with Richard nor was she ready for a permanent relationship with Dale although she could not bear to imagine life without him if he lost his job. She had so loved all the secrecy and excitement of their illicit meetings and all the weird and wonderful situations they had enjoyed together. No, she was not going to change her world and decided there and then that a policy of *laissez-faire* would remain in her life for as long as she could manage it. If it meant becoming some child of hell from St Trinians once a month for some silly old pervert from yesteryear then so be it. It would be a secret that George Banyard would scarcely divulge to anyone else and so her humiliation and embarrassment were very much of a personal and private nature. For this she was grateful. Scooping up her newly-acquired clothing she slowly made for the sanctity of her own dressing room.

CHAPTER FOURTEEN

'I'm coming to *Clover Leys* for dinner next week,' Dale remarked casually as he gazed at the beautiful body of Stella as she stood in front of him with nothing on but her white boots. He had felt it wise to leave her hands bound behind her at this stage in case of an adverse reaction once she had found out with whom he was coming.

'What…On Friday evening?' Stella said. 'I didn't see you on the guest list that Richard gave me to check. It's mostly local farming folk from what I could see and the Fanshawes', and that lady vet Amanda something or other.'

'Amanda Broughton,' said Dale, and then added, 'She's invited me to accompany her and I thought it a great opportunity to meet Richard socially in an environment where he couldn't actually ignore me. You never know… he might actually like me.'

'You never told me you knew Amanda, that trollop from Ash, that lady with a sexual record as long as anybody in the County.' Stella spoke with a slightly louder voice than was necessary in the quiet confines of Dale's apartment and felt a wee bit guilty as she really did not know too much about the wretched woman other than Jamie Donald normally 'fell' for good-looking females without too much brain between their ears. However she was a vet after all and so she must be quite intelligent.

'I don't really know her,' Dale answered quite truthfully. 'I met her in the Chequer Inn at Ash and we started talking and she told me she had received your invitation with the request that she "bring a partner along with her to make the number of guests an even one". I was asked and readily agreed. I don't know anything about her being the scarlet lady of East Kent darling.' The truth was beginning to fade into obscurity as he blathered on to Stella who was strutting up and down, furiously attempting to get her hands free in order that she could then place them tightly round Dale's throat and squeeze until death did them part!!!

In fact he had rung Amanda and had been pleasantly surprised by the enthusiastic response he had received from her. They had been out for a drink and she had invited him back for coffee. They had kissed and parted. It had been a sound first date and Dale's fantasising had made the evening most enjoyable as Amanda had been, in sequence, *a Pirate Queen, a Lady Fire-fighter* and, rather surprisingly,' as he had tired, *a motor mechanic in the ATS*. This was not a normal fantasy and went way back to a photo he had first seen as a boy, of the then Princess Elizabeth in dungarees working on an army vehicle. He had scolded himself for getting involved with royalty and HM Forces. Two days later she had rung to ask him to be her escort.

'I'm not sure that I can cope with this Dale,' she cried. 'Hells Bells! How do you think I'm going to feel if the stupid bitch starts making any overtures to you? It is going to be hard enough having you there let alone start worrying about what's going to happen once you get her back to her brothel! Oh Dale, how could you? I'm suddenly not feeling in the mood for you and your shenanigans… untie me at once!'

Her mood change was so typical of Stella and chuckling inwardly Dale took in the picture of this most beautifully shaped goddess as she stood defiantly in front of him with her hands still bound tightly behind her back. Dale carried her to a deep padded stool and sat down despite several very near misses from her flailing boots. Slowly but surely he calmed her down and as his hands stroked her anger away she straddled him gaining maximum penetration and then locking her legs around him she extracted the most wonderful purchase by bending over backwards as Dale's strong arms held her safe.

'God almighty Dale,' she sobbed, 'you are the most wonderful lover in the world… it's a pity you're such a little shit at the same time. Promise me that you will not lower yourself to try and "have a bit on the side" with this awful woman!'

'Of course I will promise you that darling,' he lied. 'It's only a dinner party and for me the most important person there will be your husband. I'm determined to make him like me. If I have to get in "through the back door" as it were then that's fine by me. In any case I think she's got the "hots" for Jamie Donald. When I first met her she was all over the bloke and he wasn't exactly protesting too much either. Now darling, is it safe to untie you?'

'It's safe,' she whispered. 'But make sure you keep your promise.'

"Bollocks to that," thought Dale as he rolled her over on her tummy and commenced untying her wrists.

Stella greeted Richard with a big kiss as he arrived home.

'Richard, I hope you won't mind but I've invited Jamie and Kate Donald to join our dinner party next Friday. I'm doing *Boeuf Bourguignonne* so a couple more mouths to feed won't worry me at all and they really do need a good social evening out together. I gather that Jamie has been playing away from home again.'

'All right by me darling and I'm delighted that you don't mind an extra guest or two 'cos I've invited old Banyard this evening. He's such a loyal old stick and I gather he leads a very lonely life these days since his sister passed away.'

"Not on the third Wednesday of every month he doesn't from now on," Stella thought.

'No darling, I'm sure that I can squeeze Mr Banyard into my plan, my table plan that is, and put him beside someone interested in the collection of matchbox labels and the growing of orchids… that is, provided there is indeed on this planet earth another human being with similar interests! Was he close to this sister then?' she enquired.

'Oh yes! They were utterly devoted to each other. They never married and lived with their mother until she died some ten years ago. Edna Banyard was about ten or fifteen years younger than her brother but led a sheltered life and her death, caused by an inoperable brain tumour I believe three years ago, has left him very badly scarred and alone.'

'Not on the third Wednesday of every month is he bloody alone,' Stella sighed under her breath.

She wandered upstairs once they had eaten and Richard had settled down with the *Daily Telegraph* and a large balloon of brandy on the little pie-crust top mahogany occasional table beside him. Going to the back of her 'walk-in' wardrobe she collected her 'schoolgirl' gear and placed them on her dressing table. The gymslip and shirt were by no means new but were in pristine condition as were the two Panama hats and raincoat. On the back of the gymslip she found a faded name tag which had printed on it 'E Banyard' and a similar tag on the collar of the raincoat. The sandals were highly polished but the soles were worn and the buckle straps frayed. The highly glossed brown wellingtons were almost replicas of those she had worn at her own convent school and when leading the Stella Ward Gang. They too had worn soles but, again, Stella found the name 'E Banyard' clearly written in indelible ink at the top on the inside of both boots.

"I'm going to be wearing Edna Banyard's old school uniform," she thought "God knows what is going through old Banyard's mind but I seem to be playing the principal role." She smiled as she replaced the school clothing and wondered if the wellies would ever be playing a part in another room at another time.

'Dale would just love to see me in these!' she laughed. 'Just like old times!'

Friday evening saw Stella looking anxiously for Richard who, as usual, was late. She was a splendid hostess and there really wasn't much for her husband to do other than decant the port and un-cork the *'73 Chablis Grand Cru* and the *'71 Volnay Premier Cru* which would be fine travelling companions for the *Tweed fished Smoked Salmon and Boeuf Bourguignonne* respectively.

Her table setting was simply magnificent and she knew it. Antique silver was everywhere, the central floral display sprayed out of a huge Georgian fruit bowl and a matching pair of 5-branch candelabra with olive green candles in place were set at either end of the fourteen foot magnificent solid oak carved refectory table which was slightly unusual by the span of its width, which was almost five foot. George Banyard would be placed a long way from her but she realised that it would be unfair to place Dale too far away from Richard even if it meant giving Amanda Broughton an easier ride than Stella would have wished. At any rate Amanda and Kate Donald should make the party go with a swing if enough alcohol got into their systems. If Jamie Donald queried the invitation she would merely say that Richard had wanted them to come and he had invited Amanda without knowing anything about Jamie's recent dalliance with the lady yet.

By seven thirty all the guests had assembled. Dale looked absolutely wonderful and Stella wanted to take him in her arms and vanish upstairs without further ado. Amanda Broughton was attractive and her auburn curly hair went perfectly with an olive green fairly low-cut cocktail dress.

"God, her tits are far bigger than mine!" Stella thought "They are almost fitting into the dress she's wearing."

Toby and Sophie Fanshawe were so different that one could only wonder how they ever got together. Toby, as usual, looked rather like an un-made bed whilst his elegant wife was a picture in very high heels and a pretty black lace cocktail dress. Toby had the look of a perambulating distillery as he wandered rather aimlessly around the Reception lounge with a large tumbler of scotch in his long, thin fingered right hand. In such a state Toby Fanshawe could be guaranteed to 'bore for England' if called upon so to do.

'Good Evening Stella,' said George Banyard. 'It was kind of you to invite me.'

'Good Evening George,' Stella replied. 'I didn't invite you but I suspect that you knew that already.'

'Mind you don't slip up and call me "sir" by accident,' he laughed, enjoying every second of his newfound power.

'No chance of that George,' she said, then smiling to herself added under her breath. 'But I can think of a few bloody names I'd like to call you ... you... you... smug bastard!!!!'

The Donalds' entry was fairly noisy and it appeared that not all was well by their demeanour. Kate had seen Amanda's Range Rover outside and the brain had disengaged from 'normal/sensible' to 'totally over the top and having jealous tantrum despite the fact that the bitch is here with somebody else.' When she noticed Dale she calmed down seeing that Miss Broughton only had eyes for this most agreeable male and quite enjoyed seeing the reaction of Jamie who said to her and Sophie Fanshawe:

'Blimey that was quick. I only introduced the bugger to her a week or so ago,' adding quickly, 'Dale and I were having a pint in the Chequer when in she came... it was obvious he fancied her like mad.' Silently he cursed the man. Dale Ingram had always been able to pull the girls and now here he was with the lady who figured daily in all his erotic thoughts.

"Life's a bitch at times," he thought.

The other two couples were neighbouring farmers who were older than Richard. Jim and Diane Cook had been great pals of Richard's parents and although a wee bit younger they had holidayed with them several times. They were very fond of Richard and had always called him Rick, much to Richard's displeasure. Roy and Gwen Thompson farmed alongside the Donalds and enjoyed a good relationship with them. They were a devoted pair and strong members of the local Farmers' Union.

Richard decided that he would try and get to know this Ingram chap and immediately got into a deep conversation about the problems all Brewers were having with bootlegging hooch from across the Channel. To his surprise Ingram was extremely eloquent and talked good common sense on the subject. He also praised his Company's products being particularly strong in his defence of the 'hoppy' bitter that the Brewery was now producing. Dale agreed that many tenants were getting wines and spirits from France directly against the terms of their Tenancy Agreement and he felt sure this was a general movement and all the Brewers with a Tied Trade Estate were suffering. Dale talked at length about Richard's father and related one or two stories about him at the time when Dale had been a very young and terrified pupil valuer. All his words were to try and impress on the Chairman that he, Dale Ingram, had been around for a considerable time and that he did have something to offer. They talked of the local rugby club and Dale was able to confirm that the rival Brewery Company at Faversham were one of their main sponsors. Richard admitted that he was not particularly interested in rugby football but felt that it would make sound sense to try and get a foothold into the County Cricket set-up in view of the success the team were enjoying in recent seasons. The nationally-based Brewery Companies tended to 'hog' such things themselves but there was no doubt that Messrs Wetton Ackeson were a very popular name within the County and as Dale put it:

'I really believe that the present committee would look very favourably on a move by your good selves to get involved… **after all, such people as yourselves are Kent, and that is what it is all about!**' The Chairman smiled and thought to himself:

"We could use this chap on our side of the fence. I like his style and I like his ideas."

At that moment Stella and Amanda joined them.

'Come on you men,' cried Stella. 'Stop talking business and chat to we ladies.'

127

'No my dear, I have just been getting some ideas out of Dale here and he has certainly given me and the Board something on which to contemplate.'

They chatted on all manner of topics with Sophie Fanshawe and the Donalds joining them. Stella noted that Amanda couldn't take her eyes off Dale but had to admit to herself that she seemed a really pleasant lady. She wasn't to know that Dale belonged to her and to nobody else but Dale had better make a few things clear to this lady veterinary surgeon before too long. The dinner was a great success with the seating plan a positive revelation. Toby Fanshawe found a kindred spirit in Roy Thompson and even stopped drinking for periods of up to five or so minutes as he discussed in great detail what was wrong with the French as a nation and then began to talk about them individually starting with a certain gendarme who had had the temerity to question his driving ability in a one-way street in Montreuil.

'I told the old froggie. You've got to be a bloody good driver to miss all those vehicles coming at you from all angles but he wasn't impressed. I mean to say… how was I to know that they've copied our road signs? Why can't they make up some "one-way" signs of their own?' Toby's innocence tickled Roy Thompson right through the meal and his wife Gwen was delighted to see her husband roaring with laughter every few minutes. Being a farmer, and a hard-working one at that, Roy enjoyed anybody having a go at the French. Jamie and Kate Donald were sitting opposite Dale and Amanda and it was clear that Kate was pleased to see Amanda with Dale. Jamie, on the other hand, tried hard to get into conversation with them both and score a few 'brownie points' for himself. However comments such as:

'Tell me Dale, what happened to that blonde bombshell you had with you at the Hockey Club Dance a few weeks ago?' or 'You must have had more blinking girlfriends than Errol Flynn!' tended to impress rather than deter Amanda Broughton. She was a girl with style and confidence and she wanted to get to know Dale Ingram as quickly as possible. Sophie Fanshawe had also noticed Dale Ingram but she had also noted the interest that their hostess was taking in him. Philo Billshot had remarked to her that Stella had been very taken by the young Broker from Tremletts and it was clear to her that Stella's eyes were constantly turning to him. She thought she caught a smile passing between them on more than one occasion but supposed that it could just have been a friendly grin.

"I shall have to follow this one up," she thought to herself. "Has the 'ice maiden' started melting after all this time?" It was pretty common knowledge in her circle that Stella was not exactly married to the most exciting man in the world and being such a stunningly attractive woman it had long been the gossip of the huntin', shootin' and fishin' brigade that one of these days she would 'have a fling' with some fun-loving individual. To date there had never been the slightest whiff of a scandal where Stella Rigden-Ackeson, JP was concerned. She turned back to carry on her conversation with George Banyard about the one hundred and sixteen match-box labels he had collected from the USSR… it was all 'go' tonight for Sophie Fanshawe!

Gradually the dinner came to an end with Taylor's '54 Vintage proving a wonderfully fulfilling climax to the evening. Kate Donald kissed Dale and whispered in his ear, 'I think she's lovely Dale… and obviously mad about you. Mind that old back of yours tonight won't you. Don't want you on my list for treatment tomorrow!!!'

Stella kissed Dale and reminded him of the promise he had made to her. 'I accept you may have to stay the night for you're in no state to drive but don't let me down with her. I love you Dale and you say you love me.'

'Darling Stella,' he whispered back. 'Nobody is more important in my life than you. You are everything to me and without you I have nothing and am nothing… trust me.' He wandered off to the parked cars seeing *Amanda in the black leather of Honor Blackman's Cathy Gale as 'the Avengers' theme played and Amanda fought against the chains that bound her across a beer barrel in the cellar of the Chequer Inn at Ash.* "Bloody hell!!" he thought.

'Goodnight Stella,' said George Banyard, 'thank you for a splendid evening. I look forward to seeing you again soon,' and added after checking nobody was within earshot, 'but looking and sounding a little different eh? I can't wait.'

Stella watched him climb into his car and still couldn't believe what was going to take place between her and this creepy individual in less than two weeks' time. She had always liked old Banyard and although she and Richard had laughed about his serious manner there had never been any doubt about his loyalty to the Company and to the Chairman.

"I can't really say there's any doubt about his loyalty to Richard now," she thought. 'It's just so humiliating that I'm being punished for the sin of falling in love for the first real time in my life... or since my childhood," for those days in Whitley Bay and Monkseaton were now so clear in her memory and the thoughts she had entertained then about young Dale constantly flooded her mind.

The Donalds took the Thompsons with them and Jim and Diane Cook accepted a lift from George Banyard. As per usual Toby Fanshawe was most reluctant to leave and Richard sat with him at the table trying to persuade him that 'home was best' at this late hour. Sophie saw that Stella appeared a little agitated and said, 'I love the new man in your life Stella.' It was a silly thing to say but she was out for a reaction, knowing that it could be put down to too much alcohol if Stella took offence tonight and that she would be forgiven the next morning.

'What on earth do you mean Sophie,' she cried. 'Who on earth are you talking about?'

'Why Dale, Dale Ingram, the dish from the Brokers' Men who could hardly take his eyes off you all evening,' she lied, for Dale's eyes had only occasionally strayed to catch Stella's glances. 'Oh come on Stella… do tell me all! It will be our secret.'

Stella tried to keep her composure feeling thrilled that Dale had betrayed his feelings for her by his constant loving looks, looks she had obviously missed as she kept the conversation going on all sides. 'I honestly do not know what you are talking about Sophie. Dale came with Amanda Broughton who was our named guest. We told her to bring a partner to even up the numbers. You are such a gossip Sophie. I promise you that if I ever do fall out of love with my darling Richard then you will be the first one to know!'

Sophie slumped as her ploy not only appeared to fall on stony ground but was swiftly booted into touch by Stella for good measure. 'Oh well, maybe I'm not a witch after all but I could have sworn there was chemistry between you two this evening. I must be losing my powers.'

'Well I'm glad that's settled,' said Stella, thinking to herself, 'She doesn't need a car for transport, she could fly home on her bloody broomstick!!!'

Eventually the Fanshawes departed and after a quick tidying up of crockery and cutlery into the kitchen for Mrs Defferary to deal with on the morrow Stella and Richard climbed the stairs utterly worn out from their efforts. It had been a wonderfully successful party and he murmured, 'I take my hat off to you…superb meal and good company too. I really believe old Banyard enjoyed himself, got on like a house on fire with Roy and Gwen. Oh, what a prick old Toby is. How Sophie puts up with him is quite beyond me. I must say I take back all my thoughts about Dale Ingram. He's got a bloody good head on his shoulders and obviously is fond of the old Company… he knows my old man you know…. used to be terrified of him,' he laughed. 'He could do a lot worse for himself than the vet lady couldn't he… she couldn't take her eyes off him all night.'

'Goodnight darling,' said Stella. 'I'll kill him! **I'll bloody kill him!!!!'**

CHAPTER FIFTEEN

In actual fact Dale had behaved fairly well after the dinner party at the Rigden-Ackesons' in that he had accepted a bed for the night at Amanda's and, after coffee and some amusing chat about the party and their fellow guests, had retired for the night by himself. Amanda had not made any overtures to him and sensing that she was a 'class act' and well worth waiting for he put Stella's final goodnight plea to the forefront of his conscience and being tired himself was more than content to curl up in her spare room and was sound asleep in minutes.

By the time he awoke it was almost ten o'clock and Amanda, on call all day, was nowhere to be seen. He did notice a card propped up on the laid breakfast table and read: *Dear Dale, Didn't want to wake you. Thanks for escorting me to the party last evening… it was lovely and I enjoyed your company so much. You are a perfect gentleman and they are a rare breed these days… Do ring me and let's arrange another evening out… Just shut the door after you when you go as I've got my key… love A.* 'Yes,' he mused. 'A class act is our Amanda,' whilst still recalling what Stella had told him about her cavorting in the Donald cow-sheds with old Jamie. 'But still a real "go'er" all the same… you wait my girl, just you wait!!!'

There was a telephone message flashing for him by the time he got home. It was from Stella who wanted to know where he was and what had he been doing all this time. It was worded cleverly but the message was there. With a perfectly clear conscience he rang and was able to reassure Stella that he had slept in the spare bedroom and had merely pecked her a goodnight kiss and been left a 'thank-you' note upon waking up at ten o'clock.

'If you want me to swear on the Bible or the lives of small children I will, I will,' he cried. 'My darling Stella, I will never let you down… you must know that.' For Dale the term 'letting down' had a connotation of sexual performance… he knew that and if Stella didn't realise it, well, she jolly well should have.

Christmas was approaching fast and Stella would be entertaining her in-laws and, joy of joys, Toby Rigden-Ackerson, his wife Angela and their two daughters aged ten and nine. Toby and she still retained a great friendship from university days and were capable of being very silly when together in each other's company. He had never really grown up and was teaching in a public school in North Yorkshire. He adored his brother and yet had refused all Richard's and his father's attempts to bring him back into the Brewery. Angela was a lovely lady with 'mummy' stamped all over her. It would be a great festive few days but Stella pined secretly that she would not be seeing Dale except for a brief session at his flat on Christmas Eve morning. He had told her she would enjoy the festivities he had arranged and this was enough to make her feel warm all over.

Wednesday December 16th was a cold cheerless day, and as the Rolls purred out of the drive on its way to London, Stella shivered with anticipation of what lay in store for her. She tried to comfort herself in the knowledge that it was after all said and done, "Only George Banyard… Dear old George Banyard," but somehow this did nothing to allay her fears. She had confided in no-one, feeling that this was just something she had to get on with and it really wasn't that much of a deal. "Nobody is going to get hurt," she thought but, it has to be said, with little or no conviction.

She showered and decided against using any make-up. She wandered around the house in a warm dressing gown for over an hour, read the newspapers, tidied up the bedroom and the bathroom… anything to take her mind off the small pile of school clothing that was neatly arranged on the bed. At twenty minutes to midday she commenced transforming herself into a schoolgirl of the

1950s. The bra and knickers fitted but Stella was glad that the elasticised legs had perished somewhat in view of her now ample thighs, the gymslip was also a perfect fit as was the white blouse underneath. Aided by a pair of her own 'pop' socks she pulled on the Wellington boots which were her size but were much tighter over the calf than when she had last worn such things. The raincoat was belted and shapeless. She crammed the Panama hat on her head and allowed the elastic strap to fit a wee bit too tightly under her chin. Turning to the dressing mirror she looked at herself.

'Oh my God! I am a child of St Trinians! I look quite awful!' The gabardine raincoat came down below the tops of her boots and so the only sight of skin that George Banyard would see would be her red scrubbed shining face peering from under the brim of the brown winter Panama. She walked along the landing corridor and caught sight of herself again in a full-length mirror at the top of the stairs. As she approached the mirror she had to admit that she did look like a schoolgirl. The coat and hat, the boots, they all had combined to bring about this change in her. Stella was no longer the smart sophisticated lady of the manor but a tousled-haired young lass ready for an interview with Mr Banyard... sir.

Stella found herself looking out at the drive like some expectant child on her birthday waiting for the postman. She did not have long to wait as George's car swung into the drive at noon precisely. He got out of the car and walked briskly up to the front door and rang the bell.

She opened the door and they stood looking at each other for what seemed to Stella an eternity. George Banyard took in every inch of her as he let the vision of this now young hoyden sink into his inner soul.

'Good morning Stella,' he finally spoke in a slightly croaking voice. 'My goodness, you do look a picture this morning and no mistake.'

'Good morning Mr Banyard sir,' she spoke through gritted teeth. 'As you can see I'm ready for school, snow and sleet. Would you like some coffee and biscuits... sir?'

He followed her into the kitchen and watched whilst she made the coffee. She felt more ill at ease with herself than at any time in her life. As she busied herself over the preparation of the coffee she felt George Banyard's eyes probing her body, piercing through her mackintosh safety blanket. She felt utterly humiliated and ridiculous. They went into the conservatory and sat down facing each other.

'No! No! My dear... you come and sit cross-legged in front of me so that I can take you in... take all of you in. I'll put your coffee on the carpet here beside me and do take off your raincoat, it's far too hot in here for such things.'

"Ah well," thought Stella. "So much for the 'no sight of skin' theory." She plonked herself on the carpet in front of George and as she crossed her legs so her gymslip rode up exposing almost two feet of bare leg and, horrifically, the end of her knicker legs. 'I'm glad you like the look of me sir 'cos I think I look awful.'

George Banyard was having the time of his life. He had admired Stella for years and had lusted after her in the quietness of his room. He refused to let the fantasy fade or Stella spoil these dreams. She was made to talk respectfully to him about her life up north and what her parents were like. He listened most attentively and made no attempt to touch her which, in a way, was just as well for to have done so would undoubtedly have seen this Enid Blyton young adventurist turn, by some strange metamorphosis, into a savage cannibalistic Amazonian warrior intent on the total annihilation of all human beings born with a penis.

As the time drew near for his departure George, with not the slightest hint of embarrassment un-zipped his flies and asked, 'And now for that kindness my dear before I leave.' His excitement was all too obvious to even the most casual of observers.

"Damn me, he's not inhibited in the least," thought Stella, "and here's me shaking in my boots… literally!"

'Do you really want me to go through with this George… I mean, sir? Do you really want me to do this… this thing for you?'

'Yes of course I do my child,' George retorted. 'I'm sure you are going to make me very, very happy. Now let's get on with it and no more questions.'

'Well I'm going to wear my marigold gloves as you agreed.'

'Rubber is *your thing* my dear, not mine, and if it makes you happy then it makes me happy too!' George was wallowing in the situation and Stella knew it.

Stella went over to the sideboard and feeling a little like a surgeon preparing for theatre she took out a pair of bright yellow kitchen rubber gloves which she pulled on and turned back to face her tormentor who had seated himself on an upright chair with his legs wide apart.

George had thoughtfully provided a condom for her in order to avoid unnecessary mess and the whole thing was over in very short time. Stella had to confess to herself that George was well-endowed but the wretched man was far too excited by all that gone before and Stella's far from gentle handling, ('I'm only twelve for God's sake') meant that it was a case of 'touch and go'. Stella rose, thinking to herself "George, the man with the hair-trigger, quick-draw Banyard, the fastest prick in the West. I trust he enjoyed it."

George had enjoyed it all, and although cross with himself for not being in control for those vital moments he knew that he would improve… and so would that little madam's handling of the situation! He made her dispose of the used condom and put on her raincoat for their walk to the front door and as he stood there Stella dutifully spouted the words of farewell that he had demanded earlier.

'Thank you very much for coming sir. I'll look forward to seeing you again on the third Wednesday of next month.'

'Not at all my dear,' replied George. 'I've really enjoyed my time with you… you are a very special schoolgirl you know Stella, and you will remain a very special schoolgirl for me for many, many years to come.'

She shut the door and stood resting with her back to it. Gradually she slumped to the floor and howled as the full force of what she had had to submit to was finally allowed to come out of her system. This man, this old man, had humiliated her in a way that she had never thought possible. He had taken away every vestige of pride that she had built up over a lifetime and quietly laid bare her soul. She had some very careful thinking to do now. "Could it be right and fair that he degrade her in this fashion for years to come? Was her marriage that special? Was her relationship with Richard that happy? Did she want to be with Dale all the time and to hell with everything else? Could George Banyard really destroy her happiness?" All these were questions that had to be answered, but perhaps now was not the right time for considered judgements. She got up and climbed the stairs, again catching sight of herself in the large gilt-framed mirror and recalling the feisty little schoolgirl tomboy of all those years ago Suddenly the old Stella Ward burst out as she stood with her legs apart and with yellow gauntleted clenched fists punched the air and screamed into the mirror, 'Yesssss!! I did it! I actually did it!'

Having bathed and wallowed in the warm water for almost an hour Stella got dressed for riding and within half an hour she had saddled Chance and was cantering on Thompson land feeling a whole lot better. On a sheer whim she made for the main road and trotted into the village of Ash where she espied Amanda's Range Rover outside her cottage surgery. Dismounting she entered the surgery and found Amanda talking to a young assistant who was holding up a rather bedraggled and unhappy-looking puppy. She waved to Stella and the young helper walked off back to the inner sanctum of the surgery.

'Hello Stella. This is a pleasant surprise. Have you ridden here?' Stella explained that she had been riding close-by and thought that Chance was favouring one of his front legs.

'Could it be a loose shoe or am I being totally paranoid about my darling Chance,' she lied, knowing full well that there was absolutely nothing wrong with her mare.

'Let's go outside and have a look at the old girl,' said Amanda. She examined all her feet and then got Stella to run her up and down a few times in front of her. 'She appears as sound as a bell Stella but it is always best to check on these things. No, I don't think you have anything to worry about. Have you time for a coffee?'

They went inside and Stella allowed Amanda to do the talking. She had so enjoyed the dinner party and Dale had been a perfect escort. 'I had heard from Jamie that he was a bit of a lad with the ladies but he was the perfect gentleman that evening and slept in the spare room. Mind you I wouldn't have struggled too hard had he decided that my room was far more comfy... Gosh! He's a real dish isn't he!' Stella was thrilled to have Dale's story confirmed by this lovely lady but disconcerted to find out that yet another rival for his affections had seemingly arrived on the scene.

She wanted to give her a really hard slap and warn 'Keep away from my Dale! He belongs to me and you can't have him' but instead she retorted, 'Well I think you must have caught him on a bad night because I gather his reputation is one far removed from that of a gentleman.' It was a rotten thing to say and Stella felt awful as soon as she had uttered the damning words. "God, jealousy is a dreadful cancer to have inside one," she thought. "Why am I so awful whenever I have to deal with anything that is to do with dear Dale?"

However the two girls chatted and Stella realised that in Amanda Broughton she really did have something about which to worry. On a level playing pitch Stella knew deep down that she and Dale would always have something so special but it wasn't level was it. She was married and leading a very respectable life with one of the most admired and wealthy gentlemen in the County. Amanda was younger than she, single, a highly successful professional lady with a reputation that was growing by the month. She had no serious man in her life and the fact that she had rolled in the hay with Jamie Donald meant that the inevitable 'ropes and rubber' of Dale Ingram would hold no fears for this particular lady. 'Oh dear!' she sighed inwardly.

They arranged to meet for a drink and a sandwich in the 'Red Lion' at Wingham on the Friday. Stella was on the bench that morning and Amanda was only on duty until noon. As she rode back to *Clover Leys* she realised with relief that she really hadn't given the wretched 'Mr Banyard… sir' one single thought since she had saddled up Chance. 'If that's what he wants then that's what I'll give him on a monthly basis.' She laughed out loud and answered all her previous doubts and worries in that one defining moment. 'One never knows… maybe it really is good for the soul to be utterly degraded and servile to a master from time to time?' Then with her mind hovering on the subject of servility and masters she wondered what Christmas surprise her real 'Master' had in store for her?

Amanda hadn't seen Dale for a few days but they were going out for a meal that evening. "Damn," she thought. "I forgot to tell Stella." She wanted to look absolutely stunning and lay in the bath wondering if her hero would be a little more forthcoming tonight. They were going to a popular eating house in the village of Bridge and Dale was picking her up at seven thirty. She admitted to herself that this was the first man for ages that had got her juices flowing and she regretted her ten minutes of madness with Jamie Donald in case Dale got to hear about it from a jealous Mr Donald. She liked Jamie who was fun to be with but he was not Dale and never would be. Jamie rang her every day in an attempt to get her in the cow-shed or wherever again, but she repulsed his advances very firmly.

The evening at the 'White Horse' was wonderful and Amanda had over-reached herself, looking utterly enchanting. Her auburn hair looked so pretty and her black silk trouser suit and black patent leather high-heeled strappy sandals completed a picture that had men turning their heads as she made her entrance into the bar. Sitting her down in the middle or 'Snug' Bar in front of a blazing log fire in the large ingle-nook fireplace Dale went to order drinks from the landlord, the portly John Emerson, who had watched his Broker's entrance with a mixture of envy and inner good-humour for he had seen this young man with quite a collection of ladies over the years.

'How do you bloody do it Ingram? Here I am, a fine handsome figure of a man and yet an ugly bugger like you ends up with something like that! **Please** can I have her when you've finished with her? My old Dutch wouldn't mind at all... well not so long as she never found out about it!!!' he chuckled.

'John, you couldn't pull a bird like that as long as you've got a hole in your bottom,' laughed Dale. 'Now do stop slavering, there's a good chap and pull me a pint of your excellent bitter and a Noilly Prat, ice and tonic for the lady.'

They moved into the dining room and spent two hours talking, drinking and eating a quite superb meal. John's wife, Kim, was a marvellous chef and with fresh vegetables guaranteed and all her own soups and sauces they had made a real name for themselves over the past five or six years. Dale knew he was, maybe, just over the limit but was sensible enough to know that provided they didn't have an accident with some idiot or have the sheer bad luck to be caught in a road trap he would get back to Ash without too much bother. He had eaten well and allowed Amanda to drink the major portion of the Claret they had ordered to go with their main course.

Settling down in Amanda's cosy little lounge in front of a wood-burning stove Dale began to prepare his plan of attack for, whether she knew it or not, tonight would be a whole lot different to the last time he had stayed with her. He slowly but surely brought the subject round to what excited her and then what excited him. He talked of rubber and the fascination the smell and the texture had for him. Amanda listened, utterly spell-bound as he wove the word patterns around the joys of bondage sex and how the sensations of same could not be bettered in any situation.

'My God Dale... you are the kinkiest man I've ever met!' she said. 'I can't believe this is the man I've just been out with and spent such a glorious evening together. Do you mean to say that you want to tie me up before sleeping with me?'

'Well only if you want me to Amanda,' he replied. 'I just thought you should try something a little bit different that's all. I guarantee you'll enjoy it.'

Amanda thought long and hard and then said, 'OK. If it's this good then let's do it. Mind you it had better be good Dale after the build-up you've just given.' Amanda had no decent rubber boots so was soon spread-eagled in exactly the way that Stella loved so much with pillows under her back to make everything that much tighter and that much more enjoyable. Going to his case he took out Stella's bathing cap and despite Amanda's protests she was soon tasting the rubber strap in her mouth as so many had done before. With all his skills and the aid of his vibrators Dale gave his partner the most wonderfully exciting and fulfilling sexual experience of her life. Once free she could not stop herself from demanding more and more from this stranger who was now becoming so important to her.

Dale, of course, was confident that she would respond as she did for, to be quite honest with himself, it would take a very strange woman who would not like what he had just accomplished with Amanda. These were basic sex needs and to have the timing of same taken away from you and placed in the hands of an expert must end up in joy all round.

Amanda couldn't get over it all and kept on and on about it into the early hours until tiredness forced her to relax in Dale's warm embrace and sleep sounder than she had done in yonks.

The next morning Dale had to be in the Medway Courts early so he was up and out of Amanda's cottage by 7 o'clock. He refused to let her get out of bed and took her a coffee before leaving.

'Thanks for a lovely evening Amanda. I enjoyed the whole thing from start to finish. You really are some woman.' Dale kissed her and went to go.

'Dale,' Amanda whispered. 'Thank you for last night. I learned so much about myself and had no idea what love and sex were really all about. I don't really know what your feelings are for me but don't play around with me Dale because I think I could fall in love with you… deeply in love with you. Please don't hurt me, will you?'

Her words stopped Dale in his tracks. Nobody had ever spoken to him like that. Dale Ingram wouldn't hurt anybody intentionally; it was not in his nature to hurt anybody. How could he hurt so lovely a creature as Amanda Broughton? He loved her, admittedly not quite in the way he loved Stella for Stella was so special, but he did love her with an intensity that astonished him.

'Of course I'll never hurt you Amanda. Why would I want to hurt you? You're gorgeous!' he said, chuckling as he added before vanishing out of sight, 'Particularly in a bathing cap!!!'

Amanda lay there trying to take in all that had happened since they had walked into her lounge last evening. She knew, of course, of certain men's love of rubber and everyone knew of bondage sex, but nobody could possibly know just how wonderful she had felt as Dale had played with her as though she were a priceless and delicate musical instrument, tightening here, loosening there, being so aware of each body shudder or convulsion and knowing her moment of climax to the micro-second. She had fought the cords that held her firm throughout the whole session but only so that when free she could wrap herself around her tormentor. Obviously the rubber cap had been a huge turn-on for Dale but such knowledge merely made Amanda more resolved to ensure that she would soon be the possessor of the sexiest rubber wardrobe in the County!

CHAPTER SIXTEEN

Stella was late for her lunch with Amanda owing to a rather pedantic and ever so slightly theatrical performance from the solicitor acting for the defendant in her last case. William Golightly would have made a passable Shakespearean actor in most of the 'Tragedies' but his efforts were slightly wasted when trying to wring compassion out of the Bench in a case involving a serial bicycle thief, who appeared heartily bored with the whole thing anyway, and just wanted to be given his 'medicine' and be out of the Courtroom and into a prison cell or the nearest bar without further ado. A police psychiatrist, brought in to the case in an attempt to try and reach into the innermost caverns of the felon's mind, gave his evidence most succinctly pointing out that his examination had not lasted too long... 'The Accused, your Worships, is a man of few words but he did give me the benefit of two of them!' The smile on William Golightly's face as he duly and quite properly lost his case resembled, Stella thought, that of the smile of the Lady Mayoress the week previously when she had officially opened the new wing of the local abattoir!

Stella had made a real effort, determined to look her best for the meeting and was wearing a smart fitted light brown two-piece suit and an ankle-length cashmere camel coat with caramel high-heeled boots in the softest of leather. She looked stunning and knew that her entry into the lovely old thirteenth century Inn had caused a stir. Amanda was wearing a check shirt, jeans and a pair of rather muddied sensible shoes, her tweed jacket was hanging over the chair behind her. With a grin from ear to ear Amanda jumped up to greet her crying:

'Oh my goodness Stella, you look wonderful! Talk about "Beauty and the Beast"! You sure you are not too embarrassed to be seen with me?'

They ordered sandwiches and drank shandy as they chatted about their current arrangements for Christmas and the New Year. Stella had said how much she was looking forward to seeing her brother-in-law and his family and admitted that the next few days would be very hectic as she finalised last minute shopping and liaised with her 'lady' over the catering side of things. Amanda had admitted that she was still unsure of her exact plans, hinting that she was hoping for some sign that Dale Ingram might want her to feature in his own plans somehow. Stella went cold at the thought but realised that Dale, like everyone else, had a perfect right to enjoy his festive holiday and it would be utterly impossible for her to play a part. She had thought he may well be travelling north to spend some time with his family and told Amanda this, adding that he still had a great affinity with Northumberland.

'I can't say I've ever been up there,' she remarked, 'but didn't I hear you say that you are from that part of the world Stella? You would never know from your accent... totally different to Dale's northern burr.'

Stella explained that she had left Northumberland as a girl in her early teens and any accent she might have had had been ironed out of her over the passage of time. She told Amanda of her childhood and how she remembered 'young Dale Ingram' a pleasant lad who had lived quite near to her in those childhood days but omitting to mention the intimate relationship they had both enjoyed at that time. Amanda was enthralled and wanted to know all about the Dale she remembered. Stella admitted that they had played together with a crowd of other local kids but did not say anything about her 'Gang'.

'Don't you find it exciting in a way to come across him after such a long time?' Amanda asked.

'I don't know that *exciting* is quite the word I would choose,' Stella replied. 'More interesting than anything,' she lied as the epithets *ecstatic, overwhelming, kinky, breath-taking, fantastic and utterly amazing* hovered on her lips. 'He's certainly made an impact on the female population around Canterbury and District if all that my spies tell me is correct,' she added, once again hating herself for the jealous bitch she was.

Her solid defensive playing of Amanda's bowling was suddenly shattered when her pretty young lunch partner casually asked:

'You are into riding Stella. Tell me, where would the best place be to buy a pair of riding boots… not leather ones as they are far too pricey for my budget. I just want a pair of rubber ones with a good gloss on them for smartness.'

"Oh my God!" thought Stella "He's either had her or he's about to have her!!!"

Stella said, calmly enough, she thought, 'I normally buy all my riding gear up at Harrods. I really don't think you pay any more for it and it is always first class. You will be agreeably surprised at how cheap a pair of leather riding boots can be provided you don't select from the top of the range… they will last you far longer than rubber boots and stay smarter despite the bashing they are given.'

'No thanks Stella… I think I'll stick to rubber ones,' replied Amanda.

"Brilliant!" thought Stella. "Just bleeding brilliant!!!"

'Oh well, in that case you'll be able to buy them at any of the equestrian shops in the area. They are listed in *Yellow Pages* and there are quite a number of them around,' Stella informed, by now utterly resigned to the fact that her Dale would be watching this gorgeous young damsel either strung up or tied down in her brand new shiny rubber riding boots before the New Year had been welcomed in.

They sat and chatted for another quarter of an hour and then made for the car park at the rear of the premises.

'Do have a wonderful Christmas Stella,' said Amanda. 'I'm so glad that I have met you and do hope that we can build on this friendship. I look forward to seeing you in the New Year.'

'Likewise,' replied Stella. 'You know that I'm here if ever you want to talk to someone who cares about you, don't you? Happy Christmas to you too, my dear.'

As Stella drove back from the 'Red lion' to *Clover Leys* she permitted a small tear to trickle down her cheek as she thought of the unfairness of the world in which she lived at present. It was galling to have to admit that she couldn't really blame Dale for feeling how he did about Amanda for she was a sweet girl and totally innocent of the intensely private relationship that she and Dale enjoyed. Any reproof from her to her lover could be met fairly and squarely by the three words 'What about Richard?' and she had no answer other than to protest that what she did have did not bear any comparison to the sheer uninhibited joy any woman but particularly **this woman** would enjoy when in the company of Dale Ingram. Richard was a man who looked upon himself as a good provider and that his appeal or his charisma, as far as he was concerned, was the successful career that he had made for himself. He was important and he was a man whose stature made him respected wherever he went in the South East of England. Stella had a great life because of him and he felt that theirs was the soundest of unions because of these facts. She couldn't help wondering if she was placing too much importance on the purely sexual nature of her liaison with Dale. He took her to heights she had never known existed before and when one has tasted the euphoria of the ozone up there it's very hard to settle for a 'bouncy bonk' once a month *if the moon's in the right quarter and there's an 'R' in the month*!!! She could not visualise ever losing Dale but she accepted, very reluctantly, that he would have to have a life for himself away from her at this time and if she were to make a scene every time she heard some bloody female extolling his virtues then she would begin to corrode the passion that they shared.

"It's not as if I'm not wanted," she thought. "I've always got George Bloody Banyard on the third Wednesday of every month!!! Oh dear! Oh dear! Oh dear!"

Dale was still unsure of his plans for Christmas. He would like to pop home for the two-day festivities and check that his Dad was fit and well and also call and see his sister and her family. It was a long journey but his father was now approaching eighty and was not in the best of health. Sadly, his mother had died in 1973 from cancer and he had not reached Monkseaton in time to say 'Goodbye' to her. She had been a wonderful mum to his sister and he and their home had always seemed a meeting point for all the youth of the town in those early to mid-fifties. Sandwiches and tea were produced to order and Mrs Ingram was the lady to whom young men and girls alike would go to and discuss their dreams and their nightmares. She never betrayed their innocence and tried to offer advice if required. Never a day went by when Dale did not think of his Mum and thank God for the time he had with her. His Dad, on the other hand, had always been a 'man's man' and although intensely proud of his family could never be accused of spending too much time with them. He worked hard as a Regional Manager for a Tobacco Company and played hard after work with a huge crowd of lovely men who were similar in their outlook on life. For Ingram Senior the pub beckoned at 9 o'clock every evening, and Saturday was a rugby match and Sunday was golf. He was a born comedian and Dale could not remember a time when his Dad was not making people laugh at his antics. He never saw him the worse for wear, drink-wise, and he never saw him shout at his mother or chastise his sister or he. As he got older and wanted to be doing the things that all teenagers get up to Dale would be told by his Dad, 'It's OK by me son but for Christ sake don't go and upset your mother.' Every Christmas Eve he would get home from the pub at two-thirty and tell his kids that he was popping out to get Mum something nice for her present. He would return half an hour later having purchased yet another handbag to add to the collection she had been receiving from him for the past twenty odd years... it wasn't that he didn't love her... he was just hopeless where the female sex were concerned.

Finally Dale decided to drive up to the North East on Christmas Eve, after seeing Stella, and return to Canterbury on the 28th. He telephoned Amanda and was pleased to find out that her plans almost dovetailed with his own. She would be going home on the 23rd to her parents and would be back on duty in the surgery on the 27th. They agreed that Dale would pick her up on New Year's Eve and take her to a party somewhere or a pub celebration if no party could be found. Dale made a few 'phone calls before deciding that the best option looked like the *Hogmanay Banquet* at the 'Red Lion' in Wingham. Peter and Barbara Martin were excellent *Mine Hosts* and their fare would sure to be authentically Caledonian from start to finish. Added to this the village of Wingham was only five minutes from Amanda's village of Ash so a taxi there and back would not be excessively expensive. Once safe in the cottage they could celebrate the coming of the New Year in their own unique way.

Amanda was thrilled to get Dale's call and upon learning of his plans she informed him that she too was away for a short while but would be back the day before his return. In actual fact she had not made any final arrangements with the Veterinary Practice in Sandwich which was much larger than her own but had promised to give them holiday cover in return for allowing her two or three days away from Kent. She had waited, desperately hoping that Dale would make contact. Now she could give them times and dates and wallow in the anticipated thrill that Dale would be taking her out on December 31st and, far more importantly, bringing her back home again in the early hours of January the First! Her new rubber riding boots lay in their box in front of the hearth... it was all so exciting and she was so happy.

'I have an incredibly kinky boyfriend and I'm loving every minute of my time with him,' she mused. 'If only my friends knew what we were getting up to, they would never believe it!' A 'phone call to her parents would confirm that she had been able to organise her timetable and see them for Christmas, so there would be joy at Number Twelve, Gilbey Road in Pinner in a few minutes' time too.

CHAPTER SEVENTEEN

Messrs C G Tremlett & Son did not actually do very much about Christmas festivities. The Reception gang hung up a few very tattered paper decorations that had been around since the end of the war and some of the departments went out for a drink during the lunch breaks on one of the days leading up to the actual holiday. Nothing seemed very organised and 'Gee Gee' did not treat this period in any other manner than normal and was totally against any early office closure on Christmas Eve despite the fact that very little actual work was done on the day.

Dale went for a wander round the office on the 23rd of December and talked to some of those members of staff of whom he saw very little. There was nothing of the 'them & us' about Dale, who could not bear snobbishness at any level of society and he genuinely enjoyed bringing himself up to date with the lives of the accountants and their clerks, the stocktakers and their clerks and the typing pool girls. He had done this for several years now and during the course of this time Jacob Growser had taken it upon himself to accompany him and point out any personal facts about the staff which he felt would make good conversation pieces. Felix Chapman resented Growser's interference into the realms of the stocktaking department and during Dale's meandering he was aware of a constant bickering between the two elderly gentlemen. Mr Tremlett never ventured upstairs and really did not know many of the folk who worked up there. Meeting people in the corridor or catching them coming down the ornate staircase to the entrance hall he would automatically beam at them as a precaution, not knowing if they worked for him or were clients of the firm.

Colleen Manwood ran Reception most efficiently. Aged forty-six she had been the senior secretary for almost fifteen years lasting longer than had any of Mr Tremlett's secretaries in living memory. Whether this was because she was super-efficient or because the Guv'nor had softened somewhat in old age was debatable but the clients, her fellow workers and all the Partners liked her. She had long dark hair and a strikingly attractive body upon which she wore, on most occasions, pin-striped grey two-piece suits and very high heels. Dale had noticed her in a pair of burgundy 'baggy' high-heeled knee-length boots during the run-up to Christmas and upon complimenting her on how nice she looked in them received the rather curt reply.

'Oh well Dale, I'm glad someone approves. "Gee Gee" has just asked me if I was going to make a habit of riding to work or was this just a one-off?!!!'

Julie Swift was a great supporter of Colleen and tended to model herself on the tall unmarried but much sought-after Senior Secretary. Dale, being aware of her fierce loyalty to him, had bought a bottle of perfume for her, a large box of chocolates for Colleen and tins of assorted toffees for the remaining Reception ladies. All the girls liked Mr Ingram and individual cards from them all were placed on his desk with warm greetings. Nobody was busy, so Dale asked his Secretary and Colleen to join him for a sandwich and a drink at lunchtime. Mr Tremlett was out bestowing gifts of wines and spirits to some of his oldest clients and Dale had organised the annual 'turkey run' for eight o'clock the next morning. At this time all those with a car from the firm would gather in a local supermarket and have a list of addresses of Brewery Area Managers from all over the South East to whom they would deliver a turkey. It was something the firm had been doing for over sixty years and being a well-known and traditional gesture of goodwill they had stolen a march on their rivals who were forced to do something similar but with not the same festive flavour about it.

Dale collected his two ladies at one o'clock and took them over to the 'White Horse' at Bridge where John Emerson was quick to pull his leg once again.

'I don't know how he does it!' he cried, winking at Colleen whom he had recognised from his many visits to the office to try and sort out his tax returns. 'Every time he comes in here he's got a right "bobby dazzler" on his arm. Today he's outdone himself and come in with two!!!!! Can I hold the blonde one until you're ready for her?' he roared, his tubby shape shaking with mirth. The rest of the inner bar enjoyed the joke and both the Tremlett ladies took it in good humour for John was an immensely likeable cove. Dale ordered drinks and a platter of prawn sandwiches. The dining room was over-brimming with office Christmas parties and two of the bars were also catering purely for this annual festive source of revenue. A table became clear as a jolly crew were called to their dining table in the bar adjoining the dining room and the three of them sat down. Julie's long fair hair had been plaited into one thick coil which ended half-way down her back. She too was wearing high boots and a smart suit and as they chatted to him about this and that Dale found himself *refereeing a no-holds-barred wrestling contest between Colleen the Cobra in the red boots and Julie the Welsh Dragon in the black boots. They were wearing nothing else and in his attempts to ensure the contest was clean he got totally enmeshed in their hot sweating bodies and…and…'*

'I was telling Julie, Dale, that Mr Tremlett would never consider an office party at Christmas,' Colleen piped up a little more loudly sensing Dale's concentration was slipping.

'Not a snowball's chance in Hell I'm afraid!' he laughed. 'It's not that he's an old Scrooge, he just hates the office routine being disrupted. Growser told me that they did have a party in the office in 1949 but one of the lady stocktaking clerks had been given three glasses of sherry and told the Guv'nor that she "loved a man in spats!" The old man was horrified and ordered the trollop to be sacked at the earliest opportunity and never permitted a celebration party to be held in office hours since. I gather that one or two of the Partners talked him round saying that the poor soul had never drank alcohol before and had not remembered anything about the party at all. Her innocence was found to be questionable some weeks later when it was found out that she was six months pregnant and that the father was 'some soldiers from the barracks'. Mr Tremlett decreed that 'it must have been the gaiters that attracted her!' I tell you ladies, our old Guv'nor could tell you stories about our firm for the next six months and still have a fund of tales untold.'

He chatted to them about their Christmas plans and found out that Julie and Morgan were travelling down to Wales and hoped to be there by midnight whilst Colleen was going to an hotel in Eastbourne for three days with a friend. She would not divulge the gender of her friend but Dale felt certain that this attractive woman would not be going all the way to Eastbourne unless there was some 'nookie' at the end of the journey. In answer to their questions he told them that he was driving up north to see his elderly father and would also see his elder sister and her family who lived in Northumberland too. 'However I'll be back in Canterbury by the 30th and will see you then.' He confirmed for the office would be re-opening for two days before the New Year's Day Bank Holiday but reminded them that Felix Chapman and his merry band of stocktakers would be working from dawn until dusk on that day which was always the busiest day in their year being the end of financial year for so many of the clubs and hotels for whom they acted.

The two ladies were thrilled with their 'outing' which had created what Dale hoped would be a more regular occurrence as both were really nice lasses. They thanked him and as they walked back into the office both gave him a kiss and wished him a 'Happy Christmas'. Dale's mind blurred as he followed them in wondering whether either of them had ever been strung up *as had been Jane Russell in 'The Outlaw' which had thrilled audiences back in the forties as Director Howard Hughes ensured that his heroine showed all her finer points, or, at least as much of her finer points as the British Censor would agree to!* Dale recalled standing outside the 'Picture House', as it was imaginatively named, on the Whitley Bay seafront, looking at the eight photographs which depicted scenes from the film now showing. All seemed to be of this sultry cowgirl either laying in straw or strung up between two trees. As an 'X' rated film only adults were permitted into the cinema to view it. Stella had seen them too and he had vague recollections of the gang trying to do the same to their leader without too much success it had to be admitted, as their knowledge of knots and rope tying was pretty poor with the necessary 'sheep-shank' being way beyond their capabilities.

Dale had dealt with his own short 'turkey run' and was back in the flat awaiting the arrival of Stella who was calling prior to a hair appointment in the city at two o'clock. Dale had told Mr Tremlett that he would be back in the office by one thirty and maybe they could walk over the road and have a beer before he set off for the north. He surveyed the parcels he had arranged and became excited just thinking about the contents of same.

Stella arrived dead on time and walked in looking absolutely stunning. A black Russian Cossack-styled fur hat was pulled right down to her eye line and a full-length military great coat in slate grey covered the rest of her body. From below the hem of her coat Dale could clearly see black high-heeled boots. 'God you are amazing Stella!' he said. 'Just when I think you can't make me love you any more than I do you turn up looking like this and my legs buckle once again!'

He kissed her lovingly and lengthily and then explained that his gifts for her would necessitate her removing all her clothes and then opening her gifts one by one.

'You won't be needing your flight bag today darling, I promise you.'

Stella did as she was asked and soon stood stark naked in front of him. He passed her the first parcel which was small and had a familiar feel to it. It was a bathing cap, but in pillar box red which she refused to don voicing all the usual objections that Stella made over this one item, for she loathed wearing it except when in bondage and preferred Dale to fit it over her head than do it herself. The next gift were bright red elbow length rubber gauntlets which Stella felt certain had come from a sex shop as she had never seen a more erotic pair of 'marigolds' in her life. Finally she extracted from their box a pair of German-made bright red, glossy, pure rubber high-heeled thigh boots that took her breath away.

'Oh Dale! These boots are simply too much. I can't possibly wear these outside your bedroom. Where did you find them?'

'I sincerely hope that you will be able to wear them outside darling but for the present just pull them on and let's see you in them.'

They fitted her to perfection and being rubber they did not need any support and stayed up caressing her thighs as she posed in her outfit. Dale went into the bedroom and after a few seconds came out with what appeared to be an old tubular steel hanging-rail skeleton wardrobe, the sort one sees in Departmental Stores holding twenty odd dresses or coats. Stella's heart started thumping inside her as her lover motioned for to approach the unit. It took a few minutes but soon Stella surveyed her plight. Her new cap fitted tightly over her head, her wrists were extended to the extreme and were level with her shoulders and bound to the steel uprights with silken red cord, her thigh-booted legs were stretched to the limit of what was comfortable for her and red cord again prevented any movement. Her blue ball-gag was in place and Dale stood in front of her wearing only a pair of swimming trunks that were bulging with excitement and his own rubber riding boots.

His hands explored everywhere and Stella, helplessly and hopelessly, could not stop her juices from flowing. She felt so sexy herself and could only imagine what Dale was thinking. Since their meeting Stella's belief in herself had increased four-fold and she now recognised herself as being a woman who could look and did look very sexy on occasions. The vibrator, as always, performed its duties with exemplary efficiency and soon she was tugging at all her bonds in a frantic attempt to avoid this helpless jerking and wrenching that was part and parcel of Dale's planning for her. As always Dale was on hand to stop things before they got out of his control and removing the whirring toy he kissed her through the gag and allowed her to almost hang there in front of him as she recovered slowly but surely from her date with a near climatic destiny.

Standing up straight and thoroughly pee'd off that he had stopped things yet again she attempted to scold him.

'**Grrrrrug Gruuu Gahcod!!!**' she screamed '**Aaaaaggll Crroogggh Goo Gah Gahcod!!**'

'What's a "Gahcod" when it's at home darling? he enquired with a straight face. 'I've a feeling that it is something rather rude. Am I right?'

'**Goo grooghin Gahcod!!**' she screeched back and then fell silent as her tormentor removed his trunks and approached her. '**Gor! Gloddy Gell!**'

Undoing her ankle bindings he entered her immediately and Stella, now supported by Dale's strong arms around her waist and back swung her thigh boots up and around Dale's torso allowing herself full leverage to take advantage of the monster that had now invaded her. Both were far too excited for their lovemaking to last too long and after three or maybe four minutes they were lying on the bed with their arms around each other but temporarily too exhausted to continue.

'Did you enjoy that Mother Christmas?' he enquired 'Even though I am a bit of a "Gahcod" at times?'

Stella laughed at his mockery of her outrage and pointed out that at that moment she could have killed him. 'You have no idea just how infuriating that bloody gag is Dale. It's not all that uncomfortable but you just cannot say a bloody word that is understandable… although you seem to have understood "Gahcod" OK.'

They made love three times with Stella remaining in all her new festive rubber gear. 'Does my face match the colour of my cap?' she asked. 'It's probably a far better sight than the white ones isn't it?'

Dale assured her that the white caps were going nowhere and would be on duty again at their next session. He would keep the boots here if it was going to be an embarrassment to her at *Clover Leys* but Stella insisted that they were her new boots and she would keep them safe at home. "I can just see Amanda Broughton, Veterinary Surgeon Extraordinaire, strutting about in these… no chance!" she thought to herself. "I bet they cost him a fortune."

They said their goodbyes and Stella left with a tear or two trickling down her cheeks. It was hard to imagine that throughout the coming festivities she would see nothing of him and it didn't help to know that Amanda and he would be up to loads of mischief in the meantime. She tried to remember exactly what her life had been like before this kinky idiot had come back into her life but could only words such as 'boring' or 'unproductive' or 'ungratified' appeared before her. She just adored the man and refused any thoughts that this was some mad infatuation brought about by his outrageous sexual demands on her. She loved her sessions and being trussed up like a turkey was a sensation that she realised had been missing for far too long in her life. In the Canterbury library she had looked into 'bondage' and found out that it was something the male enjoyed far more than the female as a general rule. There was nothing sado-masochistic about Dale for he abhorred the merest suggestion of any pain and only wallowed in pleasure when he was quite sure she was comfortable. Frustrated? Yes! Furious? Yes! Helpless? Yes!

Uncomfortable? Not at all. She had become a very confident and sexy lady in these short months and really *wanted* to wear her thigh boots outside the flat if the opportunity arose. Such a thing would never have happened six months ago although she had to admit to herself that had she seen them in a shop then she would have been sorely tempted to try them on.

Mr Tremlett was back in the office before Dale and had given some final dictation to Miss Manwood thanking clients for the Christmas gifts they had been kind enough to give him over the past few days. There were bottles of scotch, gin, brandy and two or three bottles of liqueur too all lined up on the carpet behind his desk to which Colleen had attached labels showing him who had given him what. He rose to greet Dale with a beam and wished him a 'good afternoon… or is it evening young Dale?' in order to make the point that his young valuer was some twenty-five minutes late for their appointment. Dale apologised and explained that he was behind time as 'one wife had been hanging about doing other things' and this had caused the delay.

Mr Tremlett got up again and said, 'Young Dale, you are a real asset to the firm and I'm very proud of you. You work long hours, never complain, never ask for overtime or bonuses and don't you think for one moment that I'm not appreciative. Our clients seem to like you and I realise that you have a great rapport with our friends from the various Brewery Companies for whom we act. This is the time of goodwill and I have something for you.' He turned towards the direction of the small 'off-licence' stores behind him.

Dale thought to himself, ''Please make it a bottle of brandy, Dad loves brandy, although to be fair he loves gin as well.'

'Gee Gee' continued his slow walk and ignoring the rows of carefully labelled bottles he disappeared behind the safe and came out with the most decrepit old attaché case he had ever seen in his life. It was dusty, one of the buckle clips was not working and an old leather belt was fastened round it in order to keep it closed. Holding it out in front of him Mr Tremlett advanced with the solemnity of Black Rod at the official Opening of Parliament and proffered it to his open-mouthed young Partner.

'This is for you young man. It belonged to my father and I'm sure he would have wanted you to have it.' He spoke in hushed tones.

Dale took the dilapidated object and keeping it at arm's length said in equally sombre tones:

'I don't know what to say sir. Sometimes, words fail one and this is one of those times sir. A mere "thank you" seems not enough but it will have to do.' Was that a tear trickling down the old boy's cheek? Dale left the room in a daze and was half way up the main staircase before he realised that the old rascal had 'conned him once again and was at this moment probably rolling all over the carpet kicking his legs in the air in hysterics at the gullibility of his ex-pupil. Dale loved the old man and even though a bottle would have been nice he knew that the story he could tell of this latest encounter would keep people laughing for many, many years to come. As time was getting on he rang down to the Guv'nor and asked if it would be OK if they had their drink after Christmas as he wanted to get off for the North of England and be through the London traffic before dark. Mr Tremlett wished him a safe journey and looked forward to seeing him on the 30th adding that he would be in the office every day 'just to check that nobody wants some valuation work done in a hurry', knowing full well that the chances of such a request were so slim as to be virtually nil.

Dale rang Amanda on the number she had given him and confirmed their date for New Year's Eve. She seemed so happy to hear from him and said that she was really looking forward to their night out together. They wished each other a 'Very Happy Christmas' and Amanda whispered 'I love you' as she replaced the receiver. Dale was so full of the thigh-booted 'Crimson Pirate Queen' of that morning that Amanda's simple loving farewell on the end of the line brought him up sharply and made him realise just what a fortunate man he was to have the love of two such elegant and exciting women.

'Am I a bastard?' he asked himself. 'Should I be doing this to them? Is it fair?'

'Yes! Of course it's fair you idiot,' he answered. 'We are all adults and we are all having a ball!'

CHAPTER EIGHTEEN

He arrived in Monkseaton just before eight o'clock and was welcomed by his father who insisted that they go round to the 'Black Horse' for a couple of pints. They sat down in the bar and Dale listened as his Dad brought him up to date with all the happenings of the family and local news. The beer was good and two became four before the two men were being reminded that it was 'TIME' to depart. For a man approaching eighty Guy Ingram still remained remarkably alert and mentally active. He had Dale laughing as they walked home with a fund of silly, very silly and then totally obscene stories.

The two of them were going to sister Daisy and husband Frank's house for Christmas Day and had been invited to stay the night in order that they could both partake of alcohol. Frank was a pilot with British Airways, flying 757s out of Newcastle on domestic flights and to short range European destinations. He loved the job and knew all there was to know about the history of man and the aeroplane. Their two daughters, Jill and Kirsty, aged 17 and 13 respectively, both adored their uncle and grandfather.

Christmas Day proved to be a day of laughter, good food, goodwill, alcohol galore and very little exercise. Daisy and Frank Cowell lived in a gorgeous detached house on the outskirts of Gosforth and their combined salaries, for Daisy taught Geography at a local Grammar School, ensured that their lifestyle was extremely pleasurable. Frank was a down-to-earth Northumbrian and had worked hard for all he had achieved. Dale and he had always got on famously and their mutual love of Newcastle United meant that there never was a time when they hadn't got anything about which to talk. Dale had always kidded him that being he was such a good bloke 'how on earth did you get mixed up with my bloody sister?' Needless to say he adored his elder sister but would never confess to such a thing.

His Dad bought Daisy a handbag, much to the merriment of the two girls and Uncle Dale, and the perfumes that Julie Swift had selected for Dale to give Daisy proved just right. Dale, being Dale, had bought the girls black leather knee-high boots with high-ish heels which they just loved.

'Dear Uncle Dale,' sighed Jill. 'For such an old man you really do know about what women want.'

'Tell me about it!' sighed Dale inwardly. The sight of the two perfectly formed young females prancing about in their baby doll nighties and very little else other than their new boots was far too much for Uncle who retired for a bath and a shave. The hospitality of the Cowells was endless. Frank had just returned from a trip accompanying senior men over to the maker's field in Seattle to bring across a new jetliner to add to the existing fleet and his stories about the flight and the jet itself were most interesting. He loved the 757 and having flown Trident airliners in the early part of his career he always tended to feel that the new plane had a surplus of power to it. Daisy had cooked a wonderfully plump goose, knowing her father's fondness for same, and the smells that had been emerging from the kitchen for almost three hours had meant all were more than ready for their lunch. Kirsty refused to take her boots off and wandered around in them till bedtime. Scrabble, Cleudo and Monopoly were all played by some of the party some of the time and Dale met Jill's boyfriend, Kevin, when he turned up for tea at about seven o'clock. Kevin took a bit of a battering from Frank and Dale who started on his name. 'What sort of a name is Kevin for God's sake?' and then to his clothes with terminology of 'un-made bed' and 'three sizes too big for you' being thrown at the poor soul. When it became known that he was also a fanatical Sunderland supporter Jill realised the game was over and cried at him, 'I told you *never* to tell my Dad that you supported Sunderland! Do you realise what a life I am going to lead from this time?'

It was all good badinage and with the wine and the port flowing all day Dale was a very tired man when he finally crept up the stairs to bed leaving his father animatedly discussing the price of the new Rover 2000 with a rapidly wilting pilot.

The next three days saw Dale and his Dad visiting various public houses around Whitley Bay, Tynemouth, Cullercoats and Monkseaton. Dale also called on his old House Master and found him still mentally alert but dreadfully crippled with arthritis. Mr 'Flogger' Douglas was a second 'Mr Chips' and had stayed as a working teacher for several years after the official retirement age. His memory of Dale's years there were crystal clear and of the sporting success the school had enjoyed as a band of very talented cricketers and rugby footballers had all arrived on the scene at the same time. 'Annus mirabilis my boy! Annus mirabilis! Do you remember our 1st X1 dismissing the Grammar School at Whitley Bay for nine runs? Annus mirabilis indeed!'

Dale's father was so proud of his son and wanted everyone to meet him. 'When you are my age son most of your pals have gone and very few are interested in you any more. It is so nice to be able to introduce you and let them realise that I do have a family and that we all care about each other. I miss your Mum every day of my life. I was hopeless as a husband and why she put up with me is quite beyond me. I see how Frank treats Daisy and I shudder with embarrassment… there's one of life's true gentlemen, son'.

'She put up with you Dad because she loved you. It's as simple as that.'

The two men embraced as Dale prepared to leave the North East and his Dad thanked him warmly for coming up. 'I love you boy and I'm very proud of you… always have been and always will be.'

Those few words made Dale's trip so worthwhile and he vowed that he had got to get up North a little more often as his father grew older. Daisy was wonderful and kept a watchful eye on the old boy but he needed to see him for himself and knew that his visit had been a real tonic for this 'man's man'.

He called in at Gosforth on the way home and said goodbye to Daisy and the still booted Kirsty. Jill was out in Newcastle with the dreadful Kevin exchanging her presents from Grandfather Ingram, Kevin and Kevin's parents. 'Did she keep my boots?' Dale asked Kirsty.

'Oh yes Uncle! But I think she may change them for a grey pair to go with her winter coat!'

Daisy thanked her brother for making the long trip home for she knew her brother and was quite sure there were females in Kent who would have given him a delightful and restful festive holiday. They had always been a close pair in adulthood and her family were as close as Dale had got to being part of a family since the death of their Mum. Dale confirmed that he would be up to see them again in the not too distant future for he had already begun to make provisional plans for a brief sortie up to possibly, Holy Island, with Stella if she could somehow wangle it. To have her alone for just three days would be wonderful. He had mentioned his meeting with Stella 'Ward' to Daisy who remembered the little tomboy leader who although only being a year younger than Daisy had never had much to do with his sister and her very 'girlie' friends. 'She was a strange girl was our Stella,' said Daisy. 'Didn't seem to want to dress as a girl or play the sort of games we wanted to play. You were quite besotted with her weren't you and whatever Stella Ward said had to be the gospel truth. Does she still insist on wearing Wellington boots in the middle of August?'

'Whatever she was or was not she is a cracking looking woman now Daisy. I can't believe that we have been living within ten miles of each other for over twenty years and never met. She's married to the Chairman of a Brewery Company and has a wonderful life.'

'Dale… you're not mucking about with her are you?' the term 'mucking about' was about as rude as Daisy got. 'I know you and your love for the opposite "what's it",' here again the word 'sex' did not figure in Daisy's vocabulary, 'and I trust that the adoration you once had for her has disappeared. It really is time you started thinking about settling down. You are over forty and should have a wife, a home and a family by now. This lady vet sounds nice. Why don't you bring her up and show her the scenery of Northumberland. Only Cornwall can match our beaches and where else have you the castles, the rivers and the Cheviot Hills?'

Daisy was off on her bandwagon for she truly loved her County and it made her so cross that few people in the UK had ever been up to see England's most Northerly County. Dale stopped her short.

'Daisy you don't have to convince me for heaven's sake! I was born here and love the place dearly. I am thinking of coming up for a few days and may well bring a companion up with me. I must get up to Holy Island and throw my hat in one or two doors to see if they still remember me.' As a young man, fresh out of National Service and with no serious girlfriend, Dale had been up to the island regularly for a week's break at least twice a year and had made many friends. He had taken Carol Cooper there and they had spent a wonderfully hot fortnight in August lounging in the towering sand dunes and drinking in the pubs into the early hours. She had returned to work looking as brown as a berry and had convinced them all in the office that she had been to the Costa Brava.

On the long journey back to Kent Dale mused about what Daisy had said. It was true that he was now beginning to look at himself and see what he was missing. So many of his old rugby and cricketing pals were happily married and totally involved with the upbringing of their children. He was having a great deal of fun sexually but was this becoming a rather short-term policy? The idea of full commitment to one woman had always frightened the life out of him. There were so many lovely ladies to whom he was no threat and with whom he could taste so much enjoyment. Stella was the most wonderful lover he had ever experienced and the one who, in tight bondage, excited him most. She was simply superb and her fiery temper only enhanced the final moments of their lovemaking. Amanda was one of the nicest people he had ever met and her love for him was worrying in that he did feel very strongly about her too. In character she was a much softer person than Stella but her strong body and obvious delight in reacting to her first bondage session with him made him sure that Miss Broughton and he would be chums and lovers for a long time to come. It still niggled him that she had queried whether or not he might actually hurt her, not physically of course, but by treating her shabbily. Nothing could have been further from the truth and the fact that such things worried him again made Dale realise that Amanda Broughton was also very special to him.

The weather steadily deteriorated as he drove south and by the time he had reached Canterbury it was pouring with rain and blowing a gale. His flat was warm enough and he sat on the settee with a scotch and soda munching a packet of crisps and opening a few Christmas cards that had arrived either on Christmas Eve or been delivered since Christmas. Mostly were late arrivals. One from the Scotts at Charing and written in Annie's hand had the postscript: *Hope that we are not both too tied up to go riding soon!* whilst a card had been slipped into his letter box which read: *Darling Dale, Hope you had a lovely Christmas with your family. I'm thinking of you constantly and wish I could see you. Thank you so much for my new red boots, which I shall treasure and wear for you as much as I can…where did you get them from? Do get in touch soon won't you. All my love. S.*

He was tired and strangely dissatisfied with things as he went to bed. Too many balls were up in the air and no long-term plans were in his head. The New Year, he decided, must see some changes in his life.

The Office was noisy on the re-opening day with girlish chatter filling the corridors as presents were shown or talked about and celebrations relived. Mr Tremlett was not yet in and most of the noise would die immediately his foot hit the brass threshold plate. Julie came in looking a picture in a slate grey two-piece fitting suit and her knee boots. Perching herself on her chair she handed him about six letters and asked that he deal with these now as all needed swift replies. She crossed her shapely legs and *suddenly he was facing Miss Ann Baxter once more in the old western 'A Ticket to Tomahawk'. Tied to the railway tracks once again as the massive steam engine thundered down the tracks towards her and he, the villain, licked his lecherous lips as she fought the ropes that bound her. Dionne Warwick was singing 'I'll never love this way again' to a huge orchestral backing.*

'Dear Mr Payne,' he began, thinking to himself, "Aaahh! I'm feeling better already!"

Dictation over, he wandered downstairs and knocked on Mr Tremlett's door and entered quietly. The Guv'nor was reading a letter and looked decidedly pleased with himself. 'I've just been called the youngest octogenarian on the planet,' he chortled. 'Mr & Mrs Hopkins from the "Newport Arms" are "thrilled to bits" with the job we've done for them and want me to go over and have lunch with them… they are a pleasant pair and I'll ring them up and arrange a visit next week.' Dale smiled knowing that he had actually worked solely by himself on their valuation and had seen the job through from start to finish. It had been a very difficult exercise and old Bernard Brazier from Spatwell & Creed had not given him an easy ride having had a most difficult client with whom to deal with himself. However the days of the Guv'nor's many 'triumphs' were few and far between these days and the fact that their clients had decided to heap the praise on the senior man did not alter the facts and had made the old boy very happy.

Mr Tremlett confirmed he had been in the office every day but reported that nothing of any real importance had been delivered.

January was always a busy month for the Brokers as many Licensees held on for 'one more Christmas' before handing in their notice. Sale particulars of the Houses had to be circulated to the hundreds of would-be tenants, interviews arranged with themselves and then the Brewers, inventories prepared and the court applications signed typed and despatched to the relevant Clerks to the Justices' offices. February and March were the months when many of the 'physical' changeovers took place with tenants leaving having been paid for their inventories of furniture, fittings and effects together with their wet stocks and then things quietened down as the South East prepared for the summer months and the increased trade that followed. Not only were Kent and Sussex popular holiday counties but the fact that they were very much agricultural areas too meant that there was plenty of casual farm work and overtime being paid and therefore more money in everyone's pockets. Much of this cash went into the tills of the publicans and helped them through the rather barren months at the beginning of each year. As Autumn approached so the 'notices' would come flooding in from those tenants who had opted for 'one more summer' and ensuring that the months of October, November and December were hectic ones for the valuation departments of the Licensed Property agents. C G Tremlett & Son were fortunate in that having a large Stocktaking Department the poor trading months of the valuation side contrasted with the busiest time of the year for Felix Chapman and his band of brothers. All the seaside houses needed weekly stock checks as the casual 'rogue' barmen were sorted out and sacked. It was quite common for these men to find employment all through the season but be hounded from place to place by the efforts of the stocktakers. Chapman was a great organiser and ran a very tidy ship. He did not like interference from anyone and his verbal battles with Jacob Growser were constant as the old Ledger Clerk tried to flaunt his seniority over the Department Chief. Chapman was a Junior Partner but Growser was not and this fact niggled away at the old chap for he could remember young Felix coming to work for the firm in 1948 at a time that he had been employed for over twenty-five years. He would keep on saying that 'It was all very much better when Miss Sopswith ran the stock-taking… we all knew what was happening in those days!' Miss Sopswith had been a friend of Mrs Tremlett in the late twenties and had 'twittered' about for eighteen months leaving just in time to avoid being murdered by the father of the present Senior Partner. Young Growser, as he was in those days, had fallen madly in love with the pretty 'flapper' but realised that she was far too highly born to notice him and merely attempted to assist her whenever he could.

Nobody really knew much about the Accounts Department at the top of the building. The three Junior Partners, Tom Spackman, Bill Southbourn and Barrie Brightling, were all quiet and private people who had worked extremely hard for the firm for between twenty-five and forty years and apart from nodding to other members of staff and fellow partners they did not take much interest in anything other than the tax affairs of their clients. Mr Tremlett occasionally summoned one of them down if a client had written or 'phoned expressing dissatisfaction over the amount of tax he was being asked to pay but was always confronted by all three who would put up a united front and an argument that placed them 100% in the right and the 'idiot' client 100% in the wrong. It was a pretty pointless exercise so, unbeknown to the 'three musketeers', Mr Tremlett would send off a letter of abject apology saying that the man responsible had been severely reprimanded and that if his standards dropped once more he would be summarily dismissed. He lost very few clients.

Dale popped upstairs to wish the Accounts Department the compliments of the season but was met by their normal defensive wall of suspicion and distrust. He did get a smile out of the senior typist, a lady who had been with the firm for as long as Dale and as a most buxom wench had been taken out by a very young and raw

Geordie lad in the late fifties, and been fondled in the back row of the Odeon Cinema as they watched or rather she watched and Dale groped his way through 'The Nun's Story' with Audrey Hepburn. She had been courting for almost a year but decided that a trip to the cinema with this good-looking young man from the North was worth experiencing. Dale didn't think they had repeated the exercise and she had married shortly afterwards but Mrs Pickard always had a knowing smile for Dale as if to say: 'Look what you missed!' As far as Dale could make out he had missed out on being lumbered with 224lbs of pinkish blubber and a pair of legs that could have held up a grand piano! The past twenty years had seen Mrs Helen Pickard give birth to five children and acquire an extreme fondness for pints of lager and lime. As he left the top floor the three accountants had gathered in Spackman's doorway and were talking earnestly amongst themselves.

"Probably debating what I actually was getting at by asking them if they had had a good Christmas," he thought and then pondered, "or am I getting paranoid about the three of them?"

He rang Amanda and left a message with one of her 'vet'lets' as he had nicknamed the two young lasses who assisted in the surgery. Amanda was attending to a difficult calving at one of the local farms. Dale knew she would be really chuffed to have been asked to attend as she had admitted to him that a lady vet was still something of a novelty in East Kent and despite her excellent qualifications she was still regarded in some quarters as being 'nice lassie but not what you could call a *proper* vet!' It was all very frustrating but such an operation as the one she was performing at present could do nothing but good for her reputation and her career. He hoped it was not at the Donald Farm 'cos he still had memories of Jamie's frolics in the hay with her not too long ago. He trusted that things had changed for Amanda since that time.

His worries were in vain for she had not been to the Donald Farm and all had gone splendidly well.

'You didn't end up in the hay again with a grateful farmer did you darling?' he asked.

'Shame on you Dale, I remained professional throughout and the fact that the farmer was old enough to be my grandfather was also a factor I'm afraid. Please tell me you are a wee bit jealous Dale... that would make my day!'

'I confess it. Somewhere deep down in my inner psyche is a little devil who presents me with dark pictures and I distinctly saw you and Jamie Donald, a flurry of rubber boots and much merriment in the hay!! It was awful.'

'Darling Dale, that you care enough to even think such things makes me want to hug you here and now but that will have to wait until tomorrow evening. I have made a purchase since you were last here and I trust you will approve... right up your street!'

'You haven't bought the Newcastle United Annual have you?'

'No I have not! These are something that will hopefully give you a great deal more pleasure.'

'These? Therefore there must be two of them,' he teased. 'Now what two things could you buy that I would find right up my street? I know, you've bought two entries into the Rugby Club's '200 Club' swindle haven't you. I bet old Dickie Coverdale has been on to you and you couldn't resist his rustic charms.'

'I can see you are not going to be serious so you will have to wait and see. As it happens Dickie did catch me in Sandwich a week or two ago and left me with £12 less in my purse as I contributed to the improvements at your blessed rugby club. Since I've been seen with you it seems I am now fair game for anything that might loosely be labelled 'assisting Dale and his chums'. He told me you had got a ticket... I jolly well hope you have or you are both in trouble. Are you going to take me to watch Canterbury play before the end of the season? I do love the game and I promise I won't let you down with any silly girlie comments about so and so's legs etc.'

Dale warmed to the girl even more at this last comment. Good old Amanda actually liked rugby football and didn't mind standing in the cold watching his club's 1st XV as they performed to the best of their abilities on most occasions. A pipe dream would have been to walk into the clubhouse with Amanda on one arm and Stella on the other… enough to make some of his old team-mates, now long-time married, weep into their beer! He promised that he would take her up to the club when there was a good fixture and they ended their conversation in most affectionate tones.

A quick call to Annie Scott organised a morning's ride in three days' time. She was delighted to hear from him and gave the distinct impression that she could not wait to be in his company again. They had had a simply wonderful Christmas and were fully booked for the New Year's Eve festivities. Vincent Scott could be heard in the background and Annie passed on his best wishes stating that they would love him to come back for something to eat after their ride. Dale told her he'd pick her up at 9 o'clock.

CHAPTER NINETEEN

Dale had let himself into the cottage and had been invited to pour himself a drink by Amanda who was still preparing herself. They chatted, he sitting at the foot of the stairs and she floating between bathroom and bedroom. He heard hair dryers drying, sprays hissing and atomisers doing what atomisers do. Eventually she appeared at the top of the stairs.

'Oh darling! You have never looked lovelier!' He gasped as this vision stood before him.

Amanda was wearing an Yves St Laurent black silk cocktail dress and very high-heeled patent leather black strappy sandals. Around her shoulders was a mohair stole in the distinctive green and black tartan of the Black Watch Regiment. Dale just looked and looked at this beautiful woman as if unable to take in just how gorgeous she really was. Amanda tended to dress sensibly rather than fashionably on most occasions but when she made the effort… Wow!!!!!

Their taxi was a little late but this allowed Dale time to tell his lovely date just what he thought of her. Their entrance into the 'Red Lion' caused the stir that Dale had thought it might. One or two of the local farming fraternity were there and seeing their practical young veterinary surgeon transformed into this elegant goddess saw mouths open and jaws drop. Dale noticed James and Philo Billshot who were chatting to William and Maggie Gunnerstone.

'Now there's a sight you don't often see Amanda,' he said. 'A Tied-Trade Director not only standing next to a Managed House Director but actually talking to each other… and in another Brewers' house. I expect they want a quiet life and they certainly wouldn't get that in a Wetton Ackeson hostelry.'

Philo waved them over and started chatted in her normal animated style. She was a pleasant soul and Dale liked her. She it had been who had rescued him from the clutches of one or two who could have 'bored for Great Britain' if given the opportunity at various Licensed Victuallers' Banquets and Balls around the County. These Social Annual events were sometimes wonderfully successful and at other times mind-numbingly boring. Dale always tried to get on a table with other Brokers or a few Area Managers as neither group tended to bring partners with them to such functions but quite often he found himself sitting with publicans he didn't know or couldn't remember but who knew him and would spend the entire meal telling him and the assembled company how either their Brewery Company or their Broker had twisted them out of 'a fortune' and how different it would be when they left! Philo Billshot was a great supporter of her husband and they were seen at all the Kent Banquets and a few down in Sussex too. He did not know James Billshot too well but the man was extremely straight and that is all one could ever hope for in any business dealings. His lack of humour had always amused Dale as he recalled how on so many occasions at Brewery functions the beer had flowed and he and the crew from A W Spatwell & Creed had made the whole assembly, with the exception of poor old Billshot, roar with laughter as they recounted the outrageous antics of their clients, old Mr Tremlett or old Mr Spatwell and themselves. James Billshot would look round the room at the hysterical faces of his fellow drinkers with a blank look on his face wondering what was so funny. William Gunnerstone was from the North and was proud of it. He did not take it kindly when Dale had suggested, again after a good drinking session, that Lancashire was not really 'North' but more 'North Midlands' and that he had to drive due south from his home in Northumberland for nearly an hour and a half before he reached Yorkshire! However Bill

Gunnerstone was a good operator and ran a very profitable if somewhat small Managed House Estate. His wife Maggie was not intellectually too bright but she was a mass of nervous giggles and had planted a great big 'New Year's Eve' kiss on Dale's lips as soon as they arrived which showed she was a friendly soul.

Amanda had been collared by a party of farmers and seemed to be enjoying their good-natured leg-pulling. As Philo twittered on he looked across at his lovely partner and found, to his horror, that *the dress was slowly but surely being replaced by a leather thong and the sandals by Stella's new thigh boots as she stood there chatting to her band of admirers... Cilla Black was singing 'Anyone who had a heart'...* Oh dear me, yes! It was a nightmare indeed.

Eventually Peter Martin called for all his guests who were dining to make their way to the dining room at the rear of the premises and Dale was pleased to be back with his lovely Amanda once more. The tables were laid out in two straight rows with small gaps every eighth person to allow movement to and fro the bar and/or toilets. The Martins had surpassed themselves and entering the room was like breathing in the heather from a Highland wedding party. Large linen napkins in various tartans, two large Standards of St Andrew were draped at either end of the room and the skirl of the pipes sounded as a Pipe Major entered the room in his full regalia giving a rousing rendering of 'Scotland the Brave'. The printed menus showed that much thought had gone into ensuring the guests all received a true Hogmanay dinner:

Smoked Tay Salmon wrapped around prawns in a piri-piri sauce
*
Scotch Broth
*
Smoked Haddock with Cream & Egg Sauce
*
Lime Sorbet
*

Fillet of Aberdeen Angus Beef
(Parsnips, Leeks, Kale and Roast & Mashed Potatoes)
*

Drambuie Flummery
*

Cheeses (Served with Oatcakes)
Stilton, Crowdie, Orkney & Dunlop
*

Coffee & Petits Fours
*

WINES Chassagne Montrachet & Medoc
Tawny Port 1970
*

Malt Whiskies by order only = Macallan, Highland Park & Pittyvaich

Dale and Amanda ate and drank and talked and laughed. Their nearest fellow diners were not known to them but were approximately the same age as Dale and both had a great sense of humour. They had just returned from a trip down to Cornwall and had really enjoyed it. Steve and Angela had wanted to go in the winter months, thereby dodging the holiday crowds and had spent five days exploring all the coast line either side of Land's End.

'You really should go,' Angela remarked enthusiastically, 'and if you go prepared for bad weather then you won't be disappointed. Make sure you have strong waterproof clothing and wellies with you.'

'Oh, I'll certainly have my rubber boots with me on any trip,' piped up Amanda giving Dale's knee a nudge under the table. 'I suppose that being a vet I've always got them handy.'

'You look so elegant Amanda,' said Steve, 'that somehow I couldn't imagine you in anything but the sort of things you are wearing tonight. We both remarked on how stunning you looked this evening didn't we darling?'

'You would be surprised at how good she can look in whatever she's wearing,' laughed Dale. 'In fact I'd go as far as to say I bet Amanda would look bloody good wearing only Wellington boots… what do you think Steve?'

Poor old Steve could not cope with the vision suggested by Dale and despite Amanda's fond scoldings he blushed hugely, which made Angela, Amanda and Dale laugh all the more. The evening passed far too quickly even though the various courses were served at sensible intervals allowing tummies to recover and wines to be sipped through jovial banter. The Tawny Port served was eight years old and virtually in prime condition, but some buffoon three places down insisted on purchasing two bottles of Vintage Port for an awful lot of money and then proceeded to drink it as though it were light ale.

"There's always one at every dinner party," thought Dale. "What a prat!"

Dale could tell that Amanda was in seventh heaven and his heart warmed as he felt the heat of her love for him invade his very being. It must have been so hard for this young lady to have forced herself into contention at the time she took over the established Practice of her predecessor, Walter Bigley, who had retired in 1974 at the age of sixty-five. Walter had been the absolute antipathy to Amanda in that he called a spade a 'bloody shovel' all his career and did not take kindly to young farmers questioning his judgements on anything… and that included sport, religion and politics!! Obviously he had liked Amanda from the outset and had been very good in introducing her to all his clients not only by letter but, in many cases, by taking her to the various farms and letting people see who their next vet was to be. True she had lost several good clients immediately but this was not Walter Bigley's fault and she still received the odd letter from he and his wife as they enjoyed retirement in the little hamlet of Bosham, by the river near Chichester in West Sussex. Dale had no doubts that around the farming mafia tomorrow and the following days there would be comments flowing backwards and forwards concerning 'the stunning appearance of Amanda Broughton at the 'Red Lion' Hogmanay do'.

With glasses charged, Mine Host, Peter Martin, tuned his relay system into the BBC and as the assembled company counted down the last ten seconds of the old year Dale wondered to himself what 1979 would bring about. The next second Amanda was in his arms wishing him a Happy New Year and he was kissing her, Angela, the lady on his left and a rather dumpy waitress who happened to be within grabbing range. Amanda, too, was having an enormous amount of good wishes kissed into her but appeared to be coping very well. Dale gave a silent toast to Stella as he wondered what she was doing at this very moment.

Not many folk saw the entry of another year as being the reason to end a very good party, and few looked as though they were leaving for some time yet. Pints of bitter, pints of lager, bottles of red and white wines, another bottle of vintage port for old 'prat face' along the table, and pots of steaming coffee flowed out of the bar, the cellars and the kitchen as Peter Martin's grin got wider and wider. The evening had been a set price affair but his guests had drunk way and above the excellent options he had extended to them and for the next hour or so it would be all extra profit. Dale congratulated Barbara and Peter on the excellence of the evening saying it had been quite the best Hogmanay he had ever attended. This coming from a Northumbrian was praise indeed for this night in the County of his birth is celebrated still with all the fervour of those over their northern boundary line.

'If we could do this every week Dale we could retire in five years,' said Peter. 'It is so bloody frustrating when you know you've got the wherewithal to put on events like this but don't just get the support. Barbara has really loved organising the whole thing and we haven't had one complaint apart from some prat who felt the port was a little inferior.'

'Is that the fellow drinking it out of a half pint tankard over in the corner?' Dale enquired.

Dale and Peter collapsed with laughter at this sight knowing that both of them would be telling this particular story for many days to come. Amanda breezed through the door and asked if the taxi had arrived. They had booked it for quarter to one but realised that there would probably be delays. Dale ordered two glasses of iced lemonade that the two of them sipped in the passageway leading to the car park. Almost to order as they finished their drinks the taxi driver put his head in the door and shouted, 'Taxi for Mr Ingram'. Saying farewell to Steve and Angela and agreeing that they would have a meal together soon, waving goodbye to the quartet from Wetton Ackeson and receiving big kisses from Philo who was very merry, and Maggie who was very drunk took a few minutes but eventually they were being whisked back to Ash and Amanda's cottage.

Dale had got such big plans for the two of them but their evening had been just so good that all he and his darling Amanda wanted to do was get undressed and curl up in bed together. Amanda could not resist trying on her boots and posed for him in them loving the huge erection the sight of her in them caused her lover. They made love together quietly in front of her dying wood-burning stove and lay in each other's arms caressing and feeling the depths of their passion.

'You have given me the most wonderful night of my entire life Dale. It has been so lovely having you with me and feeling the strength of your love for me. I can't believe it can get much better than tonight can it?' she asked.

Dale confessed that he too had enjoyed the evening and that the pride he felt on having Amanda on his arm had made him the proudest man in the room. 'You really are a very special little lady,' he whispered, 'and now I'm going to take this very special little lady to bed before we both collapse down here.' So saying he picked her up in his arms and closing the doors to the grate with his foot he climbed the stairs and gently placed his gorgeous naked sweetheart on the bed. He pulled off her new boots and placed them by the side of the bed confirming quietly that they would be seeing plenty of action in the morning.

'I can't wait to see what you're going to do to me you terrible man,' Amanda hissed as she cuddled up to Dale her hands finding those places that Dale wanted her to find and then as he talked quietly to her about the evening she dropped into a deep slumber, purring with contentment.

"What a night!" thought Dale. "What a bloody wonderful night!"

The shrill tone of Amanda's bedside telephone disturbed them at eight o'clock the next morning. It was a distraught lady from Ickham who had found her horse most unwell and needed Amanda's attention immediately. Kissing Dale on the forehead she tumbled out of bed and disappeared into the bathroom coming out a few minutes later dressed for work in her jeans, checked shirt and heavy green pullover.

'I'll be home as soon as I can darling,' she cried ruefully. 'Please don't get up... just go back to sleep and dream of me.'

Dale did get up and had a bath, shaved and tidied up around the house. One thing he really could manage in the catering stakes was a good old cooked English breakfast and he found all the ingredients in the fridge and set about grilling sausages, tomatoes and bacon whilst preparing the frying pan for the eggs and bread. He turned the oven on in case Amanda was going to be gone longer than he had anticipated and had just placed his grilled bacon and tomatoes in same when she burst in through the door. It had appeared the panic was a wee bit unfounded as the mare had not seemed unduly bothered by the time she arrived and normal tests had revealed all the symptoms of a perfectly healthy animal. The owner had promised to ring back should anything untoward happen during the day.

Amanda slipped her shoes off and sipped the hot coffee Dale had prepared.

'We are a domesticated gentleman this morning aren't we?' she laughed. 'I had no idea that you were capable of such culinary expertise Dale.'

'When you've been on your own for as long as I have my dear, you pick up an awful lot of tips on the best way to survive. Funnily enough my Mum taught me how to cook a good breakfast… always reckoned it was the most important meal of the day. I've never been able to get my head round eating muesli and that sort of stuff. I'm sure it's brilliant for you but I prefer the cooked breakfast and try to eat one most days… time permitting.'

They sat down and ate Dale's breakfast, which received a most complimentary tribute from Amanda and then sipped coffee and chatted on the settee until almost midday. A father and daughter turned up with their Springer Spaniel who had a deep cut in her paw and needed stitches which Amanda inserted quickly and dressed the wound giving the excitable animal a padded drumstick of a hind leg.

It was almost one o'clock when Dale sensed that Amanda was relaxed and ready to enjoy more of the lovemaking they had experienced just before Christmas. Returning to the bedroom he gently removed her clothes and as she pulled on her new rubber riding boots he went to his case and brought out some red cords. Amanda waited patiently as her wrists were tied firmly behind her back and then winced as the bathing cap was brought out.

'Why do you want me in the hat Dale? I just can't understand how it can be a "turn on" to look at a bald woman? I really would like to get inssshhhide your mind assshh issshh a real missshhhtery,' she pleaded as the chin-strap was playfully flipped into her mouth causing a lisp to occur immediately. Elbow cords were fastened and pulled firmly into place causing her lovely rounded breasts to push out proudly.

'I have told you the basics of fetishism darling. It is the sight and the touch and the smell of rubber that can drive some men to distraction. Bondage tends to go with rubber or leather but in the case of the latter I'm afraid there seems to be a great deal more pain taken and dished out. The joy of the rubber fetishist is to titillate, to frustrate and to give genuine painless pleasure. But you, my dear, have been asking too many questions so it is out with your strap and in with a proper gag.' Dale replaced the chin-strap to its proper position and watched Amanda's face as she was presented with the blue ball-gag.

'Oh my God! Is that going in my mouth?' she asked. 'Is this absolutely necessary Dale? I'm at your mercy, isn't that enough?'

Dale assured her that it was not enough and for her own good she must now be silenced. Fitting it into place took seconds and her outburst was very similar to that of Stella when muted for the first time. Dale then fastened her ankles together with more red cord and picking her up carried her downstairs and stood her in front of the front door.

'Now then me booted beauty! What have you got to say about that?'

Amanda, horrified that she was now in full view of anyone coming to the cottage, struggled on the spot to give vent to her anger.

'**Gooo glooochhy gahcod!'** she cried.

'Don't you call me a gahcod!' exclaimed Dale, trying hard to keep a straight face.

'**Gooo glooochhy gahcod! Aaarrll gurrrcha goo! Aaaarrll gloocchy gurrrcha goo!'**

As with every case Amanda realised the total useless waste of energy as she fought to make herself heard and lapsed into silence allowing the glares from her reddened face to get across her message. A small vibrator was produced and inserted with masterly aplomb.

'**Gleeeze goern gurnk ick gong… Gleeze,**' she pleaded in vain as it was clicked on and started behaving in its normal devilish fashion. Dale had been able to see the approach to the cottage the whole time and could easily have taken Amanda upstairs before any spying eyes could see her but his casual air did not give his terrified captive that consolation. Now he took her up the stairs and laid her gently on her tummy causing the vibrator to intensify its probings and whirrings. Amanda started to simulate the butterfly stroke body and leg movements despite her bound elbows and wrists and was in perfect co-ordination when Dale extracted the wretched toy and untying her completely turned her over and drew her to him. Amanda was so excited and in such a highly sexed state that she impaled herself on Dale within a second or two and resumed her rhythm this time allowing herself the groans and high shrieks the gag had denied. Dale had been highly aroused himself by this, oh so feminine body in bondage and before too long they had reached their pinnacles of desire and subsided into each other's loving embrace.

Amanda lay there breathing heavily and at total ease with herself and her emotions. This man, this bully, this awful article had transformed her in about twenty minutes from a cool, calm, professional woman into a wild, sex-crazed creature with only one thought in her mind… and she adored him because of it. He seemed to know when to do everything and, once again, it had worked to perfection. She snuggled her rubber-covered head into his face allowing him to smell the special aroma the hat gave out and marvelled as she saw his member harden almost imperceptibly to the eye but not to the grasp. Still experimenting she rubbed her boots up and down his inner calves and again her hands felt the surge that went through him.

"My goodness!" she thought to herself. "It really is true. Rubber really is his thing and it is a perfectly natural reaction."

They embraced again and Dale gently began to arouse her with a series of stroking, caressing and kissing her most sensitive areas. She could not believe the firmness of her breasts and nipples as he explored her and was soon spread-eagled without ropes as she urged her lover to take her to heaven once more. To Dale's astonishment Amanda suddenly placed her chin-strap in her mouth and licking through it she used her tongue to persuade him to treat her as if she were a tart from Warsaw or wherever.

'Come on big boy! Why gon't you give meeshh the fushing I deserve?!'

Dale could no longer resist her taunts and mounting her gave her what can only be described as a 'good bonking'! As they lay on the bed Dale could not stop laughing at this incredible female who could change so much in her efforts to satisfy herself and her lover's cravings. He had had no idea that there was a side to Amanda that only sexual desire could bring out in her and then only when she was utterly aroused.

'Well you are a surprise packet and no mistake.'

'Oh I'm sorry Dale darling but it's your entire fault. You make me wear this rubber gear and get me far too excited for my own good and then I go and make a complete ass of myself and will no doubt be reminded of this day forever more.' She took off her cap and lobbed it onto a stool by the dressing table.

'Darling, don't *ever* apologise for saying or doing anything when in the midst of making love. What happens at such times is completely natural and to stifle any deep feelings or emotions is like trying to put the cork back in a champagne bottle. To get full satisfaction you have got to be totally relaxed and allow yourself to be yourself... not somebody who you think you ought to be. If you want to scream "Fuck me!" then scream it to the heavens. What possible harm can it do and who can it upset?'

Dale's soothing words allayed fears that she had somehow let herself down and she cuddled into his body as the adventures of the day and the lateness of their retirement to bed began to take effect. Within minutes the two of them, with Amanda still wearing her new boots, were snuggled under the quilt and fast asleep.

CHAPTER TWENTY

Stella's Christmas had been a happy and successful gathering of the Rigden-Ackeson Clan. She, with the help of Mrs Defferary it must be said, had provided meal after meal of appetising goodies and Richard had been the perfect host. Richard's parents were very easy guests, loving the family around them and being more than happy to fit in with whatever plans their children had for them. Stella loved having Toby in the house because of his still youthful outlook on everything. His wife Angela was younger than her husband by about five years and was full of boundless energy which she deployed very sensibly in amusing her two daughters, Claire aged ten and Jayne one year younger. The two girls were totally different in that Claire was a real tomboy in the 'Stella Ward' mode whereas her younger sister was rather like a piece of delicate Dresden porcelain and loved music and painting above anything else. Claire could ride anything and was utterly fearless whilst Jayne was already an accomplished pianist and had passed all the examinations she had sat so far with flying colours. Their differences stifled any sibling rivalry and the two were great chums both aware of and proud of, their sister's prowess.

Kate Donald had seen enough of young Claire's ability to permit her to ride one of her boys' ponies and so Stella and Claire along with old Simon on a couple of occasions had a daily ride which blew the cobwebs out of their heads. Angela and Jayne spent their free time walking and did spend the whole day of the 27th in Canterbury where they exchanged gifts that were too big, too small, the wrong colour or just not suitable. The Sales were on and some genuine bargains were bought up with Angela being particularly pleased with a smart black trouser suit she had found in Riceman's, the big departmental store at the top end of the City. Jayne exchanged one or two long playing records for several tapes and they both agreed that Claire must have a new pair of smart shoes, whether she liked the idea or not!

Toby and Richard were seldom out of each other's company and visited one or two hostelries over the holiday period. Richard, unlike two of his fellow Directors, always preferred to drink in his own pubs and visits were made to the 'Beehive' and the 'Brindling Arms', where his presence was much appreciated by the tenants and their customers especially when the Chairman bought drinks for the entire house! He found it hard to talk of anything but the family business and Toby was once more subjected to much hard selling of a position for himself on the Board, with the prospect of a comfortable existence for he and his family.

'Richard, my dear chap, I was born to teach. It's something I've always wanted to do since I can remember. Everything that went before was merely a preparation for the main event… teaching! I love my life and if I say so myself I'm bloody good at it. You can never understand the genuine kick I get out of watching enlightenment dawn on the furrowed brow of a thirteen-year-old as he suddenly realises what it's all about or the grateful thanks of a 'loser' at thirteen who becomes a 'winner' by the time the 'O' or 'A' level papers have been marked. You feel that you've left your mark on that boy and, just possibly, he may remember old 'Toby Jug' or 'Riggy' Ackeson for the rest of his life. Come on Richard don't you remember the names of the masters to whom you still feel indebted?'

'"Riggy" Ackeson,' exclaimed Richard. 'You don't let the little so and so's call you "Riggy" Ackeson do you? Yes! Yes! Yes! I hear what you say and I suppose old Bates, Brennan and Reid all had a definite say in my education although I certainly didn't appreciate it at the time. Bates had gone by the time you arrived on the scene but he was one hell of a man. I recall him converting a ball from the halfway line when he must have been over fifty. The power of the man tended to concentrate one's mind on the particular Latin or Greek verbs he was trying to force into our intellect.'

It was all good stuff from the memory banks and just being with his big brother gave Toby the injection he needed for he admired him enormously. Stella had popped into Canterbury on the 28th with Toby and after slipping a notelet through Dale's letterbox she arranged to meet up with her brother-in-law again in the bar of the County Hotel. She wandered through the Reception and smiled to herself as she recalled her 'ordeal' in the telephone booth with that dreadful man Ingram. 'Wonder what he's doing?' she mused. 'I wish I was with him or going to meet him in a few moments' time.'

Toby was in the bar and greeted her with all his usual enthusiasm. They had just settled down in a corner of the lounge with their drinks when Philomena and James Billshot waltzed in accompanied by George Banyard. They had met in the High Street and decided it was time for a drink. George had known Toby from his schooldays and the Billshots had met him on one or two social functions over the years so there were no introductions to be made. Stella found great difficulty in looking at George Banyard, feeling inwardly debased by his presence. The hold he now had over her demanded absolute politeness on her part, however, and her outward show of friendliness to him could not have caused any suspicions from that quarter. She had got so used to calling him 'sir' that Stella found herself thinking very carefully before saying anything directly to the wretched man. 'Philo' was on top form and had them laughing about some of the 'disasters' she had been given for Christmas whilst James Billshot, knowing of his Chairman's wishes on the subject, quizzed Toby as to the possibility of joining them at the Brewery. 'Philo' announced that they were going to celebrate the New Year at the 'Red Lion' at Wingham where Mine Hosts were putting on a quite fantastic banquet. 'It's purported to be an *authentic* Hogmanay Dinner but we shall see,' she exclaimed. 'We're going with Maggie and Bill Gunnerstone from Managed Houses so he'll be able to spot a mile off any product that's from the local Frozen Food Wholesalers! Let's face it most of the menus in his own houses are based on their products anyway,' she laughed.

As the others chatted, George whispered to Stella, 'How's my little schoolgirl this morning? I trust you are fit and well and looking forward to welcoming me to your home next month?'

'I'm very well George and must say that the thought of dressing up for you in January makes me so excited I think I've wet myself and I can see from your trousers that you can't wait either.' She spoke softly with a perfectly straight face and giggled inwardly as the lecherous old beggar hastily glanced down at the front of his trousers.

'Touch and Go George! Touch and Go!!!'

On New Year's Eve, Stella and her faithful Mrs Defferary cooked a superb dinner with a prawn and sliced avocado starter, rabbit baked with tamarind and yoghurt served with lashings of pilau rice and a mild vegetable curry as a special treat for Richard's father and mother and then either a Banana and Lime Pavlova or Chocolate Roulade to finish. Richard and Toby had taken care of the cheeses with the Chairman producing two decanters of a '54 Vintage Port that even had his father, an absolute connoisseur of such things, drooling. As they raised their glasses at midnight and kissed and hugged in the New Year, Stella left her glass in the air for that extra second as she sent a silent good wish to her lover.

'God bless you my darling Dale and keep you safe… wherever you are.'

Stella knew that she was not behaving very well and hated her duplicity. She had been married to Richard for over twenty-two years and had never strayed an inch over the border of respectability. It troubled her desperately that her husband was being treated so shabbily by her and try as she might she really could not justify her behaviour. She felt that only Dale Ingram could possibly have brought about this situation, his knowledge of her former loves and his straightforward determination bringing all those childhood memories quickly back into her life. Two years ago she could not have envisaged in her wildest fantasies that she would have been party to all the wonderfully kinky and mad antics that, together, they had enjoyed. But now she realised that no matter how deeply her conscience troubled her, if Dale rang and said he wanted her in nothing but her rubber riding boots in the car park of the 'Red Lion' at twelve o'clock her only query would be, 'midday or midnight?'

The George Banyard Saga was frustrating and hugely embarrassing but it was not something about which she really suffered too much anguish. She had got herself into the mess and it was such a private affair between her and this sad man that an hour of unbelievable play-acting once a month was not too high a price to pay. In a perverse way she felt that it was a period of punishment that she had to suffer to pay her back for her treatment of Richard. Possibly her husband's complete lack of any real sexual awareness of her needs had increased the initial feeling of sheer joyous completeness that she had experienced as Dale re-introduced her to bondage and added the masterly skills he had gained over those missing years, teasing out of her the lust and passions that virtually all women possess but few are able to confess they have fully understood or experienced. She and Dale had been careful, and apart from the telephone booth in the County Hotel and her nightmare in the Turk's Head Hotel, they had left no hint of her infidelity.

'I'm not a bad person,' she consoled herself, 'and I deserve to have a hobby like everyone else. I wonder if there's a name for a collector of sexual orgasms?'

Toby and Angela left for their home in the Yorkshire Dales on the second of January. Claire and Jayne hugged their Auntie and Uncle in turn and it was clear to all that the girls had thoroughly enjoyed their break at *Clover Leys*. Already Claire was extracting promises out of her Dad that they would definitely be down in Kent during the summer. Richard and Toby's parents had gone home on

New Year's Day in order to prepare for a winter cruise they were taking early in January. They too were full of praise for Stella and Quentin had actually taken Stella aside and thanked her for the supportive role she always appeared to be playing beside his son.

'All we men are only as good as the lady beside us you know my dear. I thank God every day for giving me Kathleen over sixty years ago and I trust Richard does the same thing in respect of you. You are one hell of a partner my dear and I hope he knows it!'

'Oh dear! Oh dear, oh dear,' sighed Stella inwardly. 'I really could have done without that.' But she smiled and thanked her father-in-law for his kind words knowing that they were spoken from the heart.

Checking her diary when at last alone, she rang Dale at his office to organise a meeting. She didn't mind if it was for a coffee or two or three hours in his flat… she just wanted to see him and to touch him and to hear his voice. Dale was agreeing a valuation on the telephone and his secretary felt it might be some time before he was free so she left a coded message that ensured he would ring her back as soon as possible. It was two hours before she heard from him but he was his usual lovely self and they agreed to meet at the flat at six o'clock that evening. Richard was at a Board Meeting that would be followed by dinner and had informed Stella that it would be about ten before he was home.

Their first meeting of 1979 was not quite as straightforwardly sexual as usual. Stella wanted to talk about her inner guilt and did get quite a few of her worries across even though she was losing much of her clothing as she did so. Dale listened and encouraged her not to take things quite so seriously as the final articles of underwear came off. Going over to her bag he found she had brought her red cap and gauntlets but the thigh boots had not made the journey and so he tossed over her riding boots and watched as she pulled them on. Stella came over to him and turned with her now rubber clad hands dutifully held behind her back allowing Dale to secure her wrists together with some of his red silk cord. Never one to put on her cap herself Dale retrieved it and to her usual moans about expensive hair-do's, the heat and tightness of the thing and how awful she looked in it, he nevertheless pulled it over her head and having fastened the chin strap in place then flicked it over her chin and let the strap settle tightly between her lips.

'Now then darling, what was it you were blathering on about?'

Stella glared at her lover as he quickly undressed and went into the bedroom to pull on his own boots. She followed him in so that she could get across to him how unsettled she was about all this deceit trying at the same time to place the strap on her upper lip so that she could talk to him without lisping all the time. Her attempts were to prove singularly unsuccessful and she hated hearing herself say.

'Issshh all wight hor you. You don't 'ave a husgang to deesheeesh!' Dale turned round and she was able to see just how excited he had become as her 'uniform' had gone on. 'Cor you'ssshh missshed me.' She gasped as he sat on his bedroom stool and allowed her to straddle him. Their lovemaking lasted for almost ninety minutes as they told each other of all their innermost secrets and fears. For most of that time Stella had been free but she had made no attempt to remove her rubber wear knowing Dale's love of seeing her in it. Eventually they had to stop and she wandered into the shower leaving her cap on in order to keep her ruined hair dry if nothing else. Dale made some coffee and they sat until almost nine o'clock telling their Christmas tales and professing their love for one another. Stella hated the fact that he had seen in the New Year with Amanda Broughton but knew deep down that it was inevitable and was at least happy that their two Christmas breaks had been spent with their respective families and not in bed together.

Dale admitted that the Hogmanay Banquet had been wonderful and although only touching on the subject did give Stella the distinct impression that Amanda had looked pretty sensational and had made many of the farmers present and who knew her, sit up and take notice. He told her he was riding with Annie Scott on the morrow and was looking forward to it. He was not sure whether this was a good move or not but he hoped it would help to stifle any jealous thoughts that Stella might be having about Amanda. He was wrong.

'What on earth are you going out with Annie Scott for?' she asked. 'Hasn't she got a new pub to run? I thought you were going to give her an introduction to your farming buddy and let her take it from there.'

Dale explained that she was still unsure of the rides and he had promised her husband that he'd keep an eye on her for one or two more times until she was more confident.

'She didn't seem to lack any confidence when I last saw her,' Stella remarked. 'Does she wear breeches and boots Dale?'

'Yes of course she does Stella… and she keeps them on the whole time. I'm not interested in Annie Scott I promise you, for heaven's sake… she's a client!'

Stella's jealousy was something she always regretted and quickly she apologised, knowing that she had yet again gone over the barriers of unreasonable behaviour. Dale, as always, was quick to understand and forgive.

'You are so mixed up darling,' he whispered, 'you are not some kind of a monster you know. You just happen to have found the man you loved in a strangely childish but nevertheless quite profound way thirty years ago and sexually we make the sort of music that neither of us has heard before. I'm not asking or demanding anything from you Stella, but I do love you, and I'm not going to suggest that we stop seeing each other because that's just plain daft.'

Stella drove home feeling so good in herself and with some of her nagging doubts removed from her mind. Dale was such a clear-thinking individual and tended to work on the theory 'if you are not hurting anybody then where's the problem?', which was fine provided nobody ever did get hurt. She had undressed and was reading in the bedroom when Richard finally got back. The chauffeur had brought him home and it had obviously been a good meeting as he was in high spirits and talked with great animation about the plans they had put together for the coming year. The time, his mood and the place were right and Richard's sexual foreplay commenced by removing his pyjama trousers and pulling Stella into his arms whereupon he started stroking her body with great enthusiasm and then flattened her to the mattress and began pumping her up and down in furious fashion as his face became redder and redder. After about three minutes of this battering he exploded into her and rolled off with a gasp of sheer delight and certain that his darling Stella would be going off to sleep shortly wallowing in the joys of their intercourse together. The fact appeared to have escaped him that Stella had not climaxed or even become remotely excited during his 'bouncy-castle' performance.

Stella thought to herself as she stopped her theatrical gasping and saying 'Yes! Yes!' in her husband's ear. "Well on the blissful orgasm scale of one to ten I guess that rated about minus three but he's so happy I can't complain." She was asleep within minutes.

CHAPTER TWENTY-ONE

Dale thoroughly enjoyed his ride with Annie and was delighted that she talked so openly about their relationship and how much she had enjoyed kinky booted sex with him last time. She appeared to have no hang-ups and he wished all women would accept things as easily as did Annie Scott. They talked of her move and it was clear she was so happy that Vin and she were now in Charing.

'It's a funny thing you know Dale,' she confided, 'but if your Mr Tremlett hadn't popped in for a beer and a bit of bread and cheese last June we would still be in Rye. He expressed surprise that we were still in Rye considering the success we were enjoying in what, let's face it, is a pretty average public house.'

Dale smiled as he listened to Annie's description of a scenario he knew only too well. For as long as could remember his Guv'nor had been using this ploy to provide the firm with much-needed changes of tenancies. As his pupil, Dale was instructed to commit the landlord to a deep conversation about sport, the trade, politics, the Brewery or whatever, allowing 'Gee Gee' to talk to the landlady. During the course of this chat the old Broker would casually drop into the conversation the immortal sentence: 'In a way my dear, I'm surprised that you are still here. I've always felt that you and your husband were far too good for this house and would be going after something with a great deal more potential within a year or two!' He never elaborated and having planted his seed into the minds of his, up till then, perfectly happy clients he then waited patiently for his telephone to ring. In most cases the telephone would indeed ring within two or three weeks and it would be that particular tenant asking if they could be placed on the mailing list and receive sale particulars of all houses on the market. Mr Tremlett would organise a date for Dale to attend to prepare their new sale inventory and valuation and would replace the receiver with a throaty chuckle.

'Never fails my boy! Never fails!'

Arriving at the secluded copse of their first meeting they dismounted and Dale spread his tartan rug on the mossy grass. He had been determined to introduce Annie to the bathing cap this time as well as tying her up, and in view of her refreshingly uncomplicated outlook on all matters sexual he had little doubt that provided she was happy with the end result he'd have nothing but enthusiastic support from this cheerful bouncy character.

The length of cord he produced brought an immediate response from Annie.

'Oh my goodness! You really mean to tie me up don't you!' she squealed. 'I can't believe this Dale. I really can't believe this is happening. What are you going to do to me?' She wasn't frightened but this was an absolute 'first' for her. Since their last meeting she had thought quite a lot about bondage and had found that the subject excited her. Dale gently helped her off with her breeches and boots and then watched as she dutifully pulled her boots back on again. Leaving her jacket on, he secured her wrists behind her back and then produced the rubber cap from his pocket. Annie looked on in absolute horror as he placed the hat on her bare knee.

'You know that your boots are a real turn-on for me Annie. Well this cap has exactly same effect on me I'm afraid, and you are just going to have to get used to wearing it.'

Annie had never been helpless in her whole life and tugging futilely at her bonds she realised that this man, this awful man, could do and most certainly would do, almost anything he wanted to her.

'Dale, what if I beg you not to put that bloody thing on me. I'll look awful. I wouldn't wear a bathing cap when I was thirteen because of how it made me look and I don't intend to start now!'

'Oh I'm afraid you do my dear Annie,' said Dale as he gently but very firmly placed the hat over her curly hair until no tresses showed and her flushed face glared out from the stark contrast of the white rubber surrounds. The chinstrap, almost inevitably, went straight into her mouth as it was clipped into place.

'It's not a real gag,' he explained, 'but it makes you look sensational and very sexy!'

'Dale you bashtard, pleeshh don't do thissh to me. I can't beleeshh that thisshh isshh happening. I musssh look awful!' For the first time Annie's total besottedness with Dale broke as she lashed out with her free legs in sheer frustration at being made to look so unattractive by this awful man. Quickly Dale proceeded to employ all his skills on Annie and quite quickly, in all the circumstances, she had forgotten how she looked, where she was and even who she was as her body reacted so favourably to his touch and wonderful technique. After almost an hour it was time to think about returning and Annie, by this time only wearing her boots, with her shirt and jacket some five yards away and the cap lying only a few feet from the stream that she had intended to land it in once her hands had been freed. She was exhausted but oh so excited by the experience she had just undergone.

'God, you make me so randy Dale Ingram! I'm just a normal woman for the vast majority of every day but when you start talking and doing things to me I become some bloody sex maniac. I don't love you, you bugger, and sometimes I want to kill you but you drive me so bloody wild and I can't stop myself. If my old Vin could see me now he just wouldn't believe it. I can hardly believe it myself!'

She was sitting up on the rug, still stark naked despite the chill in the air, and chatting away non-stop as the whole episode continued to keep her adrenaline flowing far too speedily. She was still chatting away as they approached Tony's stables and Dale sensed that Annie Scott would be quite a handful for poor old Vin that night. She was genuinely exhilarated by the whole thing and was going to have great difficulty in calming herself down.

'Have you got anything else you're going to make me wear Dale?' she asked. 'Any other little surprises for me once you've got my hands tied?' she teased.

'That's for me to know and you to find out my dear Annie,' he laughingly retorted, 'but thanks again for a lovely morning's ride… you were quite superb!' Annie kicked hard and the two of them raced across the remaining meadow down to the farm.

Tony Cracknell was waiting for them on their return and helped Annie dismount. Dale always insisted that they assisted in the stabling of the horses but as his daughters were both at home Tony assured them that there was no need. He had decided to sell 'Dixie', the younger girl's horse and wanted to know if Annie was interested as it was obvious she had a great rapport with the young cob. Annie Scott was most interested and especially when Tony said that he would allow her to stable the animal at the farm for the going rate. On the drive back to the pub she chattered about the horse, the ride, the 'bloody cap' and the enormous enjoyment the morning had afforded her. Dale stayed for lunch and helped to persuade Vincent that the purchase of 'Dixie' was a wonderful idea much to Annie's delight. She came out to the car as usual and thanked him for another lovely day. 'You are a remarkable man Dale and I just don't know how you have never married. Still I'm not complaining and I reckon there's a few ladies like me who aren't either. Don't let it be too long before you come out again but, to be fair, I really can go by myself now and certainly will do so if Vin allows me to buy "Dixie".'

The following weeks were busy ones for Dale as there were so many licensees leaving their houses either to take other tenancies or seek fresh employment. The trade always seemed to reward those that possessed the intangible 'something' that turned them from ordinary pleasant folk into successful publicans. Dale recalled the

Guv'nor talking about it and how he just did not know what the secret ingredient was that brought about this metamorphosis in some people. At interview they didn't seem any different from the next couple but as soon as they were given their pub the change in their fortunes was almost immediate. And this 'something' did not always travel well. A Brewer would reward a couple like the Scotts who had done so well in their first house by giving them a bigger or a better pub or one with far more potential. Sometimes the couple would continue to find success, as in the case of Vin and Annie Scott, but just as many will fall flat on their faces despite not changing their style one iota. It is always a case of horses for courses and some folk are really just suited to serving one class of people.

Mr Tremlett decided to attend the 'change' of the Talbot Arms near the village of Chartham. It had been a case of outgoing and ingoing tenants simply loathing each other from the outset when Mrs Goode had caught her would-be successor, Mrs Sinclair, running her index finger along the mantelpiece in the private living room and finding dust on it. The two men were at odds over Mr Sinclair's refusal to purchase three out-houses made of breeze blocks that the Brewery would not allow on the inventory decreeing that it was not an essential trade item and therefore must be treated on an optional basis. The Sinclairs, feeling that Mr Goode could do nothing about the situation, were advised by some idiot who did not know the present landlord very well to say they didn't want them.

'What can he do about it? Can't take 'em away can he?' they were told.

As Tremletts were acting for both parties, having brought in an independent valuer to value the inventory on behalf of the incoming pair, the Senior Partner decided Dale could do with more help than his young pupil could give him and so attended personally. To be entirely correct one should add that the old boy loved a battle too and he sensed that World War II would have nothing on this if the ladies really got started.

Their arrival at the house found the Sinclairs standing in the field at the rear of the premises looking at what used to be three breeze-block out-houses, that was before Mr Goode blew them up the night before! There were bits of breeze-block everywhere and the roofing had disappeared altogether. Mr Goode told Dale that he understood they didn't want the stores and so he'd got rid of them.

'They didn't think I was going to *give* them away did they Mr Ingram?' he asked blithely.

Mr Tremlett took him to court for the Protection Order application and Mr and Mrs Sinclair travelled with Dale, complaining all the way about the awfulness of their predecessors. Dale did point out that the advice they had been given about refusing to consider the stores had been fatally flawed in that their mentor did not realise the sort of man that Albert Goode was.

'If you had pleaded poverty and offered him £20 in notes he would have accepted it I'm certain, but he realised your tactics and now you see the result.'

'I'll bloody swing for your bloody father one of these days!' Tom Sinclair snorted at his wife. 'If there was a gold medal for getting it bloody wrong on every sodding occasion he'd be in a bloody class of his own!!!'

The court application went off OK but Goode, when asked if he had any objections to the application, admitted he did not but then in a stage whisper that all but the Magistrates heard added, 'But I bet the villagers of Chartham and the Hatch will before the year's out!' The Hatch, being Chartham Hatch, the adjoining village.

Once back at the house the two warring families, because the parents, sons and a daughter were now involved as well, continued to argue about everything under the sun. This went on until about three o'clock with very little being achieved at which time Mr Tremlett performed his 'party piece', a little cameo that Dale had seen him carry out on several similar occasions. When certain that both parties were in earshot he suddenly rose to his feet and slamming his case shut he roared, 'I am not prepared to put up with this behaviour one minute longer. One thing is certain… (pause for dramatic effect)… **there will be no "change of tenants" here today!!** Good day to you all.' So saying he stalked out of the bar and drove off in the direction of Canterbury. Both parties were devastated. There were large pantechnicon-vans loading and unloading on the car park and the Goode and Sinclair clans realised that things had gone far too far for the 'change' to be postponed at this late hour.

Mr and Mrs Goode and Mr Sinclair approached Dale who had adopted the guise of the 'friendly old broker' by this time and begged him to try and get the transaction back on the rails. In the space of ten minutes compromises that had seemed impossible earlier were being suggested and accepted with a rapidity that had to be seen to be believed. Dale made his call to the supposed 'office' knowing that the Senior Partner would be waiting for him, sitting in the bar of the 'Artichoke' along the road, and told him that the differences had been sorted out and would he reconsider his decision and allow the 'change' to take place.

To the great joy and relief of everyone including the poor Area Manager, Tubby Norton, Dale was able to announce that his Guv'nor would return and promptly got on with the paperwork that was still outstanding.

'Well done Mr Tremlett!' Tubby whispered to Dale. 'I was beginning to think he wasn't going to pull the **"There will be no change today!!"** routine out of his bag of tricks.'

'Tubby, my dear chap,' replied Dale. 'If you engage the services of the best then you get a successful "changeover" every time.'

On the journey back to the office Dale told his pupil, Ben Herbert, that another trick the Guv'nor would pull if the clients on both sides were getting fractious or the fees were likely to be exceedingly high, would be to get into a terrible row with the other Broker, often old Spatwell, who was in on the act, and in a matter of minutes the whole changeover was in jeopardy with cases being slammed and clients pleading with their Agents to stay and finish the job.

'I'm here to see you are treated fairly Mr Bloggs and it would seem that the other side are a load of collusive knaves dealing in skulduggery at the highest level. We shall see how the legal position about all this appears in the morning. I will not have you treated in this manner sir!' Old Claude Spatwell was saying similar things to his client and before long, with legal fees now having to be considered, both clients could be seen talking and eventually an agreement was resolved with both Brokers ensuring that their client felt he was coming out of the transaction on the credit side, thanks to the noble efforts of their dear old Broker. Past squabbles or high fees were forgotten in the relief of actually being allowed to leave or take over the tenancy that day.

Young Ben Herbert was laughing his socks off at Dale's description of the 'changes' of yesteryear but understood that he had witnessed that afternoon the actions of a supreme professional. Mr Tremlett was delighted that everything had gone so well and left the office for his nightly game of snooker at his Club in high spirits.

Dale had mentioned to Stella that he would love to retrace their childhood haunts and pop over to Holy Island if the chance arrived and in mid-February an excited Stella informed him that Richard was going to be away in Scandinavia for a week from next Tuesday and she had hinted to him that she may use the time he was away to drive up to Northumberland and visit the street in which she lived as a child and see some of the County at the same time. She told him she had thought about inviting a friend but had then decided that this arrangement would cramp her plans. Richard was most enthusiastic, feeling with unashamed selfishness, that by doing so he would avoid having to go there with her at some time in the future. He did not holiday much and the North East of England was not a spot in which he would choose to spend leisure time.

Dale swiftly altered his diary around and by telling Mr Tremlett and dear Amanda a small white lie about his father's health he was able to confirm within an hour or two that the trip was 'on'. 'Leave everything to me darling. Pack your bags, including your flight bag full of goodies, and leave your car in the park behind the flat. I'll see you at 9 o'clock on Tuesday morning… it'll be bloody marvellous!!'

To have Stella to himself for three or even four days with no fear of discovery would be simply wonderful and it was a very excited Dale Ingram that greeted Stella on a cold and wet Tuesday morning. She was wearing tight black trousers tucked into her high heeled black leather boots, a black polo-neck heavy wool jumper and a tan leather travelling coat which came down to just above her knees. Dale and she decided that her BMW was much the more comfortable car in which to make the journey and so Dale transferred his valise into the boot of the other vehicle and tucked his own Rover at the back of the car parking area. If Amanda did use the park during his absence he would tell her that he had gone up by train and Stella agreed that this was the best policy.

CHAPTER TWENTY-TWO

HOLY ISLAND

Arriving in Monkseaton, Dale drove straight to his Dad's house and he watched as Stella got out of the car and looked up the street to her own house which had not changed all that much since the time of her departure. 'Everything seems so much smaller than I remember,' she cried. 'I thought our Crescent was a really wide street but it is quite narrow isn't it.' His Dad was out so they walked over the railway bridge and down to where James' field had used to be with its five-bar gate entrance where they had been subjected to humiliation from the Goofy Grafton Gang all those years ago. It was all housing estates and fairly old-established ones at that. Red House Farm appeared to have disappeared too.

It had begun to rain so they wandered back to the house and found his Dad admiring Stella's car. He was overjoyed to see Dale and remembered Stella with vivid recall.

'You were ahead of your time my dear,' he laughed. 'Some of we Dads could never get our minds round the fact that our boys were being bossed around by this little chit of a lass, but I must say our Dale worshipped you. Dale tells me you're married to the boss of a Brewery Company. Does he know you are up here with Dale?'

Dale warned his Dad not to be so bloody inquisitive and pointed out that he and Stella were merely sharing a few days of nostalgia together and that was all there was to it.

'I am happily married Mr Ingram,' she volunteered, 'and have no intention of wrecking a very good marriage. Dale and I are great pals, having met up again last July and we tend to do a lot of things together as my husband is a workaholic and hasn't much time for such things as holidays or even weekend breaks.'

They stayed and chatted to the old man for about two hours and then departed assuring him they would be calling back on their way down to Canterbury in three days' time. Guy Ingram looked fit and well and Dale knew he would have been given a great boost by seeing his son again so shortly after the Christmas break. It was dark when they left and Dale made straight for the A1 and the road to Scotland. Stella had never visited Holy Island and coming across the Causeway at night was always a little creepy for those who did not know the geography of this quite unique island. The sea, coal-black, is never far from your car on the right hand side as you make the drive into the village and the towering sand dunes of the North Shore and The Snook loom out of the darkness on the left. The island is rather like the shape of an obese comma laying on its side with the village, the Castle, St Mary's Church, the ruins of the Lindisfarne Priory, the Winery and the harbour all scattered at one end with a few narrow lanes joining up the various points of interest. The three public houses were The 'Northumberland Arms' known as 'The Tavern', The 'Castle' known as 'The Hotel' and the 'Crown & Anchor', which was always called 'The Croon'. This could cause any amount of problems for visitors and particularly for those from outside of Northumberland, as the Holy Island burr was very broad and difficult to understand made doubly so when the islanders would be directing you using the names they used for the various hostelries and not what the house signs proclaimed. However, the island was so small that one could not get too lost within the bounds of the village.

The main industry was fishing but many of the houses took in 'Bed & Breakfast' lodgers during the season and all the small hotels on the island were full throughout the summer months. Several boats went out into the North Sea every morning in the early hours and returned at various times in the afternoon and early evening. Their main catch would be of crabs and lobsters with those lucky enough to have a licence also netting salmon trout off the Tweed estuary. As with most fishermen their lives were steeped in tradition and superstition and they would never refer to a pig as anything other than an 'article' and the sight of a priest or a female on their way down to the boats would mean a swift return to bed and no fishing would be done that day. The 'pig' superstition goes back too long for anyone to know the origin, but the sight of the priest and/or a woman at that time of the morning would generally mean there had been a death and a 'laying out' had taken place and therefore ill-fortune had intervened in their walk to the harbour.

The Causeway enabled the island to be accessible for two fairly long periods during daylight hours but as soon as water appeared on the stretch immediately beside the mainland then it was extremely foolhardy to attempt to drive across with several cars being lost every year and drivers scrambling for safety in the towers provided.

Dale had told Stella as much as he could about the island and the folk who lived there and she confessed she was looking forward to exploring the length and breadth of Holy Island during their short stay. Dale had booked in at the Lindisfarne Hotel, a small family-run hotel where good wholesome food and cleanliness were priorities and after a wash and change of clothing they had dinner and then went for a stroll around the silent and darkened streets. It was a clear night and the stars were shining brighter, or so it seemed, than they did down in Kent. Dale felt that it was the fact that in Kent it was so difficult to distance oneself from artificial lighting, which diffused the brightness of the heavenly lights but Stella pulling her coat round her tightly thought that the bitterness of the night air was the answer.

'I'm freezing darling,' she cried after about ten minutes, 'let's get in a pub or a bed or something warm!'

They walked up from the harbour and popped into the Northumberland Arms or 'The Tavern' and were given a warm greeting by the landlord John and his pretty wife Terri. Dale had enjoyed many crazy, zany nights within these walls, firstly when the present landlord's father had held the licence and in recent years during the son's reign. The beer was wonderful and the 'crack' or chatter was always amusing. Stella's entrance caused one or two heads to turn but then Stella would always create a stir because of her looks and her confident way. She sat down in a corner by the fire and Dale approached the bar to order only to be waylaid by a couple of the fishermen whom he knew well and who were pleased to see him. Their comments were as blunt as he would have expected and were mainly along the lines that 'what the hell was he doing in the pub when he had someone that looked like that with him and that there was plenty of time for talking tomorrow… it was now time for humping!!!'

After chatting briefly to the landlord he returned to Stella who had understood a little more of the conversation than the fishermen had realised.

'There you are darling, they think we should be in bed and so do I,' she laughed. 'Mind you it's so warm in here you are going to have a job getting me out of the pub and into the cold night air once more.'

The fishermen were off quite early as of course they were on the sea in the early hours. Dale teased them that he and Stella would come down to the harbour to wave them off and received the anticipated reply as to what would happen to the bonny wee lady if she put foot outside the hotel before eight o'clock!! Stella did not understand what her fate was to be which was just as well, the burr defeating her and Dale on this occasion but causing instant mirth from the other islanders present.

Back in the hotel Dale put his head round the entrance to the small and intimate bar and found the owners, Clive and Sue, sitting with a couple of bird watchers from their native Yorkshire and discussing the plight of their beloved cricket team. As Kent had won the championship the previous season, Dale felt it right and proper to enter the fray and both Stella and he partook of two glasses each from the remarkable collection of malt whiskies that adorned all the display shelving above the decanter counter before giving way to genuine weariness and leaving the 'pro-Boycott' and 'anti-Boycott' lobbies still at loggerheads.

Dale could see that Stella was virtually out on her feet and instead of suggesting that it was now time for fun and games he took her in his arms and laid her on the big double bed and pulled the blankets and eiderdown over her divine body. Turning off the bedside light he crept under the clothes himself and found Stella's back searching for his warm body into which she snuggled and was asleep within seconds.

Wednesday morning was windy but dry and Stella finally woke up at quarter past eight with the lines of deep sleep still etched on her face. Dale was at the window with his binoculars and had showered and dressed for the day ahead wearing heavy corduroy trousers and heavy soled brogues, shirt, crew-necked sweater and his Harris Tweed sports jacket was laying on the bedside chair.

'Morning darling,' she murmured sleepily, 'you were very quiet, I didn't hear a thing.'

'Stella, I think I could have marched the Band of the Coldstream Guards through this bedroom and you wouldn't have woken up. My God you must have been tired.'

'You should have woken me darling. You know I'm always happy to be woken up by you. Why don't you get undressed again and let me show you how much I'm loving this break.'

'Good heavens darling,' Dale cried, 'you don't think you are going to be allowed to make love in bed do you? On this blessedly quiet and sparsely-populated island? My dear, prepare for some real adventures this morning... the dunes and Sandham and Coves Bay await you! I've got the cord so all you've got to do is get into some suitable clothing and put your cap in the haversack although it's probably too cold for you to go swimming. Mind you there are folk who actually swim all the year round up here provided it's not dangerous so to do and it couldn't be better today!'

"Oh my God," thought Stella. "What on earth has he got planned?" Stella said, 'I'm starving and will just have a shower and then I'll be down for breakfast.'

They ate a full English breakfast including, to Dale's delight, fried bread and had a large pot of steaming coffee to themselves as Dale suggested that they walked out to Castle Point and then went along the coastline to Sandham Bay to see the seals at play and then on through the dunes to his favourite spot of all, the small picturesque Coves Bay.

'We can visit the Castle and Priory etc if the weather gets bad but let's use the fine weather to walk.' Stella had dressed in an olive green windcheater, her black polo neck jumper and had tucked her tight black trousers into her rubber riding boots. She had a black cloche hat pulled right down to her eyebrows and looked sensational. Dale decided against his sports jacket and opted for his own green and blue windcheater jacket that had a hood tucked away in case of rain.

The walk to Castle Point took them past the small but imposing Castle set on high ground and surveying the whole island. Stella recalled that it had been used as the scene of much macabre happenings in the Polanski movie 'Cul-de-Sac' and still thought it looked a wee bit scary. It really was a lovely brisk February morning and soon both Stella and Dale were as warm as toast as they made their way along the coastal path towards Sandham Bay. Protected on all sides by sand dunes Dale made his way to the golden sanded bay itself and laughed as Stella, protected by her boots, walked into the lapping tide as it turned and stood while her lover took two or three photographs of her in the North Sea.

'My God! I can feel the cold even through my boots!' she cried.

There were no seals on view and so they walked the length of the bay and then set off into the dunes again and made for Coves Bay. Finding a high dune that gave them full protection from the wind, Dale asked Stella if she would pose for him for a few seconds in a swimsuit and cap.

'It's the one chance I have got of getting a genuine photograph of you in your gear and who's to know that we took it in February darling? Please?' he begged.

Stella realised she should have checked the haversack far more carefully before she came out for there was one of her costumes all ready for her to get into. After extracting a promise from him that she would only pose for photographs and that he would only take a few seconds doing so she quickly stripped off and donned her black bathing costume and then pulled on her cap. She could feel the goose-pimples beginning to invade her exposed body as she attempted to smile at Dale as he fiddled with his camera.

'Do hurry up darling, it really is bloody freezing and...'

'Eee by gum Edith! We never believed 'im at the hotel when he said people swam all the year round but 'ere she is... the living proof! Wait till we get home and tell them! They won't believe us. I bet you don't stay in there long, love eh?' The pleasant Yorkshire couple from the hotel were standing on the top of their towering dune looking down in amazement at poor Stella. They were dressed for bird-watching and wore matching green and white bobble woollen hats

'Don't you let us keep you love! You get in there before you catch your death!'

'Eee luv... I think you're a real little champion,' echoed the female 'twitcher'.

Stella looked at Dale and breathed fire through her flared nostrils. 'You bastard Dale Ingram! You utter bastard! What the hell am I supposed to do now?'

'I guess as you're dressed for it the best thing to do would be to get in and out as fast as you can darling,' he suggested rather pathetically, whilst trying hard not to let a smile flit across his face. 'It will be warmer in than out and I've got a big towel in the haversack.'

'If you laugh Dale, if you even smile, you are *dead*!'

Stella set off for the sea very reluctantly and very slowly, looking back to see if their fellow guests had moved on only to receive vociferous encouragement from the pair of them as they cheered her pathway to the white tipped rollers as they broke on the shore. She was a strong swimmer and realised that what her idiot lover had said was true. The sooner this was over the better. Seeing that the water was shallow and the beach sandy she ran the last few yards and plunged into the North Sea for the first and last time in her adult life. The icy coldness of the water took her breath away as she rose to her feet only to be knocked sprawling by the next wave. Fighting for her breath she plunged into the next wave and was carried by it almost to the shore where it deposited her as a piece of flotsam on a bed of seaweed. Dale ran down the beach and wrapped a towel round her now tinted blue body and began rubbing her down with a series of powerful up and down strokes.

'You were brilliant darling, quite brilliant!' he exclaimed with genuine admiration.

'I am s-s-so c-c-cold!' She shivered as the two enthusiasts waved their woolly hats in the air and shouted 'Bravo!' 'I ne-ne-never r-r-realised the North S-S-Sea was s-s-so b-b-bloody fr-fr-freezing!' Dale didn't think the time was ripe to admit he had two brilliant action shots of his Stella 'frolicking' in the waves and hated himself for suggesting that she should now pose for him.

However Stella was warm again from the vigorous towelling he had administered and Dale took three or four shots of his darling as she stood with her back to the sea, pouting and posing, her legs apart and her hands on her hips. He would treasure these snaps forever and Stella was well aware of this fact but, alas, ignorant of the fact that the two distant 'Tykes' were in possession of a very expensive camera with a zoom lens which only that morning had taken shots of a Black-legged Kittiwake (or *Rissa tridactylia* as Kevin would trip off his tongue) and had also enjoyed snapping her various poses.

'Dale. I love you dearly but why do you keep getting me into these scrapes. I cannot believe that I have just swum in the North Sea… **it's bloody February for God's Sake, and if those two idiots don't stop waving and cheering I shall scream!!'**

Gradually Stella recovered from the ordeal of having to take on the power and the cold of the sea in Northumberland and as they walked back along the farm tracks towards the village she began to laugh.

'Well Dale, I expect when Pinky and Perky tell their tale I shall be a minor celebrity on this lovely island. I saw their cameras clicking when I walked down to the sea so they will have something to show the folks back home won't they? I seriously wonder how many women have ever swum at Coves Bay in the month of February? Are you sure that there are men and women who actually do go for a dip throughout the year up here?'

Dale confirmed it for he remembered several people who swam every day when he was a boy. By the time they arrived at the village Stella had a real glow to her and felt absolutely wonderful. Dale sensed that she was going to 'milk' this situation to the maximum effect. They called at the Post Office and bought two daily newspapers. Ian, the pleasant Post Master, who knew Dale, at once greeted them in friendly fashion and remarked on the weather.

'I see you've brought your Kentish weather up here with you, Dale.'

Stella smiled and answered, 'Yes, it is my first visit to Holy Island and Dale had warned me about your harsh winter weather but it's lovely and the sea was positively gorgeous when I swam out at Coves Bay this morning… I really didn't want to come out but Dale feels the cold and ordered me to get dressed again… what a wimp!'

Two of the island ladies were in the shop and heard Stella's words. Southerners were always tolerated on the island for visitors were the lifeblood of the community but they were the subject of good-natured badinage and Dale, despite having been born in the County and having lived there for eighteen years had to accept a certain amount of ragging because of his life in Kent. The idea that this southern lady in her lovely clothes and high boots could have taken on the North Sea in February at Coves Bay was something to talk about. When was the last time anybody had swum there in February?

They wandered round to the church and saw the depth of history unravelled before their eyes. The famous old island families lay buried there and the names of Douglas, Patterson, Kyle, Luke and Cromarty figured largely on the gravestones around St Mary's Church. Dale told Stella of the old superstitions concerning weddings on the island and how each new bride must leap from a large stone in the church grounds immediately after the wedding ceremony, normally supported by two of the island men. She and the groom must then pay to have the Church gate unfastened and finally, once outside the Church grounds they must walk through two ranks of the island 'shooters' who fire their shotguns into the air to ward off all evil spirits. Being a small and intimate island virtually the whole population is involved and a wedding is a real social event. Dale had attended one some years previously and had not been sober for two days. Stella was enthralled by it all.

They sat in the manicured grounds of the ruined Priory and looked at the remains of what had been a thriving Priory. The tiny museum was full of interest and gave visitors a complete story of how the Vikings had been a constant threat to the holy people of Lindisfarne.

The Crown and Anchor was their next port of call and Dale ordered two pints of 'Heavy', a brew from Edinburgh, and two rounds of crab sandwiches. An old pal of Dale's had run the pub for several years but had now left the island and returned to his native Berwick-upon-Tweed, so the new tenants were not known to him. However the sandwiches were as delicious as crab sandwiches always were on Holy Island, which was not really surprising as most of the crabs had been in the North Sea twelve hours earlier. Stella tackled her pint with great gusto despite the fact that it looked rather like a gasometer in her small hand. Dale could tell she was thoroughly enjoying her trip back to her native County.

'I hear you've been swimming Miss,' said one of the old-timers. 'I can't recall a February swimmer for some years. Did you enjoy it?'

Stella told him that it had been wonderful and that she had enjoyed every minute of it.

'I don't think it lasted quite one minute darling,' Dale whispered and then fell silent as her left boot came into contact with his right shin. The landlord, whom Dale gathered was not from the island but couldn't work out from his accent from what part of the country he did hail, insisted on buying Stella another drink and was delighted when she complimented him on his beer and said she'd have another 'half'.

Eventually they returned to the hotel for a rest only to be greeted by Clive who had heard of the stout-heartedness of Stella from the birdwatchers, Kevin and Edith, and reported that they had gone into Berwick to have their photographs developed so that they could give some of Stella to them before they left on the morrow.

'I gather you just ran down the beach and plunged in as though it were a sunny day in August... and let me tell you... you wouldn't get many islanders plunging in the sea at that time either!'

Stella was growing in confidence as tales of her swim got round and Clive was sat down on his bar stool whilst Stella gave him chapter and verse, over a malt whisky and ice, as to the strokes she had performed, the waves she had dived under and how disappointed she had been when Dale, standing on the shore with a towel had complained he was getting cold and had ordered her out.

Their lovemaking lasted most of the afternoon. Firstly Stella was spread-eagled and tormented to distraction before Dale undid her cords and allowed her to give full vent to her passion. She was on a complete high and was insatiable in her demands, keeping her rubber cap and gloves on the entire session in order to keep her lover's libido at full stretch. Eventually she heaved a sigh of utter contentment and rolled over on her back, too weary to undress herself from her kinky wardrobe. Dale leant over and removed her cap allowing her to shake her lovely dark tresses free around her shoulders and then pulled off her gloves and boots. She glistened with sexual sweat and her stomach moved in and out in a slow rhythm as she came down from on high and flirted with sleep.

'Oh Dale, this is so wonderful, I'll never forget this trip to this blessed isle... never!' She spoke no further words as she drifted off into a deep slumber and Dale, exhausted by her demands, was not long in joining her in the land of nod.

When they awoke it was dark and almost time for dinner. 'It's so quiet here,' Stella cried. 'I can't believe how silent this place is. It's as though the island were deserted for most of the time.'

Dale explained that in the summer months the island was full of tourists with coach after coach coming on to the island and disgorging its passengers all over the island.

'When I first came here people were staying in every cottage and house during July and August. The Hotels were full and the Boys' Camp was full too. Not so many are resident holiday makers these days, tending to come for the day but of course the birdwatchers will always be here in their hordes during the winter months. I used to stay at a boarding house called 'Castle View' in Fenkle Street and run by one of the most remarkable ladies it has been my privilege to meet. Wonderful cook, wonderfully kind and Christian in her outlook. She is one of the true 'characters' of the island and is loved by everyone. I will take you to meet her this evening, her name's Annie.'

Sue had cooked a splendid dinner and they sat and chatted to two or three other couples who were staying on the island for the umpteenth time. They had all heard about Stella's swim and she wallowed in the praises of the men and their wives as they expressed their incredulity at her valour. Kevin and Edith were late arrivals having been looking for some little-seen owl but soon photographs of Stella 'standing in the dunes', Stella 'walking down the beach', Stella 'plunging into the waves' and Stella 'lying on the shore-line' were being handed round to the assembled company together with, to Stella's dismay, a series of her post-swim poses showing off her pouting stances very clearly for Kevin was a fine photographer.

'Bloody Norah,' said one of the older male guests, sitting down quickly and grabbing a tumbler of cold water.

'Oooh, I think you are sensible to wear the old-fashioned swimming hat,' said one of the ladies, 'they are so ugly but they do keep your hair dry. My Fred would have a fit if I put one on wouldn't you dearest. I didn't know they still made them.'

'Oh yes,' sighed Stella, 'they still make them.'

'I wouldn't have a fit if you looked like this in it,' replied Fred, looking at the shot of Stella standing in the dunes, looking very sultry, fulsomely feminine and distinctly sexy.

"Bless you Fred," thought Stella, "and bless all the men here," for she could see the gathered males present were all taking a great deal of time to hand the photographs on and this included Dale.

'Bloody Norah!' sounded once more from the far right hand table, followed by a deeper voice from the left of the room. 'Eee well our lass... I'll go to the foot of our bed if that isn't the finest sight I've seen this twelve months. Last time I saw peaks like this they 'ad snow on 'em! She's a bonny female and no mistake!'

It was a cold dry night and it only took two or three minutes to arrive at Fenkle Street with its quaint collection of different-shaped cottages and houses. 'Castle View' was the largest house in the street and had a greyness of stone about it that went well with the green woodwork. Dale took Stella round to the back entrance and found Annie sitting in front of a black and white television set with a cigarette stuck on her bottom lip. She was delighted to see one of her old visitors and they embraced warmly. Dale introduced Annie to Stella and watched in amusement as he saw Stella's face desperately attempting to work out what Dale's old landlady was saying. Annie was as broad in Holy Island dialect as any soul on the island and even when she attempted to help the visitors by speaking slowly she was still virtually impossible to understand fully. She brought Dale up to date with all her family news and gave him the island gossip too for she knew that Dale was interested in all that went on around her. Dale scolded her on her chain-smoking and advised that if she stopped smoking she would be able to buy herself a colour television set.

'Mr Ingram,' she replied, in her broadest of tongue, 'if I gave up smoking I could put a collar television in every room in the hoose, including the hen hoose across the road!'

She did not take in visitors much nowadays but Dale had a sneaking suspicion that had he wanted a room in August she may well have found one for him for he loved this very special lady and he felt she knew this. When they got up to go Annie hugged him and then gave Stella a kiss and told her to take care of her Mr Ingram. Stella did not catch the full meaning but agreed and smilingly told her that he was well able to take care of himself. Dale was delighted that he had been able to introduce Stella to this lovely lady who had given him so much loving care over the many years he had been coming to the island during the summer months. Annie Ramage would always be a jewel in his crown. She had not looked too well, but, then again, she normally looked as though she had just emerged from some sort of a giant blender! As Dale's visits seemed to be getting less and less he was glad they had had their meeting.

Their entrance into the Northumberland Arms was greeted by applause from the landlord and his wife. 'What's next Stella?' called out John. 'Are you going to attempt the Channel Crossing? It'll be a doddle after swimming at Coves in February… or are you going into next month's edition of *Playboy*?'

'I love the swimming hat Stella,' exclaimed Terri. 'We've seen the photographs this evening. The couple from Wetherby were looking for you.'

Stella went into her well-rehearsed statement about keeping her hair dry and she didn't really care what she looked like when having a swim but did not seem to convince Terri one iota.

'You would have to tie me down to get one on my head!' cried Terri.

"Tell me about it!" thought Stella

John made it very clear that if Stella was swimming tomorrow he wanted to be there and would hold her towel, along with three other 'herberts' who were chuckling into their beers.

'You remind me very much of a client of mine near Canterbury, John,' Dale said. 'He's twice your weight but John Emerson thinks along the same lines as do you.'

Dale recalled his first ever visit to the 'Tavern' at which time he had gone in and asked a very young and newly married Terri for 'a pie, a pint and a kind word!' Having been granted the first two requests his attractive barmaid turned away to get his change and Dale reminded her of his third request, 'what about the kind word?'

'DON'T eat the bloody pie!' came back the response, as quick as a flash, from one of the Patterson brothers. This was the humour of the island that Dale had grown to love so much.

They had a few drinks in the 'Tavern' and then set off for the Lindisfarne Hotel and sleep. Clive and Sue were in the bar and after a 'medicinal' malt whisky each and a brief chat with their hosts and a couple of fellow guests they made their way to bed. They were both yawning like mad and both agreed that it must be the fresh air that was beggaring up their systems. Stella was in bed in about five minutes and Dale followed soon after. Stella's hands were cold but soon found something warm to hold on to and before long she had aroused him and was being stroked and fondled in all her 'right' places. She got on top and directed operations giving herself room to bend as far backwards as was possible increasing the leverage of their contact and bringing her to a blissful climax within seconds of feeling Dale's body shudder with joyous satisfaction also. Placing her back into Dale's stomach she hugged his protective arm and was asleep within a minute or two.

Friday was a terrible day and reminded Dale of the sort of weather Northumbrians have to suffer for so much of each year. Stella wanted to visit the Winery where Lindisfarne Mead was produced together with a very special marmalade and one or two other items. After another terrific cooked breakfast they made their way round to the factory and showroom and bought some of the Mead and some marmalade too. It was pouring with rain so they left the island and drove to Berwick-upon-Tweed and saw the town and the lovely River Tweed without getting out of the car because of the constant downpour. They then pushed inland to Coldstream where they had a good lunch in a High Street pub, and in a brief let-up from the rain Dale was able to take some nice photographs of Stella by the Tweed. Despite the weather she looked terrific in a long white mac' and her black high-heeled boots. They meandered along B roads back to the A1 and then got back on the island with about half an hour to spare before the Causeway was impassable.

The rain did not let up and so their walk to the 'Tavern' was made with the help of Dale's huge MCC coloured umbrella. John and Terri gave them a warm welcome and they spent a couple of hours laughing about all the fun and games that had gone on in the Tavern from the early sixties. It had been a lovely time in their lives as the young fishermen, their wives and girlfriends, the publicans and the visitors all seemed to gel and create pandemonium in whichever hostelry they happened to meet up. Dale sensed that it had become a quieter place over the past year or two but maybe that was because he was getting older himself. Certainly John and Terri never changed and it was with genuine sadness that they finally said their goodbyes.

'I really have enjoyed myself up here,' said Stella, 'all that Dale told me about the island and the islanders has been found to be true. You have made me very welcome and I do hope we will see you again.'

'Do say goodbye to Lacky over there won't you,' asked Dale as he saw that one of the fishermen, a real character and a complete 'one-off', had gained the attention of two young and pretty school teachers in a corner of the bar and was getting them to teach him how to read and write. He'd been using this ploy for years and it seemed to bring him either spectacular sexual success or depressing failure. 'His mind's on the job in hand and I wouldn't want to cramp his style!' he chuckled.

It had stopped raining for their walk back to the hotel and Stella begged to walk around the harbour before turning in. The tide was going out and the water was still with only the sounds of sheets rapping against masts and the gentle lapping of the tide on the sloping shoreline. They walked across the field Dale always called the 'Herrin Whorls' because of the rotating iron gates. He was never sure of the spelling or the derivation of the name but it certainly had sounded like 'Herrin Whorls' when he had first heard it. It was cold but they were well wrapped up and with his arm round her Stella could have walked for hours in this silent and peaceful haven.

Clive was still up when they arrived back and insisted on giving them a malt night-cap which did finally put the hat on any more lovemaking as dear Stella was again almost out on her feet and asleep as soon as her head hit the pillow. Dale mused that they had not made love at all that day and yet he had so enjoyed himself in the knowledge too that his beloved Stella was so happy just 'being there' with him.

Tides demanded a fairly early start and after thanking Clive and Sue for their warm hospitality they left a rain-lashed village and were soon back on the mainland and heading towards the South. They called in for a coffee with Daisy who was not surprised to see Stella as her father had told her of their meeting earlier in the week. What did surprise Daisy was the change that had transformed the little tomboy into this elegant and sophisticated lady. Daisy always said it as it was and had Stella laughing as she described her friends' and her own feelings concerning the Stella Ward Gang.

'There were we, all a year older than you, playing with dolls, going to dancing school and generally doing the things that little girls are supposed to do whereas this odd little girl in her shorts and brown Wellington boots was constantly getting into all sorts of trouble with her awful gang. We thought you were all quite dreadful!'

'Yes Daisy, I do seem to recall my father, bless him, asking me on more than one occasion as to why I insisted on being with a bunch of hooligans when I could be playing with that nice Daisy Ingram and her friends. I confess I thought you were a soppy lot.'

Daisy told Dale that their Dad would not be there this morning as he was away on a coach trip with some of his old golfing cronies. Dale doubted whether his father would actually play but he would doubtless be the life and soul of the party in the 'Nineteenth Hole'!

Their journey home was fast and uneventful and it was about seven o'clock as they turned into Dale's car park. Stella turned down Dale's offer of coffee, knowing full well that he was itching to play with her, realising that she had told Richard she would be returning home at tea-time on the Friday.

'Darling Dale,' she spoke softly to him, 'I have no idea what the future holds for us but one thing is for sure. You have given me three days of absolute bliss. I am now a legend in my own lifetime because of my swimming prowess and it was simply wonderful to have you to myself for three whole days. Thank you darling and I'll ring you tomorrow.'

They embraced and Dale hugged her close to him. He too had enjoyed the trip but it continued to nag at him that this was not what he wanted. His love for this remarkable lady knew no bounds and yet her marriage to a man she did not criticise or vilify in any way did not appear to be rocky in any way. It was frustrating and left far too many questions unanswered.

CHAPTER TWENTY-THREE

Dale popped over to see Amanda on the Saturday, but she was on duty all day and seemed to be really busy so he went back to Canterbury and watched the Canterbury Pilgrims defeat the Dover Second XV in a rather one-sided affair. He had a few beers with his old pals and then made for home and an evening in front of the telly for the four-day break had taken its toll on him and he knew that a good night's sleep was the remedy. Amanda rang to see if they could meet up tomorrow and Dale's invitation to come to lunch was readily accepted.

Dale was able to tell her over lunch of how he had found his father and mentioned that he had popped up to Holy Island and renewed old friendships on the Thursday. Amanda was disappointed that she had missed out as his occasional references to this island off the coast of Northumberland had made her determined to visit the place. They 'played' for about an hour after lunch had been fully digested, with Amanda looking absolutely wonderful yet again in her new boots. Dale placed her in the rack from which his 'Crimson Pirate' had been suspended and got very excited at the sight of this gorgeous female standing splay-legged in front of him and totally unable to prevent him bringing her up to the point of climax after climax without allowing her the satisfaction of achieving such joy. Eventually he released her and had all his time cut out in attempting to hold her at bay whilst he prepared himself for their joint fulfilment. It was seven o'clock before they ventured out into the cold dry air and a walk along the quaint Mercery Lane into the Burgate found them in front of the main entrance to the Cathedral and standing in the Buttermarket. Dale opted to turn left and they wandered down the narrow Sun Street and popped into the Seven Stars Hotel, which was a popular Whitbread Managed House with a name for good home-cooked food and excellent beer. Dale introduced Amanda to John Hogan, the cheery Manager and his very attractive wife Rosaline whilst their teenage twin daughters, as alike as two peas in a pod, studied the lovely Amanda from the kitchen entrance. They sat in a corner and drank a pint and a half pint respectively of the excellent bitter. John came over and asked if Dale was at tomorrow's 'changeover' of friends of his at the 'Bluebird Inn' at Dover, and when told that both he and old man Tremlett were attending he informed him that he might just get over to see them out… 'Provided, that is, that the old battle-axe and her two henchwomen allow it!!' he chuckled.

Dale had never seen anyone who looked less like a 'battle-axe' and tried desperately to keep *the sight of this lovely lady as Linda Evans being bound to a chair in the 'Big Valley' as Dionne Warwick warbled 'Walk on By'*. Pulling himself together he told John that he would enjoy his company if indeed he did manage to make the trip down to Dover for the 'change' itself looked to be a fairly grim affair. They stayed for about an hour and then made their way back to the flat where Amanda collected her things and kissed Dale goodbye. 'Oh I have missed you Dale. Please don't go away again without me. I love you so much despite the awful things you do to me, or maybe,' she chortled, '*because* of the awful things you do to me!'

As so often happens when doom and disaster are forecast the 'change' transaction at the 'Bluebell' went off without any hitches and much to the satisfaction of Eric Walkington the Tied Trade Whitbread Area Manager who was a Yorkshireman and had been dreading the nightmare situation of the outgoing couple not having enough money to settle his final account and the ingoing pair not having got all their cash together in time for the change day. Mr Tremlett popped another priceless gem into Dale's memory banks when, after being confronted by the two stocktakers and asked 'how do we value a haystack sir?' promptly looked around the bar and having picked up a 'long arm' (which is the name given to that long pole with a brass hook on the end for opening skylight windows etc) stalked out across the field behind the pub followed by the two gormless stocktakers, one skinny and well over six foot tall and the other fat and decidedly vertically challenged. A more than interested Bernard Brazier and Dale brought up the rear of this odd-looking procession.

'What the hell's he going to pull this time?' asked Bernard, blinking nervously from behind his steel-rimmed spectacles.

'Haven't got a clue Bernard but it will be worth the short journey just to watch him,' Dale promised.

'Gee Gee' reached the rather dilapidated, ill-constructed and decidedly ancient hay stack and after a most theatrical twirl above his head he thrust the long arm right into the belly of the stack and giving a dramatic twist extracted the pole which now had what appeared to be a pile of rank smelling manure on the end. Inspecting it from all angles and smelling it deeply he glared at the two stocktakers and bellowed 'Fourteen Pounds!' before stalking off back to the house.

'You going to argue the toss about this Bernard?' queried Dale.

'I may look silly old boy but I'm not entirely without a morsel of commonsense. Of course I agree totally with Mr Tremlett's assessment!'

'Very sensible old chap. Damned difficult to extract a long arm from your anal passage I should imagine,' chuckled Dale as the two Brokers made their way back to the warmth of the bar. Yet again his Guv'nor had demonstrated the art of thinking on one's feet and added to the myths and legends that had grown up around him during his career.

CHAPTER TWENTY-FOUR

George Banyard was due in half an hour and Stella was right on time with her planning for the day. Amanda Broughton and she were going riding in the afternoon as this seemed the perfect antidote to the date she had with her elderly blackmailer. She put her gymslip on and had just tugged on her wellingtons when the doorbell sounded. George was early. She buttoned up her raincoat and ran down the stairs to open the door cramming her Panama hat on the top of her head as she went.

'You look lovely my dear,' George greeted her.

'You're early… sir,' replied Stella breathlessly. 'I'm only supposed to wear these things for you for one hour… sir, as agreed, so we'll be finished at 12.45 won't we… sir?'

'We will be finished when I say so my dear and not one second earlier,' George remarked very softly but very firmly.

'Whatever… sir,' sighed Stella.

Their hour of play-acting was nearing completion when, to Stella's utter astonishment and dismay, the door to the Conservatory opened and Mrs Defferary, who was not supposed to be on duty today, stood in the entrance.

'Oh 'allo Mr Banyard. I didn't know you was here,' remarked Stella's rather rotund housekeeper, then seeing Stella on the floor in front of him asked, 'and who might you be young Miss?'

'This is my niece… Edna,' replied George quickly, smiling grotesquely.

'Pleased to meet you I'm sure young Edna,' replied the housekeeper. 'Well, Mrs Upshott's here to see about the Royal

226

Society for the Prevention of something or other and she's barged in through the back door and is waiting in the kitchen. I know that Madam's in 'cos her car and old Chance are here but I can't find her anywhere.'

George Banyard, wallowing in the situation of Stella writhing with embarrassment at his feet cried out, 'Quick sticks my dear! Up you get young Edna and try and find Mrs Rigden-Ackeson for Mrs Defferary. She can't be far away for she opened the door to us not long ago.'

Stella got up and rushed across the room with the Panama pulled down over her face, anxious to be out of the room and the nightmare, only to be pulled back by Mrs Defferary who called sharply to her.

'Now then, now then, don't you go haring about like some mad thing young Edna. Walk like the young lady I'm sure your parents are paying a lot of money for you to become,' she cautioned, 'isn't that right Mr Banyard?'

'Quite so Mrs Defferary… quite so,' spluttered George.

'Yes Mrs Defferary. Sorry Mrs Defferary. I'll remember in future Mrs Defferary,' squeaked Stella, thinking to herself, 'I'm going mad… I'm really going quite mad!!!'

Once out of sight of her housekeeper she rushed along the corridor into the shower room, flung off her gymslip and shirt, tore off the Panama, wrapped a towelling robe around herself before finally placing a towel round her head, turban-styled. She tore back down the passage and then floated into the kitchen trying to look as casual and elegant as possible. She caught sight of the formidable Dorothy Upshott looking out of the window, her tweed suit and very sensible shoes portraying perfectly the woman she really was. Stella apologised profusely for keeping her waiting explaining that she had been taking a shower, but then noticed with growing dismay, that Mrs Upshott was staring with a fixed expression on her face down at Stella's feet.

"Oh Jesus!" thought Stella. 'I'm still wearing Edna's bloody wellies!!'

'Er… I see you've noticed my boots. I… er… I have a wretched verruca on each of the soles of my feet and have to keep my soles… er, dry. Doctor's orders.'

Dorothy Upshott nodded rather half-heartedly it has to be said and then started discussing the forthcoming Charity luncheon with great gusto whilst still inspecting from time to time Stella's feet which the owner was desperately trying to hide beneath the folds of her just too short towelling robe.

She eventually was able to bid the good lady farewell and then it was back to the shower room to transform herself once more into the guise of 'Edna Banyard of the Lower Third'.

George had seen the funny side of her predicament and had chuckled at her frantic dash to the ground floor shower room and thence to the kitchen and complimented her on her speed of thought and movement. He had still insisted on his sexual gratification however and had shown much greater will-power and inner resolve than on previous occasions. However Stella was more than a match for him over such things and sensing resistance she sat back on her haunches inevitably allowing her gymslip to ride up alarmingly showing warm pink flesh from boot tops to knicker legs… Game, set and match to Mrs Stella Rigden-Ackeson in a matter of seconds!

'Goodbye Stella my dear,' said George as he departed. 'It's been a most satisfying and entertaining morning. As a 'quick-change' artist you could earn a good living on the stage my dear.'

'Goodbye sir… and I look forward to seeing you on the third Wednesday of next month at noon,' Stella dutifully replied, albeit in a dull robotic, monotonic voice.

She closed the door and made for the staircase, a spring in her step and a song in her heart. 'It's over for another month,' she trilled silently.

Mrs Defferary appeared at the back door, laden down with a huge pile of washing from the line.

'Here young Edna,' she cried, 'just who I need. Do come and give me a hand with these here clothes whilst your uncle is seeing Mrs Rigden-Ackeson. I need them separating for ironing tomorrow. I shouldn't be here today by rights but I left this lot on the line overnight and I knew they would be dry by this morning. I don't want to be late home as my old Defferary will be expecting me to sort his lunch out for him... proper spoilt he is and no mistake.'

'I'll do them for you,' piped Stella in a high-pitched tone, wondering if her agony was ever going to end. 'I'll sort 'em out for you and leave 'em on the table in the Still Room.'

'That's a good lass Edna. I'm truly grateful and will tell Madam about you... and Mr Banyard when I next see him. That'll make him happy won't it my dear.'

"Bloody ecstatic I shouldn't wonde," thought Stella but staying in her character she giggled, looked down at the floor and scuffed her feet in embarrassment. Mrs Defferary waddled off talking to herself as Stella mused, 'That's right Mrs Defferary, you go and catch whatever spacecraft takes you to the planet you're living on these days.'

After seeing to George all Stella wanted was to shower and wash the wretched man out of her life for another month. Her unexpected meeting with Mrs Upshott had been utterly farcical but she had just about pulled it off and had it not been for the bloody wellingtons Dorothy Upshott would have almost certainly have believed her story and not left with the firm opinion that Mrs Rigden-Ackeson was going slightly dotty. She couldn't believe that in the rush she had forgotten to remove her rubber boots. Mrs Defferary would no doubt complain to her about the rather boisterous schoolgirl she had come across at their meeting tomorrow but no problems there as Mrs Defferary was already one or two sandwiches short of a picnic and

Stella would be able to reassure her on any other points about which she may be concerned.

"Wonderful housekeeper," she thought to herself, "superb cleaning lady… but barking mad! Totally, utterly barking mad!"

Amanda and Stella had been riding for almost an hour and a half and were in deep countryside not too far away from the villages of Eastry and Woodnesborough. The two women had become such firm friends and despite Amanda's continual tales of Dale Ingram and what a wonderful fellow he was, Stella really enjoyed her company. She was also able to keep track of most of Dale's whereabouts through her friendship. Stella tended to see Dale about once a week and his passion for her never seemed to wane, a fact that delighted her immensely. He could not wait to see her in rubber and lying there in comprehensive bondage she was thrilled at the sheer magnitude of his passion for her. Their lovemaking seemed endless and joyous and she could not remember a time in her life when she had been happier. Amanda was a girlfriend for him and she was pretty sure that Amanda too was being tied up at fairly regular intervals, but she had to accept all this because of Richard and the restrictions her marriage placed on Dale and herself.

Stella was shaken from her reverie by the unmistakable sight of one of Wetton Ackeson's green and white dray lorries, parked on the forecourt of the 'Bracken Inn'. Despite the late hour of the afternoon there were several cars in the car park of this rather remote country inn. Her suspicions were aroused by the fact that the 'Bracken' was a Charrington house and she knew more than enough to realise that the Company dray had no reason or purpose to be where it was at this time.

Richard had been going on and on about the bootlegging that was going on between the Kent coastal towns and France and was most concerned that some of his own workers and tenants may be heavily involved. Dismounting, she said to Amanda, 'I'm not happy about our dray being in the car park of the "Bracken Inn". I'm going down to have a look and see what's going on. I'll be quieter if I go down on foot so just keep hold of Chance for me. This shouldn't take long… I hope.'

Before Amanda could issue a word of warning Stella was off and scrambling down the wooded hillside. Amanda watched as her friend crossed a field and then stealthily approached the lorry.

Stella quickly unfastened the straps securing the dray's side panel and peered in.

'Bloody hell! It's Aladdin's bloody cave,' she hissed in anger. The lorry was packed from top to bottom with illicit spirits and cigarettes. It had come back from France and was obviously on its way to a depot somewhere for un-loading and redistribution.

'Well! Well! Well! What 'ave we 'ere then?'

Stella had been so totally absorbed in the treasure trove she had discovered inside the dray that she had been unaware of the silent approach of the three thuggish-looking characters, who now effectively, blocked her passage of retreat.

'I think I had better explain,' she said as calmly as she could, her heart beating far too fast and alarmingly forcefully inside her. 'I'm Mrs Rigden-Ackeson, the wife of the Chairman of Wetton Ackeson and I wondered what one of our drays was doing outside a Charrington public house. Has it broken down?'

'I think you had better come inside love and explain a little more closely why you've been spying inside the lorry,' said the shaven-headed lanky one.

'No I think not,' said Stella, moving away to the left.

'Yes I think so,' retorted 'shaven head' and in a flash the small check-shirted yob had grabbed her from behind whilst his fat balding accomplice grabbed her legs and carted her unceremoniously into the house.

Amanda watched in horror at Stella's abduction and feeling utterly helpless she started trotting down into the village of Eastry leading Chance behind her. Chance was never easy at the best of times when her mistress was not present and took a very poor opinion of being led on a short leading rein pulling hard immediately and causing no end of frustration for Amanda as her own mare reacted to the tetchiness of Chance. Sadly, because of all this nonsense and being unlucky at finding the first two houses she passed un-occupied it must have been about thirty five minutes before she had made the 999 call and given brief details of what she had seen.

Even so, the police had arrived at the 'Bracken Inn' within an hour of the abduction and had been met by the landlord, a Mr William Sackett by name, who admitted he had seen a green and white lorry on his forecourt that afternoon but it hadn't been there long and as he'd been playing cards with the assembled company they had not gone out to investigate.

'It was out of trading hours Guv'nor so he wasn't taking up any customer parking spaces and we never thought anything about it lads, did we?' he asked the assembled group of seven ill-assorted characters and duly received blind support for his statement.

Inspector Ted Haith looked at his young side-kick, PC Solly, and shrugged his shoulders for he realised they were going to get precious little out of this lot today.

'Mind if I have a look around the premises Mr Sackett,' he queried. 'Only a lady dressed for riding is purported to have gone missing and we have received information that she was last seen being man-handled outside on your car park.'

'Help yourself Inspector Heath... go anywhere yer like.'

Ted Haith clicked impatiently as he wondered why the vast majority of this County's population failed singularly to get his name right but thanked the landlord and he and Solly began to search the house and stores outside, confident that they would find absolutely zilch... and he was 100% right in his prediction. There wasn't even a bottle of contraband hooch or a packet of illicit cigarettes anywhere to be seen.

'Do call again Inspector Hale and if I do find a lady rider wandering about the area or even 'er bleedin' 'orse I'll be sure to let you know,' William Sackett said, failing to hide the smirk that lay behind his semi-serious words.

"Smug bastard," thought Haith. 'Thank you sir,' he replied. 'Because kidnapping is a very serious offence with a long prison stretch inside for those participating in such a crime as I'm sure you all know gentlemen.'

'Absolutely Inspector.' 'Absolutely.' 'Never spoke a truer word.' The replies came thick and fast from the assembled chorus of deadbeats, losers and local wasters.

'Why the hell did we do away with good old police brutality Solly?' Ted Haith asked. 'Sixty years ago we could have sorted that bunch of misfits out before supper. There's an awful lot to be said for a good whacking. Nowadays if we even swear at the buggers they need a psychiatrist to help them through a period of being "unloved" and "persecuted". We had better get off and see what tomorrow brings.'

Amanda sorted out the horses and having spoken to Dale on the telephone arranged to meet him at her cottage. Dale said that he would leave the office immediately and would be with her within half an hour. Dale could hardly believe Amanda's story, but realised the serious nature of Stella's situation and suggested they go round to *Clover Leys* at about seven o'clock by which time Richard, and hopefully Stella too, would be home.

Richard answered the door looking decidedly agitated.

'Stella's been kidnapped,' he told them. 'The bastards are asking for five hundred thousand pounds for her safe return and I'm not to get the police involved. Got to say it's a domestic matter.'

'What have you done so far?' Dale enquired.

'I've asked Banyard to get Chief Inspector McKay to come round to see me this evening,' replied Richard. 'Bill McKay owes me a favour and I'm sure he'll sort this thing out pretty quickly.'

Amanda told Richard all she had seen, but he had already received a report from an Inspector Hoath and knew of her involvement.

'Banyard is checking on all our dray lorries with the Transport Manager and I've told him to report to this local Inspector Hoath as soon as he finds anything that he feels is vaguely suspicious. You are certain that it was one of ours Amanda?'

Amanda admitted that she was not too conversant with dray lorries, but that Stella was adamant that it was one of the Wetton Ackeson fleet.

'Have you sorted out the financial side of things?' Dale asked.

'No! I damn well have not, nor have I any intention of doing so,' snapped Richard, 'they will not get one brass farthing out of me and they must understand this from the outset. You give in to low life such as these and it never stops!'

Dale's heart sank. Kidnappers were a heartless breed of men and well known for their spiteful and ruthless cruelty if their demands were not met.

'Wouldn't it be safer to play along with them Richard?' he suggested, 'it gives everyone a bit more time to make their enquiries. The last thing we want is for anyone to do anything rash.'

'Dale. I'm telling you what I tried to tell them… they are wasting their time. Release Stella and I'll take the matter no further, or so they think.'

The telephone rang as he finished speaking. His conversation was brief and animated. He returned to them white with anger.

'It was those bastards again… no money and I'll never see Stella again… what a load of tosh! I told the rat on the other end that I'll have my turn in court!'

Dale and Amanda could hardly believe their ears. His petulant attitude was so naïve as to be positively inflammatory to an already bad and worsening situation.

'Well you two, thanks for coming but I think we had better leave this matter with the Kent Constabulary from this time and let them get on with doing what we pay them to do. I'm sure you've got things to do so I'll say goodnight.' Rising from his chair Richard walked towards the door leaving his guests with little option than to depart.

Dale was fuming when he got outside. 'The fool! The absolute fool! Doesn't he realise the calibre of the low life with whom he is dealing? If they get an inkling that they are on to a loser here they'll dispose of Stella without further ado... no body, no case to answer!'

Amanda sat in the Range Rover listening to Dale's outburst and began to realise for the first time that there was more to his frantic despair than that of an interested friend. This was more, much more than the worry of a caring chum.

'You are really fond of Stella aren't you Dale?'

'More than I can ever say, Amanda. We go back over thirty years and I've always cared about her... you may not know this but she's one hell of a woman!' Dale's voice wavered slightly as the stress he was under began to show.

The difference in the two men's emotional states could not have been more different. Richard Rigden-Ackeson was angry, furious that somebody or something that belonged to him had been taken without his express permission. He was so used to giving orders and seeing them carried out without question that this new situation was, for him, intolerable. The person or persons who had committed this mortal crime against his person must be found and suffer enormous punishment... end of story. Dale, on the other hand, was simply frantic with worry for the well-being of his darling Stella. His mind was working overtime as he tried to explore every possible avenue that might lead him to her. He was shaking with the inner black thoughts that kept flooding into his brain. Kidnappers were the scum of the criminal classes who would kill without any remorse or pity if their own freedom were in any danger whatsoever. They were well aware of the punishment that would greet them if caught.

'Do you love her?' Amanda asked quietly.

'Yes Amanda darling, I'm afraid I do. I've always loved her I suppose but finding her again last year after all these years, married to such a successful man and living a life that most women can only dream about makes me realise that it would be too much to ask for, for her to give it all up for some silly sod like me.' He spoke quietly and a little sadly.

Amanda felt inwardly shattered as Dale spoke for although he had never professed great love for her they had nevertheless enjoyed some great times and their sex together had been something she could not and would not ever forget. She loved his kinky desires and thrived on being tied up and unable to prevent him doing the most outrageous things to her. Marriage was something that had never been mentioned by her but it was something about which she had often thought. The idea of having Dale Ingram 'to have and to hold till death do us part' was simply too marvellous to dwell on. However this was not the time or place to think selfish thoughts and her compassion for this poor soul in torment beside her and her fear for dear Stella meant that her priority at this moment must be 'being there' for him at all times.

'I've got a call to make in Thanet,' he said, 'it's a long shot but I may just strike lucky.'

'I'll come with you Dale,' responded Amanda immediately.

Once inside the 'Bracken Inn' Stella was hauled into a small bar at the right of the entrance lobby. The room was empty but for a small bespectacled man who was talking on the telephone. Stella did not scare easily but she was sure her position was perilous and regretted bitterly announcing her identity to these hoods.

'Shorty' put down the 'phone and said, 'Well Miss, you have certainly got yourself into a real can of worms and no mistake.'

Stella dragged up as much self-control as she was able and replied, 'Look if there's a problem then let's talk about it. There has got to be a way of settling all this by sensible discussion.'

'I'm afraid that you "talking about things" is the problem lady and being found here is an even greater worry for us. Your fellow rider was seen and we must presume he or she has gone to tell the story of your abduction to the gentlemen in blue uniforms. So we must now abduct you Mrs Rigden-Ackeson.' Taking out a small handgun from his pocket and pointing it straight at Stella's navel he ordered, 'Let's have your bleedin' hands behind your back and your bleedin' feet tight together please.' Shorty's affable manner had suddenly dried up as the last curt orders were given.

Stella stood her ground and attempted to remonstrate with her diminutive inquisitor. Five or six minutes earlier she had been sitting on Chance and chatting to Amanda and now here she was with a revolver pointing straight at her stomach and being told to prepare herself for what was obviously going to be a most humiliating situation.

'I can't believe you are going to do this to me,' she said as calmly as she was able, 'do you realise the penalties you will be incurring by treating me in this fashion?'

'Mrs Rigden-Ackeson. I'm beginning to lose my patience with you and if that happens then God help you. Now put your hands behind your back, put your ankles together and then shut up for Jesus' sake!'

'This is utter madness,' cried Stella as 'Baldy' wound black insulating tape around her wrists pinioning them tightly behind her. 'Shaven Head' meanwhile was doing likewise with her ankles. When it was safe to approach Shorty took some two inch tape from his other pocket and with great care wound it twice round her head and mouth effectively gagging her. She glared at him as fiercely as she could in the circumstances but the only response from Shorty was to grin back at her and tweak her nostrils together for a second or two making it impossible for her to breathe and letting her know in the clearest manner possible that he was totally in charge of her well-being from this time. She could hear plenty of noise coming from the other bar as she was hauled over the shoulders of 'Baldy' like a sack of coal and carted out to an old white van and dumped in the middle of a large spare lorry tyre. Stella had noted that the van was a Citroen and that one of the two rear windows had a crack in it, she was unable to catch sight of the registration number.

'You're going on a mystery tour now love, so let's make it a real mystery tour shall we?' chuckled the bespectacled little wimp as he produced a green *Marks & Spencer* plastic bag which he placed over her head tying it loosely round her neck by the handles.

Stella heard the dray lorry start up and leave the car park going off towards Canterbury and then the van's engine burst into life and departed too in what she thought was the Dover direction. She knew there was at least one man in the back of the van with her and thought that there was only one man up front driving. The journey lasted about twenty to twenty five minutes which made her think that they were in Ramsgate or Broadstairs or maybe Deal or the outskirts of Canterbury or… "Oh it's hopeless to try and guess," she thought to herself.

As she was carried out, once again like a sack, she smelled the odour of 'Baldy' and heard the sea, very close by. A door was opened and she was carried across a fairly spacious area before another door opened and she sensed she was being taken down some concrete steps. The air was chilled and a musty smell invaded her nostrils through the plastic bag over her head.

'I'm in a cellar right by the sea,' she surmised.

Standing as best she could on tightly bound ankles the plastic bag was taken off and the little wimp stood right in front of her. Taking a long chain from his bag he threaded it through an iron loop on the wall and padlocked it firmly in place. He then placed an old two inch studded leather dog collar through the chain and buckled it into place around Stella's throat. Showing surprising upper body strength for such a small man he lifted her off her feet and walked to the furthest stretch of the chain, so that it was taut from wall loop to dog collar and still left Stella about five yards from the exit. Slicing through her ankle bindings with a Stanley knife he said, 'Now you can stroll around your prison cell my love and there's a box to sit on. Can't take off the gag I'm afraid but you wouldn't expect us to, would you darling? There is also one other point I should mention and that is that my pal here asked particularly for your legs to be nice and free. I wonder what he's got in mind for you two, tonight? You ever tasted a "bit of rough" love? You could be on a winner if you play your cards right my darling!' The little sadist chuckled at his own humour as Stella judged that he was about 15 inches too far away to have her right riding boot placed very hard in the centre of his genitalia. Baldy stood there smirking doubtless thinking of the fun he was going to have with this haughty bitch once left alone with her. Just as quickly as she had been captured so she was alone again, the light had been switched off and she was left to her own dark thoughts. Suddenly Stella felt very vulnerable and very frightened.

A tear trickled slowly down her cheek, then skated quickly across the tightly wound tape of her gag before dripping off her chin. Her thoughts were of Dale whom she knew would be aware of her plight… she did not hide the fact from herself that Richard did not appear to come into the equation. Richard would be furious of course that anybody could have dared to do this to him and he would be organising for all hell to be let loose on her captors. It would never occur to him that she could be in real danger: 'For heaven's sake, I'm the Chairman of a Brewery Company… what in heaven's name could happen to her!!?'

'Oh dear, what is going to happen to me?' she sobbed through the ghastly gagging tape. Being tied up by Dale was such fun but to be bound cruelly like this was simply awful. The threat of rape was very real indeed and in her present state she could see very little that she could do about it other than to lay back and think 'of England, Harry and St George'!

'Mind you,' she figured. 'Breeches and boots may be a turn-on for loads of men but they are an absolute bugger to get off if the wearer wants to keep them on, bound or not!' She walked over to her box and sat down, her wrists ached, her gag was loathsome and the dog collar was already chafing at her neck.

'Oh come on Dale,' she sighed by now in total despair, 'your rubber princess really could do with one of those famous rescues from bygone days... where are you my love?'

CHAPTER TWENTY-FIVE

Dale and Amanda drove straight to the 'Royal Mail' in Margate and Dale asked the peroxide blonde bombshell to let Mr Lucan know that he was here and needed to talk to he and his wife very urgently. Within seconds the landlord and his wife were down in the bar and Tony Lucan gestured for them to come through to the private quarters. Amanda could see that they were both genuinely pleased to see Dale and seemed very fond of him.

'Well what can I do for you Mr Ingram?' Tony asked.

'Not all that long ago Tony you told me that if I ever needed a favour or a good turn I was to come to you. Do you remember that conversation?'

'Of course 'ee does,' interrupted Jenny Lucan, 'wivvart you sir we wouldn't 'ave got this 'ouse and that's a fact. What can we do for you Mr Ingram?'

Dale, in words of not more than two syllables and without beating about any bushes, told the Lucans what had happened and how he now feared for Stella's life. 'This possibly isn't the place, but it is the only time I have to tell you that this lady means more to me than life itself. I know that the ransom demand will not be paid under any circumstances and I suspect that the kidnappers are now aware of this too. It is simply not in Rigden-Ackeson's character to give in to such threats and if this is the case then I cannot see the kidnappers allowing their victim to live. I'm sure this is a case of illegal but understandable bootlegging that has gone horribly wrong, and now we have men involved who may bend the laws of this country a wee bit from time to time but would never stoop, knowingly, to kidnapping. Tony, I need you to find out for me who has my Stella and where she is being held and I need to know this information very, very quickly.'

Tony had gone a little grey as Dale's words went home.

'Blimey Mr Ingram, I 'ad 'eard a whisper abart this but I never knew it 'ad gone as far as kidnappin' this poor lady,' Tony croaked a little hoarsely.

'God luv'ver 'eart, she must be terrified,' coo'ed Jenny.

'Tony,' Dale persisted. 'I know you sail close to the wind in most things. It's your way of doing things and I've no quarrel with that. I think you are aware that I'm very fond of you both and the proof of your ability is clear to see... Jenny and you have really picked this pub up and turned the trade round in a most impressive fashion since taking it over. Don't throw all your hard work away. You have my word that no one, not one single soul, will know that you and I have spoken this evening. I speak for Amanda also when I make this pledge to you both. Please use all your contacts and whilst you are doing your probing warn them all of the very deep water they are getting into if any of them are even slightly involved in this particular bootlegging scam.'

'I'll do me best Mr Ingram,' promised Tony, looking very concerned after the final warning in Dale's outburst. 'I can't promise anyfink of course but I'll give yer a bell as soon as I've got anyfink that might be useful. I promise yer Mr Ingram... I'll do me best!'

"Ee'll do better than 'is bleedin' best Mr Ingram,' interrupted Jenny, "Ee's abart to perform bleedin' miracles for yer in the next few hours I promise yer!'

Dale put his arms round this warm-hearted cockney lass and hugged her. 'I'm so grateful Jenny...so grateful.'

'Don't you worry my luv,' she whispered, 'my Tony will sort this out for yer... you see if 'ee don't.'

Dale gave them Amanda's telephone number and his own and they left by a door at the rear of the house and drove back to Ash to await Tony's call.

'Do you think he'll ring?' Amanda asked.

'Oh yes. Tony will ring and I just hope that he and a few of his cronies will be more frightened of the inevitable backlash of this crime than incurring the wrath of the thugs who have taken Stella. None of Tony's crew are vicious criminals... just a bunch of likely lads, and very frightened likely lads at the moment if I'm not mistaken, trying to beat the system.' Dale hoped he sounded as upbeat about things as he had intended.

The cellar door creaked open and Stella got to her feet immediately. Her eyes had grown accustomed to the gloom and she was able to make out the shape of the awful 'Baldy' as he searched for the light switch. Stella had decided that she must stay as near the loop in the wall as was possible in order to allow her more room for any counter attack she could make on her 'admirer'. If she was going to be raped by this yob then it was not going to be made easy for him although it had crossed her mind that many a rapist prefers the struggle and the ultimate conquest of his victim rather than the subservient approach.

'Oh God!' she thought, 'here we go Stella.'

'Baldy' had found the switch and stood on the other side of the room leering at her. Stella was almost as tall as him and she stood opposite him defying him to come into her territory, her eyes blazed naked aggression and her knees were slightly bent allowing her the movement of a spring off either foot if necessary.

'Oh come on darling,' muttered the hunter, 'you know and I know that before too long you are going to be enjoying the best fuck you've ever dreamed about. All you posh bints love a bit of "rough" so here's your chance. I tell you what... I'll even take your gag off... there I can't be fairer than that can I?'

Stella stayed exactly where she was, not fooled for one minute by the 'kind' offer. By allowing him near enough to start pretending to unwind her gag would allow him to wrestle her to the ground which would be the beginning of the end for her. He circled round her as she remained close to the iron loop and got hold of an old long-handled deck scrubber. Stella saw that his intent was to get a hold on her chain and kicked out at the scrubber head as he attempted to hook it up under the sagging chain. Once, twice, three times he manoeuvred the brush into position only to be thwarted by well-directed kicks from Stella's riding boots. She could see he was getting frustrated at being kept at bay by a bloody female with her hands tied behind her back and wondered how long it would be before the ache in his loins got the better of him and he charged at her. Suddenly though he had the chain in his brush head and then it was in his hands.

'Now then darling,' he snarled. 'You've got your dog collar on so let's have you on the floor shall we!' So saying, he jerked viciously on the chain in a downward movement almost tearing Stella's head from her shoulders. She could not possibly resist the combined strength of his shoulders and arms and as the collar bit into her neck she was forced down into a bending position and then, with one more jerk, on to her knees. 'Baldy', now in complete control of the situation, came round behind her and with the sole of his shoe planted firmly in the small of her back gave her a firm shove and watched her fall flat on her unprotected face in the cellar dirt. She felt his sweating hands undoing her breeches' belt and then groping for her vagina which, upon finding, he inserted one or two of his grubby fingers and squeezed until the pain forced her to scream through the gag.

'Oh come on darling… I haven't even started yet and you're crying already?' The bully was having a 'field day' now and Stella knew she was in for the sort of nightmare that all women think about sometime in their lives but few actually have to endure. What annoyed her more than anything else was the fact that this bastard actually thought he had made her cry. Her tears were real enough but had come naturally and automatically as his fat little hand had stung into action every tear duct and nerve end in her body by his crude and vicious attack on her most private parts. He had obviously decided that the boots would stay on and seemed intent on getting her breeches down below her knees and then making his entry from the rear.

'You've got yer collar on darling so we'll start tonight's entertainment by doing it "doggie fashion",' he chortled, as he pulled hard on the chain forcing her head off the ground. Stella's resistance was fading rapidly as her pain increased by the minute and she accepted her fate with one last furious burst of controlled aggression against this hideous balding, foul-breathed creep. Her flailing boots caught his shin or knee and he shouted in pain. Rolling over on her back she lashed out again and again and again, her sobs becoming louder and louder through the gag and her nostrils as she fought for her right to be treated as a member of the human race and not some poor animal without an intellect to protect. The chain, that bloody chain, dictated all and recovering from his pain and the shock of this bitch's assault on his person 'Baldy' heaved the chain down and down went Stella with it. He kicked her hard in the solar plexus and watched as she subsided, heaving for air desperately through her over-used flaring nostrils.

'One more trick darling like that, and I'll really hurt yer. I mean it darling… one more bloody trick and I'll break something on your bloody body. Now lie still before I really lose my temper.'

The door to the cellar opened and both Stella and her assailant swung their heads round to see who was making this unexpected visit to the inner cellar.

'Get off her you animal!' barked a voice that sounded familiar to Stella. 'Baldy' got up off the floor and slunk off out of the room leaving Stella on the ground with her breeches just above her knees and her shirt ripped and open.

'What have they done to you Stella? Here let me help you up and tidy you up a wee bit.'

Stella scrambled to her feet quite unable to fathom just what George Banyard was doing here in her cellar prison ordering 'Baldy' about. George pulled up her breeches and after tucking her shirt in he did up her belt and then proceeded to unwind her gag. He did not however untie her wrists or remove the dog collar.

'I can only apologise for the antics of that piece of filth,' George said calmly as Stella sucked in the musty air of the cellar as though it was the ozone one inhales with joy on a mountain peak.

'Good evening Mr Banyard... sir' she said as calmly as was possible in these extraordinary circumstances. 'I'm sorry I'm not dressed for you but as you can see I've been a bit tied up with other things today. Thank you for saving me from a fate worse than death itself by the way. What the hell are you doing here? I gather, as I'm still standing here with my hands tied, that you are somehow connected with this bunch of half-wits. Is it your turn to beat me up now and pull my pants down? May I please go to the little girls' room before I burst?'

'Questions! Questions! I can see that you have not lost your spirit Stella my dear and I admire you so much for the way in which you have been conducting yourself throughout this ordeal. Now let us see to the last and most urgent request before we do anything else.'

George arranged for a plastic bag to be loosely tied over Stella's head before getting 'Baldy' to untie her wrists and remove the awful collar and chain. She was then led by the pair of them up the cellar steps and after a short walk arrived at what she was told was the ladies' toilet. George warned her that if she removed the bag from her head there would be no more 'kindnesses' shown to her and assured her that although the cubicle door would have to remain open throughout her visit she would be given 'the privacy a lady deserves'. Stella did as she had been ordered and was soon back in her cellar with her wrists bound behind her and the suffocating bag removed from her head.

As 'Baldy' refitted the collar and chain, George returned to the answers to the questions she had posed.

'I'm afraid to tell you that your arrogant husband, my arrogant Chairman no less, has decided that you are not worth the twenty pieces of silver we were demanding and has disobeyed virtually every request, or demand if you like, that we have put to him. We are all going to be fried in oil, if he has anything to do with it.'

'How much did you want for my safe return?' she asked.

George waited until 'Baldy' was out of earshot before replying.

'Five hundred thousand pounds my dear. Sounds a lot I know, but not to him… not to your wealthy husband Stella. All he has done is to threaten us down the 'phone and rant on about what a load of doggie poo we all are which, of course, we know anyway. No I'm afraid he hasn't done your case much good at all. He actually had me telephoning the local police Inspector to bring him up to date with what progress had been made. Why did you have to go down and have a look in the dray lorry my dear? Why couldn't you have just turned a blind eye to it all and got on with your ride?'

'Are you behind it all George? Are you Mr Big?' she asked as she slowly sauntered back to her loop.

'Well, there is another gentleman with a keen interest but the idea was mine and it has been a very lucrative business venture which, sadly thanks to you, must now draw to a close. The sale of two of our older drays gave me the idea. I purchased them through an Agent and had them fully overhauled and re-registered. I then did all the necessary paper work for them to be accepted as genuine Brewery lorries but ensured that all documentation came to me personally. We were always correct with our weights and there was always Wetton Ackeson stocks on the outside of every load, mind you it was the same stock on every trip across the channel, whilst inside this outer layer was the real money in spirits, fags and beer cases at duty free prices. We have a huge network of retail outposts and nobody really suspected another couple of the old traditional brewery dray wagons as they trundled to and fro across the channel every two or three days. Our drivers had to be paid, I believe you have met one or two my dear, and one or two palms have been greased in order that no hiccoughs ever occurred but the main profits have come to me. I've had the money I paid for the lorries returned within weeks and over the past two years I have become a very wealthy man Stella... and now it has to stop... because of my dear little Stella.'

'Why are you telling me all this George?' asked Stella, beginning to feel very uneasy about her new position in this wretched pantomime. 'Have you got plans for me?'

'Well yes... I'm afraid I have Stella. Our beloved Chairman will not rest until you are returned to him and this is utterly impossible for obvious reasons. So I'm afraid that you are going to disappear,' he paused for a long second, 'to disappear permanently.'

Stella's heart sank as she learned of her fate. As Banyard had blathered on about his wonderful scheme to defraud the Company and HM Customs and Excise she had begun to realise that there was not going to be a happy ending for her. She remained calm and just as George, confident in his mastery of the situation but not aware of the true geography of the cellar, began to enlarge on his cleverness she leapt forward and kicked him as hard as she could between his legs.

'Take that you smug bastard!' she screamed as he sank to the floor clutching his groin. He was still within reach of the restraining collar and chain and Stella's boots went in hard and often until he had crawled out of range. 'I've been wanting to do that to you since the third Wednesday in December you sick old bastard. How do you like that, Mr Banyard... sir?' she asked.

After a lapse of about five minutes during which time George gingerly got to his feet and proceeded to feel himself all over to see if this virago had actually broken any of his bones the Company Secretary said, 'Well maybe I did deserve that my dear. You were a wonderful 'Edna' you know and I shall miss you as much as I missed her. We had a very special relationship did Edna and I and that's probably why we never married.'

'Did she have to give you a "kindness" as well George?' asked Stella as she retreated once more to her loop in the wall. 'And dress up in her school uniform for you?'

'What Edna did for me will always be our secret my dear. But now, to more mundane matters. It is now almost midnight and you are in a public house near Deal. At two o'clock you will be taken down to the picturesque bay at St Margaret's and loaded on to a small craft. You will be weighted down and unloaded in mid-channel. That will be the end of Stella Rigden-Ackeson and I shall be at the Brewery tomorrow morning to try and do all I can to help my Lord and Master in his hour of need. The two drays are already on their way out of the country for good so it would seem that every minute detail has been taken care of. I shall call round in the fairly near future to see Mrs Defferary and collect young Edna's school gear that she left at *Clover Leys* after a morning ride on the day of her visit. I'm sure the old dear will allow me to go up and collect it from your room and I may take one or two other items of your clothing as a souvenir of the time we had together… let me see… yes the white boots you wore for your first date with me at the 'Turk's Head' opening in Folkestone… very fetching they were. They will be an excellent memento of a quite astonishing sight and one that will remain with me for always.'

Stella listened as this cool hard-hearted killer rambled on. So she was to be drowned at sea, weighted down like some old piece of junk that was no longer required on voyage and tossed overboard. George shouted for help and the three idiots from the 'Bracken' forecourt appeared after a moment or two.

'Get her ready for sailing,' he said, 'and be careful with her. She's got more honest guts in her little finger than you three have got in your whole three useless bodies. Call me when she's been prepared.'

'Shaven-Head' turned to George, totally oblivious to the stinging remark he had just made and said, 'By the way Guv' thanks for the pay packet, very generous of you I'm sure. Let's hope we can do some more work for you in the future… it's been a brilliant two years.'

There was no point at all in any more fighting and struggling and Stella submitted to being roped hand and foot and then having the chain wound round and round her body before finally being looped around an old iron anchor and padlocked firmly into place.

'Do you get a kick out of killing women?' she asked. 'You will never get away with this. Somebody is bound to talk and they'll drop you in it. You'll be led away for life sentences and incensed people will bang on the sides of the prison van as it takes you away for twenty years. When you get inside your lives will be misery and… urrrggghh… urggghh!!'

'That's better isn't it darling,' said 'Baldy' as he re-taped her mouth tighter than ever. 'Don't want any water getting in there do we? We might bleedin' choke to death.' He laughed as he watched Stella lying on the floor and quietly preparing herself for death.

'What was it that Peter Pan once said?' she asked herself. 'To die would be an awfully big adventure… or something like that I'm sure.' Her thoughts turned once again to Dale. Time was running out fast and she could not imagine Dale would be able to be doing much at this unearthly hour of the morning other than lie awake and pray for her safe return.

CHAPTER TWENTY-SIX

Dale leapt to answer the 'phone but passed it over to Amanda as it was an elderly lady from the village who was concerned about her cat. The time was almost eleven o'clock and still no news from Tony Lucan. Amanda reassured her client and then moved into the kitchen to brew up another pot of coffee. They sat sipping their drink, not looking at one another and hardly speaking. Amanda desperately wanted to hug the man and tell him that it was going to be OK, but the words froze on her lips. Dale had not hidden the facts from her and she realised that his summary of the scenario was the most plausible and that Stella could well be dead by now. She could willingly have murdered Richard for his irresponsible attitude but realised too that he would have to bear the full responsibility for his actions for a long time to come if, indeed, Stella was found to have been murdered.

All that had happened that night and the frank disclosures that Dale had uttered to her concerning his great love for Stella had not diminished Amanda's love or her respect for him one iota. If anything he had risen even higher in her estimation as he had tried so hard to find out where Stella was being held. Only naturally she thought also of the wonderful and joyous relationship she had enjoyed with Dale since they had first made love together. She wondered how her life would change should Stella be found dead or emerge alive and well after her ordeal, for one thing was certain… all their lives would never be the same.

Tony Lucan's telephone call came through at ten minutes past one. 'Sorry it's taken so long Mr Ingram. We can talk later but my information is that she's being held at the "Kittiwake Inn" at Kingsdown. The landlord is a Tommy Mole and 'ee's shit scared apparently. I don't know 'ow many men are wiv 'er.'

'Thanks Tony! I owe you mate. We'll talk later!' Tony put down the 'phone as Amanda replaced her bedside 'phone too having listened to the conversation between the two men.

'Come on Amanda!' Dale shouted, 'let's get off and end this bloody nightmare once and for all!'

'What about the police?' she asked. 'You've got to tell them Dale. You can't possibly take on this mob by yourself!'

'Makes sense,' Dale agreed and duly made his 999 call asking that Inspector Hoath be made aware of his intention to be at the 'Kittiwake Inn' in the next half an hour. Amanda and he then ran to her Range Rover and were soon driving at great speed along the Sandwich to Deal main highway.

'Make it go faster Amanda,' he urged his willing driver.

'I'm touching "ninety" as it is Dale!' she screamed back. 'We're going to make it my darling man, I'm sure we're going to make it.'

The vehicle drew to a skidding halt some thirty yards from the house. Amanda doused her lights and waited for Dale's instructions.

'Stay here darling,' he cautioned, 'don't do anything until you see me coming out again. If anyone else appears then blast out of Kingsdown as fast as you can… don't stop for anything or anyone! Are you clear on this?'

'I will do exactly what you say,' she replied, thinking to herself, "He called me darling."

Dale moved towards the house and seeing a light at the rear of the property he crept to the glazed back door and peered in. A solitary man was sitting watching the television in the private sitting room. Dale tried the door but found it locked. He banged hard on the door.

'Open up Mr Mole! It's the police!' he shouted.

Tommy Mole nearly passed out at Dale's call. He opened the door, his face the colour of two-day-old ashes, but before he could utter a word Dale grabbed him by the throat and snarled:

'Where is she you big fat bastard? We know everything and unless you co-operate fully with me now then it will go ill for you at your trial. You may just be about to save yourself several years on your sentence. I repeat… where is Mrs Rigden-Ackeson? If she is harmed then it will be all the worse for you.'

'Moley' was not one of life's heroes and as the urine trickled down his left leg and then the right leg he could not talk quickly enough. He had not known anything about anything and didn't even know that he had a person in his cellar until half-an-hour ago.

'I thought it was contraband Inspector,' he whined, 'until they appeared with this lass all bound with chains. They told me to keep my trap shut or I'd suffer the same fate as her. They're going to dump her in the channel. They have gone to St Margaret's Bay where there's a boat waiting. I was frightened of them Inspector and didn't know what to do.'

Dale rang 999 and gave the police exact information as relayed by Mole and tore out of the house shouting for Mole to do nothing until his local colleagues arrived to make their official arrest.

Amanda drove like the wind along the Deal to Dover road swinging left into the village of St Margaret's-at-Cliffe and then down the winding steep slope that leads to the small cliff-bound cove from where so many successful swimmers have either commenced or finished their channel crossings. Dale saw lights on the beach and ordered Amanda to sound her horn continuously as they completed their steep descent.

Stella had lain in the dirt of the inner cellar floor for almost an hour before one of her guards decided that Banyard had better be told that 'his "package" was ready for delivery'. Because of the chains that virtually encased her from top to toe and the fact that all the fight seemed to have gone out of her 'Baldy' didn't really take much notice of her except to go on and on about how painful death by drowning must be and he did come and try and look at her breasts but gave up because of the tightness of her bonds. As an act of defiance against Banyard he did kick her once more in the midriff as she heard the approach of her executioner and laughed quietly as she doubled up as best she could and heaved in through her nostrils.

'Not such a clever bitch now are yer darlin,' he sneered.

'Stand her up Ray,' Banyard ordered, mentioning Baldy's real name for the first time, 'and let's have a look at you Stella. My goodness you do look a mess. I had been thinking of inviting you to dine with me this evening but I doubt whether old Tommy Mole would have allowed you in the dining room in this state. I must say the steak was quite magnificent, doubtless from off the back of a lorry but, then again, I doubt whether "Moley" was ever born in the true sense… almost certainly fell off the back of a lorry!' The three hoods all joined in and roared with laughter as George made fun of the landlord upstairs.

'It's now time to be off Stella my dear. Any last words before you go for your final dip in the briny? Remove her gag Ray and let our songbird sing.'

Stella winced as the tape was torn off her mouth and then said quietly and with almost a look of boredom on her face, 'Just get on with it will you. I don't honestly think I can put up with listening to you pathetic bunch of creeps any longer. There's George who can't get an erection without having his elder sister dress up in a school gymslip and Ray who's got the smallest prick I've ever come across and as for you two other losers…' The tape was rewound around her face and the total silence that followed her short address was music to her ears.

'Just put the bitch in the van,' hissed George, realising it had been a grave mistake to have let Stella have one last opportunity to put him down. How dare she talk of his dear Edna in that fashion.

He vowed that he would have the last laugh by changing his plans and accompanying her onto the craft so that he could watch her face as she went over the side instead of driving himself home to bed.

The journey was not a long one and Stella felt the van shudder as it made its way slowly down the steep 'S' bends that led to the bay. Ray put her over his shoulder and carried her to the shoreline whereupon he dropped her face down and chuckled as the seawater soaked her. There was no sign of the boat that was to take them out to mid-channel. After about ten minutes Stella heard the 'put-put' of a small engine and heard the relieved comments of the gang. She was absolutely soaking by now as nobody seemed to care that the tide was coming in and what had been the shoreline ten minutes ago was certainly now awash. The boat was now very close to the shore and Stella sobbed quietly to herself. She was so wet that nobody could possibly have seen the tears and she remembered Dale telling her of her fierce order 'Don't you dare cry!' as she and he had been waylaid in the snow, all those years ago, by Goofy Grafton and his gang.

'I'm trying not to cry my darling Dale… but it's so hard to be brave without you,' she sobbed as another wave broke over her.

Suddenly all hell was let loose as she heard the sound of a car horn blaring in the night air. She forced herself up on to one elbow and saw that another vehicle had hit the beach area and with headlights lighting up her area of the shore she saw the outline of a man racing across the rocks towards them. From round the cliffs on the Deal side the roar of a helicopter engine preceded the machine itself by a few seconds and with the floodlamps lighting up the whole of the Bay Stella was able to see Dale Ingram, her wonderful Dale charging on with no sign of stopping until he had her in his arms. The boat had turned and was on her way back into the channel as the Banyard Gang split up and ran towards the road only to see the flashing of blue lights and the sound of sirens as Inspector Ted Haith and his squad poured into the bay to make their arrests.

Dale knelt in the waves and cradled her in his arms murmuring, 'It's OK darling, it's OK. It's over and you're safe I promise.' He gently unwound her tape gag and her lips met his in a long and passionate kiss. The wail of the ambulance added to the cacophony of loudspeakers, sirens, engines and shouting as Dale picked up and carried his bedraggled and still chained-up darling Stella to the roadside. Ted Haith walked to meet them and greeted them both warmly.

'We've got the lot of them,' he started to say when Stella interrupted crying, 'Have you got George Banyard from the Brewery…? He's the boss… it's his gang.'

'Yes my dear Mrs Rigden-Ackeson we've got your precious Mr Banyard all right and all his comrades. The crew from the boat are also being arrested as soon as our launch arrives on the scene. The 'copter will keep an eye on them until that time. I don't know how you did it Mr Ingram but without you I don't really have to enlarge on what would have undoubtedly happened here tonight. You've never thought of joining us on this side have you?' he joked.

Stella was sobbing continually as she was loaded into the ambulance. Her chains had been cut away and warm blankets fought against the shock from which she was now suffering. Amanda watched from the Range Rover and felt that it was not appropriate for her to interrupt her friend's loving reunion with Dale. She would follow the ambulance wherever it was going and she would 'be there' for as long as she was needed.

The ambulance set off and Dale gazed down at Stella as she lay there being checked over by the paramedic who quietly gave Dale the 'thumbs up' to indicate that in her opinion there had been no serious damage done to her general state of health. Stella felt for Dale's hand and whispered to him, 'I love you Dale, I love you so much my darling.'

She was fast asleep before the ambulance had travelled more than two miles on its journey to the Kent & Canterbury Hospital.

Stella's injuries were mostly superficial. The tightly wound chain had left bruising to her arms and the tops of both her legs but her breeches and boots had helped to lessen the damage to her lower half. Her wrists bore deeper wounds from tape that had been tied viciously tight. Her ribs were bruised from the first of the two kicks she had received, her lips had been damaged by 'Baldy's' spiteful removal of her gagging tape on two occasions. The vicious jerks that 'Baldy' had given her dog collar had resulted in major lesions around her throat in a two-inch raw band and falling on a rock whilst being dumped on the shoreline had bruised her forehead. Despite all these cuts and bruises, despite the trauma of being within a whisper of dying and despite aching from head to foot Stella was wide awake and receiving visitors by ten o'clock the next morning.

Inspector Haith and a WPC Watkins were early on the scene and took a comprehensive statement from Stella who was able to repeat all that George Banyard had bragged to her about the scam he and his gang had been running for the past two years. She gave explicit details of what she had seen in the dray lorry, descriptions of her kidnappers and their vehicle and confirmed that she had been told by Banyard of Richard's refusal to pay any ransom and that she was going to be drowned to prevent her from talking to the authorities.

Richard had arrived from *Clover Leys* at about four o'clock in the morning and had waited for her to wake up. He was delighted that everything had worked out all right in the end and had re-assured Stella that he knew nothing would have been gained by giving in to the empty threats of her captors. Stella was too weak to argue with him and just lay there listening to him as he rambled on in his own way about how right will always come to the surface in the end.

Stella thought to herself "Bloody hard for 'right' to come to the surface if 'right' has a bloody big and heavy iron anchor attached to it!" but said nothing. She was coming to terms with her ordeal gradually and realised already that her marriage to Richard was quite possibly over. She had been in love with Dale, if she was honest with herself, since their first meeting at Croft House when he had taken her to a level of absolute bliss, both emotionally and sexually and made her realise that her marriage had been something of a charade. It had been a pleasant and comfortable life but it was a charade in that she had never been *wanted* in the way that Dale wanted her and never craved for attention from Richard in the way that she did from Dale. Richard was a decent man but he was a man for whom personal relationships were difficult and sexual encounters almost a duty rather than a time for partners to touch and lie together and join in the sheer uninhibited ecstasy of the consummation of their love for one another. To lose her would be embarrassing and annoying, the word 'expensive' also tripped on her lips but she felt that an uncharitable thought and dismissed it. This was not the time to discuss such things but discuss them she would and it would not be a pleasant meeting.

Richard left after giving her forehead a peck and ruffling her hair with a 'Well done old girl, it's good to have you back in the fold!'

As he vanished, Dale walked in still looking utterly bedraggled. He had obviously been at the Kent & Canterbury all through the night but had kept out of sight of Richard and had waited patiently for his departure before coming into her private ward.

'How are you darling?' he asked. 'You look quite amazing considering what those bastards put you through. I was so totally absorbed in getting to you that I really never had the chance to smack any of them and now I'll never get that chance... not unless they put me inside too for impersonating a police officer!'

He answered all Stella's questions without telling her of Tony Lucan's part in her rescue and had her in tears of laughter as he described 'Moley's involuntary trouser wetting as a prison sentence loomed and his own deception in bringing about an immediate confession as to the part he had played.

'Did you ever meet up with the big fat slug?' Dale asked, 'for he was adamant that he didn't know what was down in the cellar and assumed it was contraband.'

Stella confirmed that she had seen nobody but the four thugs and George Banyard and being permanently gagged had meant that she had made no sound during her incarceration.

'Didn't they even give you a drink of water?' Dale queried.

'Dale, darling,' Stella replied. 'I doubt whether any of them had anything in mind for me other than hurting me, humiliating me or having me. They were animals and despite his reluctance to get rid of his "Edna", when it got right down to it George Banyard wasn't any better.'

'His Edna?' Dale queried.

'Oh yes. That's something else I can tell you about now.' Stella lay back on her pillows and as quickly as she could, told of her 'school' days with the Company Secretary while dressed in sister Edna's clothing in order to keep the story of their encounter at the 'Turk's Head Hotel' away from Richard's ears. Dale exploded as she recounted his sexual demands and his anger made Stella more certain than ever that she had taken the wisest course of action in keeping it a secret from her lover.

'Dale. Look at you!' she cried. 'It's all over and yet you are so angry. You would have gone and beaten him up and then he would have told Richard how he had found me, having been tied up by Dale Ingram and wearing little else but a bathing cap and my white wellingtons! Can you imagine what would have happened... it doesn't bear thinking about. What could I have said? How do you explain something like that to someone like Richard? All said and done, all I ever had to do was humour the old fool and give him a wank at the end of the session wearing my marigolds! I was never in any danger and only my pride suffered I promise you.'

Dale relaxed and smilingly admitted that she was probably absolutely correct in her reading of the situation.

'Yes my darling… I suspect that a plea from you that you were trying to counter wet-rot in the bedroom when attacked by persons unknown, would fall on stony ground!'

They both laughed at the thought of such an explanation and Dale bent down to caress his extraordinary Stella. 'You have been so bloody marvellous throughout all this Stella. I am so desperately proud of you darling.' He brushed his lips against her bruised mouth and stroked her eyebrows and temple. Stella reacted to his affectionate advances and searched for his lips again and then his inner mouth and tongue.

'You saved my life Dale,' she said, quietly and fought her emotional state as her passion for this man brought more tears to the surface. 'It's something I will never forget and has changed my whole life from this time. We must talk as soon as I'm out of this place.'

Dale realised that there would be other visitors, some official, and caring friends too. He kissed her once more and told her to get some rest and he'd be up to see her when office hours were over and provided it did not cause problems for her. Walking back down the corridor he came across Amanda who was sitting reading a 'Kent Life' magazine. She looked worn out but managed a smile as she saw him. Dale gave her the good news and estimated that it would not be too long before Stella was causing chaos in her efforts to return to her beloved *Clover Leys*. As Amanda rose to her feet Dale embraced her warmly.

'You were just brilliant Amanda. I could not have done all this without you and I haven't forgotten that it was you darling, who made me stop and ring for police assistance before charging off to St Margaret's Bay. A fat lot of good I would have been rushing down the beach by myself faced by three hoodlums, Banyard and at least one revolver. If the truth be known you have saved my life as well as Stella's.'

'I was just so glad to have been there for you Dale. It looks as though I have lost you to Stella but to have lost you completely would have been unbearable… I… I… I do love you Dale and I can't help it. You have made me so happy in these past months and the thought that I'm possibly no longer going to figure in your plans is so bloody depressing,' Amanda tailed off and a tear ran down her white and tired face.

'Amanda, dear Amanda.' Dale quickly answered. '*You* will always be part of my life for as long as you want to be. You know what I'm like and you know that the sight of Amanda Broughton stretched out or hung up is one of the most exciting sights I have ever seen. You are simply superb in bondage and if Stella does not get in the way of your own enjoyment then there is no reason for you to be hanging up your boots just yet, or your bathing cap for that matter!' he chuckled. 'Don't forget that Stella is married to Richard and he ain't going to give her up, so we must live our lives as best we can. I love you dearly Amanda, no, I know maybe it is not in the same way that I have always loved Stella, but I do really love you nevertheless and the sessions we have together are brilliant.'

The look of sheer happiness that invaded her face as Dale's words sank home could not be disguised and she hugged him tightly.

'Oh Dale, I don't mind about Stella. I know I'm never going to be a threat to her place in your heart and I accept that. So many women will never have what I have and I'm just so happy that we can continue to be friends and lovers.'

Time was getting on and both realised that it was time they should both be washed and dressed and ready to deal with another day's normal duties. Amanda dropped Dale at the flat and promised she would see him up at the hospital about 8 o'clock that evening. He had a day in the office, so could easily walk up to the Kent & Canterbury Hospital and then pick up his car from outside her Ash Surgery later on in the evening.

Arriving at his office Dale found that the news of the night's adventures had broken in a big way and there were a stack of messages from a wide source of interested parties who wanted to talk to him. Julie was full of excitement and came in to his office simply bubbling over with joy and pride.

'You saved Mrs Rigden-Ackeson's life Dale! You're a hero… you've been talked about on ITV this morning and we've had reporters ringing us up since the office opened. 'Gee-Gee' wants to see you as soon as you are free,' she added.

Dale dealt with his office mail and then asked Julie to just tell any reporter who rang that he wasn't in the office and had rung in to say that he wouldn't be coming in today at all.

'Not even Richard Baker or Trevor MacDonald?' she pleaded.

'Not even Sir Robin Bloody Day!!!' he growled as he set off for the office of his Guv'nor. The old boy beamed at him as he entered, always a bad sign, and rose slowly with his hand proffered towards him.

'Well done, old chap! Well done! My goodness me I can't recall such excitement in the office. You appear to have saved the life of the lady wife of the Chairman of Wetton Ackeson and are quite the hero old chap. I'm not sure that I understand how you were involved but my wife told me that you had come across bootleggers. Is this true?'

Dale sat down and related the story as quickly as he could from the time when a girlfriend of his had rung him in great distress saying that her great friend had been kidnapped and he had taken it from that point, working with the police or just in front of them to be honest. He admitted that he had known Stella Rigden Ackeson since childhood and had met up with her at Canterbury Cricket Week last year. She was a good friend of his but he had tried not to let this friendship get in the way of his business connections with the local Brewery Company.

'Quite right my boy, quite right,' nodded Mr Tremlett. 'One has to be very, very careful with friendships because sometimes such things are misread by those involved with disastrous consequences. Have you seen Rigden-Ackeson since the rescue of his wife?'

Dale said that he had not seen the man but expected that he was spending all his time at the hospital comforting his wife. Mr Tremlett had been approached by the local press and had agreed for their photographer to take a photograph of Dale and himself at midday.

'I thought it would be a splendid piece of good public relations for the local population to see me shaking the hand of our local hero and they have promised to send a copy of the photo to the *Morning Advertiser.*' Dale could find nothing about which to complain for it seemed fair and reasonable that the firm should get some good publicity in the licensed trade's national daily newspaper. The Brewer and the Broker were seldom shown in a good light for, to be honest, there was much about which to complain from the point of view of the tenant licensee although no one reporter had ever appeared to check into the world of brokerage and found out what a highly skilled and useful job the vast majority of them carried out. It was a common misconception that the Public House Broker was hand in glove with the Brewer but nothing could have been further from the truth and 'Gee Gee' Tremlett's guiding rule had always been that the firm 'worked its socks off' for whomsoever was paying their account at the end of the day. If one was working for a Brewer then one did one's absolute best for the Company, but if it was a tenant who had engaged the services of Messrs C G Tremlett & Son then that client would receive exactly the same first class standard of work. 'Gee Gee' insisted on standards and Dale respected him for his total inflexibility over such things.

Jacob Growser knocked at the door and entered at the bidding of the Senior Partner. He was carrying four or five files and was more stooped than usual.

'Well young Growser! What can I do for you?' Mr Tremlett commanded the question rather than asked it.

The aged ledger clerk ran his fingers through his ash grey hair and said falteringly, 'I've just spoken to somebody from Fleet Street in London, sir. You know sir, where all the papers come from and some magazines I'll be bound.'

'Yes Growser... I'm sure Ingram and I don't need a lecture on what happens in Fleet Street. Just get on with it, there's a good lad.'

'Well sir, it seems that our Mr Ingram has been performing acts of great derring-do, saving damsels in distress and generally behaving like the good egg all we members of staff know him to be. This chap from London wanted to know a little bit about him but I told him it was not my place to discuss our partners with anyone from outside the firm and he then said he'd make it worth my while to "dish the dirt", I think is how he actually put it to me. I replaced the receiver sir but thought I had better let you know that there are bounders about who just may be a threat to some of the less well-off younger members of our staff. I felt it necessary to bring this matter to your attention, Sir.' Jacob Growser stood to attention and awaited his Master's voice.

'What an excellent chap you are Growser. I recall my father telling me that Growser would never make a useful addition to our staff as long as he had a hole in his bottom but I saw something in you that he didn't. Please go round all the offices and tell all members of staff that if they speak to the papers I shall sack them. Well played Growser! An absolute straight bat throughout! Now get out... there's a good chap. We have work to do.'

It was difficult to get rid of Growser when in this mood and he lingered in the doorway. 'May I, on behalf of the staff Mr Ingram, say how very proud of you we all are.'

'Growser!!!!!!' The ominous growl of 'Gee Gee' was enough to see the old retainer vanish from sight.

By lunchtime stories were leaking out from 'eye-witnesses' of passionate embraces on the shore and of Dale's trudge up to the ambulance cradling the sodden and chained kidnap victim in his arms. These were things that Dale did not want to hear and he could see that there was going to be a great deal of liaison between himself and Stella if their secret love was to remain just that.

'Gee Gee' Tremlett had a wonderful day. He fended off reporters, posed for photographs, gave statements and ordered the odd news-hound out of the office when the questions got too hot to handle. Dale went off home, but popped into the 'Shakespeare' on his way and downed a couple of pints of Kent-brewed bitter. As he sat drinking he mused that his last pint had been only twenty-four hours earlier and yet so much had happened in that short time. Most kidnappings were long drawn-out affairs with much haggling and counter bids etc… he felt that Rigden-Ackeson's attitude had been utterly reckless and but for Tony Lucan, Stella would undoubtedly be at the bottom of the English Channel. He tried to pay for his drinks but the lovely old landlord insisted that they were 'on the house' adding that had if it been the Chairman of his own Brewery Company that Dale had saved then he would be 'paying double for the bloody drinks!' The remark was in typically humorous vein and would still certainly have been made had his own Chairman been there to hear it.

Dale caught a taxi up to the hospital and met up with Amanda as she was walking from the official car park. They agreed that it would be better for Amanda to pop in first and then let Dale know when the coast was clear. Dale took her keys and went back to the Range Rover with his Daily Telegraph.

There was strict security around Stella's room and Amanda had to give proof of identity and details of her relationship with Stella before being allowed to wait in the corridor outside. She could hear raised voices and wondered whether this was a mistake, a visit too soon. After some forty-five minutes Richard came out of the room and swept off past Amanda without a sideways glance.

Amanda's presence was passed on to Stella and she was quickly ushered in. Stella's bruising was coming out and she really did look as though she had boxed fifteen rounds with Henry Cooper. She embraced Amanda warmly and immediately apologised for causing her so much distress. Dale had told her of the major role Amanda had played in her rescue and Stella tried hard to get across just how grateful she was. 'I'm so sorry that I didn't tell you the whole truth about Dale and I,' she said ruefully, 'but I didn't want to hurt you or dash your dreams away so cruelly. I had not worked out anything in so far as my marriage was concerned and could not possibly object to Dale having a girlfriend whilst still remaining the wife of Richard. I was jealous of your affair 'cos I know what he's like and I can guess how much you have enjoyed these past weeks with him. I presume you have bought your bloody rubber riding boots by now?' she giggled.

'Oh my God!' Amanda exclaimed, blushing furiously. 'You knew all along what I wanted them for! Yes I've got them alright.'

'We've been lovers since July, Amanda, and I have never been so happy. He is the man for me and from the attitude that Richard seems to be adopting it won't be too long before he gets rid of me, in any case. I think someone is stirring things up and I'm sure that the story will break soon if it hasn't already made the papers. George Banyard has requested an interview with his Chairman and I can't begin to wonder what he's going to tell him. He has nothing to lose now by giving him the truth with a whole lot of half-truths added and I can't think that he feels he owes me any favours… especially as I managed to kick him in the balls just before they chained me up. Richard will go ballistic if he only knows about half of what has been going on.'

'I can imagine,' murmured Amanda.

'Oh no you can't, Amanda. I promise you the things that Banyard could tell him are way beyond Dale Ingram. I'm not sure whether Richard will give him breathing space but if he does then he may well settle my fate for me.'

Dale made his entrance some twenty minutes later, after Amanda had returned to the car and reported that the coast was clear. Seeing the bruised condition of Stella he visibly blanched and took hold of her hands and squeezed them gently. They kissed and then Stella brought him up to date with her situation. The one good thing about her hospitalisation was that it had brought her peace and quiet. The local police were doing a marvellous job of protecting her from the media and not one member of this band of news-hounds had managed to get through to her. Obviously the court case would be asking questions about her relationship with Dale but provided Banyard wasn't spiteful in defeat then her friendship with Amanda and Amanda's 'boyfriend', Dale Ingram, may still be acceptable to all concerned parties.

As it happened George Banyard could not have been more vindictive. Richard had refused to see him but had received a personal letter from his former Company Secretary, written from Maidstone Prison, in which he gave all the data that Stella had suspected he might. It was not a long letter but utterly devastating for Richard nevertheless.

Dear Chairman,

Firstly, please accept my abject apologies for my treacherous behaviour to the Company and to you personally. I have always enjoyed my life with Wetton Ackeson and am deeply ashamed that the lure of instant money, and a great deal of it at that, proved too much for me in the long run. I have no excuses but hope that in time you will remember some of my good points and allow these recent indiscretions to fade from vivid memory.

I regret the treatment my men subjected your wife to during her stay with them. She truly was in the wrong place at the wrong time and circumstances made me take actions that I now know were wrong. However fear of arrest and certain imprisonment can make men take outrageous decisions. I must compliment your wife on the courage she showed throughout her ordeal. She truly is a remarkable lady.

However, I must make it clear to you though that my opinion of your wife's moral behaviour is not high and having found her in a bedroom at the Turk's Head Hotel in Folkestone on the re-opening day last year, wearing virtually nothing but her boots and a bathing cap, bound hand and foot and excitedly awaiting the return of her lover, Dale Ingram, put me in an impossible position. That I did not tell you was purely my loyalty to you and my reluctance to hurt you in any way. I am sure she will not deny any of this report on her devious sexual antics but cannot believe that you will be able to accept any explanation other than she is a tramp and her lover, a sexual philanderer!

I await my trial with much trepidation and will try and use the time I must spend in prison to try and better myself. Once again, sir, my sincere apologies to you and to your dear father and mother for my inexcusable behaviour.

Yours sincerely

G Banyard.

Richard was truly devastated by Banyard's revelations. He showed a copy of the letter to Stella as soon as he had received it, some three weeks after his refusal to see Banyard and asked for her comments. Stella realised that there was nothing to be gained by lying and admitted her affair with Dale and of their mutual attraction to bondage which went back to their childhood days.

'I am still in love with you Richard but what I found with Dale was something so different and yet something that my body and mind craved for. You are a decent honourable man and I'm sure you can't get your head round such things but to experience those deep basic emotions of lust and sexual longing whilst in a "tied up" state is something that has no conscience… it simply smashes its way through all conventions and niceties in its fevered and frantic attempt to reach total fulfilment.'

'Boots and a bathing cap?' asked Richard, with a sneer that was ill-disguised.

'Dale is a rubber fetishist and I guess it turns me on too,' Stella replied colouring as she spoke the words. 'Some men like stockings and suspenders, some want leather and sadism, some prefer their women to dress in gymslips. All men are different and all get their kicks in varying ways. You probably feel that the sight of me, tied up in a swimming hat and rubber boots is both ludicrous and unbelievably awful but the mind games one plays in such a state quite overwhelm one's imagination and the desire for lust is beyond any normal person's comprehension. I repeat "lust" Richard because that is what fetishism is all about. Love has little or nothing to do with it. Have you ever thought of me in a "dressed-up" state Richard, or did you always find me quite acceptable as I am?'

Richard categorically denied that he had ever had any such thoughts and told her what he thought of her and her kinky oaf of a boyfriend in quite short and explicit terms. 'Firstly I'll have an interview with that old beggar Tremlett and put an end to Ingram's career with his firm. Old Tremlett's a real stickler for standards I'm told and this little juicy tit-bit will see him go through the roof I should imagine. I'll also let him know that if he expects to let my houses in the future then he had better do what's necessary by the end of the week. I'll also make it my business to ensure Ingram doesn't get any employment down here in the South…he's a northern un-educated oaf and I'll finish the bastard once and for all! You see if I don't!'

Stella slumped down in utter despair, knowing that Richard would be true to his word. He was hurt and his pride and dignity had been savaged. This made him a very dangerous animal. She rang Mr Tremlett that morning and asked if she could come and see him and was pleased to obtain an interview that very afternoon with the

269

Senior Partner. She asked that her visit be treated with the strictest confidentiality and received his assurances on that matter.

Mr Tremlett rose from his chair to greet Stella. He beamed at her and showed her to an antique mahogany armchair with a rush seat. His whole office was full of antiquity with a massive bookcase and huge circular shaped rosewood table dominating the room. She confirmed that she was now fully recovered from her ordeal but was now in the throes of another and reported to him of Banyard's spiteful letter to her husband and of Richard's determination to 'finish' Dale Ingram. She told Mr Tremlett of Dale's and her own fond relationship back in Northumberland and how things had just exploded when they met up again. She took full responsibility for her actions and without painting Dale as a 'Saint' she nevertheless did try to make it clear that the affair had been sought and encouraged by her. 'I can't see this lovely and gentle man lose the career he loves because of my lust for him or my husband's loss of face because of him,' she cried.

Mr Tremlett rose and put his arm around her. 'Now then, my dear, now then,' he whispered. 'I can't have you upset like this. So my Dale has been having an affair with you has he? I must admit that my wife who reads most of the daily newspapers did hint to me that Dale's acts of heroism tended to show exactly that but of course one cannot make such assertions in public. Please don't distress yourself my dear, on my account. Let me make it very clear that your husband does not do the "firings and hirings" in C G Tremlett & Son... I do! And that is how it will remain until I decide to retire from the fray I can assure you.'

Mr Tremlett's long-suffering secretary, Colleen Manwood, brought in a tray of coffee and biscuits and placed them beside Stella. 'Yours is on the left Mrs Rigden-Ackeson,' she whispered. 'He doesn't take sugar in anything, says he's sweet enough,' she giggled and left the room.

As she sipped her coffee, Stella took in the old gentleman who faced her. That Dale adored him was not up for debate and she could see that his fierce independence and freedom of will would not be bowed by the bullying tactics of Richard. 'Gee Gee' Tremlett was not a man who would frighten easily and she began to gain enormous optimism as she realised that Richard had sadly under-estimated this celebrated old East Kent Licensed Property Broker. Whether or not he would throw Dale out anyway would depend on his own understanding of the situation, but it gladdened her to know that Richard would have no say in his dismissal.

After talking generally about her adventure and her schooldays with Dale she rose to leave.

'I thank you so much for seeing me, Mr Tremlett. Dale is so fond of you but I'm not sure he would approve of my actions in coming here today. He's a proud man too and I know that he was going to have to tell you all about us in due course of time. One thing is for certain… there can be no going back. We do love each other so deeply and now that our attempts to try and keep everything under cover have failed we must start planning for the future as I can't see my husband ever forgiving me, no matter what I do or say.'

Mr Tremlett beamed once more and said, 'My dear, it took great courage to come and see me today. I am not an ogre and I do accept that people fall into love and fall out of love. Dale and I will have to talk and I'll have to let him know of your visit. You do understand this don't you? Please try not to worry too much. Dale Ingram is a fine man and a great asset to my firm. I can't think of anyone who doesn't like him… although, on second thoughts, I suppose I can think of one gentleman who is not to keen on him at this moment in time.' He smiled as he shook her hand warmly and bade her goodbye.

Returning to his swivel chair he pressed Miss Manwood's number and roared down the intercom, 'I want to see Ingram the second he puts a foot inside the office!!!' He sat looking at the painting of his father and mused, 'Why oh why are young men so led astray every time they get a stirring in their loins? I've a damn good mind to murder him when he gets in.' He had liked Mrs Rigden-Ackeson and could quite see why Dale had fallen for her. She was a striking woman and the tales of her bravery whilst in the hands of Banyard's hoodlums added an air of quality to her already impressive appearance. He looked forward to his meeting with the Brewery Chairman and wondered when he would get a summons from him. 'Gee Gee' felt that he was never too old to experience new sensations and his love of a battle seemed never stronger.

Dale's subsequent meeting with his Guv'nor was noisy and very much to the point. He was told where he was going wrong in life and what a pain in the neck he had been to the firm over this affair and if ever it happened again then he would not be responsible for his actions. He then went on to say what an absolutely charming lady Mrs Rigden-Ackeson was and explain the reason she had called today to see him. 'It is quite clear that you have made a dangerous enemy Dale but you will just have to get on with it. I gather he's going to talk to me about you but I haven't heard from him yet.'

Dale was delighted by the way in which his Guv'nor had taken the news of his affair with Stella. The old boy's hackles had obviously risen at the suggestion that he might be 'ordered' to get rid of one of his partners and Dale felt he knew the man well enough to be confident that whatever happened, Richard Rigden-Ackerson would not be successful in his quest to ruin his career.

Dale was also pleased that Stella and Amanda had talked together about their own relationships with him and each other. It was so clear that the two women had enormous respect and a genuine fondness for one another and this not only made him happy in his heart but also found him hatching a plot involving these two most important women in his life. He chuckled out loud as outrageous thoughts flooded into his head. 'Stella will never forgive me,' he chortled, knowing full well that she would... as would Amanda... eventually.

CHAPTER TWENTY-SEVEN

It was Saturday, late afternoon and Stella had been prepared by Dale in his usual caring and loving way. Spread-eagled in all her rubber gear and being gently caressed by her lover she wallowed in sensual joy. Richard had gone away for the weekend and was 'killing things' in Northern France with a few of his cronies. He had hardly spoken to her since receiving Banyard's letter and had moved out of their bedroom, preferring to use the number two guest room at the other end of the landing corridor. The door intercom crackled into life and Stella, through her tight-fitting rubber cap, thought she heard a woman's voice and then to her horror heard Dale inviting someone up.

'Dale! For God's sake! Shut the door so that I can't be seen,' she cried in panic and then relaxed as he quietly closed the door as requested. 'Do make them go away Dale... I'm really ready for you darling and for anything you are going to throw at me this afternoon!'

Amanda bounced into the hall and was met by Dale who kissed her and immediately started undressing her.

'My goodness me, have Newcastle United won again?' she laughed as her clothes were thrown left, right and centre.

'Better than that,' said Dale, 'we have a real celebration to enjoy this evening. Now hurry up with your boots and let's get into the bedroom.'

Amanda had soon pulled on her boots and again they embraced as her lovely body, now exposed, nestled tightly against his. 'The bedroom!' he ordered.

Amanda waltzed into the bedroom and caught sight of Stella, her head raised in horror as her naked rival stood, transfixed, in absolute bewilderment at the vision before her. Dale entered and said quite calmly, 'It's time you girls got to know each other better. You know what you like and I suspect that you know far better than I what you really want from your lover. What have you got to lose? Love and sex are fun things and not to be taken seriously. Amanda, may I suggest, only a suggestion you understand, that Stella has her ball gag fitted now. She always has far too much to say at this time in the proceedings and this is your play so enjoy it… and make sure that Stella enjoys herself too.'

'If you try to put that bloody thing in my mouth Amanda then I will not be responsible for my actions! I hate it! I hate it! And I hate you Dale Ingram. Amanda don't you **dare come anywhere near me with that… UGGG BAGGOG GIGHGIG**.' She subsided into a resigned silence as the inquisitive and by now highly aroused lady veterinary surgeon firmly buckled the gag in place. Sat astride her captive chum Amanda gazed at the quite beautiful form of Stella and with a naturalness that amazed her she began to stroke the hills and dales of her friend's supine body. Stella's eyes, blazing emeralds, never left her own eyes as she kicked against her ropes and pulled hard against the cords that kept her wrists high above her head. Gradually the demonstration of protest lessened as Amanda's educated fingers sought and found all those places that she herself loved to have caressed by Dale. Realising how desperately she always wanted Dale's mouth at such a time she un-buckled the gag and leaned over to kiss Stella. 'Don't fight this darling Stella,' she whispered. 'Let me love you in our own way.'

As Stella's lips touched Amanda's their tongues slid automatically inside each other's mouths and Amanda's fingers played havoc with mind-blowing efficiency down below. 'Untie me Amanda! Just untie me please,' sobbed Stella. Her partner quickly undid her bonds and the two women fell into each other's arms, exploring, touching, stroking and finally climaxing together in one wonderful crescendo of sexual pleasure. Half an hour later Dale walked into the room with a bottle of champagne, three flute glasses, a bowl of peanuts and cheese cubes.

They were still booted but Stella had removed her cap and gloves, as was her custom. The two loves of his life were lying on their backs talking and laughing and, to his great relief, had nothing but smiles for him.

'Dale Ingram, you are a devious bastard but then you already know that don't you,' started Stella. 'However you are also the most remarkable man I have ever met. Did you see anything of our adventure together?'

'Not one single act of sinful deviation I promise,' he replied instantly. 'I just wanted you two gorgeous friends to put yourselves on a level of friendship that few ever attain. Because you've enjoyed a sexual encounter together doesn't mean you are now dyed-in-the-wool lesbians and will start wearing sensible shoes, smoking cigars and chasing poor old Mrs Defferary all over the house. You are wonderful females and can really admit to loving each other without any shame, for whatever the two of you got up to came naturally.

'I couldn't believe you were going to do what you did Amanda,' said Stella slowly, 'did you really get excited by the situation?'

'Yes, Stella, I think that because this blighter has put us both through the indignity of being at his mercy and knowing how randy it has always made me feel, lying there and quite unable to prevent him doing anything to my body, I just knew that despite the struggling you wanted me to take advantage of your helplessness. If I'm really honest the gagging was just wonderful. Your face! I thought you were going to explode as I put the wretched thing in your mouth. You weren't frightened were you?'

'No I wasn't frightened… I suppose I just wanted to be you instead of me if the truth be known. I just know that I would love to have you totally in my power Amanda and be able to pull that bloody cap over your head and stick the gag in that very sexy mouth of yours. I'm going back to schooldays again but the sight of a captured member of the gang always sent a thrill through me. Can you remember Dale?'

'Yes I have vivid memories of such things,' Dale interrupted. 'You were very keen on the old bondage games and all that went with them. But enough of that… fair is fair and I reckon Stella should have her chance of total domination now. Are you game Amanda?'

'What can I say? If I don't agree then I'll be labelled a spoilsport. A girl who can dish it out but can't take it! Alright Stella… where and how do you want me?'

Amanda allowed herself to be bound hand and foot in a standing position. Stella, with enormous gusto tugged the white rubber bathing cap over Amanda's lovely auburn tresses and snapped the chin-strap into position. She held up the ball-gag in front of her friend and teased her saying:

'Now you know how I felt just now my dear. Prepare to meet thy doom!'

'If I promise not to say a word Stella… not one single word would it be possible for you to allow me to not have the… **aaaagggghhhh!!**' Amanda's theatrical pleading came to an abrupt end as Stella laughingly buckled up the gag. After watching Stella examine her now passive partner, Dale made another discreet exit for the role of 'voyeur' was not in his make-up. Stella continued to torment and titillate her helpless playmate and then asked Dale for a vibrator which he handed to her through the door.

'No darling, you must come and watch this,' she insisted. 'Amanda knows what's going to happen and won't mind at all if you study her at close range… will you dear?' she asked.

'**Gorr….Gogh aargg gagh!!!!**' came the animated response.

The vibrator was put in position and switched on as Stella held Amanda close to her own body and licked her nostrils before letting her darting tongue explore those parts of her half-opened mouth that the gag permitted. Her helpless hostage to pleasure began to groan and totter on her bound ankles as the inevitable surges swelled up inside her before collapsing in Dale's arms and being carried to the bed where her bindings were removed. She lay there for a few moments only to be joined by Stella who cuddled up to her and whispered, 'I think that evens up the score somewhat, don't you?'

'Can we call it a day?' moaned Amanda. 'I think I have aches in places that I didn't think I had places. Why did I ever get mixed up with Dale Ingram and his gorgeous cruel Stella?'

They all chatted and decided that a dinner at Canterbury's major Italian restaurant would be a fitting end to a 'night of unashamed debauchery', as Dale had put it so succinctly. The three of them linked arms and walked round to the restaurant where they were wined and dined in excellent style. Their talk was of the future and what lay in store for all of them. Stella intimated that she could not see Richard permitting her behaviour to pass without hurting her in some way and Dale tended to agree that the damaged pride of the man would drive him to lash out at anyone who was vaguely interested in the case. Dale reassured Stella about his own future and went as far as to admit that the way in which she had conveyed her fears for Dale to Mr Tremlett may have gone a long way to deciding how the old boy dealt with things. Stella informed them of the instant rapport she had established with Dale's Senior Partner and how much she had liked him.

'I do hope you didn't mind me interfering in your business Dale but I just felt so low what with Richard's snarling threats and my general situation that I reckoned Mr Tremlett might just take pity on this poor wretched female in distress.'

Their dinner over the three chums strolled back to Dale's flat where Stella felt it was time she was off home but Dale insisted that she had had far too much to drink and must stay the night. A compromise was agreed and after a 'phone call to Mrs Defferary had reassured her that Mr Defferary had sorted out Chance and had also been out for a walk with old Simon only half an hour ago and had re-set the alarm system Stella was happy to stay. Dale made steaming mugs of cocoa and within minutes the three tired and happy friends were in Dale's king-sized bed. Dale had always had a 'thing' about sleeping on the right and the idea of being the 'filling' in a female sandwich did not appeal to him at all. Stella took charge and kissing him goodnight she took centre stage and after a kiss between Amanda and Dale she turned Amanda away from her and on her side so that she could cuddle her warm back. Despite Stella nibbling at Amanda's ear and playing with her nipples the two women were asleep in seconds and left Dale in reflective mood as he went back over the events of the day and decided, not for the first time in his life, on just how truly wonderful the female of the species had become or, maybe, always had been.

Amanda was on call all day Sunday and had to leave early next morning. She crept out of bed and after a shower dressed for work and was just off when Stella emerged from the bedroom looking sleep-eyed and, for her, somewhat bedraggled.

'Bye Amanda,' she whispered. 'Thanks for such a lovely day yesterday. I don't know about you but I can't believe what we got up to. I know that I am a perfectly normal female with very normal desires where sexual contacts are concerned but when placed in the situations that our wicked friend next door organised I just lost all sense of what is right and what is wrong, what is normal and what is abnormal. I just wanted you to take advantage of the position knowing damn well that had the positions been reversed then you would not have got off as lightly as did I!'

'Ooooh! Sounds very interesting,' chuckled Amanda, 'you have just expounded what I feel too Stella. Dale seems to know, instinctively, that sex should be fun and that there are no rules at all provided nobody gets hurt. I love the simple philosophy of the man and don't feel at all embarrassed that you and I have made love together... it's something I shall never forget and if the opportunity for us to experiment again arises then I trust that we won't hesitate, and you certainly won't get away with things as lightly as you did last evening I can promise! Mind you, we mustn't make old 'sleepy head' in there feel jealous… what a downer to his male ego if we had to turn him down 'cos we were otherwise engaged,' she laughed. They kissed each other on the cheek and embraced warmly before Amanda shot off to begin her day's duties.

Stella washed and made a pot of coffee in the battered old percolator which despite its decrepit condition still managed to produce the most gorgeous coffee in the County. Smelling of Oscar de la Renta she wafted into the bedroom wearing only her riding boots and a dazzling smile… it was to prove a sensational start to the day and resulted in, horror of horrors, Dale missing twenty-five minutes of the omnibus edition of *The Archers*. Dale was not a telly addict but loved Radio Four's *Test Match Special* and *The Archers* which he had followed avidly since it commenced after the old serials of the forties,' *Dick Barton Special Agent* and *The Daring Dexters* had been axed.

Richard saw Mr Tremlett on the following Wednesday. He was not at all happy with the outcome and realised that his threat to remove the firm of Messrs C G Tremlett & Son from his Company's list of accredited Licensed Property Brokers had not met with the success he had hoped. Mr Tremlett was one of the old school and Richard's bullying and arrogant manner merely hardened his resolve. Remaining totally in control of himself he asked if his firm, a firm that had tended to the needs of Messrs Wetton Ackeson for almost one hundred years, was to be thrown on the scrap heap because of an illicit affair that one of his partners had been having with the Chairman's wife? He assured Richard that young Ingram would be dealt with by himself and hurt where most young men can be hurt… by a cut in salary. Surely it was a matter between himself and his wife as to how they settled their personal differences and nothing to do with anyone else. Mr Tremlett, sounding more and more like Sir Winston Churchill, moved up a gear.

'I cannot possibly envisage a circumstance whereby one of the oldest and most esteemed family Brewery Companies in this country, or any other country for that matter, could or would become involved in any nefarious, base or churlish act of vindictive retaliation against such a small and honest to goodness firm like mine. How would the world of Brewing judge such an action? How would the *Morning Advertiser*, our national 'Daily', view such malevolent and over-oppressive behaviour when interviewing the devastated eighty-five year old Senior Partner? Can you begin to imagine the furore…'

'Alright! Alright Mr Tremlett, you make your point most eloquently,' interrupted Richard Rigden-Ackeson, 'I merely suggested to you that it was an option I may well take and feel like taking if the truth be known. Whether or not I do so has yet to be decided. I am heartened that you have decided to punish the wretch and may I make it quite clear that invitations from the Company to your firm in the future must never be taken up by Ingram. If I never see the rat again I will be well pleased.'

'Gee Gee' Tremlett gave him swift assurance on that point and sensing that he may well have extricated his firm from what had appeared to be looking more and more like a headlong plunge into a pile of horse manure he decided that he had better get out while still ahead.

'Chairman, I am truly sorry for the antics of Ingram but I will deal with him I promise. I do hope you will not attempt to punish my firm for his awful behaviour. I must employ thirty odd totally innocent and hard-working men and women who should not suffer financially because of one silly man's conduct. I sincerely hope that you and I will not talk of this wretched business again.'

The two men shook hands and Richard was left thinking what a character Tremlett must have been in his prime. He accepted, albeit reluctantly, that a total severance of business connections between himself and Tremletts' would undoubtedly receive massive hostile publicity as a direct result of the amount of organisation the old rascal to whom he had just been talking would personally inject into the story. He also realised that any tenant leaving his house with a beef against the Company would almost certainly engage the services of a hostile Broker in order to get the very best deal out of the changeover transaction and so Tremlett & Son would still continue to do business with his Company. Relations with the senior Brewers in the County, Shepherd Neame in Faversham, were diplomatically genial enough but Richard knew that any suggestion of a tactical boycott of Tremletts' would be thrown out without further ado for they were just as fiercely independent as were Wetton Ackeson.

'Oh to hell with them all!' he sighed, 'I seem to be a loser whatever I do.'

The next few weeks saw little improvement in Stella and Richard's relationship. He had poisoned any feeling his family might have had for her and even brother Toby had not made contact with Stella since her abduction. Local publicity had died down and would probably remain low until the trial of Banyard and his gang. George's letter to Richard did not seem to have been read by anyone but Richard but Stella feared that if the news of her affair did get out into the open then her husband, in present mood, would take great delight in letting the world know of her bondage games at the 'Turk's Head Hotel' in Folkestone. That would effectively end her career as a Justice of the Peace and as Chairman of a local school's Board of Governors and would sadden her as she had gained genuine enjoyment from her association with both these activities. His only reason for keeping quiet on the subject would appear to be that it might well bring down a certain amount of scorn on his own head.

She and Amanda rode two or three times a week and she looked forward to their afternoons out together. They had not repeated the performance they had given at Dale's flat but had both been able to joke about it with each other and there was no doubt that a bond had been established between the two that would always be there. Kate Donald had joined them once or twice and in the course of conversation had intimated that her intention was to start a riding school and stables in the next twelve months, as her practice now had allowed her to engage a couple of young newly-qualified osteopaths who would be taking on much more of the daily sessions. Horses were still a passion with her and she missed the daily contact she had once enjoyed. Stella, her mind working overtime, hinted that *Clover Leys* might make a suitable venue and if Kate was indeed interested in such a thing then she would discuss it with Richard. Stella loved her home so much and was already thinking pessimistically about her future with Richard. If he did indeed intend to divorce her then really all she wanted would be her home and she could not believe that Richard would be naïve enough not to agree to such an offer.

Both she and Amanda were seeing Dale but not at the same time. Dale tended to see Amanda at her cottage and would entertain Stella at his flat in Canterbury. He was very busy at work and was receiving a great deal of good-natured joshing from his clients and fellow brokers. Annie Scott had rung him telling him she was now the proud owner of 'Dixie' and asked when they could go out riding again, but he had been forced to postpone their next morning out because of the work schedule old Tremlett had given him. Eventually he saw a gap in the diary and rang her immediately. She was delighted and they made a date for the following Monday at 9 a.m. when Dale would pick her up from the 'Green Man'. 'Vincent insists that you have a spot of lunch with us afterwards Dale, please do,' she pleaded.

The two of them rode out for almost two hours before arriving at the sheltered copse of their last encounter. Dale helped her down and they spread his tartan rug on the mossy carpet that covered the entire area of the wood. As always he had plans for this most attractive and very willing young woman and soon had suggested what he would like to do.

'You know how much you enjoyed your first experience of bondage Annie.' He spoke in a matter-of-fact manner pretending not to notice Annie's eyes opening wider and wider at his words. 'Well here's what we're going to do.'

'I don't mind anything but you must promise me that you will *not* put that bloody bathing cap on my head. I cannot bear it Dale!' Annie was very serious when she spoke and as Dale did not intend to use the hat today he solemnly agreed that she would go bare-headed on this occasion, although making a mental note of how magnificently cross she was going to be when wearing it next!

Ten minutes later a still totally bewildered Annie Scott was spread-eagled in an upright position with her two wrists and her two ankles tied to two young but firm saplings about three yards apart. Apart from her riding boots and a pair of lace pants she was stark naked and feeling more vulnerable and more excited than she had ever been in her entire life. Dale stood off and looked at her from various angles as she pleaded with him to untie her. She really did look magnificently sexy and the fact that the whole thing was taking place out in the open air made it that much more exciting and rather like a film-setting. Inserting his 'killer' vibrator he switched on and watched the dramatic convulsions of *Cat Ballou or Jane Fonda as she fought the ropes, the surges* and the mounting urge to scream with joy from the top of her voice. Dale nipped all such thoughts in the bud as he rescued his battery operated gadget of the devil and releasing her from her ropes carried her to the rug where he caressed and moved her body into a perfectly controlled rhythm from which her final joy was indeed screeched out to the surrounding countryside and all who dwelt therein. It had been a superb session and Dale had enjoyed himself thoroughly. Here was a situation with no problems, no hang-ups and no commitment. Annie had obviously loved her day out but was now more than happy to return to the pub and the husband she adored. True she would never forget Dale for few women that had been subjected to his own brand of love making would ever forget him, but it was just a passing episode, wonderfully exciting and daring, but just a passing episode in her life. If he hung her up by her heels next time, wearing the dreaded bathing cap, and swung her like a pendulum she would still be there and screaming like a banshee until his gentle final acts of love-making transported her to the nearest thing to heaven that she had experienced to date.

Vincent Scott was such a pleasant chap and a first class operator. Their trade was quite phenomenal and he was, to a large extent, responsible. Annie was pretty and very bubbly in her personality but Vin had this ability to make everyone like him as well as being able to assess the best way of making a pub really 'hum'. They were now employing a chef full-time and their food trade had become popular from Maidstone to Ashford. Dale and Annie walked in and she ran to greet her husband with a big kiss.

'We've had the most wonderful ride Vin. I've seen so much more of the countryside than before and Dale has been very patient with me when I've wanted to just sit and take it all in. I do hope you can do this again Dale... I know I'm being a bit of a baby but I'm still not really confident enough in this part of the country to go off on my own yet.'

Dale promised that he would be delighted to ride with her whenever he had time and whilst all this was going on dear Vincent Scott beamed with happiness that all in his life was so bloody wonderful. Their meal was excellent and after a cup of coffee Annie came to the car with him.

'Thanks again Dale, for such a great morning. I have no idea what you are going to do next but I know that I'll love it. If ever you want me to tie you up you won't be shy will you?' she asked, 'I bet I could get you going once I've got you in my power!' she laughed.

Since gang days Dale had never been tied up and now, here with this pretty little landlady who really was very inexperienced in such matters, he was left feeling very, very excited. 'I'll have to see about that,' he joked. 'You may leave me there in the woods and I'll be kidnapped by gypsies.'

'You just think about it my lovely. I'm sure I would be a good captor and the thought of you as my captive makes me go all shaky. See you Dale and thanks again!'

CHAPTER TWENTY-EIGHT

Stella was trying so hard to keep relations between her and Richard on a socially acceptable level and was still ensuring that he had a home and a hot meal to which to come home each evening. Despite everything, she was well aware that she was totally in the wrong and a man's failure to take his wife into the realms of sexual ecstasy on a regular basis was hardly a hanging offence. If this were the case then she suspected there would be public executions on a weekly basis and East Kent would be known as gibbets'ville! He began talking to her in a normal and civil manner on the first of July and she wondered if this date had any significance for him. He did seem to realise that she had been making a considerable effort to say sorry for letting him down in the way she had and that possibly, just possibly mind you, she had got this bloody Dale Ingram out of her system once and for all. He longed to ask her that very question but could not face the agony of a hedged or negative reply. Certainly his spies had told him that Master Ingram was seeing Amanda Broughton on a very regular basis and this had to be good news for she was a most attractive woman and could give Stella at least ten years he reckoned. Unbeknown to his wife he had explored her wardrobes and found rubber boots, an incredible pair of high-heeled red rubber thigh boots, rubber swimming hats, rubber gloves, a complete schoolgirl's outfit including Panama hats, sandals and wellingtons. He found it all totally weird and could not begin to get his head round it all. Try as he might the idea of seeing Stella in any of this odd collection of gear did nothing for him at all, and the thought of roping her up before intercourse seemed to be nothing but a waste of good bonking time.

"It's the Change of Life! It's got to be," he thought to himself, for there could be no other reason for her most irregular behaviour. Dale Ingram was a very presentable fellow but was hardly in Richard's league and certainly quite unable to keep Stella in the way in which he did. Having decided therefore that she had reached that stage in her life at which time women become even soppier than normal, Richard began to feel much softer towards his errant wife and decided that he would forgive her and put the whole wretched business down to a form of temporary insanity. "Yes, that's it... hormones and things, poor old soul's been off her head for the past few months and I didn't spot it," he concluded.

Stella was so delighted with Richard's obvious change of heart and began to hope that possibly, just possibly mind you, they may be able to save their marriage after all. She knew that he would never understand her sexual desires and probably thought that she was totally bizarre in such matters but she could live with all that just so long as he forgave her for her unforgivable behaviour. She saw less of Dale in her attempt to create a feeling of trust between Richard and herself but the periodical meetings were still, oh so wonderful for her. She fully realised that one more indiscretion on her part would mean the end of her relationship with Richard, and if that happened then the life she enjoyed at present would, nor could, ever be the same.

Dale had expressed an interest in her schoolgirl outfit from time to time but she had never let him see her in it until one warm and sunny August afternoon when she had met up with him at Croft House having, for once, hatched a plan of her own. Having talked as they undressed and pulled on their boots she suddenly suggested that it was about time she did the tying up and he was tormented instead of her.

'I seem to recall that you enjoyed the last time I had you at my mercy,' Stella reminded him.

Dale was forced to admit this had been the case even though it was more than thirty years ago.

'You found feelings in me that I had never experienced before and it was probably just as well that neither of us really knew what was actually happening to our bodies.'

After a short debate Dale found his hands being bound expertly behind his back and then he was made to lie on his stomach on the carpet while his booted ankles were bound together and then looped to his wrists and pulled tight. He was hog-tied like a Christmas turkey and then saw to his horror that the bathing cap had been brought out.

'This is a bit of a girlie thing Dale but you've got to experience it to know what we go through every time we are in your power,' explained Stella as, despite vociferous and firm threats from her prisoner, she pulled the rubber cap into place and buttoned up the chin-strap. Dale felt ridiculous but noted that he was fully aroused and desperately wanted her hands on him. He also knew that the ball-gag would be produced and fitted inside his mouth next and so it proved. Stella pushed him over on to his side and was startled to behold the massive erection he already was showing.

'My! We are a big boy today aren't we…and I haven't even started on you yet!' she laughed in a throaty way which terrified him.

'Goo Gahcod!! Corr ghat kackit goo aughgat!' Dale desperately tried to clarify exactly what he wanted to do to his gorgeous captor but realising the futility of it all groaned, 'Ahh Gloody Gell!!'

'I do believe my dear little Gahcod wants to say something to me? Tough baby boy but I'm afraid that's the way the cookie is crumbling this afternoon. As they say in the pictures… *"You ain't seen nuthin' yet!!"*'

Stella laughingly disappeared into the bathroom after having put him back on his tummy and re-emerged a few moments later wearing her gymslip and schoolgirl wellingtons and nothing else.

'Does this bring back memories darling?' she taunted as he groaned in frustration at his inability to profit from her dress. Squatting down on her haunches inches away from his face she allowed him to smell the rubber of her boots and see the whole of her womanhood through the brown twin pillars of shiny rubber. 'You can see but you cannot touch Dale… but I can still touch you. If you want me to help you then lick my boots like you did the last time.' She unbuckled the gag and allowed him to gasp.

'You little bitch Stella. Will you please take this bloody stupid hat off my head? You wait my girl… just you wait.'

'My boots Dale, let's see you lick the toes all over and then I might feel generous enough to give you a little light relief. I trust your bathing cap isn't too hot? You look very fetching in it I must say. I'm certain the lovely Amanda would approve. My boots, Dale… now… or the gag goes back in.'

Dale knew he had no option and with the same view still in front of him he proceeded to lick her boot tops as fast and as comprehensively as he was able, watching her wet body in front of him all the time. Eventually she took pity on him and pushing him over on to his side once more she began to stroke him very slowly but nevertheless very firmly to an inevitable brain-bursting climax he was never to forget. He felt his very being was going to explode and as he fought the cords that bound him the precious moment arrived and his love for this remarkable woman erupted forth.

Untying him and allowing him to remove the wretched cap and hurl it to the farthest corner of their room Stella removed her gymslip, and came to him in Edna's wellingtons as he took her in his arms and started a bout of passionate love-making that was to last almost two hours. Dale was almost a man possessed as he found more and more energy and desire to show Stella how much he adored her. All the memories of the young tomboy had come flooding into his brain and he now knew, deep down, that his romance with rubber had most assuredly commenced in those early days. The scent and the sight of his lovely leader in her boots had been with him for over thirty years and today's exciting session had brought the explanation for why he was like he was to the surface of his comprehension, clearly and unequivocally.

They were physically unable to move or speak for almost half an hour after they had untwined their wet bodies, just laying there on the bed breathing deeply and occasionally allowing their hands to touch. Eventually Dale rose and said quietly:

'Stella, my darling Stella… that was quite something. Do you realise what your outfit did to me, even after all these years?'

'I don't think it would have been possible not to notice what my appearance did for you Dale. I don't know if it was the fact that you were tied up but I have never seen you so excited.'

'I just wanted to be held darling and your taunts only made it more impossibly wonderful. You do realise that you will now be licking boots for an awfully long time to come. God! It was so humiliating to be placed in such a position but I know it's something I have had coming to me for quite a time… and my goodness, didn't you make the most of it!'

Dale was still in quite a state about all that had happened and reaching over he found a piece of cord with which he bound Stella's wrists together as she lay beside him. Stella was just too weary to object and rolled over passively on to her stomach wondering what on earth he could possibly do to her after all that had gone before.

'No hurry darling but the only way you will be freed today will be after you have licked my boots in exactly the same way as I licked yours,' and so saying he relaxed once more, on his back, and gazed at the ceiling in anticipation of Stella having to do as he had ordered, sooner or later.

After about five minutes she propped herself up on one elbow and pleaded to be untied.

'I'm just deadbeat Dale darling, and honestly can't do anything else at all. Please let me off this time.'

She knew that Dale would *never* let her off, but it was worth a try and after a few minutes of being cross with him, then being sweet to him and then exploding with venom all over him, she finally got up onto her knees and bending down licked his boots from top to bottom.

'There you bugger! Are we now equal? Have you had your pound of flesh?' she asked.

Dale felt that honour had been satisfied as he first stooped to pull off her boots and then gently untied her wrists, kissing her flawless back as he did so. It had been a great afternoon at Croft House and although it had been very different from what Dale had had in mind he could not have been more fulfilled. Stella had been wonderful and the timing of her re-appearance as a schoolgirl after he had been subdued had been inspirational. They had a tray of tea and biscuits sent up to the room and took far longer than ever before to prepare to leave the hotel.

Stella was home and changed long before Richard got back from a meeting in London with the new Company Secretary, Jerome Hill, and greeted them in the entrance hall with a smile from ear to ear. The two men only wanted a coffee and a brandy each as they finalised a particular plan they wanted to put into practice concerning the tenants' responsibilities for keeping the decorative state of their properties in a fair and reasonable state. It had always been the case that each tenant would complain that he had taken over a complete 'hovel' but that now they were leaving it resembled Buckingham Palace, save for the fact that their successors were already likening the place to a 'hovel' once more! Richard had warmed to Jerome's suggestion that an annual assessment of the tenants' dilapidation charges would leave no-one in any doubt as to what it would cost them to restore the internal decorative state to a 'fair and reasonable' state of repair, and may even encourage their tenants to spend money on the premises more regularly rather than have a frantic and expensive total redecoration of the premises at the time of their departure.

After a brief stay Jerome thanked Stella for the coffee and brandy and bade them goodnight. Richard was extremely pleased to have prised Mr Hill from the Bass conglomerate, for he was a man who although still quite young was nevertheless a very experienced and canny performer. He hated admitting it but he missed George Banyard every single day as things that ought to have been done were left and his 'sounding board' for the past twenty years was no longer there to listen and advise. His successor had built up quite a reputation of being a pretty ruthless character if needed, certainly not one to 'tug his forelock' to popular demand and appeared to have made the transference from 'Big Six' Brewer to Family Brewer with great success. Mr Banyard would have been a very hard act to follow in normal retirement circumstances but his shameful departure from the Company had made such a change much easier to accomplish.

Stella was absolutely whacked and had yawned several times before Richard told her she should get off to bed before she fell asleep in her armchair. He hesitated before adding, 'I thought I might move back in to our bedroom dearest... if that's OK with you?'

'Of course it's fine by me Richard. It's where my husband should be sleeping and I've missed having you near me these past months. I realise the reason of course but we do seem to be getting our act together again and this is such a heartening move for me I promise.'

The words were true for although he was absolutely hopeless when dealing with her emotions that did not make him a bad person and he really still was the man she had fallen in love with and married all those years ago. The fact that this man from her past, this wonderfully sensual man from the backwaters of her mind had made her realise the true extent of the joy and fun there was to be had from sexual intercourse was not Richard's fault...it had just happened. The idea of making love this evening filled her with apprehension for her body had taken all it could take but in the event Richard was just happy to be back in bed with her and read his Brewers' Manual contentedly until the lights were switched out.

At about the same time Dale was switching his own bedside light out. He too, was exhausted from the sexual intensity of today's meeting with Stella but very clear in his own mind that his sexuality and the special preferences he and Stella shared were a direct result of those early juvenile sorties into the world of male and female attraction. It had been one hell of a day and Stella had bewitched him yet again… she really was one hell of a woman!

'Gee Gee' Tremlett and Dale were off to Maidstone where one of the 'Big Six' Brewers were introducing a new Tied Trade Director to the South Eastern Brokers. They had reached the bottom of the Old Dover Road and the roundabout, which took them on to the ring road that surrounded the City of Canterbury. Mr Tremlett had his own views on everything including motoring in the UK and his thoughts on roundabout manoeuvring were quite explicit… big cars must be given right of way by smaller cars! A lady in a small Ford Anglia was on the roundabout and just about to pass by their car when 'Gee Gee' shot out in front of her causing her to break frantically and the cars touched. Oblivious to the traffic around her and almost apoplectic with rage the woman tore round to Mr Tremlett's window and started screaming at him, calling him all the names under the sun and generally letting him know and the world know that he had no right to be on the road at his age. 'Gee Gee' wound down the window and beamed at her.

"Oh my God," thought Dale, "Please don't beam at her!"

'Good morning, my dear. May I suggest, before you do yourself a mischief, that you get a hold of the current edition of the Highway Code and turn to page 14. Halfway down the page you will find a paragraph in heavy black type. READ IT my dear and on this occasion I will take no further action against you! Good day to you.'

The poor soul stood there with her mouth open as impatient car horns blasted her back to her slightly dented vehicle and watched as Mr Tremlett's huge black Humber Hawk shot away from the scene of the accident.

'What does the passage in the Highway Code refer to sir?' asked Dale as they left Canterbury.

'Haven't the faintest notion my boy,' the old man chuckled. 'But neither did she and it saves taking insurance details and all that nonsense. Wretched woman shouldn't be allowed on the road. If I had my way I wouldn't let any female loose on the highway in charge of a motor vehicle except for my daughter who is an extraordinarily competent driver. It's a proven fact that they are different to we chaps. They are temperamentally not able to deal with tricky situations like roundabouts and passing other vehicles. For heaven's sake, I don't blame the ladies, it's just the way they are!'

Deal smiled to himself for he had heard the Guv'nor's views on the female of the species and the motor car on many occasions and particularly after he had produced some quite unbelievable piece of awful driving which had left other drivers with a permanent nervous twitch and a reluctance to continue driving themselves. However his eighty-year-old brain still worked far faster than anyone he knew and he couldn't help laughing out loud as he brought to mind the look on the poor lady's face as his Guv'nor had reprimanded her. 'Gee Gee' knew what he was laughing about and the two men were still chuckling as the Humber met up with the M2 motorway.

The meeting went pretty much to norm as the young Tied Trade Director, with his degree in some obscure subject safely tucked in his belt, proceeded to let the assembled company know of his stack of new ideas that were going to justify his appointment and make life easier for everyone including the tenants and the Brokers. It was par for the course as every new Tied Trade director always had a 'refreshingly new' plan that was going to change the world of public house tenancies. Mr Tremlett always had a large pad and appeared to be making copious notes as the words of wisdom were showered on the heads of the biggest band of old cynics this side of the Thames. In actual fact he was writing a letter to his daughter in Australia but that was for him to know and for this blithering young idiot to find out. Any small quip from the eager lips of the Director saw the Brokers fall about with mirth as they jockeyed for position in the popularity stakes. The meeting over, 'Gee Gee' had a few words with his old rival Claude Spatwell and they agreed that as far as their two firms were concerned they would carry on in their normal fashion as the theorist ideas of young Master Lester Barrett BA would never work, 'not in a month of Sundays!' Both the old rascals enjoyed the buffet however and reassured Mr Barrett that he was a real breath of fresh air to the industry omitting to explain that he had very much got up both their noses!

The trial was imminent and on the way home Mr Tremlett enquired as to whether Dale would be called to give evidence. Dale told his Guv'nor that Banyard had verified the facts of the case where he had been involved in the rescue, and he doubted he would be needed. However if the Prosecution wanted him there then he would most certainly attend. George Banyard had virtually admitted to every charge levelled at him in the hope of a little less severe sentencing and the matter was not expected to last too long. William Sackett's continued assertion that he had seen nothing or knew nothing of Stella's abduction was well supported by the customers and the powers that be saw little point in taking this particular prosecution any further. Paperwork recovered from Banyard's house however clearly listed all those involved in the bootlegging exercise and this long list of publicans and illegal retailers which included Sackett, Mole and Tony Lucan would possibly be dealt with in another court at another time. Dale had been particularly keen to let the police know of the most helpful part Tony Lucan had played when told of Stella's perilous plight and he and Inspector Haith had discussed this aspect at some length. Ted Haith was a straight copper and knew the value of Lucan's underworld investigation and revelations that night. He promised to do all he could to keep him out of court without making it pretty obvious that he was getting preferential treatment, being aware that, although Tony Lucan was a rascal and a 'chancer', he was not a real criminal in the true sense and had been as horrified as the next man when news of Stella's abduction was made known to him.

'I reckon that if we can manage to quietly delete Lucan's name and about six other "minnows" from old Banyard's list of those publicans who were receiving illicit stocks and merely give them a severe warning that should take away any direct suspicion from his shoulders,' Ted Haith told Dale. 'I'll try and sort it out with my superiors before it all gets too complicated to organise.'

CHAPTER TWENTY-NINE

THE TRIAL

The Trial was held at the Maidstone Crown Court and attracted the attention of some of the National Press, although not making the front pages. George Banyard's absolute determination to plead guilty to all the charges that were levied at him made life much easier for all concerned, and meant that he would not be tried by a jury along with his motley crew, but merely sentenced at the conclusion of the trial. George remained quite sure in his own mind that he had been rendered temporarily 'money mad' because of the unexpected and very high returns he had gained over the eighteen months of the exercise. In his wildest dreams he had not visualised the wealth that would be lodged in his hidden accounts and Stella's untimely entry into his world of crime had unhinged him from normal decent feelings of kindness and humanity.

'It was as if she had ceased to be Mrs Stella Rigden Ackeson, the wife of my Chairman,' he had explained to his Counsel. 'To me she was just a nuisance, a temporary hiccough, something that had to be removed and kept out of sight and mind permanently. I can't believe that I was intending to actually do away with the poor woman and it will always be an agonising and unanswered personal question as to whether I could actually have allowed her to be drowned. Was I that insane? Could I have committed murder? I tell myself "**NO!**" but how can I be totally sure?'

George also refused to admit to there being anybody else involved at the top of the tree as it were, a fact he had most certainly hinted at to Stella, claiming that he had just made such a comment to make her believe it was a bigger syndicate than she had imagined. In view of his willingness to tell the truth about every other query raised, the matter was therefore not pursued with any enthusiasm and finally dropped from the investigation. Stella still retained doubts as to whether George had been totally truthful over this one fact although unable to even comprehend who such a person could have been. He would not, however, assist overmuch on the parts played by his small band of miscreants sensing that Stella's forthright and honest testimony and their own complete inability to avoid dropping their cohorts even deeper into the mire would be more than enough to convince any juror of their guilt.

The cases of the three dray lorry drivers, Ray Bryant (Baldy), Ciaran O'Canter (Check Shirt), Jocky Marshall (Shaven Head) and their diminutive foreman Dickie Dean were not helped, as George Banyard had anticipated, by their constant lying, counter-charging and refusal to admit to any guilt whatsoever. George took the blame for virtually everything but did confirm, as it would have been both pointless and unworthy not to have done so, that they had all worked for him since the outset and had carried out the collection of illicit goods in France and done the deliveries and collected the cash this side of the Channel. He would not enlarge over the part they had played over the abduction of Stella or on her account of the inhuman treatment suffered whilst in their hands. He did confirm that he, George Banyard, had prevented Ray Bryant's attempted rape and possible buggery of Stella by his timely entrance into the cellar of her confinement.

It was accepted that the awful Tommy Mole had not known of Stella's imprisonment in one of his disused cellars but note was taken that he had thought 'they were storing contraband down there'. It was also taken into account that he had done absolutely nothing after watching the removal of the chained Stella from his cellar and being told of their plans for her by the wretched Bryant. His plea that he was frightened of the thugs and feared for his own life if he had rung the police was taken up by the Prosecution and used against him with telling effect. There was never going to be enough evidence to convict William Sackett of having had anything to do with the abduction from his car park. His story of complete ignorance of the whole affair was backed up by far too many people and Stella had confirmed that although she could hear plenty of noise coming from the bar area she had not actually seen anybody but Bryant, O'Canter, Marshall and Dean. Sackett however was on the list of those licensees who had been receiving illicit goods from the Banyard consortium and so his future did not appear all that bright.

All in all, the Trial was a fairly low-key affair with the national press and the local weekly papers making out George Banyard to be a rather sad old man who had just 'got it all wrong'. Despite the almost horrific consequences of his ruthless actions there was a certain amount of sympathy for him because of his total honesty, his refusal to accept any circumstantial evidence for the actions he had taken and the abject sorrow he felt for letting down his Chairman and the Brewery Company that had been his life for such a long time. His Barrister was magnificent and in mitigation made much of the superbly professional and loyal service his client had given to the Wetton Ackeson Company. Knowing that George Banyard's total honesty must be used to the fullest extent he made it very clear to Judge Caroline Starling that his client pleaded guilty to all the charges and put great trust in her to take into account the state of mind that George Banyard found himself in as money poured into his coffers and in such a short time had made him a very wealthy gentleman. He praised the man's full acknowledgement of the seriousness of his crimes and reminded her that he was an elderly and rather fragile gentleman for whom incarceration would be an awesome burden to bear.

Having duly been found guilty on all counts George Banyard was given a ten-year sentence for kidnapping and false imprisonment and a further five years for master-minding the fraudulent evasion of duty on chargeable goods over a period of eighteen months, the two sentences to run concurrently. Judge Starling, in her summing up of the case, praised him for his honesty and contrite demeanour since being apprehended. However she felt that Mrs Rigden Ackeson's ordeal had been such, that any less severe sentence would have been both inappropriate and unrealistic. He accepted his sentence with stoicism and apologised yet again for his sins before disappearing from the view of the public.

The four creeps who had abducted Stella all were sentenced to five years imprisonment with Ray Bryant getting a further two years because of his vicious treatment of Stella. The long list of local Licensees who had been receiving the duty free goods was dealt with at another place at another time but there were twenty-seven names on the list and all lost their licences as a result with several receiving custodial sentences for the amount of 'ferrying' they had carried out once the contraband had been deposited with them. Mole and Sackett were both amongst this latter group with the latter's sentence causing Inspector Ted Haith great joy and satisfaction. The sentences were to play a big part in lowering the amount of contraband that was coming in through the outlet of the cross-channel ferries and into the local hostelries for some time to come.

No mention was made of Tony Lucan in this second Hearing and so it appeared that Ted Haith had been true to his word and that a small group of 'naughty minnows' had indeed been omitted from the Customs & Excise charge list thus clouding the issue and ensuring the future well-being of Mr Lucan.

CHAPTER THIRTY

CORNWALL

Following their wonderful Hogmanay evening and their conversation with fellow diners Steve and Angela, seeds had been sown in Dale's mind about a first ever visit to Cornwall and Amanda was absolutely ecstatic when he mentioned the possibility of them spending four or five days together in the West Country.

'Oh Dale! It's a wonderful idea. I haven't been down there since childhood but my memories are full of wonderful beaches and glorious scenery. Please! Please count me in. I can organise a few days off with the Sandwich gang and being a one-woman outfit it will be hard for me to get away for any longer than you suggest at this particular time in my career.'

Dale very much wanted to see Truro and so booked in for one night in early October at an hotel near the City centre and then organised another four nights at the Mullion Cove Hotel which was situated quite near to Lizard Point. He felt that this would prove to be an excellent base from which to explore the famous beauty spots of England's most isolated County. Amanda, true to her word, sorted out her duties and as their day of departure drew near she became more and more excited at the prospect of sharing five whole days with the man she had grown to adore.

Being unaware of what Cornwall would throw at her in early October she had packed summer and winter gear and so felt equally confident and capable of dealing with warm sunny days or the wind, mist and wet weather that could so easily dominate the area for days on end. Her bathing cap, rubber gloves and riding boots were all included and also, in the very unlikely event of Dale forgetting anything, she also tossed four lengths of gold silken cord into her travelling bag.

'Can't be too careful,' she muttered to herself, feeling a warm glow of pleasure surge through her at the anticipation of what lay ahead. 'I wonder if any poor female has ever been bound to the most southerly rock in England?' she mused. 'Oh my God! He wouldn't! Would he?' Her vision of herself at Land's End, spread-eagled on a craggy rock with the Atlantic Ocean pounding all around her and a huge audience of anorak-wearing bird-watchers, and American and Japanese tourists, cameras clicking like mad, had to be dispelled quickly and the shrill tone of her mobile 'phone effectively ended the nightmarish scenario of her daydream. It was Stella, who wanted to go riding with her on the following Wednesday and then have some lunch back at *Clover Leys*. The two ladies still rode out quite frequently but Stella had been putting a lot of effort into really getting her marriage back on an even keel and had gained loads of 'Brownie points' by supporting Richard at many of his Brewery functions and this had meant no meetings with Amanda or Dale for sometimes up to two or three weeks at a time.

Dale had told her of his intention to take Amanda to Cornwall. She had wept openly at the news but not in front of her lover. Her memories of her own trip to the magical Holy Island were so vivid in her mind and the thought that Amanda and Dale were off on a similar adventure was a tough blow to stomach. She had attempted to sulk but being securely bound at the time of Dale's devastating news and therefore quite unable to prevent him from making her perform like some deranged tart from the more seedier quarters of Montmartre within five minutes of hearing same tended to ruin the effect somewhat.

'I must say, you took it all far better than I had expected or could have hoped darling,' Dale had remarked.

'Oh darling, I'm just so pleased for you and Amanda. I would love to be with you but realise that I can't wangle it so that's that,' she replied, failing to add, 'and how would you expect me to have behaved with my legs stretched wide apart and that bloody wriggling, squirming, vibrating, extending and contracting mechanical toy of the Devil being paraded in front of me!?'

Amanda confessed that next Wednesday was impossible because of 'Cornwall' and waited for some acid response. Instead she was so relieved to hear her friend admit that she had 'quite forgotten about their trip' but that she 'would be very interested to hear all about it the following week'. Amanda confirmed she would meet her for lunch at the 'Red Lion' in the village of Wingham one day that week and have a 'girlie' chat about the break.

'I'll ring you when I get back,' she promised.

'Don't forget your boots and that delightful cap darling,' Stella teased.

'My God! I'd rather forget my toothbrush and hair-drier!' came back the swift retort.

Their trip down to Truro was uneventful with both sharing the driving and by three o'clock they had booked in at the Charlton, one of those lovely old hotels on the Falmouth Road, and were exploring Cornwall's capital City. The Cathedral, as in Canterbury and so many other small Cathedral Cities, tended to dominate the whole centre and most of the shopping and business fraternity saw this fairly modern Anglican Cathedral looking down on them at every twist and turn as they went about their daily lives. Lemon Street, with its Georgian Parade of beautiful residences appealed to Dale enormously whilst Amanda loved seeing round the old granite City Hall in Boscawen Street.

Amanda's enthusiasm had always enchanted Dale and as this lovely female chattered away, pointing out this and then asking about that he found himself totally absorbed in watching and listening to her. She knew so much about so many things and her comments were constantly both interesting and enlightening.

But Dale was Dale and he would never change. As she informed him that they *must* stop at the Royal Cornwall Museum he was picturing his lovely companion…*as the red-headed Maureen O'Hara in the film… oh blast it! What was it called? She was a thigh-booted pirate captain who strode the poop deck of her ship and took very unkindly to being bound in chains and brought before the Governor.* By the time he had 'rescued' her, Amanda had gone off on another tangent and was informing him that the site of the Cathedral had been Holy land for over six hundred years! They walked slowly back up the gradually rising hill that is Falmouth Road and were tired but happy holiday-makers by the time they were safely back inside bedroom number fifteen.

After refreshing showers and an hour of warmth and loving they decided to walk back down to the City centre and sample the fare of one of the many eating-houses situated there. An Indian Restaurant proved to be an excellent choice with good atmosphere, authentic cuisine and excellent lager to cool down their palates. The night air was not cold and they walked their dinner down by strolling around the narrow lanes and streets that surrounded the Cathedral. By the time they had ascended what had now become, to their tiring limbs, the mountainous climb up to the Charlton they were worn out and collapsed into bed without even making themselves a hot drink from the ample range of sachets provided. Amanda, knowing that Dale was almost out on his feet, had pulled on her cap and came out of the bathroom wearing nothing else. Dale was already in bed and lay there admiring the sheer magnificence of her body as she posed in the doorway.

'You ready for one randy little swimmer darling?' she teased.

'Just get in this bed and I reckon you will be mine in about thirty-six hours' time!' came back the answer in double quick time.

Amanda jumped into bed with a playful squeak and pushed her rubber cap right under his nose, her cold hands searching for and finding the warmth of his member which was already beginning to rise to the occasion. Dale found the scent of the cap and the feel of Amanda's warm body just too much to ignore any longer and despite the aching tiredness of his limbs he was soon wallowing in the joy of making love to this gorgeous and quite shameless young woman who adored him and all the kinks in his character. Sleep came easily to them both and it was almost eight o'clock before Dale surfaced and slipped out of bed to shower, shave and put the kettle on for a morning coffee. He glanced at Amanda's lovely face as she lay on her pillow, still deep in slumber. "My God, you are a beautiful lady!" he thought to himself. "I am so lucky to have found you."

The pair of them made breakfast by the skin of their teeth but the cheery diminutive waitress made light of the fact that the breakfast room would have been shut in three minutes' time and Dale celebrated the start of his Cornish holiday with a full cooked breakfast whilst Amanda was content to have some toast and a pot of black coffee. The breakfast passed Dale's 'tomato test' with flying colours in that the two halves were soft, very hot and slid away from their skins quite easily. Dale had a fixation about the roadside cafés nationwide who thought it proper to serve in their *all-day breakfast* half of a luke-warm tomato that was as hard as the un-cooked variety and always made his abhorrence very clear to each 'twelve year old' Manager at the time.

The Mullion Cove Hotel was even more impressive upon the approach than it had appeared in the hotel's excellent brochure. Standing in solitary magnificence on the highest land it surveyed the delightful little working harbour and cove below and stood in well-kept grounds with a sheltered open-air pool to one side. Their room was on the first floor and gave them a panoramic view of Mullion Cove and the Atlantic Ocean beyond.

'Oh Dale!' Amanda gasped. 'Isn't it wonderful, it's going to be a wonderful holiday!'

The Lizard Point was their first point of call and most impressive it was too. Dale loved the fact that England's most southerly point had not been commercialised in any way and a strong wind gave the ocean a very sinister look about it as the foam flew from the rocks that were hardly visible to the naked eye, lurking just on or under the surface in readiness to bring down any seafarer who was unaware of the perilous position in which he had found himself. Dale took a few photographs with Amanda in the foreground of the majority and then they motored round to the attractive little fishing village of Cadgwith with its cottages crammed in on every available site, built mostly of local serpentine stone and with thatched roofs of varying patterns. The main beach of greyish shingle was home to the collection of village fishing boats whose owners still fished regularly, mainly for crabs and lobsters. A lovely old inn stood nearby and having had to walk from the car park above the village proper they were ready for a beer and some food.

Amanda then insisted on dragging Dale up a very steep winding footpath to the south of the harbour having ascertained from the innkeeper that this was the route to *The Devil's Frying Pan*, a 200ft deep hole in the cliffs which had been formed years ago by the collapse of a sea cave. It was a journey Dale did not regret making as a cauldron of very angry water spat and hissed at the two holidaymakers way up above and gave him what he hoped would be most impressive photographs of Mother Nature 'flexing her muscles' as it were. By the time they had got back to the hotel Dale's calf muscles were stiffening up and he was beginning to feel every one of his forty-two years. However the enthusiasm of Amanda still continued to cascade out of her and almost before he had locked the car doors and begun to make his way towards the hotel entrance he found himself being whisked away for 'just a little stroll' along to the south of the hotel. Some twenty-five minutes later and after a fairly steep stepped footpath down they arrived at the sandy cove that was Polurrian. The place was utterly deserted but Dale's thoughts of a future visit for 'swimming' snaps was swiftly knocked on the head by Amanda who could see that there were far too many places above from where she could have been detected.

By the time they had got back to their room it was almost six o'clock and Dale ran himself a hot deep bath into which he collapsed with the warning to Amanda that 'I shall be in here for some time and indeed may never get out again!' He did indeed wallow for almost three quarters of an hour constantly topping up the hot water and singing his own totally unique version of the 'Rose' Song from Carmen from time to time. Dale, along with most males when semi-submerged in hot water, really believed that his voice resembled the pitch of Mario Lanza and was quite hurt when Amanda expressed the opinion that she was 'glad there was no smell with it'.

Dinner was a superb meal served to a full dining room and Dale and Amanda tucked in with the gusto of a couple of navvies, making short work of each of the three courses that were brought to their table. A bottle of Merlot enhanced the meal and they ended the evening by taking coffee with a glass of Vintage Character Port in the adjoining bar.

Back in their room Dale had recovered from the 'assault course' of Cornish coastlines to which Amanda had subjected him and soon his lovely partner was in her rubber wardrobe and safely tied to the 5ft bedstead awaiting his attention. Dale felt absolutely exhilarated by all that had gone on since arriving in Mullion Cove and was in a particularly playful mood. With superbly skilful use of his number one vibrator he reduced Amanda to a frenzy of demented movement as she attempted to fight her inner lustful feelings, her restraining cords and the gag that bottled up the noise she had inside her.

'Goo! Goo gloddy **Gahcod**!' she screamed at him, her white teeth gleaming behind the ball gag.

'Oh no! I'm not being accused of being a Gahcod again am I,' he laughed. 'Why don't you just come out with it and tell me what you really think!'

'**Goo Gahcod! Kye Gont Goo Guck Gee? Goo Gucking Gahcod!!!**' Amanda screeched back at him.

Dale removed the gag but quickly slipped the chin-strap between her teeth whilst his lover gulped in some air and prepared herself for whatever Dale had in store for her. Cords were loosened and the two were as one immediately their bodies in total unison as their lips met and tongues entwined despite the restrictions of the strap still straddling Amanda's open mouth. The squelching noise of their rubber boots as they rubbed against each other enhanced Dale's already powerful performance and it was almost an hour before they fell apart and lay side by side, their emotions spent and their bodies exhausted.

Pulling off each other's boots they went under the shower together and washed the sweat of lovemaking from their tired bodies. Towelled and warm, her cap finally removed, Amanda quietly lay on the top of the bed and whispered to Dale:

'Oh, my darling Dale. I am so happy. I can't believe that you have come into my life in the way you have. When we make love it is as though the world has just stopped moving and we are in a permanent state of bliss. Do you realise how much I love you? Do you understand that I have never felt remotely like this about any other man in my life?'

Dale smiled at her in his rather lop-sided way. 'Yes my darling, I think I do know of these things and I find it totally wonderful that you do feel this way about me. I suppose, if I'm honest with myself I have been waiting all these years for someone, some very special lady with whom I could share my life. I thought that Stella was that person when she came back into my life but she is married and somehow that always prevented our love from reaching the top echelon of human emotions. With us it was sex, bloody wonderful sex of course, but just sex nevertheless. I have found with you my darling that there is a much deeper emotion to delve and you have awakened fresh thoughts and feelings in me, totally new and exciting plans are constantly rushing through my brain. You are wonderful in rubber and you obviously like the bondage that I demand. You are the love of my life, also my whore and simply sensational in both roles. I really want to spend the rest of my life with you… you… you gorgeous little gahcod!'

'What can I say?' whispered Amanda, close to tears at the words she had just heard.

'Well, a **"Yes"** would make me the happiest man on earth,' Dale replied.

'Do you mean you are asking me to marry you Dale?' she asked in faltering tones, scarcely able to believe what she was hearing.

'Yes my darling, that's exactly what I'm asking you to do,' he laughed.

Hurling herself across the bed she landed on top of Dale and squealed joyously, '**Yes! Yes!! Yes!!'**

'Oh well that's OK then,' he laughingly reassured himself. 'I suppose we had better start looking for a ring before you go off the whole idea.'

They talked and cuddled each other for over an hour before Amanda turned her back and allowed Dale to place one arm over her, locking her into his embrace, and within minutes they were fast asleep. It had been the best day of their lives and they knew it.

Wednesday morning was glorious and after another real English cooked breakfast which, this time, was consumed by both Dale and Amanda they drove to Gweek at the head of the River Helston and visited the National Seal Sanctuary, the largest of its kind in Europe, and saw the well-equipped hospital, the spacious outdoor pools and the underwater observatory. Amanda was most interested in the hospital and having introduced herself was welcomed in and given a very special tour whilst Dale camped by the sea-lion pools and watched the antics of several of the species who were, for various reasons, unable to be returned to the open seas. Next stop was the small harbour town of Porthleven where they lunched at the impressive Harbour Inn and walked the total length of the harbour area. By the time they arrived at the popular holiday resort of Perranporth the sun was burning with the intensity of an August afternoon. Seeing a shop in the main shopping street advertising WET SUITS FOR HIRE – ALL SIZES Dale was quick to persuade Amanda to take advantage of the weather and to try their hands at the art of surfing. The Atlantic rollers were certainly rolling but not too intensively and they had soon used the changing huts provided and with 'baby' boards tucked under their arms the long walk down to the water across a three mile stretch of golden beach commenced. Amanda looked sensational in her black and maroon wet suit that emphasised the sheer perfection of her body and Dale's black and yellow suit fitted him far better than he had dared hope. As they got halfway between the shoreline and the promenade Dale produced Amanda's white cap and tossed it to her.

'Are you *ever* without a bathing cap?' she queried.

'You never know when you might need such things darling and let's face it, it will keep your hair pretty dry during our surfing experience won't it.'

'And allow you to take several "on the surface" perfectly legitimate photographs of me in rubber from head to foot I have no doubt... you haven't got my boots tucked under your suit somewhere have you by any chance?'

Amanda pulled on her cap and Dale took several shots of his darling fiancée-to-be as she struck a series of provocative poses with a backdrop of the foaming surf enhancing the realism of the whole thing. A passing American couple volunteered to take a photograph of them both and ended up taking about five shots as they hugged each other.

'Do you want one without your hat on honey?' enquired the large Texan lady.

'Oh no,' sighed Amanda. 'Let's allow the picture tell the story as it is.'

'Well you sure look mighty handsome in any case my dear,' her husband added comfortingly.

'Hear! Hear!' cried Dale.

'GAHCOD!' came back the reply and thanking their transatlantic cousins the two lovers left their towels and camera on the pretty deserted beach and ran hand in hand into the surf. The water was cold but the protection of the neoprene suits allowed them to spend a joyous hour trying and failing hopelessly to conquer the art of surfboarding. As the afternoon wore on so the temperature began to drop but a jog along the water's edge soon had them both warm as toast and thoroughly exhilarated by their adventure.

Back in the hotel and after warm baths the two lay on the top of the bed and discussed their day and the plans for tomorrow. Amanda was absolutely vibrant and happiness oozed from her. She teased him over his kinky habits and listened intently as he explained some of the things that had governed his sexual way of life over the years.

'I suppose you could say that Stella as a schoolgirl was a role model for the vast majority of women with whom I've ever had any relationship. She was intelligent, a brilliant organiser and an extremely practical individual. She did however adore being tied up by we lesser mortals and suffer the pangs of humiliation as the male stood over her helpless body. I have always thought, and most men with whom I have discussed the matter agree with me, that the female of the species is vastly the more superior force in any partnership. It seems to me that only the feminists of this world don't appear to have got the message. One has only to look at the creatures of the animal and bird kingdoms to see exactly the same procedure occurring. The male of the species will strut around preening himself, roaring, breaking wind and generally doing bugger all to assist the welfare of those nearest and dearest. His mate however is organising, making the home, having the babies and making it all work. I see you as this very special body of human beings who just wallow in being tied down or tied up and made to accept and deal with very natural sexual urges that are gently but very insistently nevertheless brought to bear by your captor. Rubber is Dale Ingram but this I put down to Stella and the Wellington boots we always wore for her games, the aroma never ceases to arouse me and I suppose it always will. You don't really mind do you darling?'

'Dale, I fell in love with you. I fell in love with all of you, every part of you. I love wearing all my gear and seeing the effect I have on you. Did you realise how excited you looked in the wet suit by the way? Hope the bulges don't show in the photographs. I had never been tied up in my life until that night in the cottage but the sensation of being completely at your mercy but in no danger whatsoever was, simply, the most exciting period in my life and I honestly doubt whether any woman could or would object to similar treatment from one she loved. A few may huff and puff in public but the bedroom is an inner sanctum, a very private place and I feel so lucky to be the lady with whom you want to settle down, for you really are a superb lover.'

Dale was so thrilled to hear the words tumble from Amanda's lips. She was an uncomplicated lady and tended to speak exactly as she felt at all times. He had never really questioned or regretted the kinks in his character feeling that the joy he experienced and appeared to give to his partners over the years justified everything. He had never hurt anyone and would have been mortified if he had been responsible for a rope 'burn' or an attack of cramp for instance. No, his game was one of mutual pleasure... first, last and always.

The hotel owners, Jim and Elizabeth Bones, toured the dining room that evening and seemed to know who everyone was, which in a way, was typical of the homely atmosphere of the whole place. They both knew the Hotel L'Horizon at St Brelade's Bay in Jersey, an hotel to which Dale had given valuation services over a number of years, and were delighted when Dale assured them that their attention to detail had reminded him very much of the L'Horizon's General Manager's way of doing things.

A very tired couple fell into bed that night and despite an attempt by Amanda to stir some life into her contented partner she was so sleepy that she herself was fast asleep before Dale. He mused over the day and turning on his side relaxed and placed his arm gently once more around the body of his beloved Amanda.

Their arrival at England's most westerly point, Land's End, the following morning was a wee bit of a disappointment to Dale who did not like, but fully understood, the commercialisation that had taken place over the years. However once they had got through the shops, shows and general waffle the sheer rugged beauty of the dramatic coastline lay before them. The day was cool with a really strong wind coming off the sea but the clearness of the day enabled them to see not only the Longships lighthouse some mile and a quarter away but also the Wolf Rock lighthouse which stands over eight miles from Land's End. Their surfing of the day before seemed a distant memory and Amanda was delighted she had chosen to wear her bright green wind and rainproof jerkin, black corded breeches and riding boots. On her head she had a black cloche-styled woollen hat similar to one she had seen Stella wearing to great effect. She looked wonderful and Dale took several photographs and also arranged for a snap to be taken of her standing beside a signpost pointing to New York in one direction with the mileage from Land's End showing 3147 miles and to 'Ash' in the opposite direction with the estimated mileage of 362 miles.

They then drove to the popular seaside resort of St Ives and were pleased that this was an 'out of season' visit as the place was still very busy. Beautiful beaches surrounded the town and a picturesque harbour with yet another sandy beach remained the central hub of the resort. Pubs, tea-shops, art galleries and china shops were everywhere and Dale sat by the harbour wall and demolished his first-ever traditional Cornish Pasty. Amanda had selected a 'medium' sized pasty for him, much to Dale's disgust, but he was grateful to her in the end as it proved to be very filling. Dale was anxious to try and find an engagement ring, but none of the many jewellers in the town appeared to have exactly what he was looking for and he accepted that possibly Canterbury or Maidstone might be a better bet. After an hour and a half of touring the shopping centre and all the twisting and turning narrow lanes that are part and parcel of the town they popped into a tea-house boasting 'Original Cornish Cream Teas' and enjoyed featherweight scones, home-made strawberry jam and quite the most delicious cream either of them had ever tasted. The jolly waitress was very taken with Amanda whom she made sure was 'one of them fillum stars' and simply *made* their day by telling Amanda, 'Well me dearie, iffum you're not a fillum star then you jolly well should be 'cos you're the prettiest thing oi've had in me shop all year, and that's no word of a lie!' As they left she was busily telling two other tourists that, 'She may fool some folks but she hasn't fooled me. She's a fillum star alright but obviously she wants to remain synonymous and incontinent!'

The rain was beginning to fall as they drove back to Mullion's Cove and they were more than happy to return to their bedroom and wallow in a very hot bath before getting under the sheets for a couple of hours before dinner. Amanda placed her arms around Dale and hugged him for all she was worth.

'Oh I have so enjoyed today darling. When I'm with you I feel so good in myself. I have never thought of myself as anything but an ordinary, run-of-the-mill kind of girl but with you I feel so sexy and so bloody female it's not true.'

'Oi think you look like one of them fillum stars me dearie,' Dale sleepily replied only to wake up with a start as the bathing cap was clamped over his nostrils to the accompaniment of a screech from his wicked partner as she climbed on top of his supine form.

'Like the smell me dearie?' she asked. 'Like to sort me out once and for all me dearie?'

They loved and laughed and loved again finally falling into a deep slumber that almost made them miss the dinner 'deadline'. Elizabeth

Bones was in the dining room as they fell through the door with a minute or two to go. She laughingly looked at her watch and cautioned, 'You are obviously not taking into account the bracing Cornish air… I can't think of any other reason that would make you so late?'

Their dinner was a leisurely affair and washed down with a bottle of Claret that, temperature-wise, could not be faulted. The idea of returning to Kent in another day or two seemed unthinkable to these two happy lovers and their chatter was of weddings, family life and their future together. Sleep that night came easily and once again Amanda backed her body into the warmness of Dale's embrace murmuring as her tiredness dominated. 'I love you so much my darling, darling Dale.'

The rain was coming down in 'stair-rods' the next morning and so both Dale and Amanda wore their warmest clothing and rubber boots. Dale was determined that the day not be wasted and they set off for nearby Poldhu Cove where they parked the car and pulling their rainproof jerkin hoods tightly over their heads they set off on a marked ramblers' trail and two hours later had arrived back at the car park, having inspected the Marconi Monument erected in honour of this very site where Marconi sent the first transatlantic radio signals on the 12th December 1901. They had also come across the Wesley Stone which commemorated John Wesley's preaching here to a group of Methodists who met on the site in the latter part of the eighteenth century and passed Polurrian Cove, Polbream Point and Men-y-Grib Point en route. The rain never ceased but the intensity of same did abate somewhat and by the time they were back at the car both Amanda and Dale were as warm as toast if somewhat bedraggled. It has to be admitted that the bedraggled state of Amanda had been brought about as much by Dale's attentions on her as by the weather itself. Finding a coastal and sea bird look-out 'hide' near Men-y-Grib Point and being fully aware that they had seen nobody on the walk to date, Dale soon had Amanda's hands tied behind her back and the bathing cap back on her head once more.

Slipping her stretch breeches down was not a problem and bending her backwards over the rough timber table they made love quickly but by no means quietly as Amanda's screams of delight dove-tailed beautifully into the sound of the multitude of various gulls that soared overhead in the air currents that lay above the coastline. Dale re-dressed her, leaving her hands still bound and then re-covered her capped head with the hood of her anorak and tied it tightly in place so that none of the white rubber was on show. Slipping the strap into her mouth he pulled her amber and black woollen scarf over the bottom part of her face. Amanda had allowed all this to go on without protest, doubtless wondering what in hell's name this madman was going to do next. But as he opened the door of the Hide and made it clear that she was going to carry on the walk the boots flashed out at his shins in real Stella fashion causing him to leap clear to avoid contact. Obviously she was not in a position to dictate and kicking and struggling, she eventually had to accept that her 'boots were made for walking' as Dale's gentle but firm hold guided her into the open air once more.

'One of theesh daysh I am going to gurder yoosh!!!' was one of the more comprehensible threats that Dale heard from behind the scarf but all went well, despite a continuous stream of furious lisped abuse from the muffled Amanda until, quite suddenly, a couple of hardy fellow ramblers appeared on the near horizon coming towards them. Amanda panicked and attempted to turn and run off in the opposite direction but was quickly hauled in by Dale who untied her hands and told her to 'just act naturally' as they got to within 200 yards of each other.

'Act nashherally! ACT NASHHERALLY! **HOW THE BLOOSHY HELL DO GOO EXPECSH ME TO ACT NASHHERALLY!!!'** she exploded from behind the scarf as the chin-strap got in between her teeth and her tongue, every other word.

Dale was almost beside himself with heavily disguised mirth as they passed the other walkers.

'Not a day for the faint-hearted!' he cried out.

'Too true Squire,' replied the taller of the two men. 'We've been out for almost three hours and you are the first human beings we've seen. Can we offer you a *Fisherman's Friend* lozenge? They really do warm you up although your good lady looks lovely and cosy to be sure.'

'Thank you most kindly sir,' replied Dale enthusiastically. 'We would love one wouldn't we darling?'

Dale heard something that sounded vaguely like 'sucking gahcod' come from behind the scarf as with great aplomb he took two of the warming boiled sweets and slipped one into Amanda's mouth almost in the way one gives a sugar lump to a horse. As soon as the two men were out of sight Amanda removed the hood and took off the cap and for the remainder of the short walk never stopped talking as her tirade against his outrageous behaviour put the position from her point of view very clearly and most firmly.

Dale let her do the talking and kept on nodding and shaking his head in what he hoped were the right places. There was no point in trying to interrupt her in full flow and by the time they were back at the car she subsided and left the stage clear for his response.

'Darling you were simply fantastic! Only you and I knew the state you were in and there was no way anybody else was going to find out... now am I right? You know I love you in your hat and the excitement of showing you off, albeit in a rather sneaky way, was absolutely wonderful. Don't be cross with me for loving you in my own way darling.'

Amanda was now calm again and now that the pulse-quickening adventure was over she was experiencing those joyous feelings that had invaded Stella after the escapades in the 'phone booth at the County Hotel and on the beach at Coves Bay on Holy Island. Yes, of course, she was now totally exhilarated by exciting her lover and she realised that this last episode was merely yet another chapter in what was going to prove a most thrilling life-style from this time forth.

'I'm not cross with you my darling Dale. I've never been so frightened in my life but I suppose I've just got to learn to trust you. I know deep down that you would never let me down or hurt me but I've got to tell you that you are a master at walking the tight-rope of potential utter humiliation. I adored being "taken" in the bird hut by the way, even tho' I'm sure I've got a splinter in my bum!'

'*Hide* darling, they call it a *Hide*.'

'Oh alright then clever clogs,' came back the reply. 'I've got a splinter in my *Hide*!'

Removing their soaking outer jackets they drove back into Mullion and walked around the twisting streets and narrow lanes before rain again forced them back into the car. Dale had been really enchanted by the rugged splendour of Lizard Point and so they drove the few miles back to where their holiday had started and sat in the car watching the power of the ocean as it roared against this, the most southerly point in England.

'When you see Mother Nature like this it makes you realise just how pathetically impotent we humans are. She has us in her grasp at all times and it will always be she who will call the tune to which we all dance,' Dale said softly, then changing the mood, he suggested another visit to the pretty village of Cadgwith and another chance to sample the excellent bitter and pub grub that was available there.

No more rain fell on their final day and before going back to their room they walked down the gradually sloping path from the hotel to the Mullion Cove Harbour and sat by the wall watching the ocean crashing against the black cliffs that attempted to shelter the small harbour from the worst of the battering. Amanda cuddled up to her Dale and squeezed his hand.

'It's been a wonderful day Dale. I know I went on at you but that was just my terror coming out and you know I love you so much really. Let's go back and have our hot baths now and have an hour or three in bed before the 'Last Supper'.'

As they lay together the two lovers talked of their four momentous days in South Cornwall and of the changes it had brought about in their lives. Their lovemaking over the past hour had been simply wonderful with Dale at his most caring and attentive. Amanda had been made to feel the most desirable creature on God's Earth as every erogenous zone of her body had been caressed and licked by this man who had asked her to be his wife. She had been totally naked the whole time with Dale not asking or imposing any code of dress for her. She had become almost comatose by the sheer unremitting love that Dale had expressed to her, both in his actions and by spoken words, and lay in his arms, half awake, half asleep and day-dreamed of the life they would share from this time. Stella, her dear friend and Dale's lover, would have to be told. Amanda's confidence had grown so much during her holiday and she now felt quite capable of ensuring that her rival ceased to be just that… a rival.

Dale was simply at ease with himself and his life. He had never been more sure of anything in his life. Amanda was great fun to be with, she was simply wonderful in bed and appeared to love rubber and bondage games as much as did he. She was a beautiful woman with intelligence and style and she was as keen to start a family in the coming years as was he. To make babies together and share the joy of family life was the something, he realised, that had been missing for these past years. Turning on his side he gazed at the lovely form of the lady who had agreed to be his wife, her bared breasts moving almost indiscernibly as she breathed in semi-slumber. He saw her lovely face, lips slightly apart and her auburn hair still damp from the hot bath and their exertions of the past hour. This was a woman to cherish and he vowed quietly to himself that this was a woman he would indeed cherish.

Amanda sensed his attention and opened her eyes. Still half asleep she murmured, 'Hello you darling man, do you want me to put on my cap or something?'

'No my darling lovely lady,' he replied with a lop-sided grin on his face. 'You keep that bloody cap out of sight. I just want you to get up and get dressed so that we actually make the dining room without having to race down the stairs and tumble into the place at the very last moment. All the time you lie here looking like this I will want to make love to you and so it's up to you to be the strong-willed one in this partnership.'

The next morning, after another excellent cooked English breakfast with the tomatoes coming up to scratch yet again, Jim and Elizabeth Bones were both around to wish them *Bon Voyage* in the manner that friends or relatives would do after a visit. But this was perhaps absolutely typical of the way in which the owners chose to run their business. It was as though their guests were 'family' for the duration of their stay and both Dale and Amanda felt that anyone coming to the hotel and falling in love with the charm of the place, as they themselves had, would be back time and time again.

It was a cold and showery journey of almost seven hours back to East Kent but with a good stop for lunch and shared driving duties the two lovers were in good shape by the time they got back to Amanda's cottage. Amanda brewed up a cup of coffee for them both and they sat and relived their adventures. Amanda had so loved her surfing at Perranporth and being given a *Fisherman's Friend* lozenge in what for her were most dramatic circumstances whilst on their circuitous ramble by Poldhu Point.

'Oh Dale, it is such fun to be with you. You are quite mad but I love every second of your madness and can't wait to find out what's going to happen to me next. Thank you for quite the best time I've had in my life. I am so thrilled that you want me to be your wife and can't wait to wear your ring and flaunt it to everyone unashamedly.'

Amanda was on duty first thing Saturday morning so Dale did not stay too long and arranged that he would see her the next afternoon and take her up to watch Canterbury's First XV play the might of Maidstone. 'Wrap up warm darling,' he warned, 'Our

Merton Lane Ground can be a very chilly place once the leaves start falling off the trees.'

He stopped in at the office on his way back to his flat and saw that he had a busy week ahead of him. 'Gee Gee' had left a hand-written note on his desk pointing out that he wanted to accompany him to a Change of Tenancy in Sevenoaks on the Monday and would Dale pick him up from his home at eight o'clock. Dale relaxed in the knowledge that by the time they arrived at the public house he would have been brought right up to date with all matters appertaining to the business. He knew the old boy would be thrilled to bits with his personal news and was aware that his affair with Stella had disturbed his senior partner not a little. He rang young Ben Herbert, his pupil, and organised that he made his own way to the house and got on with checking the trade inventory in order to check that all the items passing from outgoer to ingoer were still there and in working order. It was always a grotty job but so important that it was carried out with the utmost professionalism. Ben was a willing worker and a damn good centre three-quarter for Canterbury so his career was assured with the firm for the foreseeable future, or at least until he stopped playing in the first team! He was in the side for the morrow's match and Dale wished him well adding that it made it so much easier for him in the coming twelve months if Canterbury could put one over on the motley crew from Maidstone. Dale had quite a few old adversaries whom he saw from time to time and who were not slow to point out the sadness of supporting Canterbury as their own club won the annual fixture with depressing regularity. A victory over Maidstone was a rarity but something that must be savoured like vintage port and with Amanda on his arm, and later behind the steering wheel, he would be able to savour a few pints of Shepherd Neame 'vintage' bitter if the victory were indeed gained.

CHAPTER THIRTY-ONE

RUGBY

Saturday morning was dull and wet but by lunchtime the clouds had lifted and a weak sun was trying very hard to make some sort of impression on the proceedings. Dale put on his warmest winter coat, corduroy trousers, heavy brogues, his 'Broken Bones' club tie, and a warm shirt for he was well used to the gradual body-numbing coldness the damp ground produced over the course of eighty-five minutes of rugby football. Amanda was waiting for him and looked absolutely stunning, as he knew she would. She was wearing a black polo-neck sweater, a dog-tooth black and white check jacket, black stretch corduroy breeches and very shiny black rubber riding boots, which had obviously been cleaned and leathered since their walk around Poldhu Cove. On her head she wore her woollen cloche hat and her old country waterproof jacket lay on the side of the entrance porch.

They took the Rover and arrived just after the kick-off. Dale introduced her to all the old stalwarts, some fellow ex-team mates and others who were older and who had watched Dale perform in days gone by. Her staggering good looks provided a great deal of good-natured banter from the assembled company and Dale, who was very good at dishing it out, had to take their chiding in good spirit. All males present were utterly united in one respect... it had all been very much better in their day and they had all been a great deal more talented than this crowd of nincompoops who were wearing the black and amber hoops today!

In the end the superior goal-kicking skills of the visitors gave them a narrow and perhaps just about deserved victory, but it had been very close right up to the 'no-side' whistle and the relief on the faces of the old 'farts' from West Kent ensured that Dale's life would be tolerable for the next year. Young Herbert had enjoyed an excellent game, much to Dale's delight. In the bar Amanda chatted to the friendly gang that crowded into the Vice Presidents' Bar and impressed them by her comments about the game and the home side's showing.

'Christ almighty Dale!' muttered Bob Rook. 'You've picked a winner here haven't you. Not only is she bloody drop-dead gorgeous but she actually knows about rugby football! I don't suppose she'd go in for a "gang-bang" would she? Not that I could do much myself these days but I could hold the coats and get enormous pleasure by just watching!' Bob was a lovely man and openly confessed to the doubtful honour of never ever having been a Welsh schoolboy international. Dale had never met any Welshman with the exception of dear old Bob who had not played for his country at schoolboy level and had supposed that being almost impossible to prove or disprove it was a method used over the years by those from across the Severn, as a means of ensuring that upon joining a new club they would not have to start at the bottom and take half a season to find their playing level.

The beer flowed and Dale lost Amanda for long periods as all the randy old men of both Maidstone and Canterbury attempted to tell her what a bastard old Ingram was and how she would be much safer with them! It was all good fun and she thoroughly enjoyed herself. Dale eventually suggested they leave and have some supper at the 'Red Lion' in Wingham on the way home.

Peter and Barbara Martin were delighted to see them and were able to fit them into the fully-booked dining room as it was still fairly early and having extracted a promise from Dale that he would be away again within the hour. Dale was so happy just to have Amanda all to himself once more and was so pleased that she had enjoyed her first visit to his old club. She explained that her father had been a very keen player and committee member of his club and she had been forced to watch rugby since about the age of ten.

'I grew to actually love the game and all my early boyfriends were daft about rugby so my interest never waned until I was in my last two years at University and got involved with a hockey player…

'Oh God, *not a bloody hockey player!*' Dale interjected. 'Amanda, how could you? It is a well-known fact that all hockey players drink BABYCHAM and are useless in bed!' he teased.

'Not Julian, I promise you,' she retorted.

'Julian? Bloody Julian!! What sort of a bloody name is that for goodness sake? I rest my case milord,' he roared and they subsided into laughter at the outrageousness of Dale's comments. They demolished two rump steaks set in a gorgeous peppered sauce with plenty of French fries and garden peas, washed down with a bottle of the excellent 'House Red' and were on their way in plenty of time for Barbara to be able to re-lay the table for the nine o'clock booking.

'I was *so* proud of you today darling,' Dale remarked as they sat in front of the cottage's cosy wood-burning stove. Amanda was on the hearth-rug and, at Dale's request had stripped off and was only wearing a heavy red towelling robe and, almost inevitably, her riding boots. 'I know my old rugby mates and you knocked them all sideways I promise you. Over all the years I have been associated with the local rugby club I have rarely taken a female up to the ground and so it was very special for me to be able to show you off and announce to them all that Dale Ingram was in love and very deeply in love at that.'

'I'm glad that I didn't let you down Dale and I certainly don't expect to be up there too often with you I promise. My leisure time is so restricted and Saturday afternoons are normally taken up with shopping, washing and generally sorting the house out.' So saying she turned from the fire and slipping her robe off her shoulders she sat cross-legged in front of him and held her arms out towards him as the flickering flames cast shadows on her shapely body. Their lovemaking lasted into the small hours as they talked of their lives, their ambitions and their future plans, laying together, so happy and so at ease with one another. Dale told Amanda of his life as a member of the Stella Ward Gang and how he had worshipped their hoydenish and feisty leader and of his despair when she was taken away from them. She was interested in his early love affair with Peggy Graham and how easily she had adapted to his sexual demands taking into account that the 1950s were hardly the enlightened era of nowadays.

'Oh Peggy was far more aware of my needs than I was,' he laughed. 'She was a smashing lady and had I wanted her in corrugated iron she would have ordered the services of a ferrous arc-welder to produce an outfit for her. I suppose it would be fair to say that had National Service not taken me away to Germany for two years then we would have married and it would have been an excellent union for she was a very special lady with whom I was very much in love. He told of her appearance in a rubberised mackintosh, sou'wester and new wellingtons on the morning after she had realised his liking for rubber and had Amanda chuckling as he related the terror that went right through him as the enormity of his 'oddness' was brought to the surface.

'It seems to me that in the years between Peggy Graham and me you have not really enjoyed a lasting and deep love with any other woman. I am aware of Stella of course but I have to put that down to a form of childhood enchantment that became magnified in your inner sexual psyche because she was removed from your life, Wellington boots, ropes and all, when you were at such an impressionable age. I can quite understand the thrills you have experienced since meeting up with her again after all these years. For God's sake, I'm not some Sibylline lesbian and yet I found the sight of this oh so classy lady, spread-eagled in front of me and completely at my mercy one of the sexiest things I could ever have imagined… I couldn't wait to torment her. But that was lust on your part Dale, mingled up with deep affection and wonderful memories of the days of your childhood. You never did get the chance to get Stella out of your system did you?'

Dale found it hard to disagree with anything Amanda had said, knowing that the feelings he had for her were totally different to any emotions he had ever felt before. Sensing that tiredness was invading her he reluctantly decided that their evening must draw to a close and taking her in his arms he picked her up and climbed the stairs to her bedroom where he laid her down gently and went off to lock up, close the stove doors and generally tidy up. By the time he had cleaned his teeth and returned to the bedroom Amanda was purring softly in deep contented slumber. Feeling under the bedclothes he found her boots and gently pulled them off without disturbing her. Dale always had tended to lie awake after retiring to bed, taking stock of his day and musing on the events of the morrow. He was asleep in seconds this night as Amanda's back found his body and the comforting touch of his embrace.

CHAPTER THIRTY-TWO

CORNWALL THE AFTERMATH

Amanda had rung Stella and arranged to go riding on the Monday morning after her Surgery. She felt that things had to be discussed between the two of them in view of the way her relationship with Dale had progressed so fast and so wonderfully during their visit to the West Country. She fully realised that all the times that she had enjoyed with Dale had been duplicated by her lover and her friend but that was then and now it was different. She desperately hoped that Stella's disappointment would not cause a rift between them or a change in her feelings for Dale.

Arriving at *Clover Leys* she parked and strolled over to the stables where she found Stella in deep conversation with her old groom.

'Oh dear,' she laughingly told Amanda after finally sending Defferary on his way. 'Mrs Defferary is concerned about George Banyard's niece, dear young Edna, and was wondering if they should invite her down to stay in case she has no one to care about her now that her uncle looks like being away for some considerable time.'

Amanda knew of Stella's blackmail and the monthly forfeit she had had to pay as a result. As they rode out of the drive she was still laughing at the thought of Stella, dressed as Edna, staying for a week's hols at the Defferarys'. 'Knowing you as I do Stella, I really believe you could actually pull it off!'

They were well out towards Nonington when Amanda suggested they stop and let the horses have a breather. Sitting on an ancient tree trunk she began to tell Stella of all that had happened in Cornwall and how her feelings for Dale had become so much more intense as a result.

'I know that Dale loves you Stella and that he will always love you. You were his first love and the pair of you fashioned each other for all time in so far as sex is concerned. I know that deep down his love of rubber stems from you and the sight of you spread-eagled and helpless possibly excites him in a way that I could never hope to achieve…'

'When you saw me in that state did I excite you too Amanda?' interrupted Stella.

'Yes, you bitch, you jolly well did… and well you know it. There is something about you. I don't know what it is, maybe the way you stand or the way you move? It could be the fact that you are always so superbly elegant and unwittingly superior in everything you do and everything you say that makes you look so wonderful in bondage.'

'You look pretty good in rubber yourself Amanda, so don't put yourself down so much.'

'As I was saying,' persisted Amanda trying hard not to blush from the compliment that had been paid to her, 'Stella, you are married to Richard and you want your union to continue. You have worked so hard to save the marriage and both Dale and I are happy for you. You have a wonderful life and clearly you do not intend to slip up again. But what about Dale and I, Stella? What are we supposed to do with our lives? I want to get married and I want to try and have children. I love Dale with all my heart and I know he loves me but we both love you and don't want to hurt you in any way. When we do get married, and it really is beginning to look that such an event is not too far away, then I just couldn't bear to think that he is still meeting up with you and doing all those wonderful things that I know you do when together. I want it to stop Stella and I honestly think that Dale does too. He's never looked so set on anything since I first met him and I guess that the idea of having a wife and possibly children has finally got inside him and he loves the look of his future.'

Stella allowed tears to stream unashamedly down her cheeks as Amanda spoke. She had known, of course, that sooner or later this conversation was going to have to take place. Amanda was a red-blooded beautiful young woman in her mid-thirties and the urges she now felt were the most natural emotions for any female to have. How much she had longed for children herself. Richard and she had cried themselves to sleep so many times after yet another disappointment. Dale was the most gentle man she had ever met and would make a superb husband and a loving father. She realised too that everything that her friend had said was perfectly fair and absolutely true. She had enjoyed the most unforgettable sexual sessions on a regular basis since that chance meeting at the St Lawrence Cricket Ground. These were times she would never forget and could bring to instant recall for the rest of her life. He had awakened in her deep, primeval and basic feelings of lust of which she was not ashamed in the slightest and because of which she was now a much more confident and sexy woman. She liked herself and was delighted at who she saw looking back at her in the mirror. Amanda was just right for her Dale and now that she appeared to be losing him she knew, deep down, that she really only harboured feelings of joy for them both. "Mind you," she thought, "I will see Dale one more time and say goodbye properly."

'I do understand dear Amanda and I'm happy for you. I suppose I've known all along that you two would finally get your act together and that my contribution to Dale's idyllic existence would become surplus to requirements eventually. I'll say my goodbye to all that when I next see him Amanda and you have my promise that I won't be in the equation after that time. As you so rightly observe I do love Richard and he really didn't deserve the wrongs I have done him. I'll have my memories and I'll still have your love and your friendship. Does Dale know that we are talking about this by the way?'

'Yes! I wanted to talk to you first and give you my thoughts but he does know how I feel and I sense that for the first time in his kinky old life he really wants to become a loving "one-woman" man. I have a feeling that there have been one or two dalliances apart from us, you know.'

'I will miss being transported to this plateau of sexual heaven that Dale has always been able to provide Amanda and I won't pretend it's going to be easy 'cos it isn't. Isn't it just wonderful to be put through the agonies that Dale insists we suffer knowing deep down that eventually it's going to be just so good… you are a very lucky lady to be marrying such a man but, there again, I consider myself very fortunate to have experienced such love and such passion over these past months.'

Amanda was saddened by Stella's obvious reluctance to forfeit Dale's lovemaking but pleased that she had been realistic enough to know that it would neither be fair or possible for the situation to carry on as it had been for several months now. She trusted Stella implicitly and knew that if Stella said it was over then it was over. She didn't really want there to be a 'farewell' between her friend and Dale but did not push her feelings on this point. They must be allowed to finish the relationship by themselves.

When they got back to *Clover Leys* Stella invited Amanda in for a coffee and excused herself, leaving Amanda in the conservatory. She returned with a tray of coffee and biscuits and told Amanda that she felt like Edna every time she walked anywhere with the tray.

'I've got a present for you my dear and I hope they will bring you the same sort of joy they have certainly brought me.' She produced Edna's brown wellingtons and handed them over with a smile. 'I have no idea really why they continue to be the biggest single "turn-on" for Dale but it could be something to do with the fact that they are virtual replicas of my own boots that I wore in the "gang" days. Wear them Amanda and prepare yourself for a series of wonderful experiences.'

Amanda held the soft shiny rubber boots up and looked at them. They were unremarkable but she realised that what Stella had said would be absolutely true and the fact that she knew that by wearing them in front of Dale would make her become the most desirable female on the planet did a great deal for her own confidence and gave her a huge boost of anticipated joy.

'Thank you so much… I'll treasure them,' she murmured.

'Let's have a shower,' suggested Stella who was delighted when her pal quickly agreed. They washed each other with much laughter and paid much attention to those parts that Dale was so efficient at soaping and stroking. Once out and dry Stella suddenly suggested that they have 'a wrestle' with the loser having to wear the wellies and a cap and then submit to the winner. The last time Amanda had fought anyone had been in the fourth form when she had unashamedly goaded the school 'goody-goody', a certain Gillian Eyre, into a fight which had got them both brought up before Mrs Barton, the Headmistress, and as a result of which they had received hundreds of lines to write before being allowed to leave school. The look of mortification on Gillian's face had made it all worthwhile. The last time she had heard of her she was engaged to a Chartered Accountant. "Serves her right!" she had thought at the time.

Looking like the female equivalent of Messrs Oliver Reed and Alan Bates in their epic naked battle in front of a roaring fire in the film of D H Lawrence's book 'Women in Love', the two girls squared up and were soon struggling like mad to gain the ascendancy on the deep pile carpet of Amanda's bedroom. Stella's technique was far superior but Amanda was strong, very fit and twelve years younger. Gradually, to Stella's dismay, the younger woman's strength and fitness began to tell and after about five minutes she sat astride her hostess and pinned her hands to the floor.

'Game, set and match I think Stella… GET 'EM ON!'

'Don't suppose you would agree to the best of three falls?'

'GET 'EM ON!'

Stella dragged herself off the floor and reluctantly pulled on the shiny brown rubber boots and her white cap. Amanda, now in her tall riding boots, had gained the upper ground. She was the prima donna, the dominatrix and Stella the thwarted bondswoman.

'Oh well then, where do you want me?' she asked rather sulkily for she had really wanted this role play to be reversed, feeling confident she would have been able to subdue Amanda without too much trouble. Soon, and with great expertise she was spread-eagled on her bed and being tortured with the vibrator and stroked into an unbelievable sexual frenzy by her friend who had not gagged her but merely slipped the strap in her mouth making sensible talk virtually impossible.

'Thisshhh ishh jusshh great you bitsshh,' she crooned as she fought her cords and looked at Amanda's lovely face above her. The lady vet had learned her lessons well from the master and a climax was denied her twice before she shrieked. 'For God'shh shake Amanda! Pleassh finissshh me off!'

Slipping her free of the restraining cords Amanda was ready to receive the embraces of the by now fully aroused and very excited Stella. Their lovemaking lasted for over an hour as they played, kissed, fondled and laughed together. Lying on their backs, soaked in the sweat of their exertions, the two held hands and talked of their future. Amanda was so full of Dale and her plans that Stella allowed her to do most of the talking and felt genuine pleasure for her two pals. Stella had her memories and she knew that Amanda would be her best friend for the rest of her life.

'Let's have my magic boots back darling,' Amanda said at last, getting off the bed and tugging off the brown wellingtons from her friend's feet. 'I'll look after them I promise.'

'I bet you will, you bitch,' laughed Stella as she removed the bathing cap that had remained on throughout the recovery period and shook free her crumpled dark mane of hair. The two females stood facing each other, taking in the other's gleaming body with genuine admiration. Quite spontaneously they came together and hugged each other. 'Dale is such a very lucky man,' Stella whispered as she squeezed the hands of her pal that she had pulled behind her back allowing their bodies to rub closely against one another.

They eventually dressed and went downstairs for a drink and were met by Mrs Defferary who again brought up the subject of 'young Edna'. Stella advised her elderly housekeeper that Edna had an open invitation to visit *Clover Leys* but apparently lived a very full life and didn't seem to be able to find the time to come down to East Kent.

'Ah well, that's alright then madam,' she replied. 'Just as long as she's happy. She was such a nice girl, bit daffy if you knows what I mean madam, but nice just the same.'

After a couple of long iced Noilly Prats and lemonade the two friends parted. Stella had not enjoyed the emotion she had felt upon learning of Amanda and Dale's plans but it had happened and she must just put up with it. She had a fine life in every other respect and maybe she could organise Richard a little better in the future. "I mean to say, he's a man and I'm a woman so the ingredients are all there!" she thought. Amanda drove home feeling absolutely great. She had told her friend the truth and it had all tumbled out of her mouth exactly the way she had hoped. 'And I beat the crap out of her in the fight too!' she roared.

Dale was having one of those days at the office. He had several visits to make and telephone call after telephone call kept him chained to the desk. Julie was off sick so Colleen was trying to help him as well as see to the Guv'nor's needs. She waltzed in wearing a lovely fawn two-piece jersey suit and tanned high-heeled boots becoming *Barbara Stanwyck in 'Forty Guns' in which she was described as 'a high-riding woman with a whip'* before she had got halfway across the room. '*Do you know the way to San Jose?' trilled Dionne Warwick* in the back-waters of his mind.

'Have you any urgent things for me Dale?' she asked.

Dale quickly came out of his dreaming and started dictating immediately whilst undressing, then dressing-up and finally re-dressing their attractive Senior Secretary. Another 'phone call from a client held up Colleen and he for another ten minutes during which time she crossed and uncrossed her lovely long legs seventeen times and left Dale utterly exhausted by the time he recommenced his letter to Tubby Norton explaining that the couple he was promoting for the tenancy of 'The Gamekeeper' in Eastry were quite the best pair he had interviewed this year, were on his 'special' list and how it would be absolute folly not to select them. Tubby knew of Dale's style and realised that the 'special' list had to be some 300 pages long if every person the Broker had encouraged he and his fellow Area Managers to interview during the past year were actually on this mythical list.

He eventually set off for the Isle of Thanet and some thirty minutes later he was inside the 'Royal Mail' in Margate and chatting to Tony and Jennifer Lucan. Tony had received a very stiff lecture from Inspector Haith and the Licensing Officer, Inspector Devine, and knew that Dale had definitely 'saved his bacon' in respect of losing his licence. However Dale was aware that without the help of this couple Stella would be at the bottom of the English Channel and for that he would always have a very special bond with them. Their success at the 'Royal Mail' had not gone unnoticed by other Brewers and Dale had been asked by one of the rival Area Managers to approach them with a view to taking one of his own Thanet tenancies. Tony was very interested but Jenny expressed great doubts about such a venture pointing out that they might have proved themselves financially successful but so far as the local Constabulary were concerned they were a complete disaster.

'Let's stay here for a while Mr Ingram and re-establish a bit of goodwill wiv old Andy Devine. 'Ee finks we are a couple of complete plonkers and it's up to us to show 'im that we're the biz when it comes to running a bleedin pub. I want to see our own Brewery trying to persuade us to take a bigger pub this time next year.'

Dale agreed with her train of thought and told her so. He felt sure that he would be acting for them within the next twelve months, as they really were quite capable of running a much bigger house than the 'Royal Mail'. He also felt that with increased profits Tony would not be quite so keen on bending every canon in the Brewery Book of Rules. He would make it his business to keep the Area Manager very much aware of the couple's growing reputation and the interest other Companies were showing in them. Tony Lucan would have 'a friend at court' for as long as he was in the licensed trade.

Having left the 'Royal Mail' Dale made his way over to Dr Kavanagh's who had telephoned him in the week and suggested that it was about time he underwent a little 'refresher' course in his battle against sexual insecurity and self-doubt.

Maeve greeted him wearing a pair of green fishing waders, a pea green bathing hat and a deep olive towelling robe.

'My God, you look er… really, er… green,' he said.

'All for you, Mr Ingram. All for you.'

'Now what's all this about a refresher course?'

'Come along through to the gym and you'll see.'

The small well-equipped gymnasium that Wilfred Skinner had installed was most impressive. Maeve was very quickly, at her own instruction, spread-eagled on the wall bars and as Dale, with an eye on the clock it has to be admitted, 'bonked' the very being out of her, she screamed vengeance, howled protest, threatened and generally described in graphic detail what she would like to do to her master and his 'bloody rhythm stick'!

The good doctor had amazing powers of recovery and seemingly minutes after being unfastened from the wall she was giving her patient a cup of percolated coffee whilst still in her thigh-high wading boots.

'Oh dear, I do really love helping you like this Dale Ingram. It's so good to know that one can be of real assistance occasionally. So much of my time seems to be spent trying to wring secret doubts and misgivings out of sad folk with far too often no real progress being made.'

Dale stroked her green rubberised thighs and murmured, 'Dr Kavanagh... keep up the good work. I feel so much better every time I see you.'

Stella and he had arranged to meet at Croft House on Friday at one o'clock and Dale was looking forward to seeing her for it had been almost three weeks since they had met. He knew of Amanda's ride with her and that she was not going to fight their decision to bring their sessions to an end.

'She was wonderful about it all Dale,' Amanda had related to him on the evening of her day out with Stella. 'Sad of course but she knew that what I asked was not unreasonable and I got the impression that she had not given up on Richard in the sex stakes and was going to try and get him rejuvenated in some way, though to be honest, why a woman like Stella has to *try* and rejuvenate him is quite beyond me... she's so stunning!' Amanda had not shown Stella's thoughtful present to Dale and had asked Stella to keep it a secret from Dale. She would pick her moment to pull those magic boots on and surprise the man who had asked her to marry him.

Room Eight on the first floor of Croft House had so many lovely memories for both Dale and Stella and as they sat by the window sipping from a bottle of Veuve Clicquot, Dale talked with so much affection and candour of his love for the girl he had worshipped for so many years but made no apologies for falling in love with Amanda and asking her to become his wife.

'I suppose I had been looking for you, in my mind, for almost thirty years. Peggy Graham, my first real girlfriend, soon realised I had this thing about rubber and reacted marvellously but we never really understood why. I had thought about you so much and always got an erection when I remembered our "tie-up" games and what we did to each other but it really and honestly wasn't until you wore those brown wellingtons in my flat that I knew for certain that you and you alone were the reason for my perverse nature. I don't regret it for one second for I've had so much fun over these months and can't ever recall any lady not liking my brand of lovemaking. It seems unbelievable that we are now saying goodbye to all that but I know you will understand that Amanda is quite adamant about it and I do feel that it will enable us all to remain great friends, albeit unbeknown to Richard of course… Will you miss me Stella?' he posed the question suddenly and almost caught her off guard.

'Of course I'll miss you… you great fool. Do you think I don all this rubber gear because I don't like it? I've never had so much fun in my life since meeting you. I still recall the absolute terror I felt when you casually dropped the bathing cap on my tummy as I lay tied to this bed all those months ago. I really didn't know what you were going to do to me. You are the gentlest lover in the world and I will remember and cherish all the hours we have spent together. Holy Island will always be so special to me and I must say I shall hate it if I hear you've taken Amanda up there. I know you will, but just go and don't tell me about it until much later.'

Stella rose and smiled at him. 'I'm really not in the mood for any nonsense Dale but I do want to say goodbye properly'. She slowly undressed in front of him letting him take in every curve in her beautiful firm body for the last time. Going over to her bag she pulled on her riding boots and for the first time ever, apart from the farce at Coves Bay that is, put on her cap herself ensuring all her hair disappeared and pulled on her rubber gauntlets.

'God you are so beautiful!' marvelled Dale. 'I will never forget you Stella. I never could forget you.'

His 'Rubber Princess' stood in front of him and placed her feet slightly apart so that he could take this image of her and store it in his memory banks. This was Stella Ward. This was the lady of which dreams are made.

They stayed together for three hours and explored their bodies and their minds. Stella cried with sheer joy and then sheer agony as their parting drew near.

'You have saved my life. You have made my life. You have been my life. How am I going to cope with all this Dale? I am going to get through this aren't I?'

Dale held her close and squeezed her gently as he promised her that she would indeed get over this and would go on to enjoy her life. They showered and dressed and walked slowly down the staircase together. It was the end of a fairy story and they both knew it. Dale was off on the biggest adventure of his life with a lady who adored him and was determined to provide him with children before too much time elapsed. He was ready for this act of total commitment and was even relishing the thought of it. Amanda was superb in rubber and in bondage and craved for his touch and his expertise. 'Gee Gee' was not getting any younger and the firm would be in his hands within a few years… his future looked rosy.

Stella was returning to the life she had never really left. True she had this brief wild flirtation with this incredible man but here she was, still the School Governor, still a Magistrate and still a hard-working member of several charitable institutions. She was also very keen to get involved with Kate Donald and felt sure that she could easily accommodate a riding school set-up at *Clover Leys* if Richard agreed to such a venture and Kate's enthusiasm remained with her. Plus, and it was a big plus indeed, she had retained the open friendship of Amanda and the slightly less than open friendship of her darling Dale.

They kissed warmly in the driveway before making for their respective cars. As they drove back to Canterbury both had tears trickling down their cheeks as they realised the enormity and the finality of the decision they had made.

'God bless you, darling Stella… and keep you safe forever!' he whispered to himself.

Stella arrived back at *Clover Leys* and went immediately to her dressing room where she changed and sat in her bay window surveying the stables. Defferary was busying himself outside Chance's stall and her dear old Simon was eyeing him from a sunny spot as he lazed around awaiting the possibility of a walk with the old man whom he adored. Suddenly, almost without knowing why, she started to shake uncontrollably as her despair at losing Dale's constant love and attention hit home. She had wallowed in the sheer outrageousness of all that Dale had demanded of her and for the first time in many years she had felt totally at one with herself. Yes, she adored kinky sex. Yes, she knew that she really was a lovely looking female and that men did lust after her. Why oh why had it all had to stop? Throughout her marriage she had hidden from Richard the deep grief she suffered at remaining childless but this exciting year with Dale had pushed this sadness to one side. Now, in her despair, this failure to bear a child loomed up once more and tears came irrepressibly as she sobbed quietly to herself.

Her gloom lasted for almost two weeks and Richard tried hard to get to the bottom of it all by kindness and constant questioning. He had guessed that her barrenness was at the root of her unhappiness and Stella was content for her husband to try and assist her, working along those lines. Richard tended to categorise so many things of which he had little understanding under the heading of 'women's things', and really hadn't a clue how to provide real help but she noted that he was home early most evenings, he had taken her out to dine two nights running and had booked up to see a musical at the Marlowe Theatre in Canterbury on the coming Saturday. She had not heard from Amanda but knew that she must not get paranoiac about this, as her pal had told her that for the next three weeks she wouldn't be riding because of extra duties connected with the Surgery at Sandwich. Gradually she began to feel a little more resigned to her new life and with a very hectic week of magisterial duties and an important RSPCC meeting to attend in London, Stella started to realise that there was a future for her and she was jolly well going to try and love every minute of it.

CHAPTER THIRTY-THREE

A WEDDING

Wednesday, June 19th 1980 dawned fair and warm. Amanda and Dale, after much heart-searching, had decided on a wedding in Pinner. This pleasant little suburban town had been Amanda's home from birth until her move to Kent and the ties she had with friends, relatives and the parish church of St John itself, laying at the top of the quaintly old-fashioned High Street amidst a host of horse chestnut trees were decisive factors. It was here that she had been christened and confirmed and she knew their decision would please her parents and family immensely.

'Old John Jeffcoat will be well-pleased also,' Dale had remarked at the time, knowing his old school pal lived in nearby Northwood and would have no difficulties with travel or possible overnight accommodation. 'I hope he'll be able to organise David Welch and drag him down from the North by offering him free board and lodgings.' Both these old schoolboy pals were long-time married and had children but the fourth 'musketeer' Ian Lee Francis was working and living in North America and tracing him might prove a little difficult. As far as Dale knew he had not married but news of Ian filtered through only periodically and as Dale had found out for himself when one falls in love then there are no real rules or regulations and he had found the seven months to this day extremely long and tiresome. He desperately wanted to be able to shout to the world at large:

'Look at me! Look who I've just married! The most adorable female in the world! I'm the luckiest man on earth!'

Jim and Alison Broughton had taken to Dale on sight and were so thrilled to see how happy this new man in her life was making her. She had always been a loving and uncomplicated daughter and that she was marrying a handsome man who so obviously worshipped her gave them a warm feeling about the future. Their wedding arrangements had been planned with military precision and it was almost as though the sun had been told to 'appear at twelve noon precisely and stay out until further orders'.

Dale's Best Man was an old friend of over twenty years, Tony Ambersell, a local farmer and fellow Canterbury player with whom Dale had enjoyed many many happy hours. The Bridesmaids were two teenage nieces, one from each side, who matched each other in height, age and size. Kirsty Cowell had promised not to wear her high boots underneath and looked absolutely gorgeous as did Amanda's elder brother's daughter Denise, in gowns of emerald green, designed and made for them by one of Amanda's old friends, Sophie Snow, a most attractive lady and well-established on the London fashion scene. Dale had asked John Jeffcoat to be the Senior Groomsman where his knowledge of the locality would prove so useful and Frank Cowell and another old rugby pal now living in Wales, Gerald Harries, agreed to support him.

Being the third Wednesday in the month Stella had had no problems about accepting her invitation, handed to her by Amanda with a veiled threat of what she and Dale would do to her if she did not attend. She looked simply wonderful in a suit of pale blue silk with an enormous navy blue hat and the highest of high-heeled shoes. She had travelled up with Kate and Jamie Donald who had assured her that they would not be staying late and would have her back at *Clover Leys* by early evening.

Dale's pupil, Ben Herbert, had volunteered to drive 'Gee Gee' and Mrs Tremlett up to the wedding and take them back to

Canterbury straight afterwards and this had pleased Dale so much. He laughed constantly with his old Senior Partner but never at him for the respect he had for this old warrior would not permit such things. Dale had also planted in young Ben's mind that his niece Jill Cowell from Northumberland was an extremely 'tasty' young lady and as she only had a dim-witted boyfriend called Kevin who supported Sunderland there had got to be a chance for him. Ben always appeared to be lolloping around like some demented old bull-mastiff after some poor wretched female at the Rugby Club or in the office but seldom seemed to find success from what Dale could make out.

Amanda was the beautiful bride that everyone knew she would be. She had lost a little weight in the months leading to the wedding and her dress, which appeared fashioned in liquid silk showed off her lovely figure in marvellous style. Dale had turned far too quickly than was normal thus allowing himself more time to follow her entrance and elegant walk to join him for the ceremony on the arm of a very proud and emotional Mr Broughton. His smile of greeting was from ear to ear as he whispered, 'You look stunning my darling.'

The Reception was at a nearby Hotel and was well organised by a bossy Manager and caring staff. In the 'line-up' Stella's approach saw Dale and Amanda break ranks and the three of them hugged each other with a fierceness of passion that escaped no one's attention. These three had been through so much together over the past two years and it was just so reassuring to them all that their friendship had survived all that had happened to them.

'Be happy you two,' Stella had whispered to them as they kissed her. 'And you look after her Dale for she's a special lady.'

'No more special than you Stella,' replied Amanda, 'you will always be very special to Dale and I, and well you know it.'

'I love you Stella,' Dale said quite simply. 'You have been my inspiration and you have made me an acceptable husband for this gorgeous wife of mine. Thanks for everything.'

The reunion had to stop as the long line of well-wishing guests continued to pour through the entrance doors of the Hall and possibly it was just as well as Dale could see Stella's lower lip begin to waver as his words of loving tenderness took her so unexpectedly. Later in the proceedings she was to scold him in true Stella style for almost making her cry.

The speeches that followed a perfectly satisfactory meal were well above average with an uncle of Amanda's having the room in stitches with a seemingly unrehearsed but nevertheless very professional delivery. Tony Ambersell continued to make laughter the order of the day with a wonderfully cruel and funny character assassination of his friend, the Groom and then Dale, in very subdued mood, let the assembly know of his love for Amanda Broughton and the gratitude he felt towards all those friends and relatives who had supported them not only today but throughout their lives. He thanked the new 'in-laws' for giving them such a splendid day and also for giving him their daughter, promising to look after her and, hopefully, not give them a moment's worry about her from this time forth. Finally, he spoke of two elderly gentlemen present today, both in their eighties, without whose help and guidance over the past forty years he would never have been standing here today. His father and Mr Tremlett were thanked quietly but so sincerely for the considerable parts both had played in his life and his career. His father wept unashamedly at the spontaneous applause that echoed round the room at his son's words whilst 'Gee Gee' stood up and waved to his fellow guests.

'If he had some business cards with him he'd be bloody showering us with them!' laughed Bernard Brazier to his wife and Tommy Thornhill.

By five o'clock the Bride and Groom were ready to leave and would be on a plane to Naples in two hours' time en route for a fortnight's honeymoon in Sorrento where they had booked in at one of those gorgeously decadent hotels on the cliffs overlooking the

Mediterranean and the busy harbour. As their car, driven by John Jeffcoat, roared off towards the nearby Heathrow Airport, Stella stood at the back of the happy throng and watched the joy on the faces of Dale, her Dale, and Amanda as they kissed and thanked and cuddled and laughed. For just one second Dale's face seemed to look up as though trying to make eye contact with someone but the moment passed in a blink of an eye and was gone forever.

'Goodbye you two darling people… and thank you for everything… it's been a "ball"! ' A tear trickled down her face as she mouthed the words.

'You are just like me Stella,' sighed Kate Donald who had noticed her friend's emotional reaction to the happy couple's departure. 'Weddings always make me cry!'

CHAPTER THIRTY-FOUR

STILL FRIENDS 1981

It was the third Wednesday in the month and Richard was off to his Brewers' Meeting in London. Stella was excited but nevertheless went about her preparations quietly and systematically. The four crimson cords that would soon secure her to the four bedposts were laid out on the bed together with the ball gag, the multi-movement vibrator and her red bathing cap. She was naked save for her white towelling robe.

Promises had been made and she had accepted the fact that Dale's future lay with Amanda. They were set on starting a family and her decision to try and make a new life for herself with Richard did not really permit too much straying away from the role of the good supportive wife. Yes, she felt guilty and yes, she was behaving in a weak fashion but this lovely man had awakened in her these deep passions that had lain dormant for so long. She needed to be captured and tied up, she needed to feel her captor's hands on her as she fought to try and prolong the inevitable sexual climax that her helpless state could not prevent. Surely, provided they were discreet and nobody else ever knew of their monthly sessions, there was no real damage done. Her Pandora's box had been opened by Dale and now, if she was to get through her new styled way of life and keep her sanity then the third Wednesday of every month was going to be an essential ingredient.

The doorbell sounded and running to the window she saw the familiar car in the driveway. Pulling on her red rubber high-heeled thigh boots and discarding her towelling robe she tore downstairs and opened the door.

'God, I'm so excited!' she cried. 'You just can't imagine how much I've missed you. I can't believe it's only been four weeks ago that we were together.'

Her visitor was wearing a brown hacking jacket, check shirt, jeans and rubber riding boots. 'You are looking wonderful Stella but, there again, you always do. Now let's get you up these bloomin' stairs and get this show on the road!'

Stella and Amanda Ingram ran up the wide staircase, holding hands and laughing in anticipation of spending another two or three hours together because, surely, that's what friends are for?